Liz Carlyle

The Bride Wore Scarlet

AVON

An Imprint of HarperCollinsPublishers

AVON BOOKS
An Imprint of HarperCollins*Publishers*
10 East 53rd Street
New York, New York 10022-5299

Copyright © 2011 by Susan Woodhouse
ISBN 978-0-06-196576-0
www.avonromance.com

First Avon Books mass market printing: August 2011

Avon Trademark Reg. U.S. Pat. Off. and in Other Countries, Marca Registrada, Hecho en U.S.A.
HarperCollins® is a registered trademark of HarperCollins Publishers.

Printed in the U.S.A.

10 9 8 7 6 5 4 3 2 1

PROLOGUE

*Regard your soldiers as your children, and they
will follow you into the deepest valleys;
look on them as your own beloved sons,
and they will stand by you even unto death.*
Sun Tzu, *The Art of War*

London, 1837

The lamps were turned low in the dark, old-fashioned house in Wellclose Square, the servants gliding like silent specters, eyes downcast as they moved through passageways musty with the scents of liniment and camphor—and of what might have been death drawing nigh.

Above, in the mistress's grand suite, the fire that was laid from September to June had been banked for the evening, and the circle of plaguing visitors—teary-eyed relations, gloomy priests, and nattering medical men—had finally been sent away with a sharp, if somewhat diminished, tongue-lashing.

She lay now like a spun-glass ornament in a box of cotton wool, all but lost in the massive medieval bed that had seen seven generations of her family pass from this world to the next, its walnut finish gone as black with age as once the old woman's hair had been. But age had not lessened the hook in her nose, the fire in her eyes—or the indomitability of her will, much to the consternation of her family.

Against the costly, hand-embroidered silk of her nightdress, she clutched a rosary of jet to her heart, and pondered the hope of her dynasty. She was old, had been old for thirty years—or perhaps had been born old, as so many of her kind were. But it would not do, the old woman knew, to go leaving things unsaid. Hard decisions unmade. Never had she shirked her duty.

And still, though she had known with the heart of a warrior and the head of a shopkeeper what must eventually be done, she had put off the choice for nearly a decade now.

Oh, this was not her time; she was almost certain—despite her eight-and-eighty years, and the despair of the doctors who paraded daily round what they believed to be her deathbed.

But they might be right. And she might—just *might*—be wrong.

To have admitted that possibility aloud, however—ah, now that was the thing most likely to choke the last breath of life from Sofia Josephina Castelli.

"Maria!" she said sharply, holding out her hand. "Take my rosary, and fetch me the child."

"*Sì, signora.*" Her companion rose slowly on knees that creaked a little now. "Which child?"

"Which child?" the old woman echoed incredulously. "*The* child. The one. And bring me *i tarocchi*. Just one last time I . . . I wish to be sure of what I do."

In years past, Maria would have chided her, and perhaps reminded her of the family's censure. But Maria, too, was growing older now, and weary of fighting the old woman. More significantly, however, Maria was a Vittorio—a close cousin—and she knew what was expected. She, perhaps better than anyone, understood that plans must be made.

*He had taken her hand
again, and turned it up to trace
his index finger over the lines,
as if he might read her palm.*

He lifted her hand a little, almost as if he
might brush his lips over it. She looked up to
catch his gaze, only to realize he had pulled
her almost effortlessly toward him. It was
as if he'd drawn her across time and space.
An energy—a sort of tangible emotion—
seemed to shimmer in the air about them,
and every logical thought went skittering
like marbles from her head.

They stood chest to chest beneath the
rack of swords. Slowly, as if he moved under water, Geoff's opposite hand came up,
his fingers stroking slowly over her cheek.
If waking yesterday morning with her
dress unbuttoned and her corset laid open
had felt intimate, this felt a thousand times
more so.

"Ah, Anaïs, this is so unwise," he murmured. "Tell me . . . tell me we both know
that."

By Liz Carlyle

THE BRIDE WORE SCARLET
ONE TOUCH OF SCANDAL

Coming Soon

THE BRIDE WORE PEARLS

Obligations met. And that the debt which was owed to one's blood must be paid.

Maria went to the bellpull and sent a servant off to do the mistress's bidding, then crossed to the massive wardrobe to extract the *signora*'s small, ebony wood casket, which was hinged and bound with hammered copper so old it was worn nearly smooth now.

She carried it to the bed, but the old woman waved her off again. "Purify the cards for me, Maria," she ordered. "Just this once, *sì*?"

"But of course, *signora*."

Dutifully, Maria went to the small bedside chest. Taking a pinch of dried herbs from each of four porcelain urns, she dropped them into a shallow brass bowl and set them aflame with a candle. Extracting a pack of cards from the casket, she passed them four times through the white smoke, calling down the elements of wind, water, earth, and fire to guide her hand.

"*Buono*, Maria, *buono*," the old woman rasped when it was done. "*Molte grazie*."

Maria laid the cards upon the counterpane beside her. But at that instant, the door flew open, and a leggy, raven-haired girl in a starched white smock rushed in.

"Nonna, Nonna!" she said, throwing herself against the bed. "They said I mightn't come up!"

"But now you are here, Anaïs, *no*?" The old woman set a hand on the child's head, but looked past her, to the woman in gray who still lingered on the threshold, her hands clasped uncertainly.

The governess dropped her gaze, and bobbed a faint curtsy. "Good evening, Signora Castelli. Signora Vittorio."

"*Buona sera*, Miss Adams," said the old woman. "I wish to be alone with my great-granddaughter. You will excuse us, I think?"

"Yes, of course, but I . . ." The governess was looking at the cards a little disapprovingly.

"You will excuse us," the old woman repeated, this time with a steely hauteur that belied her frail form.

"Yes, madam." The door shut swiftly.

Maria had returned to the side table, and was clearing the contents from the galleried silver tray on which the old woman's uneaten dinner of beef tea and boiled custard had been carried up. Eyes solemn, the girl had set her elbows to the bed and leaned over it, her chin propped pensively in one hand.

"Come, *cara mia*, climb up." The *signora* stroked her fingers down the child's wild tangle of black curls. "As you did when you were a *bambina, sì*?"

The earnest little face twisted. "But Papa said I mustn't bother you," she said. "That you weren't well."

The old woman laughed, a raspy wheeze. "Come, *cara*, you will not hurt me," she said. "Is that what they told you? Come, curl up beside me and let us study *i tarocchi* together. Maria has found us a tray, see?"

Soon they were settled against the pillows together, the old woman having dragged herself up in bed a few inches with Maria's help. Only her left hand, fisted against the pain, betrayed what the movement cost her.

Perched on the edge of the mattress with her long, coltish legs curled beneath her, the child took the pack, cutting and shuffling over and over like a diminutive cardsharp.

The old woman wheezed with laughter again. "*Basta, basta*, Anaïs," she finally said. "Do not wear them out, for you will have need of them someday. Now, *a sinistra*. Three stacks. Just as always."

The girl cut the cards into threes across the silver, moving each time to the left. "There, Nonna Sofia," she said. "Will you tell my future now?"

"Your future is blessed," the old woman insisted, catching the child's chin between her thumb and forefinger. "*Sì*, I will read for you, child. And the cards will say what always they say."

"But you have never told me *what* they say," the child protested, her full bottom lip edging out a tad further. "You just talk to yourself, Nonna. And I cannot make it out."

"That, too, shall be rectified," said the old woman. "Cousin Maria is going to begin work on your language as of tomorrow—only proper Tuscan, Maria, not that hash one hears round the docks."

"If you wish it, *signora*." Maria inclined her head. "Of course."

"But Miss Adams says a young lady needs only French," said Anaïs, systematically restacking the cards without being told.

"Ah, and what would such a fainthearted creature know of the world, Anaïs?" the old woman murmured, watching her small hands work. "Nothing—*nothing*—of your world, I would wager. The life you will have, *cara mia*, is beyond her mortal comprehension."

"What's *mortal comprehension*?" The child furrowed her brow.

With a trembling hand, the old woman tucked a springy black curl behind the child's ear. "*Non importa*," she said. "Come, *cara*, lay out the cards for me. You know how 'tis done, *sì*?"

Solemnly, the girl nodded, and began to lay the cards out on the silver tray, forming first a large circle, then crossing it down the center with seven cards.

"Draw a chair near, Maria." The old woman spoke in a warning tone. "You will bear witness to this."

As the chair legs bumped over the floorboards, the old woman turned the first of the crossed cards.

Maria fell into her chair with a little groan, and shut her eyes. "It should be Armand," she whispered, crossing herself. "They are twins, *signora*! This should be his destiny."

The old woman squinted at her a little nastily. "*Should be, sì*," she echoed, "but *is not*. Here, Maria, you see it as clearly as I. And you have seen it before. Time and again. It never changes. *La Regina di Spade*. Always in the cross of seven."

"The Queen of Swords," the child translated, reaching out to gingerly touch the card, which depicted a woman in red wearing a golden crown and bearing a gold-hilted sword in her right hand. "Am I the queen, then, Nonna?"

"*Sì, cara mia.*" The old woman managed a weak smile. "A queen of righteousness and honor."

"But she is a *girl*." Maria had begun to wring her lace handkerchief.

"The queen usually is," said the old woman dryly. "For Armand's part, he is destined for other things. To be beautiful. To make us rich."

"We are already rich," said Maria a little sourly.

"To make us rich*er*," the old woman corrected.

"Aren't I beautiful, Nonna?" said the child a little wistfully.

The old woman shook her head, scrubbing her long white tresses on the pillow slip. "*Non, cara*, you are not. You are something altogether different."

The girl's lower lip came out a fraction. "Nonna, will anyone marry me?" she asked. "I heard Nellie whispering to Nate that you could tell."

"Bah, Nellie is a foolish scullery maid." Maria gave a dismissive toss of her hand.

"*Sì*, Nellie is *un imbecille*," said the old woman evenly. "And Nathaniel needs to cease his flirting. But yes, child.

You will marry. You will marry a good, strong Tuscan boy. This I have seen many times in my cards."

"How? I don't know any boys from Tuscany."

"Ah, but you will," said the old woman, flipping the adjacent card. "See, here he waits. For you, Anaïs, and only you. A prince of peace in a coat of scarlet, *le Re di Dischi*."

"The King of Pentacles," said Maria softly.

"*Sì*, a man of inner strength who holds the future in his hand." The old woman turned her black gaze upon the child. "Here, do you see? Your prince has transcended the mystical and is serene and powerful. You are destined to be his partner. His helpmeet."

The child screwed up her face. "I don't understand, Nonna."

"No, no," the old woman murmured. "But have patience, child. You will."

Without further explanation, the old woman slowly turned the next card, and began to speak in a voice more distant.

"Ah, *Catulo*." Her voice was more distant than warm. "The card of victory hard won. You will choose your battles carefully, Anaïs, and bear your bleeding wounds proudly."

Maria cut her gaze away. "*Dio mio!*" she whispered.

The old woman ignored her, and kept turning. "*Dischi*," she said. "The six of Pentacles. You have much effort ahead, *cara*. Much to learn. Many transformations to make. You must be *shaped* before you may go through the white gates to your next life."

"But that man is a blacksmith," said the child. "See? He is hammering on an anvil."

"*Sì*, beating his plowshare into a sword, belike," said Maria bitterly. "Come, Sofia, think what you do! This is no life for a lady—an *English* lady."

The old woman turned a beady eye on her cousin. "What

choice have I, Maria?" she asked sharply. "Time and again you have seen the child's cards. God has given her an important task. Something she is destined to do. Turn the next, Anaïs."

The girl flicked over the next card to reveal the depiction of an angel loading golden discs into a large trunk.

"*Dischi*," muttered the old woman. "And the next?"

Again the child turned. Maria had twisted the handkerchief into a knot now.

"The warrior Venturio," said the old woman with a sense of finality. "Ah, Anaïs, you begin a long journey."

"But Nonna, where do I go?" asked the girl, surveying the cards almost warily. "Will you go with me?"

For a long moment, the old woman said nothing, guilt plucking at her heartstrings. "No, Maria will go, child," she said, falling back into her cloud of feather pillows. "For I cannot. May God forgive me."

But Maria just glared at her from the bedside chair.

"Nonna," the child whispered, "are you dying?"

"No, no, *bella*," said the old woman. "Not for a few years yet, unless God changes His mind." Then she exhaled a shuddering breath. "But I think we need not turn more cards just now."

"No, we needn't," said Maria. "For your mind is made up."

"No, my cousin. Fate has decided." The old woman closed her eyes, and let her hands fall limp on the coverlet. "And tomorrow, Maria, you will write to Giovanni Vittorio. He owes me this as my blood kin. You will tell him what had been decided. Which child will be given. Promise me."

An uneasy silence hung in the air. "Very well," Maria finally said. "I write. But on your head be it."

"*Sì*," the old woman answered a little sorrowfully. "On my head be it."

CHAPTER 1

*It is only the enlightened ruler
and the wise general who will
use the highest intelligence of the army
for the purposes of spying.*
Sun Tzu, *The Art of War*

Night lay over Wapping, nearly silent, the sky
wisped with a fog that twined like languid cats
about the bare masts of the ships at anchor in the Pool of
London. Despite the hour, the rhythmic *slush*-shush-*slush* of
a receding tide was unmistakable as it washed over mud and
gravel, the sliver of shore beneath as yet a mere speculation.

Atop the embankment, Lord Bessett ground the stub of a
cheroot beneath his boot heel, then flicked up the collar of
his greatcoat, a defense against the sharp, fetid breeze that
sliced off the Thames. The gesture cut the wind, but did
little to mitigate the stench of rot and raw effluent.

Thank God it was a chilly night.

The water slapped again, more violently, exposing for an
instant the last step, slick with green algae. Just then Bessett's well-trained ear caught a sound. He jerked his gaze up,
scanning the Pool. There was nothing. Nothing save a few
distant shipboard lanterns, misty yellow smears bobbing

faintly with the tide, and the occasional spate of raucous laughter carried across on the wind.

Then, silent as the grave, a waterman slid from the gloom, cutting along the river's edge until his hull rumbled slightly aground. A bony, tremulous finger pointed toward the stairs. His passenger—a great hulk of a man in a long, dark cloak—unfolded himself, tossed a few glittering coins into the air, then leapt with a heavy thud onto the last step.

The waterman slid back into the gloom, silent as he had come, looking rather as if he accounted himself fortunate to escape.

His every sense alert, Bessett leaned over the embankment and offered a hand as the visitor ascended into the pool of yellow lamplight. He took it, stepping up onto the paved surface with a grunt tinged with weariness.

Not a young man, then.

This assessment was proven accurate when the man turned his face toward the lamp that swung from the Prospect's riverside balcony. His was a worn and weathered visage, with small, hard eyes, and a nose that hung from his face like a bulbous wad of sausage. To complete the disconcerting picture, a scar slashed from his chin up through his mouth, horribly twisting the bottom lip.

The waterman's consternation was understandable.

"Fine weather tonight, is it not?" Bessett said.

"*Oui*, but I hear it is raining in Marseilles." The voice was like gravel, the accent thick and decidedly French.

Bessett felt the tension inside him relax but an increment. The phrase was right, aye. But there could still be trouble—and he never entirely trusted the French.

"I'm Bessett," he said simply. "Welcome to London."

The man laid a heavy palm across Bessett's right shoulder. "May your arm, brother, be as the right hand of God," he said in flawless Latin. "And all your days given to the *Fraternitas*, and to His service."

"And so may yours," Bessett answered in the same.

Sensing no animosity, Bessett eased his left hand from his pocket, releasing the hilt of the dagger he'd instinctively clutched. "So you are DuPont," he went on. "Your reputation, sir, precedes you."

"My reputation was made long ago," said the Frenchman. "In younger days."

"I trust your journey was without incident?"

"*Oui*, a swift, easy crossing." The visitor leaned into him. "So, I have heard much of this new safe house you keep here. Even we French cannot but admire your effort."

"It is a good deal more than a safe house, DuPont." Bessett motioned him down the narrow passageway that linked Pelican Stairs to Wapping High Street. "We are dedicated to rebuilding this sect. We live practically out in the open, in the guise of a sort of intellectual society."

The visitor snorted with Gallic disdain. "*Bonne chance, mon frère*," he said, stepping out into the gaslight. "As you know, we in France are not so bold—but then, we have good reason."

Bessett smiled thinly. "I take your point, DuPont. One begins to wonder if the political upheaval in France will ever end."

The Frenchman lifted one thick shoulder. "*Non*, not in my lifetime," he answered evenly. "And all your fine efforts here in London will never change that fact."

"Aye, sadly, you may be right," said Bessett. "As to the house—the St. James Society, it is called—any brother of the *Fraternitas Aureae Crucis* who passes through England is welcome to quarter with us—even those who do not support the unification."

"*Merci*, but I must not linger." The Frenchman rolled his shoulders uneasily. "So, my new *Fraternitas* brother, do we walk? Have you a carriage?"

Bessett jerked his head toward the public house adjacent. "The Society has come to you, DuPont. They wait within."

Just then, the Prospect's door flew open and a pair of garishly dressed nightingales burst out, laughing, a hapless young naval lieutenant hooked arm-in-arm between them. He looked wealthy, besotted, and thoroughly foxed—the prostitute's holy trinity.

The Frenchman watched them go assessingly, then gave his disdainful grunt again. "Ah, *mon frère*, life is the same the world over, *non*?"

"Aye, he'll be pissing pain till All Saints' Day with that pair," Bessett muttered. "Come, DuPont. The brandy here at the Prospect is passable, and the fire is warm."

Inside, the front taproom of the public house was abuzz, with every scarred and beaten table surrounded by men of the dockyards, with tavern maids swishing and weaving between them, trays and tankards hefted gracefully aloft. Lightermen, shipwrights, sailors of every nationality—even the occasional shipping magnate—all of them came, eventually, to the Prospect, where a hot meal and a fairly pulled pint might be had in companionable good spirits.

Bessett waded through the human morass, the man called DuPont on his heels, and made his way round the bar and into a quieter room where the tables sat along a row of small-paned windows overlooking the Pool.

His three colleagues rose at once, shaking DuPont's hand with outward welcome. But Bessett knew them well, could see the tautness in every move of their muscles and sense—in an ordinary, human way—the age-old wariness each exuded. Even if DuPont was *Fraternitas*, he came as an agent of the Gallic Confederation, a stubborn and secretive sect.

"Welcome to England, *monsieur*." Their Preost, the Reverend Mr. Sutherland, motioned toward the empty chair. "A pleasure to meet one of our brethren across the water. My associates, Ruthveyn and Lazonby." Handshakes were exchanged, then Ruthveyn snapped his fingers at one of the girls, sending her scurrying for a bottle of brandy.

"So, DuPont, I hear from my Catholic compatriots in Paris that trouble is afoot," Sutherland began once the bottle and glasses had been situated. "Is that what brings you?"

DuPont sipped at his brandy, his scarred mouth twisting even further at the taste. He set it down at once. "*Oui*, a child has fallen into the wrong hands," he said. "We require your help."

"A child?" Ruthveyn's dark visage hardened. "A Gift, you mean?"

The Frenchman scrubbed his hand round what looked like a day's growth of stubble. "It seems so," he admitted. "Though the child is young—not yet nine years of age—the circumstances are . . . troubling."

"Troubling how?" Lord Lazonby, an inelegant, broad-shouldered man, had thrown himself casually back into his chair, set his booted legs wide, and was absently turning his glass round and round on the scarred oak table. "Can the Guardians of Paris not keep up with their charges?"

DuPont bristled. "Ours is a nation in turmoil, you may recall," he snapped. "Our King now resides here—in utter exile—and even in these modern times, we can barely keep the rabble from rolling out *Madame la Guillotine* again. No, my Lord Lazonby. We cannot always keep up with our charges. Indeed, we often fear for our heads."

Ruthveyn planted his dark, long-fingered hands wide on

the table. "Enough," he commanded. "Let us be civil. Tell us, DuPont, what has happened. And be quick about it. We mightn't have much time."

"Aye, you are to be married, old boy, in a few days' time," said Lazonby dryly, entirely unperturbed by the scold. "And home to Calcutta thereafter. I believe Bessett and I can guess who will be charged with this task."

"Precisely." Ruthveyn's voice was tight. "Now, what is the name of this child, and how strong is your certainty of the Gift?"

"The child is called Giselle Moreau. About the other, we are certain enough to fear for her. The Gift is strong in the father's blood. Her mother, Charlotte, is English."

"English?" said Ruthveyn sharply. "Who are her people?"

"Impoverished gentry near Colchester," said the Frenchman. "They found enough money to send her to school in Paris and she thanked them by falling in love with a lowly clerk in the royal household—a bastard nephew of the Vicomte de Lezennes. She has had little contact with her family since."

"They disowned her?"

"*Oui*, so it appears so."

"Lezennes?" Lord Bessett exchanged uneasy glances with Mr. Sutherland. "I've heard the name. He's often found near the center of court intrigue, isn't he?"

DuPont nodded. "Always near, *oui*, but never close enough to be blamed," he said bitterly. "He is a clever devil, our Lezennes. He has survived the fall of Louis-Philippe, and now endeared himself to the Bonapartists—even as it is whispered that he is in truth nothing but a Legitimist, secretly seeking to restore the *Ancien Régime*."

"What do you think?" Bessett demanded.

The Frenchman shrugged. "I think he is a cockroach, and cockroaches always survive. His politics scarcely matter to me. But he has taken this Englishwoman under his wing in order to use her child, and that matters to me very much. And now he has removed them to Brussels, where he serves as an emissary to the court of King Leopold."

Bessett's hands fisted involuntarily. "From one political uncertainty to another," he murmured. "I cannot like the sound of this. This is the very thing we wished to avoid, DuPont, with the *Fraternitas*'s unification."

"I understand, but this is France we are talking about," said DuPont calmly. "No one trusts anyone. The *Fraternitas* in Paris—such as we still exist—is uneasy. Lezennes is not known for his charitable nature. If he has taken this child, it is for a purpose—his own purpose, and a bad one. That is why they have sent me. You must get the child back."

"Of course we wish to help," said Sutherland gently. "But why us?"

"As I said, the mother is English," said DuPont. "Your Queen wishes her subjects abroad to be protected, does she not? You have some rights in this, I think."

"I . . . don't know," said Ruthveyn warily.

The Frenchman crooked a brow arrogantly. "You are not unknown to us, Lord Ruthveyn," he said. "Nor is your work in Hindustan. You have your Queen's ear, and your Queen's favor. The King of the Belgians is her beloved uncle. You have influence. Would you truly punish the Gallic Confederation merely because we keep to ourselves, when all we ask is that you use your influence to save our Gift from being raised by a devil? From being used for nefarious purposes?"

"Of course not." Ruthveyn's voice was tight. "None of us wants that."

"But what of this woman's husband?" Bessett demanded.

DuPont pressed his misshapen lips together for a moment. "Moreau is dead," he finally answered. "Killed but a fortnight after the King's abdication. He was summoned late one night to his office near the palace—by whom, we are not sure—but somehow, the draperies caught fire. A terrible tragedy. And no one believes it was an accident."

Lord Ruthveyn's expression stiffened. "The dead man— he was a Guardian?"

"*Oui.*" The word was but a whisper. "A man of little Gift, but of good heart and much bravery. He has been sorely missed amongst our number these many months."

"He was close to his uncle?"

DuPont's bitter smile deepened. "Scarcely even acknowledged," he said, "until rumor of little Giselle's talent began to stir through the court."

"Good God, she was discovered?" said Bessett.

The Frenchman sighed deeply. "What is your English expression?" he murmured. "*Out of the mouths of babes?* Little Giselle predicted Louis-Philippe's abdication— blurted it out very innocently, but alas, very publicly—in front of half his courtiers."

"Oh, dear." Mr. Sutherland's head fell into his hands. "How could such a thing happen?"

"A court picnic at the Grand Parc," said the Frenchman. "All the royal household and their families were invited— commanded, really. The King, of course, came out for a few moments of *noblesse oblige* with the masses. Regrettably, he ran straight into Madame Moreau, and decided to catch Giselle's chin in his hand. He looked her straight into the eyes, and would not look away."

Bessett and Ruthveyn groaned in unison.

"It gets worse," said DuPont, the truth spilling from him now. "He asked why her eyes were so sad on such a lovely day. When she did not reply, he teased her by saying he commanded her as King to speak. So little Giselle took him literally, and foretold not only the fall of the July Monarchy, but went on to say that his abdication would be followed by a second terrible loss—the death of his daughter, Louise-Marie."

"Good God, the Queen of the Belgians?"

"Aye, and that was Louis-Philippe's doing, too, 'tis whispered," DuPont continued. "He wished his daughter to be made Leopold's queen in exchange for France's acceptance of Belgian independence."

"I thought that was just a rumor," Ruthveyn remarked.

"Eh, perhaps." The Frenchman opened both hands expressively. "But the French army stood down, Leopold's morganatic wife was cast aside, and Louise-Marie was ensconced on Belgium's throne. But now 'tis said the Queen grows weaker by the day."

"So the child's prediction is again coming true," Bessett murmured.

"Consumption, it is whispered," said DuPont. "The Queen will not likely last the year, and already the King's mistress is wielding some influence."

But a sense of ice-cold dread was already creeping over Bessett. This was the very thing Guardians of the *Fraternitas* most feared: the exploitation of the weakest amongst the Vateis—their ancient sect of seers—most of whom were women and children.

Throughout history, evil men had sought to control the Gift for all manner of selfish gain. Indeed, it was the very reason for the organization's continued existence. Whatever the *Fraternitas Aureae Crucis* had been at its shadowy, Druidic inception, over the centuries it had evolved into an almost monastic militia, devoted to guarding their own. But modernity had worn away their edges—and their structure. This child—this *Gift*—was at great risk.

It was as though DuPont read his mind. "There are a thousand dangerous things Lezennes could do, *mon frères*, to gain power and influence for himself," he said, his voice pitched lower still. "Conspire with the old Bourbons, fan the flames of further revolution on the Continent, perhaps even drive a wedge between England and Leopold—ah, the mind boggles! And it will be all the easier if he can divine the future—or have it done for him by some unsuspecting innocent."

"You think he killed his nephew." The ice-cold dread hardened in the pit of Bessett's stomach until it felt more like an icy rage.

"I know he did," said the Frenchman grimly. "He wanted possession of Giselle. Now she lives beneath his roof, subsisting on his charity. Our man in Rotterdam has sent his spies about, of course, but no one inside as yet. Still, Lezennes is grooming the child, depend upon it."

"You are working with van de Velde?" asked Sutherland. "He's an old hand."

"Most dependable," the Frenchman agreed. "And, according to his spies, it looks as if Lezennes is courting his nephew's wife."

"Good Lord, he thinks to marry the English widow?" said Ruthveyn. "But . . . what of affinity and canon law? What does your Church say?"

Again, the Gallic shrug. "Lezennes will care little for the Church's opinion," he returned. "Besides, Moreau was illegitimate. What papers exist that cannot be burnt or forged? Who really knows the truth of his birth? Perhaps not even his wife."

"Worse and worse," said Sutherland. The Preost sighed deeply and looked about the table. "Gentlemen? What do you propose?"

"Kidnap the bairn, and be done with it," Lord Lazonby suggested, his eye following the swaying hips of a nearby barmaid. "Bring her to England—with the Queen's permission, of course."

"Expedient—but extremely foolish," said Ruthveyn. "Moreover, the Queen cannot sanction such a blatant breach of diplomacy. Not even for one of the Vateis."

"It won't matter if we aren't caught, will it, old chap?" But Lazonby's voice was distant, his gaze fixed somewhere near the front door. Abruptly, he shoved back his chair. "Your pardon, gentlemen. I fear I must leave you."

"Good God, man." Bessett cut his friend a dark look. "This child matters rather more than the sway of some barmaid's arse—fine though it admittedly is."

Seated at the end of the table, Lazonby set a hand on Bessett's shoulder and leaned nearer. "Actually, it now appears I was followed here," he said quietly, "and not by a willing wench. You have my proxy. I'd best go lead the hound from our scent."

With that, Lazonby skulked from the room, and melted into the sea of crowded tables.

"What the devil?" Bessett looked across the table at Ruthveyn.

"Bloody hell." Ruthveyn watched only from one corner of his eye. "Don't turn around. It's that infernal newspaper chap."

Even Mr. Sutherland cursed beneath his breath.

"From the *Chronicle*?" Bessett's voice was low and incredulous. "How can he have learned about DuPont?"

"He didn't, I daresay." Eyes flashing with irritation, Ruthveyn turned his face deliberately away. "But he has become entirely too curious about the St. James Society for my liking."

"And too curious about Rance by half," Bessett complained. "For Rance's part, I often wonder he hasn't begun to enjoy this game a little too well. What must we do?"

"Nothing, for the nonce," said Ruthveyn. "Rance has insinuated himself into a game of dice by the fire, and dragged one of the wenches onto his knee. Coldwater is still quizzing the tapster. He has not seen any of us."

"Let Rance lead him a merry chase, and ensure he does not," Sutherland suggested. "Back to the crisis at hand—DuPont, tell us what, precisely, you would have us do?"

The Frenchman's eyes narrowed. "Send a Guardian to Brussels to fetch the girl," he said. "None of you are known to Lezennes. We have taken the liberty of leasing a house not far from the Royal Palace—very near Lezennes—and put it about that an English family is soon to take up residence. Servants have been put in place—trusted servants from our own households in Rotterdam and Paris."

"And then what?" demanded Bessett. "Lazonby's suggestion aside, we cannot very well snatch a child from its mother. Even we are not so heartless as that."

"*Non, non*, persuade the mother." The Frenchman's voice was suddenly smooth as silk. "Befriend her. Remind her of England, and of the happy life she might live here. Suggest a reconciliation with her family is possible. Then, if all else fails—if she is already too far under Lezennes' thumb—kidnap them both."

"*Kidnap* them?" Sutherland echoed.

DuPont leaned across the table. "Already my private clipper goes to anchor at Ramsgate, armed with a crew of good, strong men. It will take you to Ostend in utter secrecy, and await your escape."

"This is madness," said Bessett. "Besides, if Lezennes means to marry the woman—and if he is as conniving as you suggest—then he won't let one of us befriend her."

"Not one of *you*," the Frenchman said wearily. "Your wife, perhaps? Someone who can—"

"But none of us is married," Bessett protested. "That is to say, Ruthveyn here will be shortly, but he is leaving."

"A sister, then. A mother." DuPont waved his hand with

dismissive impatience. "*Mon Dieu*, what does it matter? A female to gain her trust, that is all we need."

"Out of the question," said Ruthveyn. "Bessett's sister is little more than a child. Mine scarcely passes for English and has two small children. Lazonby is a soldier, and hasn't the subtlety for such a mission. We only use him when someone needs to be beaten into submission."

"What about hiring an actress?" Mr. Sutherland interjected. "Or perhaps Maggie Sloane? She's a bit of a—well, a *businesswoman*, isn't she?"

Bessett and Ruthveyn exchanged glances. "Trust a padre to suggest hiring a high-flyer," Bessett said dryly. "But it's true Maggie sometimes does a spot of acting."

"Yes, every time Quartermaine beds her, I don't doubt," said Ruthveyn sardonically.

"Damn, Adrian, that's cold." Bessett flashed a grin. "Even Ned Quartermaine doesn't deserve that, even if he does run a gaming hell at our front doorstep. And he won't loan us Maggie. But yes, someone *like* Maggie . . . how hard can it be?"

"Ah, *tant mieux*!" DuPont, looking relieved, thrust one of his big paws to an inside coat pocket, then withdrew a thick fold of papers. "Here is all the information you will require, *mon frères*. The address of the house. The list of servants. Details of the story we have put about. Complete dossiers on both Lezennes and Madame Moreau. Even sketches."

Bessett took the fold and shuffled through the papers, Ruthveyn and Sutherland looking over his shoulder. It was thoroughly done, he would give the Guardians of Paris that much.

"*The art and architecture of Belgium*?" he muttered, reading aloud. "That, ostensibly, is your Englishman's purpose in going to Brussels?"

The Frenchman shrugged. "Are not many of the English

dilettantes?" he said. "Politics would have been too complicated—and too threatening. A man of business? Bah, too
bourgeois for Lezennes. *Alors*, what could seem more harmless than a rich, bored aristocrat who comes to look about
and make a few pretty sketches, eh?"

"Sounds like a job for you, old chap." Ruthveyn looked
at Bessett with what passed for a smile. "Bessett here is our
resident architect, DuPont. Indeed, he has traveled all over
Italy, France, and North Africa drawing pretty sketches—
then actually building them."

Sutherland was rubbing his chin. "It does appear this
assignment will fall to you, Geoff," the Preost murmured.
"Once we've read through all this, we'll put it to vote."

"You've an initiation ceremony to prepare for," Ruthveyn
reminded him. "Here, pass it to me. I shall read it tonight."

With mixed emotions, Bessett shoved back his chair.
Though he did not know Brussels well, he wondered if some
time away from London mightn't suit him. He had been
plagued of late by a burning sense of restlessness—and
more than occasionally, by a wistful longing for his old vo-
cation. For his old life, really.

There had been a time not so many years ago—before his
brother's death bollixed everything up—when Bessett had
been obliged to earn his own living. Nowadays he did little
real work, living instead off his land, and the oft-bitter fruit
of other men's labor. Though he had known of the *Fraternitas* since boyhood—had learned its purpose and its prin-
ciples, quite literally, at his grandmother's knee—he had not
fully devoted himself to its noble goals until Alvin's tragic
passing.

Perhaps *he* had become a rich, bored aristocrat?

Dear God. That was too distasteful to contemplate.

But whatever it was that nagged at him, Sutherland was
offering a way to escape it for a time. This assignment in

Brussels was, perhaps, a means of doing good for the *Fraternitas*—for society—while escaping the shackling role of Lord Bessett for a time. A chance to be, fleetingly, just plain old Geoff Archard again.

Ruthveyn had extracted his gold watch. "I'm afraid, gentlemen, that I must leave you," he said. "Lady Anisha is expecting me home for dinner."

"And we mustn't keep your sister waiting." Bessett set his hands flat to the table with an air of finality. "Very well, DuPont, we have your direction. Should we have any questions, we'll send a man to Paris using the same pass phrase as tonight."

"Then I beg you will waste no time in doing it," DuPont advised. "The *Jolie Marie* will lie at anchor in Ramsgate harbor for a sennight. I encourage you to make swift use of her."

"Indeed, indeed!" Sutherland managed a benevolent smile. "Well, gentlemen, I fear I must take my leave. We'll be initiating a new acolyte soon, Monsieur DuPont. If you should like to remain a couple of days, I can give you the loan of a robe."

But the Frenchman shook his head, and rose to go. "*Merci*, but I go at once to St. Katherine's to meet a friend, and thence to Le Havre." Then he turned, and offered his huge paw to Bessett once again. "*Bon voyage*, Lord Bessett," he added, "*et bonne chance*."

"Thank you," said Geoff quietly. Then, on impulse, he set a hand between the man's broad shoulder blades. "Come, DuPont. The streets hereabouts are not the safest. I'll walk you up to the docks."

But the Frenchman merely flashed another of his grim, misshapen smiles. "*Très bien, mon frère*," he said evenly, "if you think my looks are not enough to put your English footpads off?"

* * *

Maria Vittorio rumbled into the Docklands well after dark in a monstrous old town coach so heavy half a battalion could have ridden atop it. Alas, she did not have half a battalion for her journey into London's netherworld; merely a footman and a coachman, both nearly as ancient as she. But like old shoes, they had grown worn and comfortable together through the years, and Signora Vittorio was known to be deeply suspicious of change.

Near the foot of Nightingale Lane, the coach rocked to a halt, harnesses jingling. A few shouts were exchanged in the street, then Putnam, the footman, clambered slowly down and threw open the *signora*'s door.

"They say the *Sarah Jane*'s offloading on the Burr Street side, ma'am," he said in his creaky voice. "We've got almost down to the King George, but the turn is choked with drays and whatnot."

Signora Vittorio hefted herself wearily off the banquette. "Circle back to the top of the lane, then, and wait. I'll send a porter through with the baggage."

"Yes, ma'am." The footman tugged his forelock. "If you're sure? 'Tis a chilly evening, and a fog coming in."

"*Sì, sì*, go," she said, waving a gloved hand. "My knees are not as arthritic as yours."

Signora Vittorio climbed out on short, stout legs, Putnam supporting her at the elbow. As her carriage clattered away, the old woman stood to one side of the pavement, just a few yards from the King George, taking in all the bustle and shouting that spilled from the well-lit yard beyond.

As she set off past the pub's entrance, however, a small, wiry man in a tatty green coat burst from the door, almost bowling her over in the gloom. His gait hitching but an instant, he begged her pardon mockingly, his breath sour and reeking of gin.

Signora Vittorio lifted her nose a notch higher, one hand going instinctively to the pearls at her throat as she moved past. But she could still feel his gaze burning into her.

"Wot, yer fat, black-eyed bitch?" he shouted after her.

Signora Vittorio did not look back.

She made her way through the morass of humanity and horses into St. Katherine's proper to see that the *Sarah Jane* was indeed moored in the east basin. And she carried an urgent cargo. Despite the evening hour, crates, sacks, and barrels were being offloaded at a prodigious rate and stacked hither and yon upon the docks, much of it being seized up again by chains and hooks, and hoisted directly into the modern warehouses above.

Signora Vittorio turned up her nose even higher at the sight. She who had grown up in the lush beauty of Tuscany's vineyards could never grow accustomed to these grim, teeming docks, or the taverns and warehouses and stevedores that went with them. Indeed, even the smell of the Thames made her stomach turn.

Some days it seemed perverse to have married into a family destined to make its living by both land *and* water, for some of the crates—most of them, actually—were marked with the symbol of Castelli's; a large, elaborate C burnt deep into the wood, and above it a crown of grape leaves. But one glance at the crates told Signora Vittorio this cargo was special.

This was the latest shipment of *Vino Nobile di Montepulciano*, the wine on which the foundation of the Castelli empire had been built. And though the company had widely diversified these past forty years, this ancient vintage of which poets and gods had sung was still distributed to Castelli's international warehouses directly from the docks at Livorno, and transported in special crates, and only in Castelli's chartered vessels.

Just then, her young cousin shouted at her through the bustle. "Maria! Maria, up here!"

Anaïs was standing on the foredeck, waving madly.

Signora Vittorio lifted her skirts and picked her way through the tumult, swishing gingerly around the crates, cranes, and grubby urchins awaiting an errand to run or a pocket to pick, for the Docklands were not known for their salubrious atmosphere.

By the time she reached her young cousin, Anaïs was standing on the dock beside a growing pile of baggage, a leather folio tucked under one arm.

"Maria!" she cried, throwing an arm about her neck.

Signora Vittorio kissed both her cheeks. "Welcome home, *cara*!"

"Thank you for coming down," said Anaïs. "I didn't want to hire a cab this time of night, and I have too much baggage to walk."

"Out of the question!" said Signora Vittorio. "And the *Sarah Jane*? Surely, *cara*, you did not come all this way by ship? You are not nearly green enough to have done so."

"No?" Anaïs laughed and kissed her again. "How green am I, then?"

The *signora* drew back and studied her. "Merely a sort of gray-green, like that mold one sees on trees."

Anaïs laughed again. "It's *lichen*, Maria," she said, settling a hand over her belly. "And actually, I came across France, the last bit by train. But I met Captain Clarke in Le Havre, for I swore to Trumbull I'd see this shipment offloaded. It is precious, you know—and already sold."

"And your brother Armand's job to deal with," added Signora Vittorio sourly. "Instead, he's chasing a new mistress at some country house party."

Anaïs shrugged. "In any case, the river was not so bad, and one must cross the channel somehow," she said, craning her head to look about. "Besides, I haven't heaved up my innards since Gravesend."

"Don't speak so bluntly, *cara*," the *signora* gently chided. "What would your mother say? Catherine is an elegant lady. And what have you there under your arm?"

Anaïs extracted the folio. "Paperwork for Trumbull from the Livorno office," she said. "Letters, bills of lading, overdue accounts from some bankrupt vintner in Paris. Clarke just handed it to me." She paused to look about. "Where is the carriage? Have you a key to the office? I want to leave this."

"I have a key, *sì*," said Signora Vittorio hesitantly. "But Burr Street was blocked. I sent the carriage round back to load your baggage."

"Well, I'll just walk down." Anaïs snatched up a small leather portmanteau from the top of the luggage heap, and stuffed the folio inside.

"Not alone," said Signora Vittorio.

"Silly goose," said Anaïs, smiling. "Very well, then. Bear me company. Clarke will send the trunks on to Wellclose Square tomorrow. If Putnam could just manage the three smaller bags?"

With a few swift orders, Signora Vittorio arranged to have them carried through the dockyards to their carriage beyond. Anaïs was still holding the portmanteau just as two large men pushed past them, conversing as they made their way toward the *Sarah Jane*.

Anaïs turned, her gaze following. "My God, that is the ugliest Frenchman I ever saw," she whispered.

"*Sì*," said the *signora* dryly, "but the other—the tall one— ah, *che bell'uomo!*"

"Really?" Anaïs turned, but she could see nothing save their backs now. "I didn't get a good look."

"And a pity for you," said the *signora* in a low, appreciative voice. "For *I* saw him. And I am old, *cara*, but not dead."

Anaïs laughed. "Ah, but I have learnt my lesson, Maria, have I not? That lesson one so often learns about handsome, dashing men? I don't bother to look anymore."

At that, Maria's face fell, all humor fleeing her eyes.

Anaïs laughed again. "Oh, Maria, don't," she pleaded. "Giovanni would be ashamed to see these long faces were he still alive. Come on, let's hurry. I want to go *home*."

Maria's smile returned. Arms linked, nattering like magpies, they set off together at a surprisingly brisk clip, weaving through the remaining crates and barrels, and going out the back of St. Katherine's quagmire and into the streets of East London.

This was familiar territory to them both, but rarely at night. Still, as the bustle of the docks fell away and darkness settled in, neither woman was especially concerned. The fog had not obscured all the moonlight, and Maria knew Anaïs never went into the East End unprepared—or the West End, come to that.

They soon turned into the high, narrow lane that led to Castelli's side entrance. But they had scarcely stepped off another dozen paces when running steps pounded after them from behind. In an instant, everything became a blur. On a loud *oof!* Maria went hurtling sideways, slammed against an adjacent doorway, hitting so hard the doorbell within jangled.

"Take that, yer haughty bitch!" In a flash, a hand lashed out at the old woman.

"Oh, no, you don't!" Anaïs threw back the portmanteau and sent it slamming against the side of his head.

Sent reeling, the assailant cursed, and set off running, turning down a pitch-dark passageway.

"My pearls!" Maria's hand clutched at her throat. "*Sofia's* pearls!"

But Anaïs was already off, hurtling the portmanteau aside as she went. "Stop, thief!" she shouted, moving so fast she was scarcely aware of the second set of footfalls in the distance behind.

She caught the man in a dozen long strides, seizing him by the collar and slamming him against the front of a sail-maker's shop. He fought hard, but she fought smart, putting her elbows and height to good use. In an instant, she had his face flat against the shop, one arm wrenched behind, a knee against his knackers, and a stiletto whipped from the sheath in her sleeve.

"Drop the pearls," she said grimly.

"Bugger off, yer bleedin' Amazon!" said the man, thrashing.

Anaïs pressed the blade to his throat and felt him quiver. "Drop the pearls," she said again. "Or I will cheerfully draw your blood."

In the gloom, she felt rather than saw his fist open. The necklace fell, two or three beads skittering away as it struck the pavement.

"Your name, you cowardly dog," she said, lips pressed to his ear.

"None o' yer bleedin' business, that's me name."

He jerked again, and she lifted her knee, slamming it up hard where it counted.

The man cried out, and managed to twist slightly in her grip, turning his once-empty hand. She heard the soft *snick!* of a flick-knife, then caught the faint glint of moonlight as the blade thrust back.

In a split second, she tightened her grip and steeled herself to the strike. But the blade never found flesh. A long arm whipped out of the darkness, catching the man's wrist and wrenching it until he screamed.

Startled, Anaïs must have loosened her grip. The flick-knife clattered to the pavement. But the villain dropped, slipped from her grasp, and bolted into the gloom.

"*Maledizione!*" she uttered, watching him go.

"Are you unhurt, ma'am?" A deep, masculine voice came from her right.

Anaïs whirled about, still clutching the stiletto, blade up. A tall, lean figure leapt back in the dark, a mere shadow as he threw up both hands. "Just trying to help," he said.

"Damn it!" she said, angry at herself and at him.

The man let his hands fall. The night fell utterly silent. Anaïs felt the rush subside and her senses return to something near normal. "Thank you," she added, "but I had him."

"What you had—almost—was a blade in your thigh," he calmly corrected. She felt his gaze fall upon the glint of her knife. "On the other hand, you appear to have been well prepared for it."

"A blade to the thigh, a blade to the throat," she said coolly. "Which of us do you think would have lived to tell the tale?"

"*Hmm,*" he said. "Would you have cut him, then?"

Anaïs drew in a deep breath. Though she couldn't make out the man's face, she could sense his movements, his presence—and the warm, rich scent of tobacco smoke and expensive cologne told her just who he was. A wealthy man, the sort rarely seen traversing these mean, meandering streets. And he was tall, far taller than she—and that was no small feat.

"No, I wouldn't have cut him," she finally answered. "Not unless I had to."

"And now," said the man quietly, "you don't have to."

He was right, she realized. He had not saved her from danger. He had saved her from herself. She was running short of sleep, dead tired from days of travel, and still queasy from the crossing. Neither her judgment nor her intuition was at its best.

"Thank you," she said, a little humbled.

In a flat high above, someone shoved a casement wide, and thrust out a lamp. Still, the feeble light scarcely reached them. But it was enough, apparently, to allow him to bend down, sweep up her great-grandmother's pearls, and press them into her hand.

"Thank you, sir," she said again, the pearls warm and heavy in her palm. "You were very brave."

But the tall man said no more. Instead, still deep in shadow, he swept off his top hat, made an elegant bow, then strode off into the darkness.

CHAPTER 2

In battle, there are not more than two
methods of attack: the direct and the indirect;
yet these two in combination give rise to
an endless series of maneuvers.
Sun Tzu, *The Art of War*

*A*ttired in the austere vestments of the *Fraternitas Aureae Crucis*, the Earl of Bessett stood on the stone gallery that encircled the Society's vaulted temple. Below, the chamber thronged with brown-robed men, and looked much as any small, private chapel might, save for the absence of pews and the almost monastic lack of adornment. Indeed, viewed by flickering sconces, the stone walls and floors appeared as grim and gray as the balustrade, with each level broken by alternating stone arches that served to cast shifting shadows over the assemblage.

The austerity of the temple was heightened by the fact that it was built underground—far below the streets of London; lower, even, than the cellars of the elegant St. James Society, for the temple had been dug beneath them, and the rubble carried out under cover of darkness. Few men living knew of this subterranean chamber, or of the sect itself, for too often over the centuries, the *Fraternitas* had been all but destroyed by the vicissitudes of religion, power, and politics.

But time and again, the Brotherhood had hung on. And though they lived now in an age of enlightenment, enlightenment was only as good as the men who stepped forth to defend it, and the *Fraternitas* had become defensively—and deeply—secretive.

His hands braced wide on the balustrade, Lord Lazonby leaned over and looked down through his sardonic blue eyes at the milling crowd as Bessett watched him assessingly. "What did you do with that lad from the *Chronicle* the other night?" asked Bessett quietly.

"Lured him up Petticoat Lane and lost him in the rookeries."

"Christ, that place may be the end of him," said Bessett. "What can he be after anyway? The reading public cannot still be interested in you. You are out of prison, and exonerated of any crime."

His gaze fixed in the distance, Lazonby rolled his shoulders restlessly. "I don't know," he said. "It has begun to feel . . . personal."

Bessett hesitated a heartbeat. "And I've begun to wonder if you aren't taunting him—and enjoying it."

"Bloody nonsense!" Lazonby's eyes flashed. "What has Ruthveyn said to you?"

It was an odd question. But over the last several months, the *Chronicle*'s reporter—and his apparent mission to dog the new Earl of Lazonby to his grave—had become an irritant to all of them. There was no denying, however, that Rance's checkered past left him vulnerable to gossip and suspicion.

"Now that you mention it, I have lately sensed a strain between you and Ruthveyn," said Bessett.

Lazonby was quiet for a moment. "Sometime past, I inadvertently gave offense to his sister," he acknowledged. "I should rather not say more."

Bessett's gaze drifted over the swelling crowd. "So Lady Anisha's ardor for you has cooled, has it?" he finally said.

Lazonby cut an incredulous look at him. "Why am I the last to hear of the lady's so-called ardor?" he snapped. "As I told your brother when *he* warned me off, Nish is not my type. I adore her, yes. We flirt a little, yes. But she—why, she is almost like a sister to me."

Bessett snorted. "By God, she's not like a sister to me."

"Then you pay court to her," snapped Lazonby.

"I bloody well might, then," said Bessett.

And indeed, it was not a bad idea. He had been turning the notion over and over in his mind for some time now.

Lady Anisha Stafford was a breathtakingly beautiful widow whose unruly children were in dire need of a father. And if a man had to confine himself to bedding one woman for the rest of his days, then one could hardly do better than Nish.

But more important than the lady's beauty and character was the fact that he need never explain himself to her. Need never be judged. She understood the thin, carefully crafted façade he maintained, that tenuous wall he had built between his conscious mind and the darkness beyond.

Perhaps that was the key to his restlessness. The thing that seemed out of order in his life. Perhaps it was just the yearning for something . . . *more*.

"I will, then," Bessett muttered. "If you indeed lay no claim to the lady?"

Without so much as looking at him, Lazonby waved his hand as if in invitation.

A little awkwardly, Bessett cleared his throat. "Are you at all anxious about the new acolyte?"

Lord Lazonby's head jerked around, an odd smile curling one corner of his mouth. "Why should I be?"

"You've seemed . . . different the last two days." Bessett set his head slightly to one side, and studied his old friend. "Distracted."

Lazonby threw back his head and laughed softly. "You cannot read me, Geoff," he answered, "so stop trying. Besides, this is a solemn occasion—or so our Preost keeps telling me."

"I find it odd that until now, you'd never agreed to sponsor an acolyte," Bessett mused. "You seemed not to take this part of the *Fraternitas* with any seriousness. Are you afraid the new recruit might forget his vows? Or trip over his own two feet?"

Lazonby crooked one eyebrow. "If the fellow falls arse over teakettle at Sutherland's hems, it's nothing to me," he said evenly. "After all, he was groomed by old Vittorio, and Sutherland's the one who made me do this."

"It *was* your turn, Rance," said Bessett.

"Aye, and now I've taken it." Lazonby's hands slid from the stone balustrade as he straightened. "And what Vittorio and I hath wrought, old chap, let no man put asunder. Remember that, won't you?"

Just then, a gong sounded, the low reverberations echoing off the vaulted walls. With a roguish wink, Lazonby threw up his hood. "Ah, the witching hour is upon us," he said. "Curtains up!"

Still, Bessett hesitated. "Damn it, Rance, what have you done?" he asked, seizing his old friend's arm. "Do you dislike the lad? Or distrust him?"

"There you go again, trying to read my mind."

"Oh, for God's sake. I don't read minds."

"No?" Lazonby turned and started down the stairs, the hem of his brown wool robe dragging over the steps as Bessett followed. "But to answer your question, Geoff, aye, I like the acolyte very well indeed," he continued over his shoulder, "but I'm not at all sure the rest of you will."

After descending to the main chamber, Bessett and Lazonby took their places in the rear with the remaining Guardians. The ceremony commenced at once, all of them responding a little mechanically to Sutherland's liturgy. The traditional prayers were said, then the chalice of wine was passed, but Geoff sipped from it with half a mind.

The truth was, though he might accuse Rance of not taking such ceremonial matters seriously, Geoff, too, often skimmed over the finer points of rite and ritual. They were both far more concerned with the practicalities of how to resurrect and restructure an organization that, just a few short years earlier, had lain scattered over war-torn Europe in tragic—and potentially dangerous—disarray.

The initiation ceremony was always performed in Latin, the language of the last formal *Fraternitas* manuscripts still in existence. Over the centuries, many of the Brotherhood's records had been destroyed—often out of self-preservation—particularly during the Middle Ages, when the Gift had nearly died out, and during the Inquisition, when many of the Vateis had been put to the rack.

Though the Vateis were neither, being burned as a heretic or drowned as a witch was not an uncommon fate for those whom history had so grievously misunderstood. And out of such cruelty and ignorance, the Guardians had sprung, in order to protect the weaker among them.

Now they were to welcome another into the fold. By tradition, the young man now hidden behind the Great Altar would be a blood relation to one of the Vateis, and born in the sign of fire and war. He might possess the Gift himself, to one degree or another. But he would have been indoctrinated from his youth by one of the *Fraternitas*—most likely one of the Advocati—or a trusted family member.

Geoff's grandmother was one such example. Although forbidden membership as a female, she had been a trusted agent of the *Fraternitas* in Scotland, where the sect had always held strong. She had also possessed a powerful Gift—one that Geoff dearly wished he could give back to her.

He was returned abruptly to the present when Mr. Sutherland ended his invocation and descended from the stone pulpit. A deep hush fell over the room, as it always did on those rare occasions when any new member was brought into the *Fraternitas*—and the induction of a Guardian was the rarest of the rare.

Going to the altar behind him, Sutherland lifted the brass key that dangled from a gold chain at his waist, and unlocked an ancient, iron-hinged box. Easing back the lid, he gingerly lifted out a tattered book, already laid open, and marked with a long, bloodred ribbon.

The *Liber Veritas*—the *Book of Truths*—was the *Fraternitas*'s rarest volume. The ancient tome set forth all the rites still known to the Brotherhood, and had been in use in one form or another since the rise of Rome.

With his right hand raised in the eternal sign of blessing, and his left cradling the open book, the Preost read a few short words, calling upon the supplicant to offer up his life to the cause, and asking God to protect him in his work.

Then he dropped his hand, and gave the sign.

Inset between two thick columns, the Great Altar began to shudder and grind, the sound like that of a millstone at work. Slowly at first, and then with surprising rapidity, the altar spun halfway around.

The first thing Geoff realized was that, oddly, the acolyte was not naked.

Although the fellow was bound just as he should have been—at his wrists and his eyes—he wore not his altogether, but a sleeveless linen tunic that hung just below his knees.

And the second thing Geoff realized was that the acolyte wasn't even a *he*.

Someone in the audience gasped.

It wasn't Geoff. He couldn't breathe.

Sutherland, too, was frozen before the altar. Eyes wide, he clutched the *Liber Veritas* to his chest as if he meant to throttle the life from it. His mouth opened and closed silently, then he uttered an odd, gurgling sound—like the last of the dishwater chasing down a kitchen drain.

Propelled by the sound, Ruthveyn shouldered swiftly through the crowd. He extracted the book, then turned to face them all.

"Just whose idea of a joke is this?" he demanded, shaking the book above his head. "By God, let the wretch step forward!"

And the third thing Geoff realized was that the acolyte might nearly as well have *been* naked, for the shift or shirt or whatever it was left little to the imagination. Nonetheless, the girl stood upon the altar straight and proud, despite the ropes that bound her wrists awkwardly before her. She was tall, with high, small breasts that were rising and falling a little too rapidly, a wild mane of inky curls that hung to her waist, and long, slender legs that looked surprisingly strong.

Surprisingly?

Everything about this was surprisingly . . . something. Not to mention erotic, what with all the ropes and blindfolds and yes, those legs . . .

The room was abuzz now. Ruthveyn had found a knife somewhere, and was slicing through the ropes at her wrists. Beside him, Geoff could hear Rance softly chuckling.

In that instant, the girl twisted a little away from Ruthveyn, causing the thin shirt to slither over her hip most suggestively. Blood suddenly surging, Geoff shot Rance a burn-in-hell look, then hastened onto the dais, stripped off his robe, and furled it gently around her.

The girl did not so much as flinch at his touch.

Then, rather more carefully, Ruthveyn cut away the blindfold, which was traditionally worn until the vote to admit the acolyte was taken.

The girl blinked a pair of dark, wide-set eyes, looked out over the crowd, and surprised everyone by speaking in a clear, strong voice.

"I humbly ask for admission to the Brotherhood," she announced in precise, flawless Latin. "I have earned this right with my Devotion, with my Strength, and with my Blood. And on my honor, I pledge that by my Word and by my Sword, I will defend the Gift, my Faith, my Brotherhood, and all its Dependents, until the last breath of life—"

"No, no, no, no!" Ruthveyn waved an obviating hand. "My dear child, I do not know who has put you up such pranks, but—"

"I did." Rance's voice, too, was surprisingly strong. "I sponsor this woman for initiation to the Old and Most Noble Order, the *Fraternitas Aureae Crucis*. Aren't those the sponsor's magic words?"

"You *what*?" Geoff found himself saying. "Mother of God, man, have you lost your mind?"

"Indeed, Rance." Sutherland had finally found his voice. "You've made a joke of an honored and holy ritual. You have gone beyond the pale."

"Here, here!" grumbled someone in the crowd of brown robes.

Geoff stepped in front of the girl to shield her, but she pushed him away with surprising strength, and stepped down onto the dais.

"*Why* is it beyond the pale, my lords?" she demanded, her accent unmistakably upper-class. "For ten long years I have trained. I have done all that was asked of me, and more, though I never asked for any of this. But because I was asked—nay, *told* that it was my duty—I have given up much of my youth, and I have sacrificed, merely to meet the tasks which were set before me. And now you would deny me my right of Brotherhood?"

Ruthveyn's dark face twisted. "And that, you see, is our very problem," he replied. "This *is* a Brotherhood, Mrs. . . . ?"

"*Miss* de Rohan," she snapped. "Anaïs de Rohan."

"Miss de Rohan." Ruthveyn lost a little of his color. "Well. As I was saying, this is a brotherhood. Not a sisterhood. Not one, big happy family." Then he whirled about on the dais. "Rance, you ought to be horsewhipped. For God's sake, call Safiyah to take this poor girl away, and find her some proper clothes."

Miss de Rohan.

Now why was that name familiar?

No matter. It was obviously dawning on Ruthveyn, as it was dawning on Geoff, that this was no ordinary female. Certainly she was an *unwed* female, which made matters rather more precarious for all of them. Moreover, she both spoke and carried herself with the air of an aristocrat—a somewhat angry and inconvenienced aristocrat. And yet she stood there before a score of men, very nearly naked, and icily composed.

Old Vittorio had taught her something, that was for sure.

Rance, however, had begun to argue.

"Where, gentlemen, is it written that a woman cannot belong?" he was shouting. "Giovanni Vittorio, one of our most trusted Advocati, saw fit to take this girl under his wing and train her in our ways."

"Nonsense," Geoff snapped. "Vittorio was ill. He wasn't thinking clearly. Would you entrust your life to her hands,

Rance? *Would* you? Because that is what you are asking every one of the Vateis to do."

"You forget I have reviewed Vittorio's documentation, and spoken to the chit at length," Rance countered. "Is that not the duty of the sponsor? To ensure that the acolyte is qualified? For I can assure you, she is in many ways far more qualified than I."

"That," said Geoff tightly, "I don't doubt for an instant."

"I resent your arrogance, old chap," said Rance.

"I resent it, too," said the girl coolly. "I am qualified. And you, sir, are an ass."

Geoff spun round to face her. She had made no effort whatsoever to pull together the robe he had hurled about her shoulders, a fact that made him inexplicably angry. He let his eyes trail hotly down her, and felt something besides anger curling in the pit of his belly.

"If you are truly Vittorio's acolyte," he said tightly, "then you'll be marked."

She jerked up her chin, anger flashing in her black eyes. "Oh, I am," she said, her hand seizing the hem of the shift. "Do you wish to see the proof?"

"Good God, Bessett," said Rance on a groan. "She's marked. I made sure."

Bessett spun in the other direction. "*You made sure?*" he echoed incredulously. "Do you mind telling—no, never mind." He turned again, and seized the girl by the upper arm. "You, come with me."

"Where are you taking her?" Belkadi, one of the Advocati, had materialized at his elbow.

"To Safiyah," Geoff answered, his voice pitched low. "For I can see, even if Rance cannot, that an unmarried female of good family cannot stand half naked in the middle of what is believed to be little more than a gentlemen's club."

"Oh, thank you!" said the girl bitterly. "Ten years of my life tossed into the rubbish heap over a point of etiquette!"

Geoff did not reply but instead hauled her up the steps and through the wine cellar, into the laboratory passageway. Another flight took them to the ground floor, and eventually to the relative privacy of the servants' stairs, the girl snapping at him the whole way.

Except that she was not a girl.

No, not by a far shot.

And what she had just done—dear Lord, it was courting ruin. Did it simply not matter to her?

"You are bruising my arm, you lout," she informed him. "What are you so afraid of? After all, I am just a mere woman."

"I am afraid *for* you, you little fool," he whispered. "Be still, before you're seen by someone whose silence we can't so easily command."

She bucked up at that, jerking to a stubborn halt on the landing. "I am not ashamed of what I am," she said, clutching his robe shut with one hand. "I have worked hard to learn my craft."

"You, madam, do not have 'a craft,'" he said coldly. "For God's sake, consider others if not yourself. What would your father think if he knew where you were just now?"

At that, a faint flush chased up her cheeks. "He might not approve, to be honest."

"*Might* not?" Against his will, Geoff's gaze swept hotly down her length again. "He *might* not approve? Of his daughter running around half naked in a London club?"

Her hard, black eyes narrowed. "It isn't like that," she said. "I simply haven't told him everything. Not yet."

Geoff hesitated, incredulous. "You mean you've told him *something*?"

Her blush deepened, but her tone did not soften. "Oh, for

pity's sake, I've been staying in Tuscany with Vittorio for months at a time," she retorted. "What do you think I told him? That I was off to finishing school in Geneva? Do I look finished to you?"

No, she did not.

She looked like something . . . wild and totally *un*finished.

Like something a man might never be finished with—though she was not precisely pretty. But she was intriguing and earthy and full of a vivacity he couldn't quite grasp. And whatever she was, she looked like no woman he'd ever known before—and he'd known quite a few.

Her father's wrath, however, was none of his concern. Oddly angry with himself, he turned as if to set off again, yanking her toward the next staircase. But he caught her unaware. One foot tangling in the hem of his long wool robe, she tipped precariously forward.

"Oh!" she cried, her empty hand flailing for the stair rail.

Instinctively, Geoff caught her, his arm lashing round her slender waist, hitching her hard against his chest.

Suddenly, time and place spun away. It was as if no one breathed—a mere instant of warmth and scent and pure, artless sensuality that seemed to stop logic dead in its tracks. And when he looked down into those eyes—eyes the color of warm chocolate, fringed with thick, inky lashes—he felt something deep inside him start to twist and bend, like metal warming to the fire of some otherworldly forge.

Her bottom lip was full, like a slice of ripe peach, and for an instant, it trembled almost temptingly.

Then the girl saved him from whatever folly he might have been contemplating. "*Oof*," she grunted, pushing a little away. "If you mean to kill me, Bessett, just pitch me over the banister and be done with it."

"Don't tempt me," he growled.

But inexplicably, he couldn't stop looking down. The

swells of her extraordinary breasts were plainly visible from this angle, and God help him, he was no angel.

Irritation flashing in her eyes, Miss de Rohan fully righted herself. "Really, my lord, do you mind?" she said, hitching up the front of her shift. "I'm not in the habit of displaying my assets unless they're corseted into a ball gown."

"And that," he said quietly, "cannot possibly be often enough."

Her face colored furiously.

"I beg your pardon," he said again. "But you did choose to wear that, Miss de Rohan. And I am, after all, just an ordinary man."

She sniffed disdainfully. "Ordinary, hmm?" she said. "I didn't think anyone here was ordinary."

"Trust me, my dear, when it comes to attractive women, all men are the same." He held out his hand to her, his actions gentler now. "Yet another reason I am afraid for you."

"You suggest I'm not safe in this house?" Her voice was sharp.

"Your reputation is not," he answered. "But no one here would do you a harm, Miss de Rohan. You may trust each and every one of us with your life—my roaming eyes notwithstanding."

With obvious reluctance, she laid her hand in his.

"Now, about your father." He kept his voice firm. "I believe you were about to tell me who he is."

"Precisely?" For an instant, she caught her lip in her teeth. "He's a minor Alsatian nobleman. The Vicomte de Vendenheim-Sélestat."

Carefully watching those chocolate-brown eyes, Geoff stood his ground. "And *im*precisely?" he pressed. "Come, Miss de Rohan. You are London born and bred, I'll wager. I may be a lecherous lout, aye, but I'm sharp enough to know when I'm getting but half the truth."

At last, her gaze broke away. "A long time ago, he was called Max de Rohan. Or just de Vendenheim. He's . . . with the Home Office. Sort of."

Well. So much for gentleness. Geoff stifled a curse, then turned to haul her up the next flight of stairs.

De Vendenheim! Of all people! Rance must be a lunatic. That little shite from the *Chronicle* had finally driven him stark, staring mad.

Geoff didn't know anything about de Vendenheim's title, but he damned sure knew the fellow wasn't the sort of man one antagonized. And he wasn't "with" the Home Office, sort of. He *was* the Home Office—or more accurately, the ruthlessness behind it. Politically, he was untouchable— unelected, nonpartisan, and more or less unofficial—the ultimate *éminence grise*.

Like a black cat with nine lives, the lean, hawk-nosed fellow had survived one political upheaval after another, having outlived the establishment of the Metropolitan Police, the Reform Bill riots, the bloody work of the London Burkers, and an entire outfield of home secretaries. By rights he ought to be dead by now, so much turmoil, strife, and violence had the man seen firsthand.

And now his daughter had been trained as a Guardian? And not, apparently, with his blessing?

Good God.

"Hurry up," he said gruffly. "You are going to get dressed *now*."

"A capital notion, given the miserable draft coming up these steps," she snapped. "Can't you people afford coal? I thought you were all rich. My feet are bare and my arse hasn't been so cold since the winter of—"

"Miss de Rohan," Geoff managed to reply, "I could not be less interested in the state of your arse."

Liar, liar, liar.

"Why, I am crushed, my lord!" she said mockingly. "Of course, I was supposed to be completely naked, according to the ceremony—but even I couldn't summon up the cheek to do *that*."

"A tiny sliver of good judgment for which we must all be grateful," said Geoff through clenched teeth. And he meant it. The last thing he needed on his mind just now was the vision of Anaïs de Rohan naked.

And yet he was already imagining it. Conjuring up those impossibly long legs in his mind, and wondering if they would reach—

No. He needed to know nothing about the length of her legs. *He needed to get rid of her.*

Thank God they had reached the topmost floor of the house, where Belkadi kept his private apartments. At the door, Geoff rapped twice, hard, with the back of his hand, still holding on to the hellcat. It took all his English civility not to sling her inside and bolt as soon as the door cracked. His Scottish half wanted to tie her to a rock and tip her into the Thames.

Safiyah opened the door, her wide, doe-brown eyes sweeping over them. "My lord," she said, startled. "Where is Samir?"

"Your brother's still in the Temple," said Geoff, hauling Miss de Rohan inside. "It has been a strange night. Sorry to barge in but I need your help."

"But of course." Safiyah lowered her gaze. "Who is she?"

"The acolyte," snapped Miss de Rohan. "And I have a name."

Safiyah colored furiously, and looked away. "I shall put the kettle on."

Geoff's prisoner looked immediately contrite. "I beg your pardon," said Miss de Rohan. "You did not deserve that."

"No, I did not." Safiyah's hands were folded serenely. "Excuse me. I shall be but a moment."

"I'm Anaïs," she replied, thrusting out her hand. "Anaïs de Rohan. Do forgive me. Being manhandled up the steps has left my temper regrettably short. And I should love a cup of tea. By the way, I do have clothes, Lord Bessett. I did not walk in off the street naked. And you *are* Lord Bessett, are you not? After all, *you* did not introduce *yourself* before hauling me from the Temple and up the stairs."

"Where did you leave them?" he asked, ignoring the rest of the diatribe.

Her eyes widened with irritation. "In a little room on the ground floor," she said. "I came in through the gardens."

Geoff went at once to the bellpull, then realized the stupidity of it. "Sit down and be quiet," he ordered. "I'll fetch them. And be kind to Safiyah. She may be your only friend here when this dreadful night is over."

CHAPTER 3

*The clever combatant imposes his will on the enemy,
but does not allow the enemy's will
to be imposed upon him.*
Sun Tzu, *The Art of War*

*A*naïs watched her captor go, rubbing almost absently at her chafed wrists. Lord Bessett was proving to be both haughty and pigheaded. But what had she expected? Handsome, rich aristocrats were rarely otherwise. The fact that he was one of the *Fraternitas* did not necessarily make him a pattern of humility—or humanity, apparently.

And she—well, she looked like an idiot in her butchered shift—now topped with Bessett's scratchy, horridly gothic robe. The coarse wool dragged the floor, and could have wrapped twice around her, but she knew she should be grateful for it all the same.

On a sigh, Anaïs fell back into the deep, comfortable armchair into which Bessett had all but shoved her, stewing in her humiliation. Of course, she should be humiliated. She knew she should. Things had gone about as badly as Cousin Giovanni had warned her they would.

But now Giovanni Vittorio was dead. Her nonna was dead. Indeed, everyone who had helped bring Anaïs to this strange, otherworldly point in life had gone on to his great reward, leaving her to muddle through the hardest part alone.

Not that Vittorio had ever believed educating Anaïs was especially prudent. He'd never said as much, of course. Never had he given her less than his full attention. But over the years, as their mutual affection had deepened, Anaïs had come to sense his worry. Once—after that bastard Raphaele had broken her heart—Vittorio had even gently suggested that perhaps Anaïs might prefer a different sort of life. An *ordinary* life. That perhaps the *Fraternitas*, the Guardians, and even the Gift itself had no place in the modern world that was evolving all around them.

But even amidst the heartbreak, she had wanted—no, *needed*—to honor her great-grandmother's memory. So they had muddled on, Anaïs doing her best to learn all that was required of her, and her much-elder cousin harboring his unspoken doubt. And just now, it felt as if that doubt had been well-placed. Anaïs realized she was almost blinking back tears.

She jerked herself up short. Besides, the sense of hopelessness wouldn't last; she simply wouldn't let it. Nonna Sofia had always said despair was an emotion for the faint of heart—useful only to damsels who reveled in distress, and poets requiring inspiration.

Still, for a moment, Anaïs let her eyes fall shut with weariness and drew in a deep, somewhat unsteady breath. But the act merely served to remind her of the arrogant Lord Bessett, for the scent she drew in was unmistakably his, held round her in a warm, oddly comforting cloud by the heavy wool of his robe.

A robe that he had kindly wrapped round her, Anaïs reminded herself. He might be pigheaded and chauvinistic, yes. He might have swept that bold, searing gaze of his down her once too often. And there was no question he'd stripped her breasts bare in his imagination. But his concern, at least, had been genuine.

He was also beautiful enough to make a girl swoon—if a girl were given to such theatrics. Anaïs was not. She'd cut her teeth on handsome men, and knew that they were invariably aware of their looks—and never above using them. Her wisdom, however, did not lessen the clean, hard lines of the man's face, and that perfectly turned jaw that looked to have been carved out of marble.

His eyes were cold and glittering beneath dark, straight brows, and his nose was faintly aquiline. Only a lush, almost hedonistic mouth saved Bessett from unbridled masculinity. Nonetheless, there were no smile lines to indicate he made much use of it. In fact, Anaïs got the oddest impression the man was entirely without humor.

Perhaps a man did not need humor when he smelled so enticingly. Again, she drew in the scent of male skin and clean citrus. He had shaved recently—within the last two hours, she guessed, which likely meant he shaved twice a day. Apparently, he took great pride in those good looks, the preening peacock.

Actually, that was unfair. And spite, Giovanni had always warned, was beneath her.

The truth was, Lord Bessett seemed almost *unaware* of his looks. Indeed, he moved like some lean jungle creature, instinctively elegant and smooth, as if he owned the world and spared it scarcely a thought. Vain, self-absorbed men were easy to understand—and easy to manipulate, Anaïs had learned.

Suddenly, it dawned on Anaïs that Bessett mightn't prove so simple. Assuming she meant to *try* to get her way with him.

But what choice did she have? He was a leader here. Giovanni had told her that much early on. Indeed, he had been deeply grateful for Bessett's efforts to reestablish the *Fraternitas*, and center it in London—here, in this house, the so-called St. James Society. And judging from the opulence that was apparent throughout, he'd spent quite a lot of money doing it, too.

Just then, a faint sound roused her. Anaïs sat fully upright to see that the beautiful, dark-haired woman had returned, carrying a tray with a tea service and two cups.

She set it down wordlessly, then with the faintest bob of a curtsy, moved as if to go.

Anaïs found the idea of such a lovely, regal creature curtsying to her vaguely amusing. "I am sorry," she said again. "I was frightfully rude earlier, and you are very kind, Mrs.—?"

At last the woman lifted her gaze to meet Anaïs's, but she did not look the least bit humbled. "Belkadi," she said quietly. "Miss Belkadi."

"And you live here?" Anaïs asked. "In this house?"

"With my brother, Samir," she said.

"I am surprised they permit you," Anaïs sourly remarked. "There has been a great deal of fuss and nonsense over *my* being here."

Miss Belkadi let her gaze drift over Anaïs's scantily clad state, but did not remark upon it. "My brother is the house steward," she replied coolly. I keep the accounts, and manage the small female staff."

Like a housekeeper, Anaïs thought.

Except that this woman looked about as much like a housekeeper as Queen Victoria resembled a costermonger. But she was dressed plainly, in a gown of dark gray merino that covered her to the neck, and her dark brown hair was caught up in the simplest of arrangements. Despite all the severity, however, she could not have been much older than Anaïs herself.

"Won't you sit down, Miss Belkadi?" she blurted. "Really, I know my manners are lacking, but I could do with a kind face just now."

Somehow, Anaïs had known that her unwilling hostess would be too gracious to refuse. "Very well," she answered, sweeping her skirts neatly beneath her as she sat. "Shall I pour?"

Anaïs smiled. "That is a lovely accent," she said. "Are you French?"

Miss Belkadi's gaze flicked up but an instant. "Partly," she said. "Do you take sugar?"

"No, nothing, thank you."

The tea was hot, and incredibly strong. Surprisingly, Anaïs found it restorative. For all her bold words, tonight's ceremony had taken a greater emotional toll than she cared to admit, and a part of her was relieved it was over.

Except it wasn't over.

Anaïs was down, but not defeated. How many times had Nonna Sofia warned her that this life would not go easily for her? There hadn't been a female within the *Fraternitas* in centuries; perhaps since the great Celtic priestesses died out.

Once tonight's shock was over—for all of them—Anaïs must simply try to convince the *Fraternitas* in London to take her. Or she could return to Tuscany, she supposed, and fall back on Cousin Giovanni's contacts. The Vittorio family had many. But like so much of Europe, Tuscany had grown increasingly unstable, and the Gift—well, there was no one left who needed her. The few who were still known had been sent abroad; to relatives, to other Guardians across the Continent, all off to higher ground in an ocean of political turmoil.

Miss Belkadi cleared her throat, recalling Anaïs to the present, and to her duty as a guest. "How marvelously strong this tea is," Anaïs remarked. "Is it something special?"

"It is a black tea from Assam," said her hostess, "near the Himalayas. Lord Ruthveyn has it sent."

"Ah, Ruthveyn," said Anaïs musingly. "I saw him tonight. What is he like?"

But Miss Belkadi's gaze shuttered at once. "He is a gentleman."

"And is he . . . a sort of Hindu?" Anaïs pressed, never one to give up easily.

Miss Belkadi visibly stiffened. "I believe he is a Christian," she said, "but I never thought it my place to ask."

"No, I meant is he—"

Anaïs stopped, and shook her head. It did not matter what she had meant. "I beg your pardon yet again, Miss Belkadi," she said. "I am not ordinarily so rude. I can plead only a stressful night."

For the first time, Anaïs saw curiosity flicker in her gaze. "I am sorry to hear it," she said softly.

Anaïs looked down at her strange attire. "And I daresay you must wonder . . ."

Miss Belkadi sat serenely, one perfect eyebrow lifted.

" . . . about my state of dress," Anaïs managed to finish. "About what I'm doing here."

Miss Belkadi's expression remained passive. "It is not my place to wonder any such thing."

Just then, a swift *tap-tap* sounded on the door, and Lord Bessett slipped back inside.

Somewhere along the way he had donned his coat, which was rather a shame when he had looked so fine in his shirt-sleeves. He had rolled her clothing into a neat bundle and tucked it under his arm, somehow leaving the lace flounce of one drawer leg peeking out the bottom.

She wanted, suddenly, to laugh. Lord Bessett, however, already looked indignant enough. Doubtless he was not accustomed to playing lady's maid.

"Is there someplace, Safiyah, Miss de Rohan might dress?" he said without preamble.

"Of course." Miss Belkadi motioned toward one of the doors that opened off the small sitting room. "In my bed-chamber."

Bessett dropped the bundle in Anaïs's lap. "I've called my carriage to take you up to Henrietta Place," he said. "I can walk home so—"

"Thank you, but I don't live in Westminster," Anaïs interjected.

Lord Bessett looked at her oddly.

So he did indeed know who her father was, even where he lived. She had suspected as much from the shift in his demeanor on the stairs. "In any case, my parents are abroad at present, Lord Bessett," she said. "At their vineyards. But I live in Wellclose Square."

At that, his eyes widened. "In the East End?" he blurted. "Alone?"

"No. Not alone." Anaïs kept her face emotionless, having decided there was much to be learned from Safiyah Belkadi. "And my coachman awaits at the Blue Posts. I'm to meet him there."

The odd glint was back in Lord Bessett's eyes, and Anaïs found herself suddenly wondering what color they were. In the sitting room lamplight, it was hard to judge.

"Well, what an interesting evening this has turned out to be," he finally said. "But you aren't walking alone to a common public house. Not at this time of night."

Miss Belkadi was looking back and forth at the two of them. "It is rather late," she said, rising gracefully from her chair. "I shall walk up with Miss de Rohan. Perhaps you, my lord, might follow me?"

Bessett seemed to hesitate. "If your brother agrees, yes. Thank you."

"My brother agrees," said Miss Belkadi. She had folded her hands neatly together again, and for the first time, Anaïs saw the strength and stubbornness in the gesture.

Bessett turned his gaze on Anaïs. "Well, it's settled then," he said, his voice gentler now. "Now kindly hurry, Miss de Rohan. If another hour gets past us, we'll be sharing the street with the morning's vegetable barrows."

The following morning, the mood within the hallowed, silk-hung walls of the St. James Society's coffee room was an odd one. Lord Ruthveyn stood at one of the wide bow windows, one hand set at the back of his neck as he stared across St. James's Place at the entrance to Ned Quartermaine's gaming hell—which was, ostensibly, a private club for the most dashing amongst the *ton*.

At Geoff's right sat Lieutenant Lord Curran Alexander, who looked as if he had not slept. Lord Manders had gone to the sideboard as if to replenish his breakfast plate, then left it there, forgotten.

Even Mr. Sutherland had abandoned his coffee cup, now turning cold upon the table.

So much consternation, thought Geoff, *over one small female*.

And Rance, of course—the cause of all this discord—had not yet seen fit to present himself, being the sort of gentleman who was rarely spotted before noon unless there was a garrison to storm or the grouse were in season.

Sutherland cleared his throat a little sharply, and motioned Ruthveyn from the window. "I think we needn't wait any longer, Adrian," he said. "As Preost, I'm here to arbitrate, but not to decide. That must fall to all of you, the Founders."

Alexander had lifted his gaze to Mr. Sutherland's. "Surely, sir, there can be no question of admitting this woman?"

"Wrong question, old friend." Ruthveyn's mouth twisted

sourly as he sat back down. "The question is whether we horsewhip Rance for that trick last night, or merely toss him out on his arse."

"Gentlemen, let us not be hasty." Sutherland drew off his silver spectacles and laid them pensively aside. He was a tall man of military bearing, who had been chosen as Preost because of his wisdom and his temperament. "Membership in the *Fraternitas* is for life. We all know that. As to this so-called St. James Society, there really is no procedure in your bylaws for dismissing a Founder. And it would be over-hasty."

"But last night was beyond the pale, Sutherland," said Lord Manders, shoving his coffee aside. "To bring a woman into our midst? Think what she has seen. Imagine the tales she might spread. As Lazonby's countryman—as a loyal Scot—I am angry."

"The Scots have no special sway within the *Fraternitas*, my lord," said Sutherland a little wearily. "The Gift runs strong in that nation's blood, aye—more so than others, I'll grant you. But we do not think any more—or any less—of a man for his race."

"Besides, there is a woman in our midst every day," Geoff heard himself saying. "You forget Safiyah Belkadi lives under our roof."

"Miss Belkadi deals only with the staff," said Manders. "No one ever sees her. She rarely speaks, certainly not to men. And she knows nothing, really, of what goes on here."

Geoff was willing to wager that Belkadi's sister knew more of what went on in the St. James Society than did half the members, but he wisely withheld that view.

"All that aside, she is Belkadi's sister, and she is to be trusted," Alexander continued. "But this de Rohan woman— I daresay she was just one of Rance's damned pranks."

"I wish, gentlemen, it were that simple."

Geoff turned around to see the Preost pinching at the bridge of his nose.

"What do you mean, Sutherland?" Ruthveyn demanded.

The Preost exhaled wearily. "I have been up all night, reading the records Rance gave me," he said. "They really are quite . . . extraordinary."

"Extraordinary?" Geoff echoed. "In what way?"

Sutherland nodded in his direction. "I'll get to that," he said. "But first let me add that I also found within the file a letter to me, written before Giovanni Vittorio's death. Rance did not pass it on, I suppose, because it would have ruined his little prank—or surprise, perhaps, is a fairer term. And it is possible Rance overlooked it, or imagined it was just a dying letter to an old friend."

Alexander, however, had gone dark as a thunderhead. "With all respect, sir, why do I suspect that you're about to make some sort of excuse for Lazonby's behavior last night?"

"Or tell us something we won't care to hear," Ruthveyn grumbled.

Geoff, too, could sense a shift in the wind—had begun to feel it, even last night, in Belkadi's suite. Miss de Rohan had been entirely too dispassionate about the entire business. Not defeated, but more . . . *resigned.* Oh, she'd lost her temper once or twice, but on the whole, it was as if she'd expected a battle royal, and this was but her opening salvo.

"What did Vittorio's letter say?" Geoff's voice sounded far calmer than he felt.

"That the girl was the great-granddaughter of his elder cousin, a seer by the name of Sofia Castelli," said the Preost. "The family has had roots deep in the *Fraternitas* for longer than written records have been kept."

"She possessed the Gift?" said Ruthveyn.

Sutherland nodded. "To a moderate degree," he said. "But her medium was a rather unusual one—*i tarocchi.*"

"Tarot cards!" said Lord Manders. "What a pack of Gypsy nonsense."

But Ruthveyn shook his head. "The Gift is often manifested in unusual ways," he said irritably. "Often ways which are tied to one's culture. In India, my sister was schooled in the wisdom of *Jyotish*—astrology, you might call it—and palmistry, too. But if you asked her if she was a mystic, like our mother, she would laugh at you."

"Lady Anisha thinks it's a skill, not a gift," Bessett interjected. "And to some extent, perhaps it is."

"To some extent," Ruthveyn agreed, "*perhaps*."

"And like her brother," Geoff added, "she refuses let our Savant, Dr. von Althausen, study it in his laboratory."

"Let it go, Bessett," Ruthveyn warned.

Geoff smiled. "Very well, so this cousin of Vittorio's, she was a card reader." He turned back to the Preost. "But as I mentioned earlier, Miss de Rohan admitted to me who her father is. How did the family end up here?"

"The Castellis were engaged in the wine trade all over Europe," said Sutherland, pensively stroking his salt-and-pepper beard. "Sofia's daughter married a Frenchman with vast vineyards in Alsace and Catalonia, but he died in the aftermath of the Revolution. Old Mrs. Castelli moved the family's wholesale business to London to escape Napoleon. She was tough as nails, and ruled her family with an iron fist."

"Castelli's," muttered Alexander. "Aye, I've seen their vans sitting out front of Berry Brothers. And they've warehouses in the East End."

Sutherland nodded. "Mrs. Castelli's grandson hated the family business and went into police work, which the old woman thought beneath him—and quite correctly, I would add. It was the cause of considerable strife within the family.

But in later life, he married well, to a widow from Gloucestershire. The Earl of Treyhern's sister."

For an instant, Geoff was certain he had misheard. He felt the blood drain from his face. Treyhern—or any member of his family—was about the last person he wished to anger. "Surely you jest?" he managed.

Sutherland looked at him strangely. "No," he answered. "They have five children, the oldest being twins, Armand de Rohan and his sister, Anaïs. And there was an elder boy, a foster son."

Lord Manders's eyes had widened. "I know Armand de Rohan," he uttered. "A very sporting fellow with pots of money. Good God. My uncle is thick as thieves with his father."

"That would be de Vendenheim," said Sutherland morosely. "We must tread carefully, gentlemen."

"I should have said we needn't tread at all," said Ruthveyn irritably. "Really, we are done with this, aren't we? Save for giving Rance a proper thrashing? Of course, there's always a concern the girl might talk, but—"

"The girl won't talk." Sutherland ripped off his spectacles and tossed them down again. "Gentlemen, I don't think you understand. Vittorio was perfectly serious in training this woman. He has tutored her extensively in the ancient texts of the *Fraternitas*, as well as natural philosophy, religion, even military tactics. She speaks six languages fluently—including Latin and Greek—and can apparently ride as well any man. Moreover, Vittorio says she is one of the best blades he ever trained."

"Good Lord," whispered Alexander. "One couldn't get a better education at the *École Militaire*. But swordsmanship? That's a bit of a dying art."

"Dying, perhaps, but not dead," Sutherland cautioned.

"One never knows when such a skill might come in handy. In any case, Vittorio claims the girl was *offered up* by her family."

"By her father?" Geoff barked. "Balderdash!"

"By Sofia Castelli," said Sutherland. "Whether the father knows the full scope of what the girl has been up to—well, Vittorio was less clear on that point. But he was very clear in saying Sofia Castelli was determined—utterly determined—that this must be done. That it had fallen to this girl to take up the Guardian's mantle. And if Vittorio can be believed, Signora Castelli was none too happy about it herself. But she *was* certain."

"What are you saying, Sutherland?" Alexander demanded. "That we . . . we should *take* her? The *Fraternitas* does not admit women—not even as Preosts or Advocati or even as Savants. Certainly they cannot be Guardians."

"I cannot counter all of your argument," said Sutherland, "but in the ancient world, there were certainly Celtic priestesses—powerful ones. Beyond that, I fear we cannot know what was or wasn't done."

"Well," said Alexander reluctantly, "you are right about the priestesses."

"Moreover, I have spent the night looking through the ancient texts, and nowhere—*nowhere*—does it say women cannot belong to the *Fraternitas*," Sutherland continued. "It does not address the issue of gender at all. I wonder I never noticed it before."

"But that is ridiculous," said Ruthveyn. "Women are completely unsuited for such work."

"I don't know." Geoff spoke before he could stop himself. "I can see your sister Anisha being a Guardian—especially if one of her boys were threatened. At the very least, I should like to see the chap who's man enough to cross her."

Sutherland set his head at a stubborn angle. "The truth

is, Adrian—and I have prayed on this all night—Miss de Rohan is *ideally* suited for the assignment which fell to us in Wapping this week."

Ruthveyn froze. "What, that business of DuPont's?"

"Just so," said Sutherland. "And I wondered . . . well, I wondered if it wasn't God's hand."

It suddenly struck Geoff what was being suggested. "No," he said, jerking from his chair. "No, Sutherland, *that* will not do."

Sutherland opened his hands, palms up. "But what if there is something here than none of us yet sees?" he suggested. "What if this child—Giselle Moreau—is truly in danger? What if something vital hinges upon her safety?"

"I do not perfectly understand, Sutherland." Geoff had stridden across the room, to Ruthveyn's former station at the window, and was staring blindly out at St. James's Place. "What, exactly, are you advocating?"

"That we listen to Miss de Rohan," said the Preost. "We all of us believe, gentlemen, in fate. What if everything leading us to this point—DuPont's coming here, Mrs. Castelli's adamance, Vittorio's dogged training of this girl—what if it is all a part of some greater, unseen plan?"

"Sutherland, with all respect," said Geoff, "you cannot be suggesting I take this girl to Brussels."

"Are we not all of us just warriors for the working day?" Sutherland pressed. "Here to be called upon when needed? Here to safeguard the vulnerable? Some of you—all of you, really—possess the Gift yourselves in one form or degree. Perhaps Miss de Rohan is no different."

Geoff set his jaw in a hard line. "And what of her reputation?"

"That is the young lady's decision, isn't it?" said Sutherland. "At some point, she chose to continue working with Signor Vittorio. She had to know where that would lead. Besides, she arrived from Tuscany but a few days ago. You'll go to Ostend on a private yacht. If she is careful—and smart—no one who matters is apt to be aware of her comings and goings."

Geoff scrubbed a hand along his freshly shaved jaw, still staring almost blindly out the window. Was Sutherland right about all this? And what was it about Anaïs de Rohan? He had lain awake much of last night pondering it—oddly obsessed by it, really.

To him, she was that most foreign of female creatures— brash, willful, and obviously possessed of an incisive mind. There was nothing demure about the woman—and very little modesty, he gathered. Yet he found her fascinating.

The truth was, he did not know many women intimately. He had kept the occasional mistress, of course, but sex was not intimacy. He knew that. But like Ruthveyn, Geoff was discriminating about whom he bedded. A man who carried the Gift strong in his blood took care where he planted his seed.

Geoff's mother, whom he loved deeply, was about as traditional a woman as it was possible to be. Hearth, home, duty, and family were everything to her, and Lady Madeleine MacLachlan had been rigidly brought up to be the very definition of ladylike restraint—and on at least one occasion, she had paid a terrible price for it.

Perhaps it was not so bad for a woman to be bold. To go after what she wanted.

Had his mother broken free of society's expectations and done precisely that, mightn't his life have been different? Perhaps he might have been spared, at least in part, a painful childhood, and the awkward certainty that he would never belong.

Still, the contrast with his mother made a woman like Anaïs de Rohan feel utterly alien to him—like that mysterious woman he'd met in the dark that night near St. Catherine's. Miss de Rohan was also far more intriguing than anyone he'd ever known. Which was a little disconcerting when one realized that Sutherland's argument made a great deal of sense.

Could he travel to Brussels with her? What would it be like to be in her company for days on end? Doubtless she would irritate him raw within hours—thereby curing his fascination, it was to be hoped.

There. Something to look forward to.

But what madness.

At the breakfast table behind him, voices were rising. They were still arguing with one another, while he . . . well, *he* was arguing with himself.

"So you believe we should accept her," Ruthveyn grumbled good-naturedly. "Very well, gentlemen. Nothing you do can spoil my happiness. My wedding day is all but upon us, after which I will be going home, quite possibly for months."

"I do not know what we should do, precisely." Sutherland was sounding exasperated now. "But I believe she has come here for a reason that even she does not likely understand. And if I have learned anything about her from my review of Vittorio's records, it is that she will not have given up."

Slowly, Geoff turned around, and silence fell over the table.

"I think you're right about that," he said. "I sensed it last night—that she was not beaten, but meant merely to bide her time. And now I am quite sure of it."

Sutherland rose a little uncertainly. "You have had a vision, Geoffrey?"

"No." Geoff's gaze swept over the table. "No. I just saw her get out of a hansom cab. She's about to drop the knocker out front."

CHAPTER 4

If you know your enemies and know yourself,
you will not be imperiled in a hundred battles.
Sun Tzu, *The Art of War*

Sutherland dragged a hand through his silvery hair. "Well, gentlemen, are we in agreement? Shall we meet with Miss de Rohan, and ask if she is willing to help us out? At least in this one thing?"

"No," said Geoff, pushing past them all. "No, I am going to speak with her myself."

"Alone?" asked Sutherland.

His hand already on the doorknob, Geoff turned and pinned them with his stare. "Does anyone else here want to go to Brussels in my stead?"

The men about the table looked at him blankly.

"Then I think this matter is between the lady and me," he said tightly.

Geoff went swiftly down the wide, white waterfall of marble stairs that spilled so elegantly into the club's vaulted foyer below, each a little wider than the last. The club was perhaps the most gracious in all of London, with its fine crystal chandeliers, lavish carpets, and the collection of European landscapes that bedecked its silk-hung walls.

They had built a lasting legacy here; he, Ruthveyn, and Lazonby, and it had been in many ways the most successful period of his life. For the first time, he had been surrounded by men like himself; by men who believed in the cause of the *Fraternitas*, and together they had accomplished much.

But he had not been especially satisfied by it all.

It sometimes seemed to Geoff as if his life could be divided into three distinct chapters. There was his childhood—those bleak, often terrifying years of not knowing what he was, or what was wrong with him. And then had come what he thought of as the Enlightenment—his time with his true grandmother in Scotland, his formal education, and eventually, his successful career at MacGregor & Company.

And then Alvin, damn him, had decided to go shooting in the rain—at a time when half their little Yorkshire village was abed with a virulent fever. And thus had begun Chapter Three.

Geoff had been waiting ever since for Chapter Four.

But why was he thinking of this now, and standing at the foot of the main staircase as if lost? Miss de Rohan had no answers for him. She could not even begin to guess at the questions.

But she was waiting somewhere within, and deserved the courtesy of an appointment.

The footman on duty informed him that the lady had indeed arrived, asked to see the Reverend Mr. Sutherland, and been escorted to the club's bookroom, a private library that was not open to the public.

By virtue of their guise as a society devoted to the study of natural philosophy—a not entirely false façade—the St. James Society often allowed outsiders, even females, access to their libraries, archives, and ancient manuscripts. The collection was vast, and housed in some half-dozen opulently furnished reading rooms throughout the Society's headquarters.

The private library, however, was a small, intimate room containing their more valuable books, and reserved for the use of members and their guests. The door stood open, and for a few moments Geoff lingered in the shadowy stillness of the passageway, simply watching her move through the room.

Bathed in a slanting shaft of morning sun, the elegant young woman scarcely resembled the earth goddess he'd met last night. Miss de Rohan was roaming along one of the bookshelves, pausing occasionally to tug out one of the volumes, flip it open, then shove it back again, as if nothing could possibly please her.

Today she wore a brilliantly hued walking dress of royal-blue silk faced with black satin, her mass of dark hair caught in a loose, untidy arrangement that looked as if she'd tucked it up as an afterthought. This precarious arrangement was topped by a little hat set at an almost rakish angle; a confection of black ribbons and blue ruching trimmed with three black feathers. To complete the ensemble, a black velvet reticule on a tasseled silk cord swung merrily from her wrist.

She wasn't precisely beautiful, no, and the dress was perhaps more striking than strictly *à la mode*. But the hat—ah, now the hat hinted at a certain impudence. On the whole, it made for an almost breathtakingly lovely vision.

She shoved the last of her perusals back into place with a quiet little sigh. "Pray do not keep me in suspense, Lord Bessett," she said without looking at him. "Are you still angry with me, I wonder?"

Startled, Geoff strolled into the room, his hands clasped behind his back. How on earth had she seen him, when she'd not once turned her head?

"Does it matter if I'm angry?" he asked.

She sighed again, then spun about to face him. "Just to be clear, I'm not one of those silly misses who goes haring about stirring up trouble for sport," she answered. "Yes, it matters. Is that really what you thought last night? That I wouldn't be back? That this was a lark?"

Geoff was no longer sure what he thought. "Miss de Rohan, might I ask—what brought you to this strange point in life?"

"I beg your pardon?" She lifted her slanting black eyebrows. "What point is that?"

Carefully he measured his words, but there were things he needed to understand. "You must know that your actions last night put your reputation in grave jeopardy," he said. "An unmarried lady of good breeding—"

"—showing her shift *and* her ankles in public?" she finished, her hands clasped almost modestly before her. "Indeed, but I know, too, what the ceremony requires, and how much your Preost values it. I did what I could bear to do. I compromised. I am not . . . *brazen*, Lord Bessett. Well, not in that way."

Geoff tried not to scowl. "If you meant to go through with such folly, you could have met first with the Reverend Mr. Sutherland and—"

"And given him the chance to refuse me straight out?"

"—and asked for a special dispensation."

She took a step toward him, hands still clasped, her black velvet reticule swinging from her wrist. "One must begin as one means to go on, Lord Bessett," she said, her voice far too husky for his comfort. "A woman cannot expect to be treated as anything near an equal if she sets out by asking for special favors. Besides, we both know that the ceremony clearly states that the sponsor must introduce his candidate *at the initiation*—a ritual that dates to the twelfth century. Tradition is everything to the *Fraternitas*.

I was not about to be the one who broke with it—not any more than I had to."

"I understand what tradition means to us, Miss de Rohan," he said, gentling his tone. "But I know, too, what a young lady's reputation means to her in England. Times have changed a little, perhaps, for unmarried females of good breeding. But not *that* much."

"To be perfectly honest, Lord Bessett, my breeding is nothing to be bragged about," said Miss de Rohan coolly. "I've got trade on one side, and a long line of rakes and rapscallions on the other. In his youth, my father actually worked for a time as a Bow Street Runner. On those rare occasions he entered a gentleman's home, it was generally through the servants' entrance. Did you know that about him? No, I thought not."

He had not known. "Well, if he was, it was because he chose to be," he smoothly countered. "He did not have to do so merely to earn a living."

She dropped her chin and looked up at him chidingly. "So, when a man lowers himself, it is a noble sacrifice, but when a woman tries to do it, it is a lark?" she suggested. "My father has an obsession with justice, yes. Watching your father being burned alive by revolutionaries will do that to you. And I could do worse than to follow in his footsteps."

Geoff narrowed his gaze. "Is that how you see this?"

She shrugged lightly. "However I see it, your concern for me is moot," she continued. "We both know the *Fraternitas* is sworn by blood to secrecy. And all of you have seen more than your share of pretty ankles before. But somehow, I'm not sure that's what you are getting at here."

"No," he said. "No, it isn't."

She strolled along one of the tufted leather sofas, pausing to draw her fingers in a slow, almost sensual gesture over a marble bust of Parmenides that sat on a little table behind it. He could not pull his eyes away from her. And today, absent the rush of temper and emotion, the woman seemed oddly familiar to him.

He was almost certain he had met her before, but he searched his mind and came up empty. He must be mistaken. She would never blend into the *ton*'s crowd of simpering, pale-faced beauties. Would never be the sort of woman a man forgot once he'd met her.

She lifted that hot black gaze and pinned him with it. "I am not going away, Lord Bessett," she said softly. "I can't give up that easily. I owe that much to my great-grandmother, and to Vittorio. I want to know if my records have been reviewed by the Preost. I want to know if there is any reason the St. James Society refuses me, other than my sex. Can you answer that for me, sir? Or must I camp on your doorstep until the Preost comes out? And pray tell him not to bother with the back gardens and that hidden passageway to St. James Park. I was on to that trick by the age of ten."

At that, he laughed aloud. The notion of Anaïs de Rohan laying siege to poor old Sutherland was . . . well, entirely plausible, really.

"I am glad, Lord Bessett, that you find me so vastly entertaining," she said.

"I must confess, you do begin to grow on a fellow." Then he sobered his tone. "But a woman will never be admitted to the *Fraternitas*. I'm sorry. I don't know why your great-grandmother thought it possible."

"But I did everything that was—"

He held up a staying hand. "And I believe you," he said. "Vittorio's records reflect it. He was the strongest of our Advocati in the Mediterranean. He was willing to fight for what he believed in, and he was no man's fool."

At that, something like grief sketched across her face.

"No, he was not. He was . . . he was . . ." Her words withering, she turned and paced suddenly to the window.

Geoff had never been especially softhearted, but something inside his chest lurched all the same. "Miss de Rohan," he said, following to touch her lightly on the shoulder. "I did not mean to—"

She was already dashing at her eyes with the back of her wrist. "It's all right," she said hastily. "It's just that . . . he was my kinsman. My mentor. And I just miss him a little, that's all."

"The entire *Fraternitas* misses him," said Geoff softly, drawing back his hand.

She lifted her gaze to the window, and stared down at St. James's Place below. He could see a hint of her reflection shimmering in the glass below his own; her wide, mobile mouth a little tremulous beneath eyes that were hollow with grief.

They were like lightness and dark seen together thus; her dark gown and black tresses against his sun-streaked hair and brilliant white cravat. It was but the most obvious of their differences, he did not doubt. There would be many more buried deeper, and far harder to flesh out.

But he did not need to flesh out a bloody thing with Anaïs de Rohan. He did not need to know her at all. He merely needed her to accompany him to Brussels for a few weeks.

Which was the same thing as saying he wished her to toss her good reputation to the four winds.

And to work and travel cheek by jowl with a woman as vivacious as she, and not get to know her? Christ, both were unthinkable.

But not undoable. Not unsurvivable. Not when there was a child's life at stake. A child who, even now, was almost certainly terrified and confused. Giselle Moreau's guardian was dead. The child had been left with no one to guide her—let alone protect her—through the most difficult years of her life, those years when she would have to come to grips with the terrible truth about herself. To accept that she was different. That she was cursed with a gift that was no sort of gift at all.

He knew what it would be like for Giselle Moreau, for he had lived through it.

The child must be brought to England, and assigned a new Guardian. She must be kept safe during this terrible, vulnerable phase. And if that meant he had to live with Anaïs de Rohan—had to look into those hot-chocolate eyes of hers every day over breakfast, and not lay a hand on the woman—then, yes. It was doable. It was survivable.

But she was looking at him in the window now, all too aware that he had been watching her. Geoff grappled for some inoffensive line of conversation.

"Tell me, what was he like, Vittorio?" he finally asked.

"Old," she said with a thready laugh. "Old, and very, very Tuscan. But from the age of twelve, I spent a few months each year with him, and came to love him like a grandfather. Even though at first . . . at first I really did not wish to go. But I know he wanted what was best for me."

Geoff gently turned her from the window. "Did he want . . . all this for you?" he asked, opening his arms expansively. "The decision was your great-grandmother's, but what did Vittorio think?"

Her gaze shuttered for an instant, and he thought she might refuse to answer.

"He had misgivings," she finally admitted. "What man would not? But Vittorio was from a different time. A different way of life. We live in a changing world, Lord Bessett. Even the *Fraternitas* is changing—and you have been the instrument of that change. Heavens, you have consolidated all the records and genealogies, built laboratories and libraries, and brought together a once far-flung group from across the Continent. Why is it so beyond you to think that a woman might have something to offer as a Guardian?"

"Women do have much to offer," he acknowledged. "They always have had. For example, I was trained by my . . . well, by a dear friend of my family. A Scottish seer. A woman who was very influential within the *Fraternitas*, and not without considerable power. She gave much of herself. Many of our most powerful Vateis are women, and always have been."

"And yet there is no place for me?" Miss de Rohan lifted her chin defiantly. "Admittedly, I am not much of a Vates, Lord Bessett. I can read the tarot—Nonna Sofia taught me—and I sometimes . . . well, I can sometimes guess what people are thinking, or feel their presence. Nonetheless, I am strong and resolute and willing. I believe in the F.A.C. and its noble mission. So I ask you again—is there no place for me here?"

"You are a friend to the *Fraternitas*, Miss de Rohan," he said. "You will always be that. Vittorio and your great-grandmother have seen to it. Over time, yes, you might become one of those women of great influence within the sect."

"And that is it, then?" Her voice dropped dejectedly. "That will be the *Fraternitas*'s final answer to my ten long years of struggle?"

For a long moment, Geoff considered what he was about to say—and his motivations for saying it. He had the oddest sensation of diving into something that looked almost bottomless. Something that would doubtless be cool and refreshing and a little shocking to the system when one hit the surface and plunged deep. But a mystery lay within those depths all the same.

"Actually, there might—if you are willing—there might be a way you could help us."

"I should *help* you?" she asked, her voice faintly incredulous. "You do not want me, but I should help *you*?"

"Just hear me out," he said. "And then . . . say no if it pleases you. I daresay you should do, honestly. And I have no doubt whatever that it is what your father would wish you to say."

"Lord Bessett." She stepped incrementally nearer. "I am a woman grown, and I can manage my father's crushed expectations—and frankly, he hasn't many, crushed or otherwise. He is not exactly your typical English gentleman."

"He isn't even English, is he?"

"Not by blood, perhaps." She flashed a sardonic smile. "But as you guessed, I'm English born and bred. I grew up in Gloucestershire and London, save for those few months each year when I went to Tuscany. But let us get back to *your* expectations—what was it you wanted of me?"

Geoff considered how best to explain. "It is awkward," he said. "I need a woman—"

She trilled with laughter. "Do you indeed?" she said. "With those gold-bronze locks and that jawline of yours, I shouldn't think it much of a problem."

"Miss de Rohan—"

"It must be those grim eyes," she interjected, circling as if he were horseflesh on the block at Tattersall's. "Oh, they are handsome, but they do not quite inspire poetry—not the swooning female sort of poetry, at any rate."

Geoff looked down at her, deliberately arching one brow. "A crushing blow indeed," he murmured. "But skill with a pen is not one of the talents I ordinarily look for in a woman."

At that, a slow, lazy smile curled her mouth. "Is it not?" she murmured. "Then perhaps you do not look high enough, my lord."

He managed a smile. "But we digress. Here, let me try and get a proper chokehold on this conversation." He motioned toward the matched leather sofas that sat opposite each other near the hearth. "Would you kindly sit down, Miss de Rohan? I should have asked sooner but something about you throws me out."

"I've been told I have that effect on people," she said. "Fine, thank you. I shall sit. And you will tell me what it is you wish me to do."

Geoff bought himself a few moments by ringing for coffee, which Miss de Rohan assured him she took hot, black, and very strong. Strangely, he could have guessed as much.

While waiting, he forced himself to make very dull, very proper conversation about the English weather, the start of the London Season, and Town society in general.

But Miss de Rohan was having little of it. She was ambivalent about the first, unaware of the second, and generally disdainful of the later—reminding him once again that no matter how hard he tried, he would likely never see her in the usual way.

Once the coffee had been poured, he gave up and got right to the point, repeating almost verbatim DuPont's story of Giselle Moreau and her father's untimely death.

When she was finished, she put down her coffee cup, now empty, and leaned back against the sofa. "And this address in Brussels," she said, "it is a town house, I collect?"

"So I'm told."

"Can you climb?"

"Climb?"

"Trees," she said. "Downspouts. Ropes. In short, are you still nimble, my lord? Or has the stiffness of age set in along with that rigid attitude of yours?"

"Good God, Miss de Rohan!" Geoff was insulted. "I'm not yet thirty." Which was true, but only just. "Yes, I can climb. What has that to do with anything?"

"Well, you could take me along with you to Brussels,"

she said. "You *are* going to Brussels, I collect? Otherwise, someone else would be telling me this story. So we'll go together. I'll befriend this woman—ingratiate myself with her, even—then manage to slip into the nursery and unfasten one of the window locks. Then you can climb up at night—or *I* can—and snatch the child whilst a carriage waits below, and we'll be off to Ostend by—oh, two or three in the morning."

"Just like that?" he said dryly.

"Just like that," she said. "It cannot be above eighty miles to the coast. Once the trains begin to run—about half past five, I should think—we can abandon the carriage in Ghent, and arrive at the port in time for breakfast."

"I begin to believe you and Lazonby should take this on," he grumbled. "One blunt instrument to beat upon another— that might drive the spike through the poor woman's heart in half the time."

"What poor woman?" Miss de Rohan's eyes widened. "Oh, yes, I see what you mean. The mother. Well, you can always send word to her once the child is safe on English soil. She probably is not complicit in any of this, but her judgment in taking up with this Lezennes character is questionable at best."

Geoff said nothing, but he could not deny the same thought had crossed his mind. Her period of mourning was scarcely out. Could she really be contemplating marriage?

"I think it more likely the lady is near destitution," he said pensively.

Miss de Rohan appeared to consider it. "All the more reason to reunite her with her English kin," she said. "Whilst we're away, have your Preost go dig up that family in Colchester—he's the genealogist round here, is he not? And an ordained minister in the Church?"

"He is both, yes," said Geoff.

Miss de Rohan flashed a mordant smile. "Well, in my experience, no one can slather on the guilt like a priest bent on finding redemption for some poor devil's soul," she said, "and Sutherland looks like he could get the job done."

Geoff set his coffee cup down very carefully. "Well, Miss de Rohan, you seem to have it all worked out," he murmured, "but you are missing one critical element."

"And that would be?"

"An invitation."

At last she had the good grace to blush.

But the truth was, he was going to invite her. She was impulsive, but she was not stupid. And she had summed him up pretty thoroughly. Moreover, the plan she had proposed was precisely what Rance would have done.

It was not, however, what he would have done.

He eyed her across the tea table. "Miss de Rohan, how old are you?"

She lifted her chin, her eyes faintly teasing. "How positively rude," she said. "A lady never tells. But then, I just claimed not to be very much of a lady, didn't I?"

"I believe you are making my argument for me."

A sly smile toyed at her mouth. "Very well," she said. "I am two-and-twenty, or will be soon enough."

"That is very young," he said. "You still possess the impetuousness and impatience of youth, I think."

"Oh, I hope so," she said. "And the optimism. That wonderful sense that all things are possible. Yes, guilty as charged. Besides, impatience is not always a bad thing."

Geoff relaxed against the back of the sofa, and studied her appraisingly. "Let me explain something to you, Miss de Rohan," he said softly. "If you run the risk of accompanying me to Brussels, you will have to live with the result."

"To my reputation, you mean." She managed a slightly acid smile. "I understand, Lord Bessett. And by the way, I am not husband hunting."

"That's good to know," he said, "because you won't find one here. And the risk, of course, might go well beyond a sullied reputation. Save for what DuPont has reported, I know nothing of Lezennes or how dangerous a man he might be. I don't even know DuPont, come to that. Our *Fraternitas* contact in Rotterdam will come down and do what he can, of course, but the truth is we might be walking into a lion's den."

"Understood," she said.

"And your family," he pressed on. "I can't imagine what you mean to tell them, but it is up to you to deal with it. If I get a glove in the face from your father, I will not be amused, Miss de Rohan."

"Please, call me Anaïs," she said, "since you are already contemplating such intimacies as a dawn appointment."

"I am perfectly serious," he said. "I know the influence your father wields in Whitehall, and I don't particularly give a damn. The *Fraternitas* is not without power. Power at the highest levels of government. Do we understand one another?"

She lifted both brows and pinned him with her stare. "I counted a cabinet minister, two undersecretaries, and a member of the Privy Council under those brown hoods last night," she said. "I am not so *impetuous*, my lord, that I do not understand the *Fraternitas* extends into the loftiest reaches of our government."

"Here is one more thing you need to understand," he continued. "If we go forward, I am in charge. I will make every decision at every turn of this operation. I will not have time to argue with you, or parry words with you. I am a plainspoken man, but I am relentless, Miss de Rohan. I will get this child back, trust me. But I will not break that poor woman's heart in the process, and I will not run roughshod over her wishes—not unless someone's very life is at stake. Do you understand what I am telling you?"

"That I am to be a mere pawn in your master plan?" she suggested.

"That, and the fact that I don't even have a plan," he said. "But I will come up with one as the circumstances warrant. And you will then keep to it every step of the way or I'll have Dieric van de Velde carry you bodily back to Ostend and put you on that clipper himself."

"Aye, aye, Capt'n." Miss de Rohan cut him a snappy salute.

"So . . . this is acceptable to you?"

A wide grin spread slowly over her face. "Did you think to run me off with your barks and your threats, my lord?" she said. "It won't work. This is what I thought I was supposed to be doing all along—helping to find justice in an unjust world."

"As simple as that, is it?"

"What, you thought I was in it for the wardrobe?" she said on a laugh. "Frankly, those scratchy brown things look as if they might harbor vermin—*medieval* vermin."

"So this is all you wanted?" he said. "Not membership in the *Fraternitas*?"

All the humor fell away then. "Oh, I definitely did not say that." Her low, throaty voice sent a shiver down his spine. "What I *am* saying is that this . . . well, this is a start, perhaps."

"A start," he echoed.

Her smile warmed like the sun. "Yes, and a rather promising one at that," she said. "Yes, Lord Bessett, I should be pleased to accompany you to Brussels, and to heed your barking and snarling as best I can. Now, am I officially invited?"

For a heartbeat, he hesitated.

Wordlessly, Anaïs de Rohan thrust her hand out across the tea table.

With grave reluctance, Geoff slid his fingers around her smaller, cooler ones, and shook it.

In the early afternoon, a London peculiar settled in along the river; a foul, foggy haze so thick coachmen passing through it could scarce see their horses' heads, and so odiferous the stench made a man's eyes water.

Along Fleet Street, the newspapermen hastening up and down the pavements in hope of making their afternoon deadlines were slamming into one another amidst curses and shoves, while below, a loaded dray rattling up from Blackfriars failed to heed an approaching mail coach.

This unfortunate misjudgment sent the dray careening onto its side, left the four coach horses shuddering and stamping in their traces, and left Lord Lazonby standing at the foot of Shoe Lane up to his ankle in loose coal. Cursing his luck to the devil, he shook the filthy black dust off his boot and strode past the quarreling drivers, each of whom had seized a fistful of the other's coat.

Picking his way across the street through the blocked traffic, Lazonby strode through the brume, then turned down the passageway that led to St. Bride's. The curses and clatter along Fleet Street were soon muffled, as if his ears had been stuffed with cotton wool.

With the cunning of a man who knew what it was to be both the hunted and the hunter, Lazonby moved around the church more by feel than by sight, then up into the churchyard. After picking his way gingerly amongst the gravestones, he chose his spot; a mossy little nook just behind one of the largest markers by the north windows.

Righteous fury simmering in the pit of his belly, the earl propped himself back against the cold stone of St. Bride's and settled in for what might be a long, damp vigil.

Perhaps half an hour later, footfalls, muffled and disembodied in the fog, came toward him from the direction of Bride Court. His jaw set tight with ire, Lazonby watched as Hutchens—his second footman for all of three months—materialized from the gloom. The damned fool still wore his red livery. That, and the sound of Hutchens's nervous, nasally breathing, made him impossible to miss.

Though he generally gave no thought to his attire, choosing instead to throw on whatever his new valet had laid out upon the bed, today Lazonby had dressed with care in shades of charcoal and gray. He blended into the fog and stone like a wraith.

Jack Coldwater, however, had worn his usual dun-colored mackintosh. The conniving little bastard came round the corner of the church, literally feeling his way past the last of the gravestones as he squinted into the gloom.

"I don't like the looks o' this, Jack," Hutchens complained when he neared. "Graveyards give me the shivers."

"Given what you're costing me, you can bloody well shiver till hell freezes over," said Coldwater tightly. "What have you got?"

Lazonby watched as Hutchens rammed a hand into his pocket. "Dashed little," he said, presenting a fold of paper. "He's to go to Quartermaine Club tonight—a regular bacchanal they're having, I hear. And I saw his valet brushing out his second-best coat, and that likely means another little pump-'n'-tickle at Mrs. Farndale's, but whether late tonight or sometime tomorrow I couldn't say."

"The man has the sexual inclinations of a panting mongrel," gritted Coldwater, snatching the paper. "And after that?"

"After that what?" said Hutchens defensively. "I told you when we started this, Lazonby don't keep to much of a schedule. You're lucky to get that." He paused to thrust out a hand, palm up. "Now where's my money?"

Coldwater stuffed the paper into his own pocket, then extracted his purse. "For this, you get half," he grumbled, poking through it.

Hutchens opened his mouth to complain. In the gloom, Lazonby leaned forward and dropped a few coins into the outstretched hand.

Hutchens shrieked and jumped, flinging the money into the fog.

"Bloody hell!" shouted Coldwater as coins rained down. "What the—!"

"That's what you're owed since Lady Day, you Judas." Lazonby glared at the footman, now cowering behind a small marble monument. "Spend it wisely, for you'll get not another ha'penny—nor a character—out of me."

"M-m-my lord?" croaked the footman.

"Indeed," said Lazonby coolly. "The fog can cover a multitude of sins, can it not? Now take yourself off, Hutchens. If you run all the way back to Ebury Street, you might be able to snatch up your things before the street urchins carry them off. You'll find them in a heap out by the mews."

The footman hastened into the gloom, the coins forgotten. Lazonby turned to see Coldwater edging backward. He followed, one hand fisted at his side, ready to plant him a facer.

"As to you, you scheming little blackguard," Lazonby said, backing the reporter up another foot, "two can play at your game. And unlike Hutchens, your clerks down at the *Chronicle* can be had for a warm pie and a pint."

Fleetingly, Coldwater was speechless. Eyes wide, he backed up another pace, but caught a heel on the base of a headstone that had nearly found its own eternal rest. The marker rocked precariously, sending Coldwater backward, arms wheeling.

Lazonby lashed out, seized his upper arm, and jerked the lad physically against him. "Now listen to me, and listen well, you little shite," he growled down at him. "If ever I hear of you so much as looking cross-eyed at one of my servants, I'll have your job. I'll *buy* your bloody newspaper, and make sure you never work again. Do you hear me?"

Coldwater was trembling, but not cowed. "Oh, aye, you and your St. James Society think you can own the world, don't you, Lazonby?" he spat. "Well, I'm on to the lot of you. I know something's going on in that house."

"You don't know a damned thing, Coldwater, save how to stir up gossip and innuendo," Lazonby snarled.

"Oh, no?" said Coldwater. "Then who was the big Frenchman at the Prospect of Whitby? The one you didn't want me to see?"

"If there was a Frenchman, you'd do well to forget it."

"Oh, I don't forget anything," said the reporter silkily. "I already know the man sailed into Dover on a French clipper carrying at least a dozen armed men. And he carried something else, too—forged diplomatic papers in a folio marked with that strange symbol of yours."

Rage and a strange mix of emotions were beginning to swim in Lazonby's head. He drew in a steadying breath. "You . . . you don't know what you're talking about."

"That mysterious mark," the reporter insisted. "The one etched in stone on your pediment. I know it means something, Lazonby. You led me a merry chase for reason."

"What the devil is your problem?" Lazonby yanked the lad so hard his teeth clacked. "For whatever reason, you seem determined to make my life hell."

Coldwater's eyes narrowed. "Because you, sir, are nothing but a murderous thug in a fine silk waistcoat," he rasped, "and it is the newspaper's responsibility to pursue you if the government cannot—or is afraid to."

And in that instant, Lazonby wanted to kill him. To wrap his hands round the man's neck and do . . . Good God, he didn't know what he wanted to do to him. Those vile, appalling emotions were surging inside him again.

Was he always to feel like this every bloody time he spent an instant in Coldwater's company? The air seemed suddenly thick with the young man's scent—fear mixed with soap and something almost familiar.

Lazonby swallowed hard, then forced his hand to let go. "No," he said quietly, stepping back. "No, this is no longer about the follies of my youth, Jack. This is about something personal."

Coldwater shrugged his coat back into place. "Perhaps I simply think the reading public has a right to know how a man who was sentenced to hang for murder is now strolling around free, hobnobbing with the rich and powerful of London."

"And by that you mean Ruthveyn and Bessett, I suppose."

"Do they any come richer or more powerful?" Coldwater returned. "By the way, I hear Ruthveyn has taken half a deck on the *Star of Bengal.* Care to tell me what the St. James Society is up to in India?"

"Oh, for pity's sake, Coldwater." Lazonby bent over and snatched a shilling from the ground. "Don't you even read your own society pages? Ruthveyn got married. He's taking his bride home to Calcutta."

But there was nothing but silence.

Lazonby straightened up to see he spoke to no one save the dead. Jack Coldwater had melted into the fog.

CHAPTER 5

The general who wins the battle makes many
calculations in his temple before the battle is fought.
Sun Tzu, *The Art of War*

Two days after Anaïs's little contretemps at the St. James Society, a small but intrepid party set off before daylight on the first leg of their journey to Brussels. They traveled by private carriage as far as Ramsgate—which was to say Anaïs went by carriage, with Lord Bessett's footman and coachman upon the box. The earl himself rode alongside, mounted upon a great, brown beast of a horse with a nasty temper and a tendency to bite—all of which put Anaïs rather in mind of its master.

For the sake of preserving their ruse, Anaïs had insisted that no servants accompany them for the crossing. Her philosophy agreed with the Iron Duke's—in for a penny, in for a pound—and no lady's maid was going to be enough to save her from the impropriety of what she was about to do.

After a long argument, Bessett finally yielded, and wrote ahead to Mr. van de Velde to ask that he employ a maid and a valet to meet them in Ostend. And so it was that Anaïs spent the whole of one day alone in Bessett's well-appointed traveling coach with nothing save a pile of magazines for company.

Given that she'd just spent a great many days journeying from Tuscany, the travel was mind-numbing. It also forced her to admit that she had secretly hoped for Lord Bessett's company—merely to lessen the boredom, of course. She hadn't a thought to spare for his shock of gold-streaked hair or strong, hard jaw. And those glittering eyes—well, she scarcely noticed them now.

But the weather held fine, the roads remained dry, and Bessett did not deign to dismount save for their occasional stops. He seemed intent upon keeping his distance.

They arrived at a ramshackle inn near Ramsgate's port to find that a stiff breeze had kicked up. Anaïs watched the inn's sign swing wildly in its bracket, and began to dread the crossing.

In keeping with her new role as a dutiful wife, she waited impatiently in the carriage until Bessett returned from having made their arrangements. In the inn yard, he helped her down, his ever-present scowl already in place.

"You do not know anyone in Ramsgate?" he asked for the third time in as many days.

Anaïs looked up at the inn's entrance. "Not a soul," she answered. "How is the kitchen here?"

"Passable, I think," he said. "I'll have dinner sent up to you at seven."

"You will not dine with me?"

"We are still in England. And I have things to do."

"Very well," she said evenly. "Just something light. Soup, perhaps."

He narrowed his gaze against the afternoon sun, and scanned the empty inn yard for the fifth time. "I chose this inn because it's not especially popular—which means it isn't the best. But they have a small suite of rooms, so Gower can sleep in a chair in your parlor."

Anaïs tossed a chary glance at Bessett's fresh-faced young footman, who had begun to unstrap the baggage. "I'm sure you mean to be kind," she said, "but mightn't it be better if *I* slept in the parlor to look after Gower?"

Bessett insulted her with a blank look.

Anaïs poked out a foot, and tugged up her skirts a few inches. The barrel of her small pistol winked up at him in a shaft of sun. "I think I'll manage."

Bessett drew his gaze back up slowly. Perhaps a little too slowly. And those eyes—eyes she'd long ago realized were ice-blue—had the oddest way of glinting both hot and cold all at once, and sending an odd frisson down her spine.

"So I see," he finally said. "But—"

"But?" Anaïs looked at him impatiently, and dropped her voice. "Look here, Bessett, do you think I'm qualified to do this or not? If we begin this mission by *your* worrying about *me* at every turn, I will be a hindrance, not a help."

"I only meant that—"

"I know what you meant," she said firmly. "Thank you. You are every inch a gentleman. But I am not much of a lady, and I can assure you poor Gower has seen nothing of the world compared to me. Now, I have a flick-knife in my reticule, a stiletto up my sleeve, and the hearing of a well-trained watchdog. But poor Gower—frankly, he looks like he just fell off a Dorset farm cart. Besides, there isn't apt to be trouble in Ramsgate."

A hint of color rose across his hard cheekbones, and Anaïs could literally feel Bessett fighting down his temper—and his concern. "Very well," he snapped. "But if you get yourself killed, I'm not waiting for the funeral."

"I should hope not," she returned. "Your only concern—and mine—must be Giselle Moreau."

Just then, Gower handed down her portmanteau to the coachman. Anaïs moved as if to cross the inn yard. "Come, walk in with me," she ordered. "I want to know where you are going and when you mean to return."

Bessett followed, his color deepening. "Playing the role of overbearing wife already, are we?"

Anaïs kept moving, but tossed him a frustrated glance. "No, I am acting like your partner in this business," she whispered. "We must both of us know what the other is doing at every turn—beginning this moment. To do otherwise is to court disaster, and you know it."

He did know it. She could see the reluctant acknowledgment in his eyes. "I'm going down to the port to check out DuPont's clipper and make sure of his men," he finally answered. "I'll be back before dark."

"Excellent. I'll get us situated here."

Bessett said no more. As they crossed through the shadowy portal and into the inn, the aproned innkeeper came eagerly across the room toward them. "Mrs. Smith, welcome!"

"Why, thank you." Anaïs tucked her arm through Bessett's. "I was just saying to my dear Mr. Smith what a charming little hostelry he has found us."

With Anaïs's smile plastered firmly in place, Bessett left matters in her hands and vanished. After directing the disposition of all their baggage, then having the innkeeper's dubious-looking sheets stripped and replaced with her own, Anaïs leaned out the window and looked over the rooftops of Ramsgate.

In the harbor below, she could just make out a few bare masts, and beyond them the lighthouse at the end of the west pier. But nearer to hand, on her left, Anaïs could see Bessett's bedchamber window, for the inn was built round a stable yard, and their rooms were set at right angles to each other. Ever the gentleman—cool and restrained though he might be—the earl had insisted upon the smaller single room for himself.

On a sigh, she withdrew from the window and pulled the thin underdrapes shut. After bathing and replacing her travel-stained clothing with something fresh, she shuffled through the wilted pile of magazines one last time. Then, with a final glance at the window, Anaïs gave in to her impulse.

The walk down the curving High Street was not long, and though the shopkeepers were sweeping their doorsteps for the evening, their windows were filled with all manner of goods designed to catch the eye. Anaïs passed them by. At the edge of town, she made her way gingerly down to the quay. A steam packet was churning its way through the harbor entrance as a small black dog ran along the pier, barking madly.

Looking about amidst the small trading vessels and ketch-rigged trawlers, Anaïs saw but one ship sleek enough to be DuPont's—a small, slender clipper with sharply raking masts that looked as if it was designed for gunrunning. Her sights set, Anaïs picked her way past the fishermen offloading the last of the day's catch, and made her way out the pier, which was devoid of tourists this late in the day. Halfway along, she paused, turned, and set a hand above her eyes to block the sun.

Yes, that was the ship. Even from this distance, the mark of the *Fraternitas Aureae Crucis*—the Brotherhood of the Golden Cross—could be seen carved into the decoration on its bow, did one but know what to look for.

The ancient symbol consisted of a Latin cross with a quill and sword beneath. *By my Word and by my Sword, I will defend the Gift, my Faith, my Brotherhood, and all its Dependents, until the last breath of life leaves my body.* Those were the words, equally ancient, that traditionally accompanied the symbol. The words Anaïs had been refused the opportunity to finish speaking.

In the British Isles, the gold cross was most often overlaid on a cartouche in the shape of a thistle. But in France and the rest of the Continent, the plainer version was more common, unless one's family had Scots blood. Anaïs had seen both forms of the symbol often during her travels—carved into pediments, painted onto ceilings, even etched onto gravestones.

Bessett and Lord Lazonby wore the symbol on their cravat pins. She wore the plainer version tattooed onto her hip. The mark of the Guardian. Like the Tudor rose, the Masonic pyramid, and the fleur-de-lis, it was one of those flourishes people almost failed to notice, so common had it become over the centuries.

Anaïs walked another few yards along the pier to better view the deck. From this angle she could see Lord Bessett standing topside, one hand propped high upon the bare mainmast, the other set on his hip, elbow out as he spoke intently with one of the crew. Another man was striking the French colors. Tomorrow, once they were some distance from shore—and the prying eyes of others—the crew would likely run up the English ensign. The *Fraternitas* was nothing if not flexible.

Bessett had again stripped off his coat, doubtless to assist in some nautical task, and now stood in his waistcoat, his white shirtsleeves billowing in the breeze, brilliant against the distant cliffs of Ramsgate. Still, it was clear from the deferential demeanor of everyone around him that he was now in charge.

Anaïs watched in fascination as his hair whipped back from his face in the wind. He wore it unfashionably long, without any facial hair to soften the lean angles of his face. Bessett was tall, too—taller and more slender than any of

the men aboard—and Anaïs was surprised by how completely at ease he appeared as he moved about the deck,
motioning at various points amongst the rigging. The man
who appeared to be the French captain nodded, turned, and
bellowed a command at two of his underlings. They would
be rigged to run hard on the wind, Anaïs suspected, absently
settling a hand over her stomach.

Ah, well. She would live.

Just then, Lord Bessett turned a half circle, his percep-
tive gaze sweeping round the harbor. Anaïs realized it the
moment he saw her. Some inscrutable emotion sketched
over his face, then he returned his attention to the captain
just long enough to shake his hand.

His business apparently finished, Bessett cut a glance over
his shoulder at her, and with a jerk of his head, indicated she
should meet him quayside.

Anaïs turned and retraced her steps toward shore.

By the time he approached the quay, Bessett had put on
his coat and restored his hair to some semblance of order.
He did not chide her as she had thought he might, but instead
offered his arm.

"Mrs. Smith?" he said, crooking his elbow. "Shall we
walk?"

He looked so very handsome in the falling dusk, even
with the lines of fatigue etched round his eyes and the look
of seriousness on his face. Oddly at a loss for words, Anaïs
slipped an arm through his. She would have been more comfortable, she suddenly realized, had he scolded her.

They wandered through the throng without speaking
until they had cleared the quay and the crowds. The silence
between them had grown expectant, almost awkward, and
Anaïs had the oddest feeling Bessett was searching for
words.

Her intuition was borne out when, at the foot of the High

Street, he stopped and turned to face her. "I have been think-ing," he said abruptly. "About your complaint."

Somehow, she managed to smile, but the heat of his gaze was intense and unexpected. "I tend to complain about a great many things," she replied. "Can you be more specific?"

A ghost of a smile lit his eyes. "At the inn," he answered, "when you said I had to trust you, or you would be a hin-drance. You were right."

Anaïs drew back an inch. "You need me, Bessett," she said quietly. "You can't very well send me packing now."

He shook his head. "No," he said. "I mean—yes, I need you. But you will have to bear with me. This is not some-thing that comes . . ."

"That comes naturally to a man such as yourself?" she lightly suggested. "Yes, I know your type—the authorita-tive, take-charge type."

This time he smiled, but it was wry. "I could say it takes one to know one."

"And I could say some men are born to authority," she re-turned, but there was no ire in her voice. "After scarcely an hour on deck, you were already lecturing that poor captain about his rigging, and having everything put your way."

"Because if things go badly—if we have any unnecessary delay—Captain Thibeaux will not pay a great price for it," said Bessett calmly. "But Giselle Moreau might."

Anaïs looked at him in all seriousness. "This child—her predicament—it troubles you on some deeply personal level, I think," she murmured. But when he made no response, she continued. "And I agree wholeheartedly with everything you said. You are not accustomed to trusting—or even working with a woman, I daresay."

"No." He glanced away, toward the path they had just climbed, one hand set at his trim waist, pushing back the folds of his coat. He looked pensive, as if his mind were running back over the confluence of events that had brought him to this place, perhaps even to this point in life. "No, I am not used to it. But you cannot be a green girl. Or a fool. Were it otherwise, Vittorio would never have sent you to us."

Anaïs turned her gaze away. "Thank you for that," she finally said.

After a moment's hesitation, he resumed his pace. She fell into step with him, but did not slide her fingers around his elbow again. Suddenly, the feel of his hard-muscled arm beneath her hand was the last thing she needed. And his kindness—yes, perhaps she could have done better without that, too.

What a sorry state of affairs this was turning out to be. Bessett's words aside, Anaïs was beginning to *feel* just a bit like a green girl—and in ways she really did not wish to think about.

At that instant, however, Bessett crooked his head and smiled down at her. "We are going to have to do better than Smith, don't you think, when we arrive in Brussels?"

"Who shall we be, then?" She kept her tone artificially bright. "I suppose we should choose something as near our own names as will feel natural."

For a long moment, he said nothing. Instead, he matched his long stride to her shorter one, and walked beside her without impatience—and without his scowl.

"MacLachlan," he said after a time, but there was a strange hitch in his voice. "I'll be Geoffrey MacLachlan."

"A Scottish name?" Anaïs remarked, and for some reason, she took his arm again.

As if it were second nature, Bessett settled his hand over hers. "It is my stepfather's name," he said. "I can always claim connection to his construction business if pressed. What about yourself?"

"My name is odd, but no one knows me," she said. "I shall just be Anaïs MacLachlan."

"It is unusual," he agreed. "But beautiful."

"Another of my great-grandmothers," Anaïs explained. "She was from Catalonia. We still have vineyards there."

"But not in Alsace?"

Anaïs shook her head. "The estate was burnt in the Revolution," she said. "My father has never even tried to reclaim the land, though he could have done, perhaps."

"So a French title, but no land," Bessett murmured.

Anaïs smiled weakly. "He never used the title until he met my mother," she replied. "He seemed to think he could not marry her without it. But I don't think titles much matter to her. She was country bred, and raised in—what is the polite euphemism? Genteel poverty? Except that poverty doesn't feel terribly genteel, I daresay, when one is living in it."

"At least she sounds refreshing." Bessett seemed to be warming to the topic of her family. "And you have a twin brother, do you not?"

"Yes, Armand."

"So, you were born at the same time—"

Anaïs laughed. "Twins usually are."

Bessett did not return her humor. "And yet he was not chosen to be the Guardian?"

Anaïs lifted one shoulder. "I don't know why," she replied. "Nonna just said it wasn't written in the cards. And perhaps he hasn't the temperament. Armand is very much the young man about town. But Maria still complains about Nonna's decision."

"Maria?"

"My cousin, Maria Vittorio." Anaïs paused to kick a stone from their path. "She was my great-grandmother's companion, and the widow of Vittorio's brother. Maria is a grumpy old dear. She lives with me in Wellclose Square—Nonna left us the house—and we used to travel together."

"Back and forth to Tuscany, you mean?"

"Yes." Anaïs sighed. "But Maria has always believed it was Armand's place to go, not mine. That I should have been at home embroidering sofa cushions and filling that cavernous house with children."

"And what do you think?"

Anaïs shrugged again, this time with both shoulders. "I haven't the patience for needlework," she answered. "Besides, Nonna Sofia lived an unconventional life. She had just one child, my grandmother, who died young. And all Nonna's husbands died young, too. So what good did convention do her? It broke her heart. In the end, she poured herself into the business and made us rich."

"An unconventional life indeed," he murmured. "But yours needn't be like that. Not if you don't wish it to be."

"I think we must be satisfied with the life fate deals us," she said. "And I have a sense of purpose few women ever have."

"But—?"

"Why do you think there's a *but* in this conversation?"

"I hear it in your voice."

She cut him a sidelong glance. "Best to turn that Gift of yours in someone else's direction, I think," she warned.

He flashed a muted smile. "I don't have that sort of ability."

"And I am not very deep, or difficult to understand," she said, resolved to change the subject. "Now, tell me, my dear husband—how long have we been wed?"

"Three months," he replied after a moment's consideration.

She nodded. "That will explain our knowing little about one another."

He crooked his head to look down at her. "So it was an arranged marriage?" he asked. "Not a love match?"

Anaïs cast him another sidelong look. "Does this feel like a love match to you, Bessett?"

"That would be Mr. MacLachlan, my dear," he said lightly.

She laughed. "So, our marriage was arranged," she said. "I was badly on the shelf, and my father paid you pots of money to marry me."

He laughed hugely. "That desperate, eh?"

"Why not?" She looked askance at him. "I'll admit, I'm no beauty. Perhaps my virtue was compromised? Or I was an outrageous flirt? You doubtless did my father a huge favor in taking me off his hands."

His expression sobered then. "Don't say those things," he said quietly. "Not even in jest."

"Careful, MacLachlan." Anaïs smiled. "I might begin to think you have a heart. So, what *do* we know of one another? I daresay we'd best decide."

"As with our new names, we should keep the details near the truth," he answered.

"Very well," she said. "I was raised primarily on my mother's farm in Gloucestershire. Besides Armand, I have two sisters and another brother, all younger and still at home, and Papa's ward, Nate, who is eldest, and on his own now. What about you?"

Bessett seemed to hesitate for a moment. "I was raised abroad," he finally answered. "Bessett was a scholar of ancient civilizations, so we traveled quite a lot."

Her eyes widened. "Did you? How fascinating."

"Yes, but he died when I was young," he said. "My mother returned to Yorkshire, and a few years after that, we moved to London."

"How odd that she should take you from your family estate to be raised in Town," Anaïs murmured.

"I was not an easy child to raise," he murmured. "She . . . didn't understand me. And I didn't understand myself. In Yorkshire, we were so isolated. In any case, I was not the heir. Bessett had a son by an earlier marriage—Alvin, my stepbrother."

"You mean your half brother?"

"Yes," he said swiftly. "He was much older than I, and we were about as alike as chalk and cheese, but I . . . I simply adored him."

"That's just how it is with Nate and me," said Anaïs, smiling. "There's nothing so reassuring as a much-elder brother, I think."

"Oh, yes, steady as a rock, that was Alvin." Bessett's gaze had turned inward. "But when he married, my mother thought it best she remove from Loughton, the estate in Yorkshire. Unfortunately, there was no heir born of the marriage, so when Alvin died . . ."

"Oh," she said quietly. "I am very sorry. A title is a fine thing, I daresay, but not at the cost of a beloved brother."

"My sentiments exactly," said Bessett, his jaw set tight.

"Has he been gone long?"

"Awhile, yes," said Bessett. "I was a man grown, and my mother had remarried. I had already come down from Cambridge, and spent a few years in business with my stepfather."

"So you built things?" she remarked.

"At first, I merely drew them," said Geoff. "And after a time, he began sending me abroad to oversee certain projects. We did quite a lot of work for the colonial government in North Africa."

"So you really have done a bit of sailing," she murmured. "Indeed, you are as well-traveled as I."

"Does that surprise you?"

"Oh, you know how most Englishmen are." Anaïs gave an expansive wave of her hand. "They think the world begins at Dover, and ends at Hadrian's Wall."

"Ah," he said quietly. "Well, trust me, Miss de Rohan. I am not most Englishmen."

She pursed her lips, and glanced up at him. *That*, she believed wholeheartedly.

"I really do think you ought to call me Anaïs, you know," she said softly. "It would be best if you got used to it before we arrive in Belgium."

He crooked his head again, and smiled down at her—a smile that reached all the way to his ice-blue eyes. "Anaïs, then," he said. "And I am Geoff—or Geoffrey, if you like."

"Geoff, then, for the most part." Anaïs managed a little wink. "I shall save Geoffrey for those moments when I am feeling put out with you."

"Both syllables, hmm?" he said, as the inn yard came into view. "I have a feeling *that* is what I had best get used to."

In London, the day was brisk, the breeze whipping at Hyde Park's spring blossoms almost violently. Such botanic brutality had not, however, deterred the last of the day's gadabouts from enjoying the twin diversions of seeing and being seen, for the London Season had commenced in earnest, and there were wardrobes to critique, rumors to be passed, and social calendars to be compared.

For most of the park's habitués, it was a pleasant if exhausting ritual. For the occupants of Lord Lazonby's black-and-gold phaeton, however, the Season held little allure. Lady Anisha Stafford was disdainful of the entire business, and about the only thing as strained as Lord Lazonby's relationship with the polite society was the conversation in his carriage.

"So, is it true you are courting Bessett now?" he asked as he cut his matched bays through the Cumberland Gate. "He must be strutting like a peacock."

"It is true I went to the theatre with Lord Bessett," said Lady Anisha irritably, "as did my brother. But so far as I know, neither I nor Lucan mean to court him."

"Don't be coy, Nish," said Lazonby. "We know one another too well for that."

"Do we, Rance?" She cut one of her mysterious, sloe-eyed glances at him. "I sometimes wonder if I know you at all. But very well, yes. Bessett asked my brother's permission to pay his attentions to me. Quaint of him, was it not?—particularly when it should have been *me* whom he asked."

"Bessett is delightfully old-fashioned," Lazonby concurred. "I think it one of his finer traits."

"Well, Adrian and I had a bit of row over it," said Anisha sourly. "I have told my brother time and again that I mean to take a lover before I take another husband."

Lazonby smiled. "Do you indeed?"

"Yes, someone different and . . . and adventurous, perhaps." Anisha's chin went up a notch. "Bessett was not quite what I had in mind, but now I think on it, his good looks quite make up for his being so archaic."

Lazonby settled his hand over hers and gave it a swift squeeze. "Look here, old thing—" He searched his mind for the right words. "I . . . I am not for you. You know that, don't you, Nish?"

Color flashed up her cheeks. "My God, Rance, but you presume a great deal!"

"I presume to account you a dear, dear friend," he said. "Shall I stop?"

Lady Anisha flounced on the seat, neatening skirts that did not need neatening, then adjusting the tilt of her jaunty little hat. "No," she finally said. Then she gave a great sigh. "Well, go on. What is it you want of me?"

"What do I *want*?" He cut a curious glance at her.

"Rance, I was married a long while, and I know how men think," she said. "You did not put on that fine morning coat—I did not know you owned anything so elegant, by the way—merely to tool through Hyde Park in front of people you could not care less about. The same people whom you well know wouldn't give Adrian and me the time of day were it not for my brother's money and title."

"Anisha, don't sell yourself short."

She cut another haughty look at him. "Oh, I don't!" she said. "I am quite as arrogant as any one of them. My mother was a Rajput princess, you may recall. London society can go hang for all I care."

"Good girl," he said, shooting her a grin.

Lady Anisha clapped a hand onto her jaunty hat as a gust of wind caught it. "So, what do you want?"

"I want you to go with me to Scotland Yard," he said.

"To *where*?"

"Well, to Number Four, actually," he said. "To visit Assistant Commissioner Napier. I know it isn't the most refined of places, but I saw you talking to him at the wedding breakfast, and I thought . . . well, I thought the two of you were getting on rather famously."

"Heavens, I wouldn't call it that," she said. "I have no use for the man whatever. But he was a guest in my brother's home, and I was polite to him."

"But he liked you," Lazonby suggested. "Either that, or he thought you were pinching Ruthveyn's silver, for he never took his eyes from you."

Lady Anisha seemed to consider it. "Oh, don't be ridiculous," she finally said. "He was civil enough, yes, but Napier was under no illusion as to why he was invited."

"Yes," said Lazonby tightly. "To make it plain to the gossiping public that Lady Ruthveyn was fully exonerated in her employer's murder. After all, he'd all but publicly accused her. It was that or have Ruthveyn rain political hellfire down upon his head."

"People are forever underestimating the reach of the *Fraternitas*, are they not?" Lady Anisha murmured, still holding her hat against the breeze. "In any case, Napier was asking me about India. He had been offered a position there."

Lazonby cast his gaze heavenward. "Please, God, tell me he is leaving England forever?"

"I fancy he had already turned it down," said Lady Anisha. "Something to do with a death in his family. No, I think you will not be rid of Napier quite that easily. And yes, Rance, I know he has hounded you unmercifully. I know it was his father who sent you off to rot in prison. And for those reasons, if no other, Napier will never be my friend."

"But you will you go with me?" asked Lazonby. "As your brother's representative, since he has left for India? Right now Napier feels a debt to your family—perhaps even a little shame. And he found you intriguing. He won't toss me out on my ear quite so quickly if you're with me."

Anisha rolled her eyes. "What about Lucan? Mightn't he go?"

Lazonby laughed. "Your younger brother has no gravitas, my dear," he said, "and you are—if you will pardon the expression—twice the man he can ever hope to be."

"Nonsense," she snapped. "He is just a boy—and a rake in the making, yes, but I shall attend to that in time. But very well, I concede he won't do."

"And . . . ?"

Anisha exhaled on another great sigh. "Choose the day, then," she said. "I shall do it—but it will cost you something dear."

"A pound of flesh, eh, Shylock?" he said, cutting a grin at her.

"It might feel like more than a pound," she said, her spine set rigidly straight. "On Saturday night, in recompense, you will accompany me to the opera."

"To the opera?" he said, horrified. "But I don't like the opera. I don't even *understand* it."

"It is Donizetti's *L'elisir d'Amore*," she said tartly. "And it's simple. They fall in love, there's a big misunderstanding, a magical elixir, and then they both—"

"—die tragically?" Lazonby flatly suggested. "And I'm just hazarding a wild guess here."

Her eyes flashed warningly. "Rance, must you be so boorish?"

Lord Lazonby laughed. "Or does just one of them die, leaving the other brokenhearted?" he suggested. "Or perhaps they accidentally poison one another? Or stab one another? And all of it sung, no less, and in some obscure language no reasonable chap would understand?"

Anisha's eyes glittered. "Oh, for pity's sake, you do not need to understand it!" she gritted. "You need to put on a proper frock coat and present yourself in Upper Grosvenor Street at seven sharp. Lady Madeleine needs another gentleman to even out her numbers—and *you are it!*"

"Ah, well!" said Lazonby softly. "Another deal with the devil for old Rance!"

CHAPTER 6

In general, the Tao of the invader is this:
When the troops have penetrated
deeply, they will be unified.
Sun Tzu, *The Art of War*

The *Jolie Marie* sailed from Ramsgate's Royal Harbor just after dawn in the wake of the morning's first mail packet. The captain, Thibeaux, was the son of an elderly French Savant who had served the *Fraternitas* well for many decades, and survived France's turmoils with his head intact. Like all the Brotherhood's Savants, the elder Thibeaux was a man of great learning; an astronomer and mathematician by trade.

By Thibeaux's estimation, the journey across the North Sea was expected to take something less than two days, and Geoff had ordered him to run fully rigged.

The trouble started, however, as soon as the Kentish cliffs disappeared from the horizon—which, given the wind, didn't take long. Anaïs, who had remained fixed at the aft railing staring at Ramsgate, began to pace the deck from stem to stern as soon as the shoreline vanished, her shawl and her hems whipping wildly about her, and it took no special gift—psychic or otherwise—to sense her disquiet. Though *disquiet*, perhaps, was not quite the right word.

Twice in passing he suggested she go below, but Anaïs shook her head. She was regretting her impetuous decision, Geoff feared. Though they had seen no one known to either of them through the whole of the previous day, the harsh reality of what she had chosen to do was likely sinking in on her now.

He had wondered—but not permitted himself the satisfaction of asking—just what she'd told her family. Obviously Maria Vittorio knew she had left England again, even if her parents did not. Quite likely her brother knew it, too.

That could prove unpleasant.

But an impetuous pup like Armand de Rohan could be dealt with in time—if it became necessary. And her brother's disposition, rash or otherwise, had nothing to do with Anaïs's present mood. The truth was, she had been distant all morning, even to the point of refusing the breakfast he had arranged in the inn's private parlor. And oddly, Geoff had found himself a little rankled by it.

He had set out on this journey trying to avoid her, it was true. The whole of his mind, he had told himself, needed to be focused on the task before him, and not on the seductive turn of his partner's backside. Watching her climb in and out of the carriage and smile at his servants at every stop along the drive from London had driven him to distraction. And he was not a man easily distracted.

But during their walk up from the harbor the previous evening, with their arms linked loosely together, Geoff had somehow begun to see more than that lovely backside. He had felt, fleetingly, as if he had glimpsed her equally lovely *inside*.

Those virtuous notions notwithstanding, however, it was

not her fine character his mind had turned to when at last he'd stripped himself naked and crawled into bed last night, saddle-weary and much conflicted. No, it was that wide, mobile mouth of hers. That husky laugh which seemed to bubble up from deep inside, then catch provocatively in her throat. Those hot brown eyes and that riotous tangle of black hair that seemed ever on the verge of tumbling down.

He watched her now as she strolled along the deck of the *Jolie Marie*, tendrils of inky hair curling wildly from the damp, and he couldn't help but imagine having it down about her breasts and plunging his hands into it. And it made him wish to the devil he'd drawn that last inch of his draperies closed last night. Or that his bed had sat under the window instead of directly opposite. Or even better, that he'd gone down to the taproom and got himself thoroughly sotted. For Anaïs, it seemed, was a bit of a night owl. Her lamp had remained lit until well past midnight.

For a time, he had merely watched her silhouette, long and graceful as it passed back and forth by her window, while he wondered what she was doing awake at such an hour. And then he wondered why he cared. She was not his type. She was young—younger and a good deal more innocent than the sort of female who ordinarily captured his imagination.

Bessett preferred experienced women who knew the game; lush, mature women with no pretense to romance and few expectations. And for that absence of finer feelings, he was willing to pay handsomely—though he rarely had to.

No, Anaïs was not for him, but capture his imagination she inexplicably had. And so he had found himself fixated upon a mere shadow, fantasizing about her even as he stroked himself, seeking satisfaction—or something akin to it—in the basest of ways. Tipping his head back into the softness of his pillow, he had thought about that hair, and breathed in the memory of her scent. And no, it was not her inner beauty that had driven him, or remained with him as he'd cried out with his release.

Even then, however, the lust inside him had not stilled.

He should have remembered his original vow—that he did not need to know the woman in order to work with her. He needed to know only that they shared the same concern for the child whom they had been sent to protect. That should have been enough. But now, as he watched her turn and make her way up the length of the deck again, Geoff felt the bite of dissatisfaction like a blackfly at the back of his neck.

And it was remotely possible she sensed it. Possible, really, that she knew a vast deal about his innermost thoughts and longings. Though it was true that those with the Gift—even a hint of it—could not read one another, there were always subtleties and layers.

Of course, as so many amongst them did, Anaïs had minimized her skill. But he'd heard the same sort of denials out of Rance, and even Lady Anisha, Ruthveyn's sister. And while it was true that few were as accursed with the Gift as he and Ruthveyn, Geoff could not escape the suspicion that a great many people took care to hide the truth.

Well, if she knew, so be it. He was a man, with a man's desires—and she would do well to remember it.

But he lost that train of thought when she paused near the hatch to seize hold of the railing, staring intently starboard as if France might magically materialize from that chalybeous infinity of water and sky. She leaned so far forward that, for an instant, he wondered if she meant to pitch herself headfirst into the churning water and swim for Calais.

But what nonsense. Anaïs de Rohan was far too sensible for that.

He relaxed, one hand upon the mast for balance, and let his gaze drift over her. She was dressed today in dark green, another of her eminently practical gowns, the simplicity of which merely served to emphasize the lean elegance of her figure. She had curves enough to please a man, he noticed, but no more, and he found himself wishing he'd looked at her a little more purposefully that night in the St. James Club. He should have liked to have a clearer memory of those small, perfect breasts to help him ease the torment at night.

In another life, he supposed, Anaïs de Rohan might have been a dancer, or an exclusive courtesan, perhaps, for though she was right in saying she was not a beauty, she fairly exuded earthly charm and celestial grace.

Just now, however, she looked neither charming nor graceful.

She looked like she was about to heave her entrails over the rail.

He had left his post by the mainmast and was hastening toward her before he fully grasped what had drawn him. By the time he reached her, Anaïs's knuckles were bloodless upon the railing, her face as pale as parchment.

He set a hand at her spine and leaned over her. "Anaïs, what is it?"

She turned her head to look up at him with a wan smile. "Merely a little *mal de mer*," she said. "I sometimes suffer with it."

He set his arm loosely at the small of her back. "So that's what's wrong," he said, almost to himself. "Look, you should go below and lie down."

She shook her head and turned back to the rail. "I've got to watch the horizon," she said, the wind whipping at the loose tendrils of her hair. "It helps. Now go. I shall be fine."

But Geoff had never seen anyone so ashen. "I can order Captain Thibeaux to slow the ship," he suggested.

"Don't you *dare*." Her voice was tremulous with emotion. "We haven't the time, and it will but draw out the misery."

He shifted his weight, and set his hands on the rail to either side of her, bracketing her with his body. The irrational fear that she might jump or fall still plagued him. He could feel her trembling. "Anaïs," he said, "do you have this often?"

She gave a pathetic little laugh. "Did I say *sometimes*? I lied."

"But . . . your travels," he murmured. "To Tuscany. To everywhere, really."

"Look, the truth is—" She had her eyes firmly fixed on the horizon. "The truth is, I can't cross the Thames without casting up my accounts. There, Bessett, you've had fair warning. Stay, and I shan't be accountable for that lovely waistcoat you're wearing."

He set one hand on her shoulder. "Then why do you do it? Travel, I mean."

"Because suffering builds character?" she suggested a little bitterly. "You know, I never much minded the long journeys across land. The being away from my family. Even the incessant political upheavals that occasionally sent me to ground. But I should rather have waded through one of Tuscany's revolutions than face a day at sea. In the end, however, England is an island, so what choice is there?"

"To stay home," Geoff suggested, then he dropped his tone. "To embroider those pillow cushions, perhaps?"

"Out of the question," she said.

"*Hmm*," he said. "Is this is why you didn't come down to breakfast?"

"Did you imagine I found your company intolerable?" She gave a sharp laugh. "I assure you, Bessett, that is not the case. I simply know better than to eat before sailing."

He let his hand slide to her waist and bent his head. "Geoff," he quietly reminded her. "Just Geoff will do. Poor girl. You must be feeling perfectly weak-kneed."

Again she gave her uneasy laugh. "What lady would not

be, with you pressed inch-to-inch down her length?" she said.

"I'm not letting you faint and fall headfirst into the North Sea," he said. "So yes, perhaps I'm a little close."

"And I wish I weren't so thoroughly unable to appreciate that fact," she said. "Oh, really, Bessett! Must we have this conversation? I seem infinitely capable of embarrassing myself. Go away now, do."

"Come midship," he ordered, gently pulling her away from the rail. "You'll find it a bit steadier there. Perhaps we can find you a seat."

She came reluctantly, and in due course, Étienne, the cabin boy, unearthed a sort of deck chair from the hold. Bessett ordered it lashed to a pair of cleats and situated Anaïs beneath a heavy blanket. The fine spring morning in Ramsgate had given way to the vagaries of the sea, and the spray off the bow was picking up with their speed.

Bessett returned to his tasks, but for the remainder of the day his gaze was never far from her. The captain repeatedly offered ginger tea—and hinted at something stronger—but she refused all offers. Later, as Bessett and the rest of the crew went below in turns to eat a little bread and cold beef, Anaïs merely shook her head, and as dusk came upon them and the temperature dropped, there was soon no horizon— blurry or otherwise—to help keep her bearings.

Finally, Geoff had no choice but to force her to go below, all but carrying her down the steep, ladderlike stairs.

The *Jolie Marie* was fitted with two private cabins; the captain's forward quarters, and a second aft for guests. This minuscule cabin held four narrow berths stacked double with drawers below, a small dining table, and a mahogany washstand with a chamber pot beneath. The last was to prove useful, for as the evening came on, Anaïs began to grow clammy, and to retch violently to little effect.

Uneasy, Geoff poured the washbasin full of water, dampened a cloth, and mopped her brow. "You should try to sleep," he suggested.

"Oh, what a miserable state of affairs this is!" Arms wrapped round her waist, Anaïs was perched on the very edge of the berth, having refused his entreaties to lie down. "I think I'm going to retch again. Please, go find something better to do, and spare me the humiliation, won't you?"

Geoff managed a weak smile. "What kind of Guardian leaves his partner alone in the lurch?" he enquired softly.

"What kind of Guardian gets seasick?"

"A great many, no doubt, under the right circumstances." He tucked a springy, wayward curl behind her ear. "This is a wicked sea today. Here, look at me. Your hair is falling down."

Anaïs reached behind as if to tidy it, pulled the wrong pin, and fully half the arrangement came tumbling over one shoulder. Muttering a most unladylike oath, she flung the pin across the cabin.

Geoff sat down on the edge beside her. "Look, turn round," he soothed. "I'm going to take the pins out. Then you *are* going to lie down."

"No," she said feebly, propping one shoulder against the wall of the berth.

But she offered no real resistance to his plan. His fingers were clumsy at first, plucking at the higgledy-piggledy pins. Eventually, however, they were out, and Geoff set about taking the other side down, marveling at the length and the texture.

Just as he had fantasized, Anaïs's hair was a glossy, springy mass of feminine glory that tumbled to her waist, and he found himself wondering how on earth she tamed it long enough to put it up.

Unable to resist the temptation, Geoff pulled out the last

pin, then ran his hands gently through it. And as he felt the warmth of it draw like satin between this fingers, it dawned on him that he'd never taken down a woman's hair just for the pleasure of it. Just for the sensual self-indulgence of feeling the warm, ropy silk draw through his fingers like air and light and water all at once.

He opened his mouth to say . . . well, something witless, most likely. But he was saved by a sharp knock at the door.

Geoff answered it to find the cabin boy, a steaming hot mug in hand. "*Thé au gingembre pour madame*," said Étienne, "*avec opium. Le capitaine*, he sends it. For sleep, *oui*?"

"*Oui, merci*," said Geoff, taking the mug. "This time she will drink it."

And she did—between bouts of insisting she would simply heave it back up again.

"You've had nothing to eat or drink in twenty-four hours," he said, pressing the mug to her lips. "That alone will make you sick. Now drink it."

Had she been fully herself, Anaïs would never have surrendered to his will. He knew that. But in her weakened state, she gave in, looking up at him between sips with round, brown puppy-dog eyes until something inside his chest did a curious little flip-flop.

Good Lord. The woman was ill, pale, and in general, a mess. What the hell was wrong with him?

He hadn't long to ponder it. After half a mug, the ginger and the opium did its job with surprising swiftness. One moment she was drinking, and the next instant, her chin hit her chest and Anaïs slumped against him with the whole of her weight.

Thank God.

She would be out of her misery until daylight, at least. And at this speed, they should sight land late tomorrow evening.

Throwing back the blankets on the narrow berth, Geoff scooped her up and settled her fully into it, wondering to what extent he dared undress her. He began by simply un-buckling the little pistol she wore round her calf, then pulling off her shoes—while trying not to stare at her legs, a matter of gentlemanly deportment at which he failed miserably.

His hand itched to draw up her skirts—all the way up—to see, amongst other things, whether she truly wore the mark of the Guardian. And it inexplicably maddened him that Rance had seen what he had not, when neither of them had any business staring at the lady's bare hip.

And in the end, Geoff allowed himself the small—and faintly wicked—pleasure of running his hand down the turn of her calf, marveling at the layers of hard muscle beneath the deceptively tender skin. Then, with a measure of reluc-tance, he took her ankles and tucked them gently under the blanket.

But the berth was so short, even Anaïs was cramped by her height. On a soft curse, he unbuttoned the front of her green gown. As he had suspected, she wore a modern corset with a bone busk. Swiftly, he popped the fasteners. Her dainty breasts shifted and flattened beneath the thin lawn of her shift, and her shoulders rolled back, relaxed. On a sigh of what sounded like pure pleasure, Anaïs squirmed halfway onto her back, and began to breathe deeply.

There. It was the best he could do. It was all he dared do.

But she was asleep, and she was comfortable.

With one last look of regret, Geoff pulled the blanket fully over her, and tucked it in all around.

And on his next breath, he suddenly wished that he had not called upon Lady Anisha Stafford the day after Ruth-veyn's wedding. Or invited her and her younger half brother, Lord Lucan, to the theatre with his mother the evening after that.

He had even gone so far as to extract his mother's promise to call upon Lady Anisha during his absence. To take her to tea, and ask her to dinner. All of which had left his mother with a speculative glint in her eye. So he had told her the truth—insofar as there was a truth to be told. He greatly admired the lady. He meant to court her.

They would likely be shopping for a trousseau by the time he got back from Brussels.

Geoff felt suddenly a little seasick himself.

Lady Anisha was, of course, a dear friend and always would be. She was so dear a friend, Geoff wished never to do anything that might leave her feeling awkward. He hoped he had not already set himself on a course toward doing precisely that.

He set one hand about the turn of Anaïs's cheek. She was like Ruthveyn's sister in that one glance at her black hair and warm skin could tell you she was no mere English rose, but a hothouse orchid, rare and slightly exotic. In every other way, however, they were as dissimilar as two women could possibly be.

He dropped his hand, and willed his mind to turn in some other direction from the one it was rambling toward.

In an effort to distract himself, he went to his portmanteau and withdrew the files DuPont had given him. In addition to the dossiers and the notes, DuPont had included a few personal items, amongst them a letter with Madame Moreau's signature, and a long, yellow hair ribbon tagged with Giselle Moreau's name.

This Geoff plucked from the packet, and for a time he sat at the little dining table drawing the ribbon pensively through his fingers. Sometimes personal effects could be of use, but because the child was of the Vateis, he would see little. The mother, however, was a different story. Her letter might open the void to him, but tonight he hadn't the heart.

He did not want to see Giselle's future, or feel her mother's fears. He did not want to know Madame Moreau's grief or feel any lingering hint of her memories.

It might all seem too painfully familiar.

He tossed down the ribbon as if it were an asp to his breast. Rising, he turned the wick on the table lamp, leaving just enough light to watch over Anaïs. Then he yanked off his boots, tossed his coat and waistcoat over a chair, and gingerly wedged himself into the bunk that lay opposite, knees pulled halfway to his chest.

Rolling onto his side, Geoff let his gaze drift over her, and heaved a sigh. He was cramped, damp, and more than a little obsessed. As Anaïs had said, *a miserable state of affairs indeed.*

Lord, it was going to be a long night.

CHAPTER 7

*In the practical art of war, the best thing of all
is to take the enemy's country whole and intact.*
Sun Tzu, *The Art of War*

*B*russels was beautiful in the spring. Pushing her
bedchamber windows wide, Anaïs leaned out over
the Rue de l'Escalier and inhaled deeply of air that was, for
the moment, fresh with the scent of rain. Sadly, it would not
last, the new butler had assured her, for the effluent of the
city, like that of London, was carried away on a river that ran
through the middle of town.

But for now Brussels was lovely and—unlike the *Jolie
Marie*—very, very still. And to Anaïs, not even a deep whiff
of the River Senne could lessen the beauty of that.

Across the narrow lane, pots of early flowers perched
almost jauntily upon the wrought-iron balconies that
marched up the street. Directly below, two elderly men were
unloading the fourgon that had followed them from their inn
at Ostend, grumbling at each other in what sounded like two
or three different languages.

Reluctantly, Anaïs withdrew, for she could feel the promise of rain. It had drizzled almost the whole of their journey

inland, but she had not minded, so grateful had she been to get her feet on land, dry or otherwise.

"And this way, *madame*, is your dressing room," said the butler's voice behind her.

Anaïs spun about with a bright smile. "Lead the way, Bernard."

The butler showed her into a wide passageway with a pair of wardrobes, storage for several trunks, and a small dressing table. In the confined space, one could still catch the scent of fresh paint.

"Through this door, *madame*, is Mr. MacLachlan's chamber," Bernard informed her. "The bathroom, it is shared, and all the rooms connect."

Anaïs felt her smile fade. This she had not considered when giving in to Geoff's argument that a sham marriage—even in front of the crew and staff—made a slip-up less likely.

"I am sure, Bernard, that it will do nicely," she managed.

The servant bowed and went out into the passageway to oversee the trunks, which were now bumbling up the steps. Anaïs watched him go, then drifted back to the window.

Bernard was far more formal than any servant Anaïs's family had ever engaged. He had come, he explained to them, directly from the Parisian town house of Mr. van de Velde, as had the two housemaids. The footmen had come from Monsieur DuPont's. The kitchen staff from someone in Amsterdam.

Though they were all trusted and loyal, they were a small group, Bernard had ruefully explained. In addition, their mysterious host—who, in the end, had not been especially mysterious after all—had brought with him a lady's maid and valet when he met them at the port.

Mr. van de Velde had turned out to be a short, fat, and

very rich Rotterdam banker with a swooping mustache and fingers in the financial pies of France, Belgium, and the Netherlands. Like Bessett, he wore the *Fraternitas* symbol on his cravat pin, albeit without the thistle cartouche.

After a warm welcome, and yet another warning about Lezennes' reputation, he provided them with maps, keys, and a list of contacts throughout Brussels, then whisked himself off again, for he was too well-known, he explained, to be seen with them beyond the privacy of his enclosed carriage.

Behind Anaïs, Bernard gently cleared his throat.

"The Royal Palace, *madame*, is that way," he said, pointing up the hill. "Madame Moreau's church is a short walk down, just through the Grand Place and flower market. Mind your step, if you please, as you go out, for all of Brussels is under construction."

Anaïs smiled. "The Revolution has been good for business, I collect?"

"In some ways, *oui*." With a tight smile, Bernard dropped his voice. "And especially good for the bankers. Monsieur van de Velde has many business interests hereabouts."

"Including this house?"

Bernard gave a decidedly Gallic shrug, and opened his hands. "Alas, the previous owner played his cards too deeply," he murmured. "He was compelled to let out the house for a year. To meet the mortgage."

"A loan for which Monsieur van de Velde held the note, no doubt," said Anaïs wryly.

Bernard lifted one slender eyebrow. "He holds many such mortgages, I am sure."

She turned back to the window, wondering yet again just how deep the tentacles of the *Fraternitas* wove throughout the governments and the economies of Europe. And van de

Velde had taken the house for *a year*? Good Lord. Surely it wouldn't take that long to make off with the Moreau family—or what was left of them.

With Maria's reluctant complicity, Anaïs could skate her way past her parents' curiosity for a while—a couple of months, perhaps, now that the growing season was here. With a little luck, Armand would be too busy cutting a swath through Town to realize she'd ever come home from Tuscany. And Nate . . . oh, Nate was like a bloodhound if he caught the scent of scandal. Even the clever Maria would not be able to put him off then. But Nate was frightfully busy, and used to her being far away.

Oh, it was true that a Guardian—even an unofficial one such as herself—often had to make personal sacrifices. She would certainly do what was necessary. But a year's absence, she considered, would burn some bridges. It would ruin her in society. And heaven only knew how she would manage under the same roof with Bessett—with *Geoff*—for that long.

It would be helpful, perhaps, if he returned to being that haughty, domineering gentleman she'd first met at the St. James Society. Instead, he seemed determined to keep her perpetually off-kilter with the occasional spate of pure kindness. From time to time, even those ice-blue eyes began to look capable of melting.

But Bernard was still standing at her elbow as if awaiting her next command.

"So the house with the red and yellow tulips," she murmured, "that is the house of the Vicomte de Lezennes?"

Bernard stepped nearer. "*Oui, madame,*" he said, dropping his voice. "Already we have accomplished much. Mrs. Janssen has made the acquaintance of Lezennes' cook at the market in the Grand Sablon, and our footman Petit is—how do you call it?—*stepping out* with the upstairs maid? They will have much to tell you of the rhythms and gossip of the house."

Anaïs pulled the sheer drapery aside, and peered more intently at the house just two doors up the steep lane. "And what of the child?" she asked pensively. "Has she been seen at all?"

"Very little," said the servant. "Most days Madame Moreau takes her to the park for a midday walk, and Lezennes meets them there, then walks them home again. He has also engaged a governess to come in each day."

Just then, Geoff's firm footsteps came swiftly up the stairs. Anaïs turned to see him striding down the passageway, one of her trunks balanced easily on his right shoulder. Today he wore his straight, heavy hair tied back with a leather cord, as if he were too busy to give it any thought. Her new French maid hastened after him, barely able to keep up with Geoff's long legs.

"Well, that's the last of it," he said, making his way through to her dressing room. "The house is splendidly situated, Bernard."

"Certainly the view across the street could hardly be better." Anaïs went to the dressing room door as Geoff set the trunk down with a grunt. "And look, my dear," she continued, crossing her arms over her chest. "Our dressing rooms connect—and we share a bath."

From his kneeling position, Bessett cut a teasing glance up at her. "Aye, well, at least there's a bit of plumbing," he said evenly. "Up in Yorkshire we still tote our water—hot and cold."

Claire, her new maid, bobbed a quick curtsy, declaring in rapid French her intent to begin the unpacking.

"*Merci*," said Anaïs.

Behind them, the butler cleared his throat again.

"Ah, Bernard," said Geoff, rising. "You said there was something in the attics you wished us to see?"

The butler gave one of his stiff little bows. "If *madame* and *monsieur* would kindly follow me?"

Much like a London townhouse, the house in Brussels was deep and narrow, and consisted of a below-grade service floor with kitchens, three main living floors, and vast attics above. Anaïs and Geoff followed the butler up the last flight of stairs, expecting to find servants' quarters.

Instead, most of the attic was open and vaulted, finished with white ceilings, a polished wooden floor, and a large, raised skylight to the rear. In one quadrant sat, of all things, a pocket billiard table, longer and perhaps narrower than an English table. In the opposite corner some distance away hung a stuffed leather bag on a rope, such as gentlemen might use for boxing practice. Between the two lay a thick, quilted mat—for indoor wrestling, she assumed, her brothers having a fondness for that sort of brutish violence.

The opposite half of the attic was empty, save for a wall rack containing an array of rapiers and *épées*, along with miscellaneous side blades and fencing gear. And at two of the dormered windows sat small telescopes mounted on tripods, like those used for navigation, along with a pair of matching chairs.

Geoff turned slowly around, and gave a low whistle of appreciation.

"A gentleman's paradise, *n'est-ce pas*?" said Bernard. "The owner is a great fan of sport."

"Hence his unrelenting indebtedness," muttered Anaïs, crossing to take down one of the rapiers.

"These telescopes are an unusual touch," said Geoff, sliding into one of the chairs to peer through the eyepiece. "Ah. I see."

"They are ours, *oui*," said Bernard. "You may wish to

move one of them to your bedchamber, perhaps. For now, we take turns here watching Lezennes' dining room, and what we believe is his front parlor."

"Seen anything?" asked Geoff, still squinting.

"Occasionally, Madame Moreau," said Bernard. "She seems to move freely through the house, and she goes out— shopping, a little, and to church two or three times a week."

"The dossier DuPont gave us says that she is Catholic," said Anaïs pensively. "Is she devout, do we believe?"

Bernard shrugged. "Her late husband was devout, certainly," he answered. "Our contacts in Paris believe she is perhaps less so. It may be that church has become an escape from Lezennes' thumb. Or perhaps the lady is praying desperately for something."

Anaïs considered it. "And she goes to where?"

"To St. Nicholas," said the butler.

"Ah," said Anaïs. "Perhaps it is time I, too, went to confession."

Geoff straightened from the telescope, and looked at her a little oddly. On one side, much of his hair had slithered from its cord.

Bernard merely bowed. "I shall go now, and get your personal servants situated. Also, sir, Monsieur DuPont has sent an envelope for you. He says it is not urgent. Shall I leave it on your desk?"

"Yes, of course." Geoff had returned his eye to the scope. "Thank you, Bernard."

As the attic door closed, Anaïs restored the rapier to its place, sliding it home with a metallic *zing!*

"No one appears to be at home across the way," said Geoff, giving up and unfolding his long, lean form from the chair.

"Yes, we're going to have to go over and make new friends soon," Anaïs murmured, taking down one of the *épées*. "I confess to being a tad anxious about it."

She turned from the rack to see that Geoff was eyeing the weapon in her hand. "Well, you look like you know what you're doing with that, at least."

With a grin, Anaïs snapped into stance, and lunged. "*En garde!*"

Geoff did not so much as blink. "Oh, trust me, my dear, I have been on guard since the moment I laid eyes on you," he said, wandering toward her with his usual loose-limbed grace. "But I did wonder if old Vittorio hadn't taught you a trick or two."

Anaïs felt her grin fade. "Yes, he was a master swordsman in his day," she said softly. "He was . . . *amazing.* And renowned throughout Tuscany. Indeed, did you ever hear—"

"—about that secret assassination attempt at the Congress of Vienna?" Admiration warmed Geoff's brilliant blue eyes. "Now, *that* exploit made Vittorio famous within the *Fraternitas.* As I hear it, the knife was intended for Cardinal Consalvi?"

"Yes, the assassin drew his weapon, but never got the chance to strike." Anaïs thrust her blade forward with a flourish. "Vittorio ran him through blind like so—"

"—whilst standing behind the dais drapery," Geoff finished.

"Yes, yes, for that was his Gift, you see!" Lowering her left hand, Anaïs dropped her gaze to the *épée*'s intricate basket grip. "Both his Gift, and his curse. He could sense the . . . the very *being* of a person; the life force, if you will. And he knew evil for what it was. He could smell it, you see, like the scent of death. He tried to teach me a little . . . but I . . . I think perhaps I did not wish to learn that particular lesson too well. Indeed, I do not envy anyone with so strong a Gift."

Some inscrutable emotion passed over his face, like an instant of pain, too swift and too raw to be acknowledged. Immediately, he changed the subject, lightening his tone.

"So, Mrs. MacLachlan," he said, "what's your weapon of choice?"

Anaïs dropped her point. "The rapier with dagger."

"Ah, the traditional school!"

"Vittorio was nothing if not traditional," she acknowledged, "save when it came to me."

"No, you are decidedly *un*traditional," he murmured. "What else did Vittorio teach you—besides that smooth lunge and blind sight?"

"I don't have the gift of blind sight." Her voice was perfectly emotionless as she drew one finger assessingly down the flat of the blade. "An eventually, yes, he hired a Florentine fencing master for me. Vittorio said he'd grown too old to do a proper job of the faster, more complex moves. That such a job wanted a younger man."

She glanced up to see Geoff was watching her hand as if mesmerized. "Did he imagine you'd ever have to defend yourself with a sword?"

Anaïs shook her head. "I think he just wanted me to learn grace and speed," she said. "Clarity of thought under pressure. And the whole sensory thing—well, my instincts are better than average, I'll grant you. Maria says I'm like a cat in the dark. But I'll never be Vittorio."

Geoff's gaze had softened. "And I wonder what that poor fencing master thought," he murmured. "Such a lethal beauty you must have seemed. He was probably half in love with you by the time it was over."

Anaïs felt heat rush to her cheeks. "Don't be ridiculous," she said, hastily turning to rehang the weapon. "He thought I had a knack for blades, and nothing more. He tried to teach me the spadone, just for the balance work, but I couldn't heft the cursed thing with any accuracy."

Geoff was staring at her with a sudden intensity when she turned round. "Why do I get the impression, Anaïs," he said quietly, "that you focus far more on your failures than your successes?"

She shrugged. "Doesn't everyone?" she returned. "Everyone, I mean, who hopes to make something of themselves?"

For a time, he merely looked at her, his head set at an assessing angle. "I think you already have," he said quietly. "Made something of yourself, I mean. But I get the sense that you push yourself—even to serve other people's wishes. Your being seasick is a perfect example of that."

"So you are suggesting I what?" she demanded. "Stay home to avoid a little queasiness? Give up entirely my great-grandmother's dream?"

She saw his jaw twitch tellingly, just the faintest of movements. "I'm suggesting that you had as bad a case of *mal de mer* as ever I've seen—and I've seen grown men weep." Geoff's voice was suddenly gruff. "And I'm suggesting that perhaps you ought to live your own dream, if you've ever taken time to decide on one."

She lifted her chin a notch. "And what of yourself?" she returned. "Are you doing precisely what you wish? And remember, I saw your face that night when you talked about your work with your stepfather."

For a moment, he looked away. "My life changed when Alvin died," he said. "Until then, yes, I had a career doing something I loved. I knew, of course, in the back of my mind that I could be called by the *Fraternitas* into service at any time, but the organization had become so fractured—"

"That in the end, you took it upon yourself to repair it," she interjected, stepping nearer. "And thereby altered your life forever."

"Yes," he said. "Yes, I daresay that's one way to look at it."

On impulse, she touched him gently on his cheek, and turned his face back into hers. "And thank God you did," she said, "for it breathed new life into the *Fraternitas.*"

"I am not sure it was begun quite so unselfishly," he murmured, glancing away. "Looking back, I think it was done out of anger. For Lazonby."

"For Lazonby?" Anaïs's brow furrowed.

"We had fallen in together in Morocco, he and Ruthveyn and I," said Geoff quietly. "Partners in dissolution, you might say. I had just finished a project for the French government, Lazonby was on leave from the Foreign Legion, and Ruthveyn—well, he was just smoking his way through the opium dens of North Africa. It was all one great bacchanalian orgy until the gendarmes hauled Lazonby off and handed him over to England. So Ruthveyn and I followed."

"And then what happened?"

"We bought a house, and founded the St. James Society," he answered. "We made good on all our high talk of resurrecting the *Fraternitas*. What good is a Brotherhood if it cannot protect its own from false imprisonment?"

"And was Lord Lazonby falsely imprisoned?" asked Anaïs. "It was a murder following a card game gone wrong, the newspapers said."

"He did not kill the man he was convicted of murdering, no," said Geoff. "But was he guilty of bad judgment? Yes. A man with a Gift such as his cannot play at cards. All manner of things can turn sour. But Lazonby was little more than a boy then—and even now, he denies that what he has is a Gift."

"But he has been marked as a Guardian by his family," she murmured.

"As have you, or so Lazonby says." For an instant, the ice returned to Geoff's eyes.

"Yes, as I told you that night in the Temple," she responded. "That was Nonna Sofia's instruction to Vittorio—that once I was trained, I should be marked and given to the cause."

"Why?" he pressed.

Anaïs shrugged. "I do not know," she said. "Toward the end of her life, my great-grandmother said only that there was something I was meant to do, and that fate would reveal it to me. And yes, I understand one can be a Guardian without metaphysical abilities. It requires only good sense, determination, and a certain amount of bravery. But Lord Lazonby's Scottish line is a strong one—most of the Scottish lines are, you know."

"Oh, aye," said Geoff tightly. "I know it well."

"And some of the French, too," she said musingly. "But truly, in parts of Europe, the *Fraternitas* had become almost ceremonial. One might as well have been joining the local Masonic Lodge—or even the Beefsteak Club—for all the good it did. But I don't need to tell you that. With all their research and documentation, the St. James Society has begun to put things to rights."

Geoff made a faintly dismissive sound. He had taken her hand again, and turned it up to trace his index finger over the lines, as if he might read her palm.

Anaïs instead folded her hand over his. "Listen to me, Geoff," she said a little fiercely. "Why do I get the feeling that you're now the one selling your good deeds short? You diminish all of us when you do that. And whatever you think of me—whether the *Fraternitas* wants me or not—I will always believe in what the St. James Society has done."

"Ah, such kind words, Anaïs!" he said softly.

"They aren't just words." Her voice trembled a little. "So often I heard Vittorio praise the work of your society. He believed it would eventually identify and keep safe all those with the Gift. Especially the most vulnerable amongst us. Like Giselle Moreau."

"Did he?" Geoff caught her hand almost roughly as she tried to draw it away.

Anaïs nodded. "I only wish that my great-grandmother could have lived long enough to see the *Fraternitas* rise from its ashes," she said. "To know that it would once again be more than just an old wives' tale. That it would resume its place as a secret society committed to doing good."

"It sounds so noble when you put it that way," he murmured, lifting her hand a little, almost as if he might brush his lips over it. "Perhaps we were just tired of feeling different, Ruthveyn and I. Perhaps we just wanted something to keep ourselves busy—busy enough that we didn't have time to look inside ourselves and question what we had become."

"I simply don't believe that," she whispered. "Perhaps, Geoff, I . . . I don't have much of a Gift. But I see *you*. And I think perhaps you know that."

She looked up to catch his fierce, cold gaze, only to realize he had pulled her almost effortlessly toward him. It was as if he'd drawn her across time and space instead of the glossy attic floor. An energy—a sort of tangible emotion—seemed to shimmer in the air about them, and every logical thought went skittering like marbles from her head.

They stood chest to chest beneath the rack of swords. Slowly, as if he moved under water, Geoff's opposite hand came up, his fingers stroking over her cheek. If waking yesterday morning with her dress unbuttoned and her corset laid open had felt intimate, this felt a thousand times more so.

"Ah, Anaïs, this is so unwise," he murmured. "Tell me . . . tell me we both know that."

CHAPTER 8

Know thyself, know thy enemy;
a thousand battles, a thousand victories.
Sun Tzu, *The Art of War*

*S*he swallowed hard, her gaze ensnared by his. "Very unwise," she whispered. "But . . ."

Her words fell away.

Oh, he was not the one for her. Anaïs knew it. And yet the moment felt inevitable.

He must have felt it, too. Sliding his left hand into the hair at the nape of her neck, Geoff settled his lips over hers, warmly and firmly. Purposefully. As if she'd surrendered her chance to gainsay his wishes, and he now meant to take his time at it.

Oh, yes, please, God, please let him take his time at it . . .

His mouth was soft, but with a strength that made plain his intent. His intent to possess her, at least in this fleeting moment. And on a whispered sigh, Anaïs gave. She melted her lips and her body to his, tipping her head fully back. Geoff bent over her, his hair a curtain of shimmering bronze as it fell forward to shadow his face.

She knew, of course, that she'd regret it—and he would, too. But when Geoff made a sound in the back of his throat and wrapped one arm low, banding her to him, Anaïs forgot about regret. Instead, she lowered her lashes and opened her mouth, nibbling lightly at the lush swell of his lower lip.

That might have been a mistake. Certainly it was an invitation, one that Geoff accepted by plunging inside her mouth with his tongue.

"*Umm*," she whispered, her hands going up—far up—to twine about his neck as she molded to him.

On a groan of pleasure, he delved deep, sinuously sliding his tongue along hers and rhythmically thrusting until her knees began to soften like so much warm butter. His right hand settled over her buttock and began to make warm, firm circles, inching up the muslin of her dress.

Suddenly breathless, Anaïs plunged her fingers into the luxuriousness of his hair, and sucked his tongue deep. As if in response, Geoff slid one hand beneath her hip, lifting her firmly against the unmistakable ridge of his erection. It was as if she could feel the hard length, the thickness, and even the throbbing hunger that lay unslaked deep inside him, and Anaïs felt herself swamped again by that profound sense of inevitability.

Scarcely aware she did so, Anaïs lifted one leg and twined it round his, then hitched it high over his hip. Geoff deepened the kiss, trembled a little in her arms, and urged himself against her in a motion that should have seemed vulgar but simply didn't. And for the longest of moments, she was simply lost in the wanting, her entire body aching for his as she pressed herself to him and felt him throb against her softness.

On a bone-deep shudder, she pulled her mouth from his. "Geoff," she whispered. "The—the mat. We could . . ."

Geoff's eyes shied toward the thick mat, and she could feel him trembling. "Good God, Anaïs," he rasped.

He closed his eyes, still holding her hips to his. Against

her belly, she felt his erection twitch insistently. She could see his throat working up and down, and smell the sensual heat roiling off his skin in waves.

"You want me," she whispered.

He gave a harsh laugh, and opened his eyes. "That's an understatement," he whispered. Slowly, he began to let her slide down his body. "You're like a flame to tinder."

Anaïs felt her foot settle onto the floor, and let her opposite leg slide down his until she was once again firmly planted in reality. Lowering her face into his shirtfront, she drew in the scent of laundry starch and unslaked lust. Geoff set his hand to the back of her head in a tender, almost protective gesture.

"I don't think," he said quietly, "that it would be wise for me to kiss you again. Ever."

She tried to feel grateful for his good sense.

She *was* grateful—or would be, as soon as her breathing calmed and that awful throb between her legs ceased.

Just then, the door hinges squealed tellingly. Bernard made another of those little sounds in the back of his throat.

"I beg your pardon," he said as they sprang apart.

"Ah, newlyweds!" said Geoff good-naturedly. "You must pardon us, Bernard."

The butler merely bowed stiffly at the neck. "But of course," he murmured. "Mrs. Janssen wishes to know what time you wish to dine?"

That evening, Anaïs locked both the bathroom doors and wandered about the small, delft-tiled chamber, taking in the strange signs of male occupation; the shaving soap upon the washing table, the gilt-handled toothbrush and matching razor upon a nearby shelf, and a small leather dressing case atop the linen chest, folded open to reveal only the most basic of gentlemen's toiletries.

So. Not such a preening peacock after all.

On impulse, she lifted a bottle from the case and pulled the stopper. The tantalizingly familiar scent of spice and citrus drifted up. Hastily she rammed it home again, then splashed a little cold water on her face. It did her no good to think of Geoff in such a way. She had come here on an important mission. She could ill afford to let her treacherous heart become her own worst enemy again.

Sanity somewhat restored by the bracing water, Anaïs set her hands wide on the washing table and stared at herself in the mirror. The truth was, she had been lucky. Dinner tonight should have been awkward, but the arrival of Petit, the footman, had saved them. Over the course of the meal, he had presented the rough schedule for the occupants of the house across the street, and told them all that he and Mrs. Janssen had learned of the household.

Lezennes, it seemed, spent most of his day at court or at various diplomatic offices within the capital. Madame Moreau's schedule was more fixed and, as Bernard had explained, consisted primarily of church and shopping. Little Giselle was barely allowed from the house. The family seemed to have formed no outside connections.

So tomorrow, they would begin in earnest. Madame Moreau would likely make her Saturday morning trip to confession, then visit the market in the Grand Place. Anaïs meant to be there ahead of her.

But when she had said as much, Geoff had looked rather pointedly down the table at her. "You will take Petit along," he had ordered. "I wish you to exercise every precaution."

With his unfashionably long hair drawn back, the candlelight had cast his lean cheeks and strong jawline in an even harsher relief, and he had looked like some imperious medieval prince upon his throne, commanding his lesser mortals. His hair looked darker, too; his nose a little more aquiline than usual.

Anaïs had merely lifted her glass of wine to her lips, and said nothing. A nonsensical order did not require a vast deal of consideration. If Geoff was angry with himself for kissing her, he would simply have to stew in it. If he was angry with her for kissing him—well, that made two of them. The man was hardly another rake intent upon seducing his way into the bed of an unsuspecting female. But that did not make her laxity any less stupid.

A little too abrasively, Anaïs finished cleaning her teeth, wondering even as she whacked the moisture from her brush if perhaps she oughtn't be hitting herself in the head with it. Or with something larger, perhaps. She cast a look at her hairbrush, then sighed.

She really did want him.

There was simply no getting around it. She had wanted him—well, not from the moment she'd laid eyes on him, perhaps—but something frightfully near it.

Anaïs closed her eyes and braced her hands on the wash table again. She could almost feel Geoff's presence in the next room. She knew he was there. Even as she lusted after him, he was roaming like a caged lion in his bedchamber, going from table to chair to window, most likely with a glass of brandy in hand.

A shiver ran through her, something deep and needy. Apparently her head was still too easily turned, for Geoff's touch had sent logic flying out the window. But this time, she needed to keep a clear head.

This time she needed to wait for the *right* man. Not the beautiful man.

She needed to remember, as Geoff obviously did, the child whom they had come to help. Little Giselle weighed on him in a way she did not quite understand. It was obvious in the way his voice caught every time he mentioned the girl.

Something else she did not understand was the nature of Geoff's gift. He never spoke of it, though Vittorio had once implied that Lord Bessett and Lord Ruthveyn were amongst the *Fraternitas*'s most powerful seers. That they were in truth mystics; throwbacks to the ancient Celtic priests from whom the *Fraternitas* was descended, and whose powerful abilities of prognostication had lain almost forgotten amidst the detritus of history and legend.

Whatever he was, and wherever he came from, Geoff obviously did not intend to let his baser emotions interfere with his work, and for that she should commend him.

On a sigh, Anaïs unlocked both the bathroom doors, then trailed back through the dressing room to her bedchamber. Her maid had gone, thank God, leaving the bedcovers folded back and the lamp turned down to a mere glow.

By the faint light, Anaïs opened her portmanteau and took from it her Bible and the ebony wood box containing the *tarocchi*, then set them on her night table. Flipping up the brass-hinged lid, Anaïs withdrew the top card, its edges worn softer than those that lay below.

With one last look at *le Re di Dischi*, she propped him up against the lamp as she always did, her gaze taking in his handsome face and his coat of bloodred armor, then swiftly, she blew out the light.

A prince of peace in a coat of scarlet.

But tonight, it felt as if her prince had forgotten her.

Or that perhaps he had not waited for her after all.

Geoff waited in utter darkness. Waited until he no longer heard Anaïs moving about in the room adjacent. Waited until the urge to go through the dressing room and into her bedchamber had passed, and he had some faint hope of perhaps sleeping undisturbed by thoughts of that heated, earth-shattering kiss they had shared.

What a bloody damned fool he was. He had known from the first it would come to this. That he would desire her. Dream of her. It would be a holy miracle if he could work with the woman at all.

But he had only to think of Giselle—to look through the mullioned glass of his bedchamber window at what Petit said was the child's nursery—and know that she might be utterly alone. Utterly terrified.

That could throw a little thing like carnal hunger into proper perspective.

When absolute silence fell across the house, Geoff rose and went to the window, pushing the arched casements wide on squeaking hinges, and leaning out into the Rue de l'Escalier to draw deep of the cool night air. But already he could smell the stench of the river settling over *le cité* like so much heavy fog. It smelled like rot and sewage—like this entire business with the Vicomte de Lezennes, truth be told.

The lights were still lit in the upper floors of Lezennes' town house, save for the room Petit had pointed out as Giselle's. After exhaling slowly, Geoff pulled a chair to the window, unlocked his traveling desk, and withdrew DuPont's most recent envelope. Beneath it he saw Giselle's yellow hair ribbon, and for an instant, his hand lingered. Perhaps it might connect him to her mother, if not the child?

Then he closed the box with a thud, lit a candle, and, for the second time that day, began shuffling through the new things DuPont had sent. There wasn't much; just a handful of overdue bills and a few letters of condolence to Madame Moreau. How DuPont had got hold of them, Geoff had as soon not know.

After flipping through the pile, he withdrew the most hopeful, a much-folded missive from her parish priest. This time, he read it slowly, focusing on every raw and painful sentiment as he held it in his hands. Trying to imagine how the letter had made her feel when she had held it in *her* hands. How she likely felt, even now.

Then he blew out the candle, closed his eyes, and opened himself quite deliberately to that infinite chasm between time and place. It felt a little like tying a tourniquet about one's arm and laying open a vein. But as the silence of the night washed over him, Geoff tried to *feel* Madame Moreau. Tried to draw in her grief and her thoughts and the essence of what was to be from the churning void beyond.

It was a task he loathed. But it was, for the most part, just a task now. Just a choice he made when no other alternative was left him.

There had been a time, however, not so many years past, when it had not been a choice. When his mind had slipped unconstrained through time and place; back and forth, slippery as an eel flicking through dappled sunlight. Like alternating flashes of blinding brightness and perfect clarity— uncontrollable clarity—that could sometimes reveal glimmers of things no child should see.

And see with complete and utter impotence.

No, he did not like to do this. But long years of practice and ruthless self-discipline had made the choice his, not fate's.

And yet tonight, he felt nothing.

On those very rare occasions nowadays when the sight came upon him unbidden, he felt a failure. And on occasions like tonight—when he could not bid the sight to come—he felt . . . well, the very same, he supposed.

He consoled himself—if the word could be used in such a context—that he did not know Giselle Moreau, and knew nothing of her mother save what they had glimpsed late this afternoon as she'd set off with her market basket. A small, tidy blonde in a long black cloak.

It was hard to grasp the threads of present thought or

emotion, let alone future events, when one had not actually touched, or at least met, the other person. But it had been worth a try.

On a sigh, Geoff tossed the letter back onto the pile. For the first time in his life, he almost missed the visions. Tonight he would be alone.

Alone with his fevered dreams of Anaïs de Rohan.

The Église St-Nicholas was a beautiful old church, tucked into a nook between the Rues au Beurre just below the Grand Place, on the edge of Brussels's more crowded, less upper-class neighborhoods. Further from the heart of royal Brussels than some, St. Nicholas was an interesting choice of churches, Anaïs considered as she roamed beneath its vaulted roofs.

But for some reason, Madame Moreau preferred it.

Perhaps it had something to do with the church's simplicity. The soothing colors and restrained giltwork. Even here, however, in this place of quiet, the signs of the city's political turmoil were apparent. The church had been repeatedly bombed and burned over the centuries, and in the Chapel of the Holy Virgin, a passing churchwarden told her, there was a French cannonball still lodged in one of the pillars.

Anaïs thanked him, but did not investigate, preferring instead to wait near the entrance and the row of confessionals through which the congregants were intermittently rotating. Instead, she lit a candle for Nonna Sofia, then took a moment to say a prayer.

Though she had been baptized in her mother's Anglican church, Anaïs had been steeped in Catholicism from an early age. As a child, she had often accompanied her grandmother and Maria to Mass at St. Mary's, for her parents had been liberal in such matters. In Tuscany, there had been no other church *to* attend. Anaïs found the religions . . . well, not interchangeable, precisely. *Complementary*, perhaps, was the word—and far more alike than some would make out.

So she settled into the Église St-Nicholas with the ease of visiting an old friend. A quarter hour later, a small, round lady with blond hair came in from the narthex carrying a market basket threaded with a bright green ribbon. The unusual basket was just as Petit had described.

Putting it down by the door, the lady pulled a scarf more fully over her hair, then went directly to one of the open confessionals. Anaïs followed, stepping up into the one adjacent.

"Bless me, Father for I have sinned," she said in French, her lips near the wooden screen. "I am Anglican. Will you hear my confession?"

The priest hesitated but an instant. "Of course, my child," he said, his voice soft. "If you aspire to a state of grace with Our Lord then you may seek the sacrament of reconciliation here."

"Thank you," she said. "It has been four months since my last confession. These are my sins. I have lied once to my father and my mother. I have several times used unladylike language. And I have had impure thoughts about a man to whom I am not married—actually, it was . . . well, a little more than just a thought."

"Ah," said the priest. "That last one—do you mean to marry him?"

"No, Father." Anaïs fleetingly squeezed her eyes shut. "There is . . . someone else."

"You are married to another?" His tone sharpened. "Promised to another?"

"No, neither, Father," she managed. "I . . . I am just waiting for the right one."

"Then you must try to be more patient, my child," the priest gently chided.

"I am sure you are right, Father," she said. "I am sorry for these sins, and all the other sins I may have forgotten."

"Very well," said the priest. "I will not give you penance. You must instead take these things into your heart to be pondered most gravely, and pray for patience in—well, in that last matter."

"Yes, Father."

Swiftly, Anaïs said her usual cobbled-together prayer of contrition. She could see out of one corner of her eye that Charlotte Moreau had stepped down from the confessional and was heading toward her basket.

"Your sins are truly forgiven," said the priest when she had finished. "Go in peace."

"Thanks be to God," said Anaïs.

She hastened down the steps then through the narthex.

Following Madame Moreau out into the brilliant sunshine, Anaïs managed bump into her basket ever so slightly. "Oh!" she said, grabbing as if to steady it. "I do beg your pardon. I mean—*zut!—excusez moi!*"

"*Mais certainement.*" Madame Moreau moved as if to sweep past her, then froze, her eyes widening at once. "Oh—but you are English!"

Anaïs feigned surprise. "Why, yes," she said. "Are *you*? I rather thought you looked familiar."

"I am English, yes." The lady's face warmed, but it did not take away the lines of grief about her eyes. "Or I *was*, I should say. But no, I think we cannot know one another. I have not lived in England for many years."

Anaïs laughed. "Well, if I were to live many years *away* from England, I might choose Belgium, too." Then she dropped her voice ever so slightly. "But you know, I fancy I *do* know you—or rather, I have seen you. Across the street, I mean. In the Rue de l'Escalier?"

The lady blinked uncertainly. "I do live there, yes."

Anaïs smiled hugely, and stuck out her hand. "I'm Mrs. MacLachlan," she said. "Anaïs MacLachlan. I think we must be neighbors."

The lady took the hand a little warily. "I am Madame Moreau."

Anaïs did her best impression of Nate's overebullient setter, without quite leaping upon the lady. "Oh, *what* a pleasure to meet you so soon!" she said. "After all, we just moved in yesterday. Isn't Brussels perfectly marvelous? Such life everywhere one looks! And the shopping." She paused, and widened her eyes. "I was just telling Mr. MacLachlan—we are on our honeymoon, you know—that I am going to bankrupt him quite utterly on lace and porcelain. And those little blue tiles—from Antwerp, someone said? In any case, I vow, I must take a trunkload when we go home." Then her face fell a little. "When we *do* go home, of course."

Madame Moreau was looking a little dazed. "Well, my felicitations on your marriage," she managed. "And welcome to Brussels."

"Oh, thank you." Anaïs smiled yet again. "Well, it was *such* a pleasure."

"Yes, a pleasure," Madame Moreau echoed.

"I hope you will call upon me someday?" Anaïs began to drift up the hill.

"Why, thank you," she said, but did not respond in kind.

Anaïs pointed up the street. "I was just on my way to the flower stalls," she said. "Is this the right way?"

"Oh, yes." Madame Moreau's placid expression was slowly returning. "Shall I show you? I was just going up to the Grand Place myself."

Anaïs tried to look hopeful. "Oh, *would* you join me?" she asked. "I do so dislike shopping alone, but the house is a little dreary, and I wanted flowers. And Cook needed a few things as well."

"I should be pleased to," said Madame Moreau as they fell into step together. "You must be in Monsieur Michel's house? One of the servants mentioned seeing baggage yesterday."

"Yes, we have taken it for a year," said Anaïs. "Though I am not sure how long we shall stay."

Madame Moreau cast her a sidelong glance. "I do hope Monsieur Michel is well?"

Anaïs lifted one shoulder. "I believe he may be traveling abroad," she said. "It was all arranged through agents and bankers. We don't know anyone here."

"Yes, I see," Madame Moreau murmured. "How did you come to choose Brussels for a wedding trip?"

"Oh, it was my husband!" Anaïs tossed her hand. "He fancies himself a bit of an artist. Or an architect, perhaps. He wished to do some drawing of all the marvelous buildings."

"And what of you?" asked Madame Moreau. "Would you not have preferred Paris? The shopping is a bit better there."

Anaïs pulled a gloomy face. "I *did* prefer it," she confessed, "but I think my husband did not."

"You think?" Madame Moreau shot her a curious glance. "But you are not sure?"

Anaïs shook her head. "I do not yet know him terribly well, to tell the truth," she said, dropping her voice as they strolled up the slight hill. "My father arranged it. He said it was time I remarried."

"Oh, you are a widow," murmured Madame Moreau.

"Sadly, yes," said Anaïs. "My late husband—well, it was a love match. Not one my father approved of, mind you, for John hadn't two shillings to rub together, but we were happy. I do think most highly of Mr. MacLachlan, though. I am sure the three of us will get on famously once we all grow accustomed to one another."

"The three of you?"

Anaïs brightened her expression. "Yes, I have a daughter," she said. "Jane is just four years old. And already I miss her so much I could cry."

Madame Moreau made a sympathetic noise in the back of her throat. "She did not come with you?"

Anaïs shook her head. "My husband thought travel would not suit her," she said quietly. "I daresay he is right. And this *is* a honeymoon. But I confess, I did not quite expect— ah, but I mustn't trouble you, Madame Moreau, when we just met. Look, this *must* be the Grand Place! Oh, my! How magnificent the buildings are!"

"Yes, let me give you a little tour," said the lady. "I think I have lived here long enough I can tell you what each one is."

"How kind you are." With a little sound of delight, Anaïs hooked her arm through Madame Moreau's.

They circled the square at a leisurely pace, taking in the guildhalls and the Hôtel de Ville with its incredible openwork spire, Anaïs oohing and ahhing at all the right moments. Soon she had one arm full of flowers, and was picking over a selection of hothouse fruit at one of the stalls in the middle of the square.

"So, do you think I should persuade Mr. MacLachlan to take me to Paris for a few days?" she said offhandedly. "Have you seen it? Is it worth it?"

Madame Moreau cut an odd look up at her. "Indeed, it is splendid," she answered. "It was my home, in fact, until a very few months ago."

Anaïs feigned surprise. "Was it? How do you like Brussels, then? What brought you here?"

They strolled away from the fruiter's stall, Madame Moreau's expression pensive. "I was widowed last year myself," she finally said. "I make my home now with my husband's uncle. He is attached to the French diplomatic corps here in Brussels."

"Oh, it *is* reassuring to have family one can count on, isn't it?" Anaïs paused to pick over a pile of lace handkerchiefs at a stall in front of the *hôtel*. "I feel most fortunate."

"A widow's life can be very hard," Madame Moreau agreed.

"Oh, yes." Anaïs selected a handkerchief, and gave it to the stall keeper. "Have you any family left in England?"

Madame Moreau bit her lip, and just for an instant, Anaïs thought she glimpsed fear in her eyes. "No," she said. "I have no one."

"Oh," said Anaïs softly as she counted out coins. "How dreadful for you. I do not know what Jane and I would have done had Papa not taken us in."

"He did take you in though?" said Madame Moreau as they set off again.

Anaïs nodded. "He declared he would not, of course," she said, "when John and I first married. And even after the babe came, his letters were cool."

"Oh, dear," said Madame Moreau. "How sad for you."

"Oh, no," she declared. "Once he actually *saw* Jane— well, what can I say? He was utterly charmed. He came for us just after the funeral. A grandchild changes everything, you know. All can be forgiven. Oh, look—is that an organ grinder?" She pointed across the market square.

"Why, yes," Madame Moreau replied, but her gaze had turned suddenly inward. "I believe it is."

"How utterly delightful." Anaïs smiled, and offered her arm. "Why do we not take a closer look?"

Just then a long shadow fell across their path.

Anaïs looked up to see Geoff standing by the opposite stall, waiting for the pedestrians to clear. His expression was dark as a thunderhead.

"Oh," she said a little witheringly. "Look. There is my husband now."

CHAPTER 9

To fight and conquer in all our battles
is not supreme excellence;
supreme excellence consists in breaking
the enemy's resistance without fighting.
Sun Tzu, *The Art of War*

It was too late; already Geoff was stalking across the cobbles, bearing down upon them like a fully-gunned frigate as he swept off his tall, very expensive hat. He was dressed today like a wealthy young gentleman of fashion in a dark morning coat, cut away to reveal the lean turn of his waist and a pearl-gray waistcoat of jacquard silk. His black stock was tied tight and high against the brilliant white collar of his shirt.

The path cleared before him as he approached, a brass-knobbed walking stick in hand.

"My dear." He tucked the hat beneath his arm and bowed stiffly, his eyes lined and hollow, as if he had not slept.

Anaïs forced a smile. "How fortuitous, Geoffrey," she said brightly. "I have had the good fortune of meeting one of our neighbors." Swiftly she made the introductions.

"A pleasure, Mr. MacLachlan." Madame Moreau bobbed a rather deep curtsy—in the face of Geoff's sartorial splendor and piercing gaze, even the Queen herself might have done so.

"Indeed, ma'am." Geoff bowed over her hand. "Might I give you my arm, my dear, and persuade you to walk home with me?" he asked, returning his hat to his head.

"Well, actually, we were just—"

But something deep in those glittering eyes stopped her.

Madame Moreau must have sensed her unease. "Please, Mrs. MacLachlan, do go," she said, again shaking her hand. "It was a pleasure to meet you."

But Anaïs held on to her fingers an instant longer than she should have. "Promise me that you will call for tea tomorrow," she blurted. "At four. Would that be convenient?"

Madame Moreau looked faintly anxious. "Well, yes . . . I daresay I might do. If I cannot, I—I shall send word."

Anaïs released her hand, and gave a little bob. "Then I shall bid you good day," she said. "Thank you for a lovely morning."

They left Madame Moreau standing a little forlornly by the lacemaker's stall and walked home past the Hôtel de Ville, Anaïs's hand tucked into the crook of Geoff's arm. And though he did not drag her, Anaïs could not but be reminded of how he'd hauled her up the stairs that night at the St. James Society.

But this time, his mood was not one of mere aggravation. It was a cold, barely restrained fury.

He spoke not a word until they were past the front door of the house. Then he slammed it shut and whirled on her. "Now, Anaïs, pray tell me," he gritted, "just what part of *'You will take Petit along'* did you not understand?"

"But Geoff, I thought that was—"

"What, ambiguous?" He hurled his hat onto the hall table. "Optional? A mere suggestion?"

"—unnecessary," she snapped.

"Oh!" he shouted, dragging the word out derisively. "Then what about '*I wish you to exercise every precaution*'? Did that instruction miss its mark as well? Was it *unnecessary*?"

Anaïs narrowed her eyes, then began to toss her things onto the coat rack. "No," she said, yanking off her scarf, "but I simply thought—"

"By God, Anaïs, it is not your place to think." Geoff's eyes drilled down into her, his voice more ominous. "Did I or did I not say that I would make—and again, I quote—*every decision at every turn of this operation?*"

One of the housemaids peeked round the corner, then jerked back again.

Anaïs sighed. "Geoff, why are you so upset? It isn't as—"

"Yes. It is." He was almost snarling now. "Now was that, or was it not, our bargain? Because the time for negotiation was then, not now."

"Oh, as if you would have entertained any thought of negotiation!" Somehow, she managed to lift her skirts and brush past him to the steps.

"Anaïs," he snapped. "*Get. Back. Down. Here.*"

His voice had grown not louder, but instead deathly quiet. She cut a glance over her shoulder to see that Geoff's eyes had a strange, unholy look about them; both distant and yet all too seeing. Something apprehensive ran down her spine.

"*Now,*" he rasped.

Anaïs shook off the sudden frisson, then turned on the steps, still holding her hems aloft. "No," she said. "If you wish to berate me, Geoff, then come upstairs and do so in my bedchamber. Not here in the front hall as if we're a pair of common fishwives."

His face going faintly pale, he strode across the hall.

"And the gauntlet is taken up," she murmured, turning and starting up the rest of the stairs.

"I only wonder it took you this long to fling it down," he retorted.

Once inside, Anaïs held on to the door and let him stride past, then closed it herself so as to keep him from slamming it. "Now, Geoff," she began, "be reasonable."

His eyes glittered, cold and blue, like a shaft of ice in sunlight. "I do not have to be reasonable," he rasped, backing her up against the wall. "*You* do."

"But why—"

"Because I say so!" Geoff gritted. "Because Lezennes is a dangerous man."

"And he was nowhere in sight!" said Anaïs, throwing up her hands.

"You don't know that." His perfect jaw twitched. "What if he was?"

Anaïs tried to rein in her temper, but it was a struggle. "For God's sake, Geoff, I'm not blind," she managed, "or witless."

"And what if he was having her followed?" Geoff leaned in, planting a hand against the wall by her shoulder. "Good God, Anaïs, what if DuPont is wrong, and she's as wicked as he is?"

"But she is not," said Anaïs hotly. "That much I do know."

"But you *don't* know," he bellowed. "You simply don't. You met her—what? Less than an hour ago? Damn it, woman, just do as I say!"

It was madness, she knew, to provoke him, but Anaïs was angry. Something worse than angry, perhaps. She could literally feel the blood thrumming through her veins as it had not in years. She came away from the wall and looked up at him, hardening her gaze.

"So I'm to just do as you say," she retorted, "blindly, without question—*or what*?"

In a flash his hand caught her, his fingers digging deep into the hair at her nape, turning her face to his. "Or so help me God, Anaïs," he rasped, "I'll turn you over my knee and wear out your backside."

Anaïs let her gaze flick hotly down him. "Oh, do you think so?" she whispered. "Why don't you just give that a try, Geoff? Yes, you're oh-so-rigid and perfectly controlled, aren't you, until someone challenges—"

His mouth was on hers before she could draw breath.

This time there was no gentleness in his kiss. His mouth opened over hers, urgent and demanding. One arm lashing round her waist, he drove her head back against the wall as his fingers tightened in her hair, stilling her to the determined thrust of his tongue.

For long moments he kissed her, pillaging her mouth and giving her no chance to respond in turn but instead forcing her against the wall with his weight. Hungrily his hand cupped over her breast, his thumb circling her nipple till it hardened. One of his thighs thrust between hers, then the lust swamped her again, leaving her sagging against the wall, yearning for more, yet still outraged.

She wanted to smack him a cracking good blow across the cheek.

She wanted to drag him to her bed, and slide her hands beneath that well-tailored façade of civility he wore. Wanted to stroke and tempt and touch until his bare skin shivered beneath her fingers.

She was strongly favoring the latter. But before she could settle the matter in her mind, he turned his face from hers and uttered a quiet oath.

Anaïs went with option one, the back of her hand.

The resulting *crack!* was not entirely satisfying for they stood too close, but it achieved her purpose.

"Bloody hell!" Eyes wide, Geoff stepped away, touching at the corner of his mouth with the back of his hand.

"Next time *ask*," Anaïs snapped.

He simply stared at her.

Deliberately, she cocked one eyebrow. "You can even ask now," she added, "so long as it's politely done."

"I . . . beg your pardon?"

"Yet another good idea," she answered. "You certainly ought to be begging my pardon. Now, are you inviting me to your bed or not? Just so I know where I stand."

"Good God, Anaïs," he whispered. "Have we both run mad?"

He turned and strode to her window, one hand set at the back of his neck, the other at his hip, pushing back his coat in that pensive posture that had already become almost achingly familiar to her. But there was still a strange, uneasy feeling in the air.

Anaïs followed, and watched him stare blindly out the glass, the muscles of his throat working up and down.

He spoke again, without looking at her, his voice mystified. "I really *don't* know whether to bed you, or turn you over my knee."

"You're far more apt to survive the first," she advised.

"Anaïs, we can't go on like this."

"I am not a child to be spanked, Geoff." She stood beside him, resisting the urge to set a hand on his arm. "If you want an invitation to my bed, ask. If you wish to send me away, try. But if you are simply angry because you desire me—and if you're going to coddle me at every turn because of it—then you're the one who risks compromising this mission, not me."

"Aye." His voice was surprisingly soft, but his eyes had taken on that haunted, otherworldly look again. "Aye, perhaps you're right. But for God's sake, Anaïs, just don't . . ."

Don't what?

She looked at the beautifully sculpted turn of his face caught in a golden shaft of sunlight, and wanted to beg him for the answer.

Oh, she wanted to beg him for more than that. But despite her anger, her swollen lips, and the hair now tumbling so wantonly down her shoulder, Anaïs still had a little pride left to her.

"What do you want, Geoff?" she asked softly. "What do you want of me? Just say it."

He exhaled suddenly and roughly, then shocked her by reaching out. He pulled her into his arms, and inexplicably, she went.

Geoff set his forehead to hers, his eyes closed. "Don't refuse to do as I say, Anaïs," he whispered. "Don't make me send you packing, do you hear? For I'll do it. I swear to God. I will."

And he could, she realized. He had warned her, in fact, that that was precisely what he would do—and long before they'd ever left London.

She was still angry, yes. But perhaps—just *perhaps*—she had not handled this well. As her mother was ever fond of pointing out, Anaïs was like her father, often well-intentioned but emotionally ham-fisted.

In a pinch, she could handle Lezennes, she felt confident. But Geoff didn't know that, and his protective instincts would likely have overridden that knowledge anyway. And he wasn't just driven by lust. He was a gentleman to his very marrow. But she was not quite ready to admit any of this nascent insight to him. No, not yet.

Geoff, however, had suddenly loosened his embrace. Anaïs looked up to see him staring out the window again, more intently this time. She let one arm fall, turning to look.

In the street below, Charlotte Moreau was hastening along

the pavement looking anxious to get home. At Lezennes' door, she set down her basket, opened her reticule, and began to paw through it as if searching for a key.

That very instant, however, the door burst open and a little girl dashed out on a cry of delight, a gray-garbed servant on her heels.

Madame Moreau dropped the reticule and swept the child up in her embrace.

Beside Anaïs, Geoff stiffened. The air in the room seemed to still, then go utterly cold.

Again, Anaïs felt that odd frisson down her spine, and this time it felt like fear. "Geoff?"

As if he hadn't heard her, he stepped nearer the glass, lifting one hand to touch it as he stared down into the street. Madame Moreau was still kneeling on the pavement, holding the little girl close. Geoff's every muscle appeared to have gone rigid, and his eyes had taken on that strange, distant look once more.

He swallowed again. "She is frightened," he said, the words deep and hollow. "Terrified. She . . . sees the blackness."

Anaïs set a hand to his shoulder blade. "Who?" she murmured. "Charlotte?"

But his eyes were not precisely focused on Charlotte. "Yes. Madame Moreau. Her darkness is—" He stopped, and exhaled slowly and deeply.

Something was wrong.

Anaïs had sensed it, almost from the moment they had stepped inside the house. No, from the moment he'd touched her hand in the market square. It was as if his emotions were so tightly tethered the rope might snap. As if he were clinging to . . . *something* for all he was worth. Or shutting something out.

And just now—that explosive temper, that raw, utterly

sensual kiss—all of it had been driven by passion and fury, yes, but something unbridled had run beneath it, like an underground stream wearing away at Geoff's emotional bedrock.

He was a man who kept his emotions shut tightly away, but today it was as if he'd edged too near a precipice.

The slamming of a door recalled Anaïs to the present. She looked up to see that Charlotte and the little girl had vanished, and Lezennes' door had shut.

Anaïs urged Geoff from the window, the better to see him.

He came, but his motions were those of an automaton. His face was rigid, all color drained away, and his eyes had taken on that eerie, icy look, like a wild creature—like a *wolf*—as if he looked through her, or far beyond her. As if he saw not this room, but another time or another place entirely.

In Tuscany, Vittorio had introduced her to such a man; a boy, really, who had been brought by his family from Malta. They had come in desperate search of answers, for the young man had lived with a mind half in the present and half in the future, and seemingly no boundary between. Dreams and visions had constantly possessed him, and upon meeting him, it was as if Anaïs could see the very portal to hell in his eyes.

But there had been little Vittorio could do, save confirm what they already knew. That the boy was not mad. He had been cursed—cursed with the Gift—an inapt name if ever Anaïs had heard one.

On the way home, the boy had taken matters into his own hands. He had tied an anchor round his ankle and leapt into Valetta's harbor, never to be seen again.

Anaïs set a hand to the soft wool of his morning coat. "Geoff?" she said softly. "How long have you been fighting this?"

His hand came up suddenly, causing Anaïs to flinch. But he merely set it to his temple, two fingers positioned just above his eyebrow. "I cannot recall," he admitted, obviously trying to focus. "Since . . . sometime late last night? I tried to see—to open to the void—and could not. But later, in the early hours, I couldn't sleep. I could feel it—the blackness—creeping in round the edges. And still, nothing came. Then . . . then I met her."

"Madame Moreau, you mean?"

"Yes," he whispered. "I met her. Touched her hand."

And now the portal to hell had cracked open.

It worked that way sometimes, Anaïs knew. She took his arm. "Come, sit by the hearth."

But Geoff didn't move. His opposite hand had gone rigid at his side, his fist so hard his knuckles had turned bloodless.

"Geoff," she said uncertainly, "come sit down. Tell me what you're sensing."

"No—just—*don't*—"

His eyes squeezed shut, and his nostrils flared wide. He still held his hand to his temple, and she could feel his entire body beginning to shudder. The sun passed behind a cloud, dimming the room, and it was as if a maelstrom of evil blew through, though the window was barely cracked.

Anaïs felt the temperature literally drop again, sending that horrid, icy shiver down her spine again, and with it a hint of nausea. The underdrapes lifted eerily on the breeze, floating around them as if borne upon an invisible cloud. Geoff's eyes flew wide, yet his gaze was eerily distant. He grabbed her by both wrists, and dragged her nearer. She began to shake so hard she feared her teeth might chatter.

"Anaïs," he rasped, "you have to stay away from her. The child. There is evil—I can feel it—all around her. *Around you.*"

Suddenly, Anaïs understood. "Who?" she whispered.

"Can you see the source? Is it Lezennes? Good God, it cannot be Madame Moreau?"

He shook his head. "I . . . I *don't know*," he said, his fingers digging into her flesh. "I cannot see. There is something— something black and potent. Like a shadow over us all. I feel it. I know it—and it knows me. That I am here."

She resisted the urge to fling herself into his arms. "G-Geoff," she whispered, "what is going on?"

And then the wind vanished, and the room fell quiet again. The surreal cold receded, and with it her strange, sudden anxiety. It was as if her blood resumed its pulse and flow, and her senses became one with the real world again. The heavy footsteps of a servant passing by her door, the smell of something baking inside the house, the coo of a pigeon upon her windowsill; all these things came back to her, the world as it should be.

With Geoff still holding her wrists, she leaned into him and set her cheek to his lapel. "It is all right," she soothed. "Let it go. Let it go for now. It will come back when it is clearer."

"God, I hope not."

He exhaled hard, almost a sigh of exhaustion—and yet it was not that at all. Anaïs could feel the last vestiges of trembling inside him settle, and the rigidity of his arms and shoulders ease as calm settled slowly around them. And when at last she felt his grip on her wrists relax, Anaïs lifted her cheek from the warm wool, and looked up at him.

"Come, sit down," she said. "I'm going to pour us both a strong sherry."

She led him to the dainty sofa before the hearth, then went to the side table where a silver tray with two glasses awaited. Pulling the stopper from the decanter, she filled both and went to join him.

"Here," she said, setting down the tray.

Geoff looked up and took one of the glasses, his face still stark and bloodless. "Anaïs," he said quietly, "I'm sorry."

She did not ask him what he meant, but instead toed off her shoes and sat down beside him, tucking one leg beneath her as she did so. "Is it always like this for you?" she asked, turning to face him. "Must you . . . invite the vision? Or does it just come to you?"

He set his wine down on the tea table, and dragged both hands through the shimmering curtain of his bronze hair. "I . . . open myself," he finally whispered. "I let what is already there come out of the . . . the amorphousness. Don't ask me what I mean, for I can't explain."

"It's as though it's behind a diaphanous veil, isn't it?" she said. "A sort of curtain in one's mind."

He looked at her for a long time with his ageless, weary gaze. "It is rather like that," he finally said. "Why? Have you—"

"No, but I met a young man once," she interjected. "His family brought him to Tuscany—and Vittorio tried to teach him how to do it. How to draw the curtain closed, I daresay, is the best way to explain it."

"It's as good an analogy as any," said Geoff. "And the young man—did he find it? Was he able to draw it shut?"

"No, I—I don't think so," she said, her voice hitching a little. "I never saw him again."

Geoff looked at her with a deep and immutable grief in his eyes, doubtless sensing her prevarication. "Ruthveyn is much the same," he murmured, "though he has learnt a few tricks over the years—not to touch people, not to look directly into their eyes, to keep an emotional distance from most everyone—and he's tried like the devil to subdue the demon with drink and opiates and worse."

"Does that work?"

Slowly, he nodded. "Oh, aye, it works," he said. "If you can stand the sort of man it makes you."

Anaïs flicked an uneasy glance up at him. "Did you try it?"

"For a while," he admitted. "Particularly when I was in North Africa. But by then I'd . . . I'd found my curtain. I'd learned how to keep up my wall for the most part. To keep my mind shut to the—the *other*—unless I wished otherwise. My mentor in Scotland taught me. All the intoxicants did for me was to—oh, I don't know—give me a few hours' respite, I suppose."

"It does sound wearying," Anaïs admitted. "As if you must ever be on guard against the . . . the strength of it, I suppose?"

"The *will* of it,' he said, frowning. "Sometimes, Anaïs, it's as if the thing wants to possess you. I don't know why they call it a gift from God when it feels more like you're wrestling with the devil."

Anaïs made a sympathetic sound in the back of her throat. "No wonder Ruthveyn turned to opium."

"Aye, speaking of which—" Geoff flashed a twisted smile, picked up the sherry, and downed it in one long swallow. "I'd take another of those if you're so inclined."

Anaïs nodded, and tipped the decanter over his glass.

They drank in silence for a time, Anaïs's leg curled up, her knee brushing Geoff's thigh ever so slightly through her skirts. There was still a sense of uncertainty hanging over the room, and the awkward weight of words unspoken. Her lips felt bruised, and her pride a little bruised, too. She was certain Geoff had not meant to kiss her. Not at first.

When her glass was half empty, Anaïs set it away and began to fumble nervously with a corded frog on her dress. She was about to do something inordinately stupid. Something she'd sworn to herself she would not do.

"Geoffrey," she said quietly, "about that kiss."

"Anaïs, I . . ." He hesitated, his gaze fixed upon the stem of his wineglass. "I meant what I said about doing what we agree to do," he went on, "or what I order you to do, if you prefer to take the harder view. But worry and a sleepless night frayed my temper. And I'm sorry. I did not have the right to . . . to behave as I did."

"Very well, next time you're wrong, I'll be sure to point it out straightaway," said Anaïs, "rather than just ignore your orders."

He cast her a sardonic glance. "Vittorio didn't teach you much in the way of diplomacy, did he?"

"Vittorio thought you could beat conflict to death with the flat of your sword," she said evenly. "But let's get back to that kiss."

He returned his gaze to the glass, the rich amber color catching the sun as he turned it round and round in his broad palms. "Anaïs, I'm no one's Mr. Right," he finally said. "I'm . . . not for you. You still understand that, don't you?"

"Oh, Geoff, I know that." Anaïs rose, and began to roam about the room, absently picking up books and trinkets. "No, you and I wouldn't suit in a million years. Not in *that* way, at least."

"No?" He pinned her with his ice-blue gaze. "So in what way were you thinking?"

Anaïs picked up a porcelain figurine of a little shepherdess. She had the oddest sense that something important—more important, perhaps, than she understood—hung in the balance now.

"Well, it's like this," she finally said, putting the shepherdess down with an awkward *thunk*. "When you kiss me, my toes curl, and something in the pit of my belly just sort of—oh, I don't know. It's your eyes, I daresay—blue as the Adriatic—and that voice, so low and so smooth, as if you could make a woman—ah, but that's not the point."

"What is the point?" His voice had gone a little husky.

"Well, all of it . . . it just makes me begin to wonder if you mightn't be . . ."

"Be what?"

"Well, not Mr. *Right*," she answered, casting a glance over her shoulder. "But perhaps Mr. *Right-for-Now*, if you catch my meaning?"

He jerked his head back almost as if she'd struck him again. "Catch it? I feel rather as if I've been bludgeoned with it." He flashed one of his odd, sideways smiles. "Once again, my dear, you put a fellow rather neatly in his place."

"Heavens, never say your feelings are hurt." She returned to the table for her glass. "Geoff, I cannot possibly be your type, either."

"Down to a type now, are we?" He let his gaze run over her, and she wondered if it warmed just a degree. "What might your type be, then?"

Anaïs drifted to the window, and wondered how much to say. "Well, he's Tuscan," she finally answered after sipping at her sherry. "And . . . regal. He has dark hair—not as dark as mine—and his eyes are kind. His nose is strong, like his personality, but his nature is calm and peaceful."

Geoff paused for a moment. "I see," he finally murmured. "Already met him, have you?"

She did not turn around. "I thought I had," she said after a time. "Once, long ago."

"And was he handsome?" Geoff's words seemed to float on the air, lightly teasing. "Were you madly in love with him?"

Anaïs stared blindly down into the street. "Yes, and yes, desperately so," she said. "But it did not work out."

"So you left him behind in Tuscany long, long ago," Geoff murmured, "and you've not seen him since?"

She wished to God she had not.

Her nails dug into the wood of the windowsill as she gripped it, the memory of her last conversation with Raphaele running through her mind. Raphaele whose life had changed so drastically and so unexpectedly, while hers had not changed at all. Certainly her mind had not. No, by God, not one iota.

"Actually, I saw him a few weeks ago." Her voice had gone cold. "In San Gimignano. He came for Vittorio's funeral Mass."

He must have caught the warning in her tone. "Ah," was all he said on that point. "Very well then, what's my type?"

At last she cut a glance in his direction and gave an undignified snort. "Beautiful," she said. "Your type is *beautiful*. Like you."

His mouth twisted wryly, and without invitation, Geoff filled his glass again. "And you are not . . . beautiful?"

She shook her head. "You know that I am not," she replied, pacing along the brass fender that guarded the hearth. "I am . . . not ugly. I realize that. But my nose is too strong, my eyes are too large, and my hair is a pitch-black, tumbling-down tangle most of the time."

He laughed. "That last one I'll give you," he said. "And are those all your faults?"

She lifted one shoulder nonchalantly. "More candor?" she murmured. "Very well. I know I'm too olive-skinned to be English, and too tall to be thought delicate. But I have grace, and a certain Continental elegance. I am at peace with that. I do not feel sorry for myself."

"No, you don't strike me as the type given to self-pity," he agreed.

She turned to fully face him. "And so we have agreed I am not your type, and you are not Mr. Right, have we?"

His expression shifted, became unreadable. "And if I concede that much—?"

She set both hands on the rolled arm of the sofa, and leaned almost over him. "Then are you Mr. Right-for-Now?"

He looked up at her over the top of his wineglass. "Well played, my dear," he murmured. "But no, I think that is not the role for me."

"Suit yourself, then," she replied.

His smile twisted. "Oh, I am not suiting myself, Anaïs." His voice was low and quiet now. "I am suiting your family. Your future. Your father. I needed you for this assignment, yes, and I pray that in the end it doesn't ruin you. But I won't ruin you on a whim, or out of petty lust."

"Is lust petty?"

"Most of the time, I think." He leaned forward, and set his glass down hard. "And for men, lust is just lust. There isn't anything romantic about it, if that's what you're thinking."

"Have you never been in love, then?" Even to Anaïs, her voice sounded wistful.

He gave a harsh laugh. "Not even close, thank God."

"You have an aversion to marriage?"

He shrugged. "I haven't an heir," he said. "Not even a distant cousin. So yes, I mean to do my duty to the title. But there aren't too many women who would care to live with a sword hanging over their heads. A man who senses things unnatural. You just saw how it can be—and trust me, that little hint of darkling was nothing."

"Heavens, Geoff, you must think all women cowards," she murmured. Then she sat back down and leaned near. "I haven't a vast deal of experience, perhaps, like some of the women you are used to. But I am no inexperienced virgin."

For an instant, naked curiosity sketched across his face. "Are you . . . some other sort of virgin?"

"Not any sort at all," she said, smiling sweetly.

"I see." He swallowed hard, the sinuous muscles of his throat working up and down. "And what about Mr. Right?"

"When I find Mr. Right," said Anaïs, leaning nearer still, "he won't give a ha'penny whether I'm a virgin or not."

Geoff cleared his throat awkwardly. "And you know that how?"

"Otherwise, he would not be Mr. Right," she replied. "Because Mr. Right is perfect for me. Destined for me. And that's the end of it."

"I think it had better be the end of this conversation," said Geoff, bracing one hand along the back of the sofa to rise. "I think I know when I have pressed my luck a little too far."

Anaïs straightened on the sofa. "What do you mean?"

"Never mind," he said. "I believe I shall go out for a walk. A very long walk. Shall I see you at dinner?"

"Oh, very well," said Anaïs. "But that won't do much to alleviate my boredom."

"Then suggest something," said Geoff, his hand already on the doorknob. "Something that does not include you and me naked on a bed."

"I love how that just rolls off your tongue," said Anaïs, turning to look at him over the back of the sofa. "And to be perfectly honest, I would love to see you naked."

"Anaïs," he said warningly. "Suggest something."

"Very well." She smiled brightly. "I think I shall go across the street and drop our cards on the Vicomte de Lezennes."

"You cannot be serious."

"Why not?" said Anaïs. "I mean to ask them to dinner. Tomorrow evening, as a matter of fact. If you cannot be persuaded, I shall hone my feminine wiles on Lezennes."

CHAPTER 10

He who is prudent and lies in wait
for an enemy who is not, will be victorious.
Sun Tzu, *The Art of War*

In the end, Anaïs did not go across the street. Over
dinner, and with very little difficulty, Geoff found
himself able to persuade her that it would look unwise to
appear overly forward; that it was better to cast one's line,
then reel the bait slowly past Lezennes, rather than simply
whack him over the head with the pole.

Anaïs sulked for a moment over her dessert—or pretended
to sulk, Geoff thought, for she came around quickly enough,
then suggested a hand of piquet afterward.

Geoff, however, was almost afraid to be alone with the
woman. Oh, he was a gentleman, he supposed—for what
little that was worth—but no one had ever accused him of
being a saint. And if Anaïs kept pressing the issue—kept
pressing her body so hungrily to his and looking up at him
with those eyes like dark pools of desire—he was apt to give
her precisely what she was asking for.

Most unwise, when she was waiting for Mr. Right. And
that, apparently, was not Geoff.

So he had excused himself and gone for another walk.

Before this godforsaken mission was over, he sourly considered, he was apt to know Brussels right down to the very gutters that carried the sewage into the Senne.

But what alternative was left to him? Getting roaring drunk was not an option; he was on a mission, and even his growing desire for Anaïs had not blinded him to that fact. Besides, intoxication was probably the surest way to find himself standing at her bedroom door in the middle of the night with one hand on the knob.

Worse still, she would likely know it.

Already he had noticed that about Anaïs. Even before they had left England, he'd got the oddest notion she had eyes in the back of her head. She might protest that she had no Gift, that she had learned nothing from Giovanni Vittorio. But she had an unerring sense about his presence in a room.

Already he had seen her address the servants to give one odd order or another without so much as lifting her head from her desk—address them by name, before he was even aware of their presence. And then there was that night— that night which seemed so long ago, when he'd walked with DuPont up to St. Catherine's.

There had been a woman in a pitch-black alley—a lady, by the sound of her voice—with a knife set to the throat of some hapless degenerate who'd snatched a strand of pearls. Cool as spring water she'd been, kicking him in the knackers, then tucking her knife away as casually as another female might straighten the lace of her cuff. Yes, he thought about it now, and he wondered.

Over the next several days, as they observed the rhythms of the house across the street, Geoff watched her more carefully—watched, that was to say, something besides the intriguing sway of her hips, or the way her eyes brightened when he came into a room.

At breakfast one morning, she asked Petit about a strange

taste in the omelet that had been sent up. The footman had hastened away, and returned faintly red-faced to admit the cook had inadvertently added sage when she'd meant to add pepper. Those eggs had been served instead at the servants' table. But the bowl had not been washed.

Some days later, they were sequestered in the attic room, taking turns at the telescopes. Occupied in thumbing through DuPont's last pile of papers, Anaïs apparently heard the latch on Lezennes' front door click open. Geoff, who had been watching a housemaid dusting the windowsills in Giselle's room, had known nothing of it until Anaïs appeared at his elbow.

"I wonder where she is going," Anaïs had mused, watching as the governess came out. "She left at four the last several days."

"It's Thursday," Geoff murmured, leaning forward to make a notation in the log. "A short day, perhaps?"

"Perhaps," Anaïs murmured, watching the tidy gray figure vanish down the street.

"You have keen hearing," he remarked, glancing up from his paper.

"Do I?" Anaïs smiled, and drifted away from the window. "Mamma always complained I had selective hearing. That I could hear a pin drop when I wished, and ignore her calls to supper when I was playing in the garden."

Geoff closed the ledger, and tried to stretch the stiffness from his limbs. "I think we've learned about as much as we are going to," he said, rising. "I believe it's time we made it a little harder for our reticent neighbors to ignore us."

"Well, finally," said Anaïs. "*Now* may we call upon Lezennes?"

"No, I think not," said Geoff. "That would be too obvious. Recall that Madame Moreau already sent her regrets for your little tea—Lezennes' doing, I'd wager."

Anaïs had drifted around the room, and back to the window. "He does not wish either of them to have contact with the outside world, I suspect," she said, arms stubbornly crossed as she stared across the street.

"And she is afraid of him," Geoff mused. "I feel it."

"It is not your imagination," said Anaïs. "That place fairly radiates evil. I am sure that is the source of what you were seeing the other day. Lezennes wants to keep them isolated."

"Aye, because if she knows no one, then she has no one to whom she can turn for help," Geoff added. "So we must manage to look as useless and benign as possible."

"Perhaps we should be poor?" Anaïs remarked.

"Aye, let's suggest to Madame Moreau that we live on a strict allowance from my father," he proposed. "That he pays all our bills, and watches our every sou."

Anaïs snorted. "Suggest it when?" she muttered. "She isn't even permitted to come across the street for tea."

"No, but she goes to the park every day at one." Geoff snatched his coat from the back of the chair, and threw it on. "And there she meets with Lezennes."

"And so?"

"So get your cloak," he ordered. "I'll fetch my easel. Perhaps it's time we met Lezennes, and showed him what harmless flibbertigibbets we are."

Located in the London heart of Her Majesty's Government, Four Whitehall Place was an unassuming house that backed onto a far more infamous courtyard, a yard that legend held had once belonged to the ancient Kings of Scotland. And while a lady might—on very rare occasions— venture through the portals of Number Four, she would on no account be seen round back, for Scotland Yard had fast become the most notorious of London's police stations, and a common point of ingress and egress for much of what constituted Westminster's relentlessly revolving rabble.

And so it was that on a lovely spring afternoon, the Earl of Lazonby escorted Lady Anisha Stafford up the steps to the slightly more proper administrative entrance, held open the door, and bowed.

Lady Anisha swept past him, nose held faintly in the air, still not entirely pleased with the bargain she'd struck. Just inside the door, there was a sort of porter's post, but it was vacant. She looked about, uncertain what to do.

"Come on," said Lazonby a little gruffly. "We'll just go up."

Lady Anisha set a hand to her chest. "What, unannounced?"

"It's Number Four, not Buckingham Palace," he grumbled, steering her toward the stairs. "Besides, you promised."

"And you promised to go with me to the theatre," she countered.

"Which I—"

"—did, yes," she interjected, "only to snore your way through Donizetti's last aria."

"That song dragged, Nish, like a crooked plow behind a lame horse," he said. "You're lucky it ended before I expired of boredom and rigor mortis set in. How would you have got my stiffened corpse back down those narrow stairs?"

"It was '*Una Furtiva Lagrima*'!" she cried. "It was heart-wrenching! And quite possibly the world's greatest tenor aria."

"I confess, I'm a Philistine," Lazonby grumbled. "Sorry if I spoiled your evening with your future in-laws. But it was your choice, Nish, to take me. You know what I am."

Lady Anisha continue to sputter and complain as Lazonby hauled her up the steps, but in a low undertone, informing him in no uncertain language that the place was a little dingy, and smelled of boiled vegetables and stale sweat. Lazonby responded by explaining—in his usual blunt fashion—that the sort of people who came to Number Four generally had good cause to sweat.

At the top of the second flight of stairs, they turned into a long, narrow chamber divided by a low, gated bar such as one might see in a magistrate's court—not that Lady Anisha had ever laid eyes on one of those, either, but she had seen Mr. Cruickshank's courtroom caricatures in the print shops round town, which was almost the same thing.

Behind the little wall sat a pair of matched clerks—or at least she supposed that they were matched, for much like a brace of footmen, the black-coated fellows were of similar height and weight—which was to say very long and thin—and perched upon stools at either side of a tall desk, which made them look rather like a set of black andirons, forever welded as one.

On Lady Anisha's side of the wall, there were a few chairs—very straight-backed chairs, with no upholstery, not even so much as a pillow.

"They don't want you to get comfortable here, Nish," said Lord Lazonby when she remarked upon the discomfort. "This is a place of suffering and inconvenience."

"Well, I seem to be suffering a vast deal of inconvenience on your behalf." Lady Anisha waved an elegant hand to forestall the frightful mélange of ink, coal smoke, and cooked turnips wafting up from the bowels of somewhere. "How long must we sit here?"

Lazonby gestured at a rather grand slab of a door at the far end of the room. "Until that door opens, and I manage to wedge my foot in it."

Being far more obliging than Lord Lazonby, the door chose that moment to swing wide. Two men came out, one portly and pretentious-looking, with a thick gold watch chain stretched taut across his belly, and a score of long black hairs wrapped resolutely round his bald head, then pomaded into a sort of greasy tonsure.

Towering over him, the second man was far more interesting. The assistant commissioner of the Metropolitan Police was a svelte, broad-shouldered fellow with a nose that resembled a meat cleaver and a thick head of dark hair trimmed to precision. His cheeks were lean and scraped unfashionably clean of whiskers, and with his hard, dark eyes, he put Lady Anisha very much in mind of a bird of prey.

She recognized him at once and came to her feet, sweeping past Lazonby. "Assistant Commissioner Napier," she said brightly, offering a bejeweled hand. "How lovely to see you again. Might we have a moment?"

The portly man having vanished, Royden Napier's gaze was now shifting suspiciously back and forth between his new callers. "Lady Anisha, a pleasure," he said stiffly. "And by *we*, you would mean . . . ?"

"Lord Lazonby and me," she said, smiling.

Napier wanted to refuse; that could not have been more apparent.

But much to his discomfort, Napier was now indebted to Lady Anisha's brother, if only a little. And he was curious—very curious—about her.

Despite her protestations to Lord Lazonby, Lady Anisha had not failed to notice Napier at her brother's wedding. Both before and after their fleeting introduction, the assistant commissioner had watched her almost incessantly from one corner of his eye. And when at last he'd approached her, he had been stiffly formal. But those eyes! Oh, they had never let up.

Perhaps she reminded him of someone from the criminal underworld. Or perhaps, like much of society, he was merely suspicious of her honey-colored skin and dark hair.

Whatever it was—as Lazonby had predicted—it was

enough to preclude him from telling them both to go to hell. Instead, he invited them into his office—which, to those unlucky few forced to come here, might have been the very same as hell for all Lady Anisha knew.

Certainly Royden Napier looked like the sort of man who might have been on speaking terms with the devil.

"Well," he said tightly when they were seated before his massive oak desk. "To what do I owe the pleasure?"

"We want you to reopen a case," said Lord Lazonby, forgoing any niceties. "The murder of Lord Percy Peveril."

"But we have already had a conviction in that case," said Napier, looking pointedly at Lazonby. "*You.*"

Lazonby jerked to his feet. "And it was *overturned*," he said, planting a hand in the middle of the assistant commissioner's desk. "But I shall never be free of it, Napier, until Peveril's real killer is found and convicted. You know that."

"I trust you'll pardon me, my lord, when I say that I find deathbed recantations a trifle suspect," said Napier coldly. "Especially when the grieving widow seems to come into a rather vast sum of money afterward."

"I was *in jail* when that happened, you fool," Lazonby growled into his face.

"Indeed, you were," said Napier, "though it took me many long years to get you out of North Africa and back behind bars. But your father, the previous earl, was not in jail. He was free to—"

"Do not you dare drag my father's good name into this, Napier." Lazonby's face had gone dangerously colorless, his hands fisted around the chair arms. "He did nothing to deserve having this vile business brought down upon his head."

"Nothing save having a hot-tempered, cardsharping wastrel for a son," Napier countered. "Lie down with dogs, Lazonby, get up with fleas."

"You damned fool," said Lazonby hotly. "I was set up to take the blame for someone else. Am I the only one who wants to know why? Does the Crown not care that a killer walks free?"

"As I recall, your case was pretty cut and dried."

"Yes, and your late father was the very chap who cut it and dried it, Napier, and he did it with about as much forethought as another man might mow down a hayfield—with no regard for what might have been concealed within the grass. Instead, he just hacked it all to bits."

"Your point, my lord?" asked Napier. Both men were standing now, Lady Anisha observed—and leaning over the desk, almost nose to nose.

"Have you even had a look in those files of his?" Lazonby demanded. "*Have* you? Or did you just take his word as gospel when you inherited this desk?"

It was at this point that Lady Anisha rose, too, clearing her throat sharply. "Gentlemen, there is a lady present," she said quietly.

Both men drew back a few inches, and Napier's face, at least, colored with embarrassment. "I beg your pardon," he said.

Lady Anisha turned a sweet gaze on Lazonby. "Rance?"

"My apologies," he said tightly, "but you knew what this was apt to come to."

"What, fisticuffs?" she asked sarcastically. "Rance, kindly leave us."

He turned on her, eyes wide. "Do what?"

"Get out," she said. "Go back downstairs. You are over-wrought. I wish to speak to Mr. Napier alone. You may come back up when I am done if it pleases you."

Lazonby half turned, then cut her a nasty glance.

Lady Anisha drew herself up to her full height—which was all of about five feet. "*Go*," she said sharply. "I mean it. You have pushed your luck with me, Rance, for the last time."

Surprisingly, he went, slamming the door behind.

Napier had paced across the room, his back now half turned to her, one hand set at the nape of his neck as he stared blindly out the window at Whitehall Place below. She waited for him to speak. She could feel the strong emotion surging through the room. She only wished she knew what it was.

"Well, is this how it begins, Lady Anisha?" Napier finally asked, his voice pitched low, and obviously angry.

"I beg your pardon?" She crossed the room toward him. "Is this how what begins?"

He turned from the window, his expression one of disgust. "Do you now threaten me with your brother's wrath?" he asked. "Or drop Her Majesty's name by way of warning?"

"Oh, my," said Lady Anisha softly. "Lofty circles indeed."

His lip curled like a snarling dog's. "Oh, I know all about Ruthveyn's 'special relationship' with the Queen," he said. "I know a good deal more than that, actually, about Lazonby and Bessett and their little coven in St. James—though I cannot quite prove all of it yet."

"I really have no idea what you are talking about," she said. "I hardly need my brother to do my dirty work, if that's what you think. I'm perfectly capable of it. As to Ruthveyn's relationship with the Queen, any loyalty he earned there, he earned the hard way—with his toil and his sweat and yes, even his blood, all given because he loves his country. And if our sainted Queen is grateful for that, then I say she bloody well ought to be."

If her unladylike curse shocked him, Napier gave no sign of it. Instead, he stood for a time by the window, backlit by the midday sun like one of Michelangelo's more wrathful angels descending from heaven. One hand was set stubbornly at his narrow waist, pushing back the front of his dark coat. Beneath, his waistcoat had shifted to reveal what looked like the butt end of a knife cleverly tucked inside the waist of his trousers.

An avenging angel, perhaps.

"Well, what *do* you want, then, Lady Anisha?" he asked coldly.

She lifted one shoulder with studied casualness. "I want to know," she said quietly, "why it is that you never stop looking at me when we're in the same room together."

CHAPTER 11

Pretend inferiority and encourage his arrogance.
Sun Tzu, *The Art of War*

By half-past noon, Anaïs was propped against a tree in the Parc de Brussels with Mr. Reynolds's latest penny dreadful open on her lap. Perched upon a folding stool, Geoff sat at his sketch pad a few feet away, his broad back half turned to her, his bronze hair shifting lightly in the breeze.

Already a fine drawing of the Royal Palace was appearing beneath his hand, the strokes bold and black and unerring. It was a view of the structure as glimpsed through the massive park gates, and Anaïs found herself fascinated by the swiftness of his movements. To look at the sketch, one might imagine he'd been at work for hours rather than a mere fifteen minutes.

"You really do have a knack for that," she murmured.

He turned and smiled—truly smiled—and Anaïs felt her breath catch dangerously.

"Thank you," he said. "I've always had a passion for beautiful buildings. It was, so far as I could see, the only saving grace of a childhood spent abroad."

"Can you draw people?"

His smile fading, Geoff turned back and removed his sketchbook from the easel. After flipping the page, he laid it across his lap, his long hair falling forward to shadow his face as he bent over it.

Dashing his hand back and forth across the paper for a few minutes, he flicked the occasional sidelong glance in her direction. Eventually, he straightened and held it a little away as if to study it.

Apparently satisfied, he ripped the paper free and handed it to her.

Anaïs took the sketch, and almost gasped.

It was the simplest of drawings, really. Just a few swift lines and a dash or two of shadow, but he had drawn her with incredible realism.

Anaïs let her gaze take in every detail. She still possessed her father's strong nose, but on the drawing it looked somehow right, and perfectly proportioned to her face. And although he had sketched her seated against a tree, one knee drawn up—just as she was—in the drawing Anaïs's hair was shown spilling round her shoulders, nearly to her waist.

But it was her eyes that were most arresting. They were large, but not overly so, and it felt as if they stared squarely, almost boldly, at the viewer. And yet they gave up nothing, appearing instead as almost enigmatic pools of ebony.

It was, on the whole, perfectly breathtaking.

"Geoff, it's lovely," she managed, still holding it. "But I fear you overly flatter me."

"Oh?" She could feel his curiosity burning into her. "In what way?"

She lifted her gaze to his, but saw no hint of equivocation there. "I'm not sure that's quite how I look."

He tilted his head and studied her. "That's how you look to me."

There was an earnestness in his face Anaïs had not

expected—and a sort of gentleness, too, though he was the sort of man with whom one would not ordinarily associate such a word. And to her extreme discomfort she felt, quite suddenly and inexplicably, as if she might burst into tears. As if the thing she had waited the whole of her life for was somehow wrong; as if she were not quite the person she'd always believed herself to be. Certainly she was not this beautiful, mysterious woman.

Abruptly, she thrust it back at him.

"You don't want it?"

"No." The word came out far too husky. "I mean—yes, I do want it. Very much. I just want you to sign it for me. And date it."

With a muted smile, he did so, scratching a bold, angular signature in the lower right corner, and the date beneath.

"There," he said, handing it back. "I daresay that's the first portrait I've sketched in a decade or better."

"Then I'm honored. Thank you."

But he had signed it *Geoffrey MacLachlan*—a precaution, she supposed, to preserve their ruse.

Just then, something caught her gaze. Anaïs laid the drawing aside. This strange and pleasant interlude was officially at an end.

"I suppose we'd best get our flibbertigibbet faces fixed," she went on, "for I see Madame Moreau turning in from the Place des Palais."

Geoff stiffened, but did not turn back around to look. "With whom?"

"A gentleman and a little girl."

Geoff nodded, and returned to his drawing. Anaïs stood as if to dust off her skirts, then looked up and brightened her expression.

"Madame Moreau!" she called out. "Oh, my! What good fortune!"

Charlotte Moreau smiled, but her eyes shied uneasily toward the thin, elegant man whose arm she held. "Good morning, Mrs. MacLachlan," she said when Anaïs hastened toward them. "How do you do?"

"Oh, ants!" said Anaïs, stepping onto the path. "I think I sat on a nest! Can you imagine anyone so witless? I seem to be imagining them all over me now, and it's utterly distracting." She twitched a bit for good measure.

Madame Moreau's smile thinned. "Mrs. MacLachlan, may I present my—er, my uncle, the Vicomte de Lezennes? And this is Giselle, my daughter."

When the full introductions had been made, Anaïs curtsied with almost comical depth to Lezennes. He was a slender, elegant man of middle age, with close-cropped hair nearly as dark as her own; a fine, thin nose, and a sharp beard that looked decidedly satanic. The child was a coltish thing who said nothing, and refused Anaïs's gaze—understandably, perhaps.

"Oh, Your Lordship, it is *such* an honor," Anaïs gushed. "A French nobleman—right here in Brussels. And a diplomat, too!"

Lezennes flashed an almost patronizing smile. "My dear lady, Brussels is awash in French noblemen, I do assure you," he said in flawless English. "And diplomats. What brings you here?"

Anaïs widened her eyes. "Oh, we are on our wedding trip," she said, tumbling over her words. "Pardon my manners. Geoffrey! Oh, Geoff, do come here. You will remember Madame Moreau, I think?"

Geoff looked placidly up from his easel, feigning slow recognition. "Why, yes, of course!" Finally he rose and came toward them. Anaïs introduced the vicomte.

Geoff pumped his hand with a sort of John Bull gusto. "Oh, I say, good to meet you, old chap," he said cheerfully. "The wife's been in alt over the notion of an English friend—can't speak a word of this odd Hollandish tongue, you know."

Distaste flitted across Lezennes' visage, but was quickly veiled. "Technically, Mr. MacLachlan, it's Flemish," said the vicomte, "but French will do as well here. Surely your wife has a little French?"

Geoff looked at Anaïs blankly. "Yes, I daresay."

"Oh, enough to stumble along, but I do dislike it," Anaïs complained, hitching her arm through his. "You must pardon my husband, my lord. We've been married but a few weeks. As to why we've come, Geoff likes to draw pictures of buildings."

"Of buildings?" Lezennes looked quizzically at Geoff.

"Yes, yes, thinking of becoming an architect. Can't live off m'father forever, eh?" Geoff gave Lezennes a conspiratorial wink. "Or so the gov'nor likes to remind me. Bags of money, that one, but tight as a parson's pucker."

"Oh, come look at his drawing, do!" Anaïs tilted her head toward the easel. "You really will be quite impressed."

Left with no polite way to refuse, Lezennes bowed stiffly at the neck. "*Après vous, madame,*" he said with a flourish of his hand.

They crossed the pathway and the clearing, Geoff yammering on about how frightfully expensive it was to live in Brussels, and wondering a trifle too loudly if Paris was any cheaper. Lezennes assured him it was not. Then the drawing was duly produced and a suitable fuss made, with Charlotte Moreau politely declaring it was quite the nicest likeness of the palace she had ever seen.

Anaïs thought it more probable it was the *only* likeness she'd ever seen, but she thanked them both profusely.

"Well, Charlotte," she eventually declared, "I hope I may call you Charlotte?"

Again, the lady cut an uncertain look at Lezennes. "But of course," she said. "And you are . . . Anaïs, was it not?"

"It is, and I was so frightfully disappointed over your headache on Sunday," Anaïs pressed on. "I so desperately wished to quiz you about the best place to buy lace. And books"—here she knelt and snatched up her cheap novel—"have you any notion where I might find a bookshop? With these sorts of English serials?"

Madame Moreau looked startled. "With English serials?"

But the vicomte was eyeing the garish cover in barely veiled disgust. "*Mon Dieu, madame*, what is that thing?"

Anaïs widened her eyes. "A penny dreadful," she whispered. "They are most exciting, my lord. This one is about a wehr-wolf."

Lezennes' lip seemed to curl. "And what, pray, is a wehr-wolf?"

"A man who changes into a wolf at the full moon," said Anaïs with a shiver. "He has sold his soul to the devil, you see, for youth and wealth, but there's a catch—isn't there always a catch when one does such a silly thing? In any case, it is most deliciously horrid. I know ladies do not normally buy them, but I am of the opinion that they should at least try one."

"Oh, she'll read just any sort of nonsense," Geoff cheerfully threw in, now repacking his things. "Have pity on us, Madame Moreau, and take her somewhere she can find a proper book."

"But in English?" said the lady, her delicate brow furrowing. "Alas, I do not think—"

"We could discuss it over tea one day?" Anaïs suggested. "If, that is, you are feeling better?"

Again, Charlotte Moreau glanced at her companion. "Well, I am not sure . . ."

But Lezennes was looking back and forth between Anaïs's

silly novel and the perfectly bovine expression on Geoff's face. "Feel free to go, my dear," said the vicomte. "I think it would be quite harmless."

Some of the tension went out of Charlotte Moreau at that, and for the first time she flashed what appeared to be a genuine smile. "I should be pleased to," she said. "When?"

"Monday?" Anaïs suggested, trying not to seem too eager. "Oh, and do bring little Giselle. She is such a pretty thing, and puts me so very much in mind of my own dear Jane."

Even at this remark, however, the child did not make eye contact, and instead pushed further behind her mother's skirts.

The vicomte, however, did make eye contact. "I am afraid Giselle is delicate, and not quite like other children." His voice was firm. "She does not often leave home."

Anaïs let recognition dawn across her face. "No, indeed, then," she said. "Of course it would not do. The poor, dear mouse. How very good you are, my lord, to be so mindful of her welfare."

Geoff looked up from the easel he was closing—and making a hash of the whole business, for he'd managed to shut his coattail up in one of the hinges.

"By gad, I've a capital notion," he said, finally thrashing himself loose with a good deal of flailing and clatter. "The two of you must come to dine! What about Tuesday? We've a smashing good cook over there. Roasts a joint as well as a proper Englishwoman. How does six o'clock sound? Afraid we're still keeping country hours."

Lezennes lifted his nose a notch. "Giselle's governess leaves in the afternoons, and Charlotte cannot be from home after that," he said. "I am afraid we could not possibly come to your house."

"Well, if you insist," said Geoff good-naturedly. "Hate to put you out, though."

"I beg your pardon?" said Lezennes.

But Geoff blustered his way onward. "Tell you what—I'll make it up to you!" he vowed. "A cask of the gov'nor's best whisky accidentally fell into my wagon as I was leaving for Brussels. What do you say I drain us off a bottle?"

"Whisky?" The vicomte literally recoiled. "Made of *fermented grain*?"

Geoff snapped his folding stool shut. "Aye, and I'll wager you'll never drink that tepid French brandy again, Lezennes, once you've had a snoot-full of Scotch glory. So six, then, at your place?"

Lezennes drew a deep, almost shuddering breath. "*Oui*, six," he said in a tone that suggested the earlier he could get it over with the better. Then he crooked his head to look down at his companion. "Charlotte, I daresay, will be glad for the diversion."

Charlotte was still smiling her genuine smile. "Oh, I would!" she declared. "Thank you, Uncle. You really are too kind."

The matter, then, was settled. After a round of polite good-byes, Anaïs and Geoff watched the three of them stroll away in the direction of the Rue de la Loi, on the opposite end of the park.

"Good God," he said when the trio was beyond earshot. "That was appalling. Even I don't like us."

"*Stupide rosbifs*, are we not?" Anaïs grinned up at him. "And now poor Lezennes must have us to dine. That was well done, by the way."

"Stepped in it like horse manure, didn't he?" Geoff grinned back. "And who knew you could be so dimwitted?"

"Or you so cheerfully crass," Anaïs added.

"Oh, I have my moments."

"I thought the coattail in the hinge was a convincing touch," said Anaïs, rummaging in her pocket. "If we cannot make decent Guardians, I daresay we might tread the boards." She produced a lace and linen handkerchief, and fluttered it at him.

He lifted one brow. "Thank you, Anaïs, but you have not reduced me to tears quite yet."

"No, silly, I pinched it from Charlotte's pocket," she said, tucking it into the collar of his waistcoat. "Vittorio taught me."

"To *pick pockets*?"

"To do a number of things," said Anaïs vaguely. "Vittorio said that sometimes a deeply personal item could be imprinted with the owner's emotions. And unless I miss my guess, that handkerchief has been damp with her tears more than once. Perhaps you will find it helpful."

"Aye, I might do, at that." Tucking it away, Geoff returned his gaze to Charlotte's back as the threesome strolled deeper into the park. "What *were* you doing with such a tawdry book, anyway?"

"Tawdry, hmm?" Anaïs crossed her arms over her chest. "Have you any notion, Geoff, what kind of money Mr. Reynolds makes selling that stuff? More than Mr. Dickens and the Brontë sisters combined, I'd wager."

He crossed his arms as if to mirror her. "And your point would be?"

"Well, I—" She closed her mouth, then opened it again. "Not that it's any of your business—"

"No, no, none at all!" he agreed, a slow grin spreading over his face.

"—but I thought, frankly, that I might try my hand at it," she finished, lifting her chin. "And do not laugh, blast it. I've known for an age you people in the *Fraternitas* would likely try to refuse me, and I must have something to do until—until—"

"Until your Mr. Right comes along?" Geoff suggested.

"Until I shove my way past your stupidity and prejudice,"

Anaïs finished. "There. I'm not giving up, Geoff. Now, let us be serious. What is your assessment of this situation in which Charlotte Moreau finds herself?"

Geoff sobered at once, and let his arms fall. "Not good," he conceded, his gaze still fixed on Charlotte's back. "She is cowed, if not outright terrified, by Lezennes. One doesn't need the Gift to see that."

Anaïs frowned. "Indeed not," she agreed. "Geoff, I have the most awful feeling that we mightn't have much time. Did you sense anything?"

He shook his head. "Only a measure of disquiet, but I feel as though I've begun to know her," he said. "To form a connection to her. And I agree with you. She is innocent, and Lezennes does not have her best interest at heart. Worse still, I don't think we have months—possibly not even weeks—to get this business settled."

"We are going to have to move faster than might be wise," said Anaïs as the trio turned from the main path and vanished into the trees. "I am going to have to be bold, Geoff. To befriend her quickly. But that may backfire if she's as skittish as I fear."

Geoff had picked up his sketch pad and was tapping it rather pensively against his thigh, in the way a stalking cat might twitch its tail in warning. His ice-blue eyes were still fixed on the distant path, and his jaw was set stubbornly again.

"Use your best judgment, then," he finally said, his voice grim. "And yes, waste no time."

"And if I fail?" asked Anaïs. "If I spook her? Are you willing to do what must be done?"

"To snatch the child?" said Geoff. "I should rather not. But without the child, Lezennes would have no use for Charlotte. He would let her go. You must try to persuade her to contact her family, Anaïs. Just in case there is some hope."

"Oh, I will," she answered. "I shall think of something, I promise you."

Still staring down the path, Geoff said no more.

It had been a most extraordinary day—a day that was leaving Anaïs more confused than ever about the man who now stood by her side. Shoulder to shoulder, quite literally, they seemed to coexist as easily and comfortably together as two people could be in moments like this.

As if it were fated.

But it was not. It couldn't be. Nonna had spelled out her fate long ago, and it would be best if she remembered that.

"Here," she said after a time. "Give me the pad and your pencils. I shall help you carry all this home."

Perhaps Anaïs and Geoff did not have fate on their side, but it was beginning to seem as though Charlotte Moreau just might. On Monday, Anaïs came downstairs for luncheon to find that the afternoon mail had brought a letter postmarked from Colchester.

Bernard presented it to Geoff on a salver with a little bow. "I hope, *monsieur*, that it brings good news?"

"It's in Sutherland's hand," said Geoff, taking it.

"Your Preost's in Colchester?" Anaïs asked, following him into the parlor.

"Aye, he left London the day after you suggested he go." Geoff took a paper knife from the desk and slit the letter open. "We are not so steeping in our—let's see, how did you put it?—yes, our *stupidity and prejudice*—that we cannot recognize a good idea when we hear one."

Anaïs leaned round his shoulder. "Oh, just read it," she insisted. "And never mind the sarcasm."

Geoff snapped the letter open, and his eyes darted swiftly over it. "Good Lord," he murmured. "That was quickly done."

"What?" said Anaïs. "*What?*"

Geoff shifted his gaze to hers. "You were right again, my girl."

"Yet another phrase that rolls beautifully off your tongue," said Anaïs. "But do go on. Precisely how brilliant was I?"

Geoff didn't even bother to rise to the bait. "Charlotte Moreau's family awaits her return with open arms," he said, a look of pure relief spreading over his face. "The prospect of a grandchild has them over the moon. And they had not heard of Charlotte's widowhood."

"Well, how could they when they cut her off?" said Anaïs a little bitterly.

"A circumstance they have sorely regretted," said Geoff muttered, looking again at the letter. "It sounds as if they have been mourning all those lost years. Anaïs, they want to give her a home."

Anaïs closed her eyes. "Thank God."

"God had help from you and Sutherland." Geoff handed Anaïs the letter. "Well done, all of you. Here, read for yourself, but don't burn it. We may yet need it."

"Thank you." She began to skim over the words, scarcely daring to believe them.

But Geoff had begun to roam restlessly about the parlor. "The *Fraternitas* has two good men near Colchester," he said, dragging a hand pensively through his hair. "Guardians both—and men whom we can trust. We can appoint one of them to Giselle; to oversee her safety for now, and later to help her understand and cope with the Gift."

With a sense of intense relief, Anaïs refolded the letter, and tucked it in her pocket. "But first we must get her there."

"Indeed." Almost absently, Geoff extracted Charlotte's

handkerchief and looked at it. "First we must get her there—and safely."

Just then Petit came in to announce that luncheon was ready. They dined in comparative silence, Anaïs remarking on little more than her hope that Charlotte would actually turn up for tea this time, rather than send another last-minute cancellation.

Geoff seemed lost in thought, but not as tense—or as cross—as he had been during their first days in Brussels. For her part, Anaïs could not escape the strong belief that their short time together was rapidly drawing to a close.

There was a part of her that would be relieved.

Geoff, too, would be glad to see England again, Anaïs thought, watching him across the table. Or perhaps he would merely be relieved to see the back of her. Anaïs did not think she flattered herself by imagining there was a strong physical attraction between them, one that had been building throughout the whole of this trip. But he had fought it, while she had not.

Well, not entirely.

Perhaps she had been lucky. A less principled man would have said yes to her offer, and shown far less concern for her.

Or perhaps it was not entirely a matter of his concern for her?

Geoff had made it plain he'd no wish to be trapped into marriage. Anaïs understood that. But perhaps it was something more complicated. A devoted mistress? A secret lover? She had not considered the possibility that there might be someone else in his life. Heaven knew it would not be the first time she had fallen into that fool's trap.

Again, she let her gaze run over him, and felt that familiar little rush, a sweet ache that went straight to the pit of her belly. With his mane of leonine hair and those intense, almost lupine eyes, Geoff struck Anaïs as some half-tamed creature, attached to no one, roaming the forests of life alone.

But there was nothing to be gained by allowing her thoughts to run in that direction, and everything to be gained for Charlotte and Giselle Moreau in getting them back on English soil as swiftly as possible. Anaïs finished her meal in silence, trying to keep her eyes on her plate, then excused herself and went downstairs to make the final preparations for tea.

That afternoon, Charlotte Moreau surprised Anaïs by arriving ten minutes early.

It was a good sign, Anaïs thought. It did not take long, however, for her to realize that the darkness had settled over Charlotte again. The vibrancy her eyes had so briefly held the previous afternoon was gone.

They settled in the front parlor by the windows that overlooked the Rue de l'Escalier and the entrance to Lezennes' house, idly discussing the weather as Petit set out the tea service.

"I was so glad we had the chance to meet your uncle in the park," said Anaïs after their plates had been filled and all the small talk exchanged. "He seems a most distinguished gentleman."

"Yes, he is," said Charlotte noncommittally. "And he has been very generous toward Giselle and me."

"What sort of work does he do for the French?" Anaïs paused to sip her tea. "Something frightfully important, I should guess."

Charlotte cut her gaze away. "I'm not certain," she said, returning her cup to her saucer. "He doesn't speak of it, and I think it is not my place to ask."

"But he must have met King Leopold, mustn't he?" said Anaïs, widening her eyes ingenuously. "Perhaps, Charlotte, you will get to meet him, too! Wouldn't that be exciting? After all, he is still so divinely handsome."

For a moment, Charlotte hesitated. "Uncle does have private meetings with the King," she murmured. "I heard one of his aides discussing it. That a meeting was to be set up—something very discreet. And I wondered, of course—" Suddenly she stopped, and snatched another biscuit from the tray on the table. "These are delicious. Will you ask Mrs. Janssen to give me the recipe?"

"She will be flattered you asked," Anaïs assured her. "As to the King, he is still deeply beloved by many in England, you know. After all, he was once intended to be *our* King."

"Well, the consort, I believe," Charlotte acknowledged. "And he was very dear to his niece Victoria, especially in her childhood."

Anaïs smiled and leaned forward to warm their cups. "One wonders though, if things mightn't have changed between them over the years," she murmured suggestively. "Leopold's position is very different now."

"Indeed." Charlotte was slowly circling her spoon in her tea. "He is a powerful king in his own right, and Uncle says that . . ."

Anaïs leaned intently forward. "Oh, go on, Charlotte, do!" she pleaded. "It sounds as if you have gossip—and who can resist a little tittle-tattle over tea?"

Charlotte flushed guiltily. "Uncle says that Leopold must now look to himself first, and take care of his own long-term interests," she whispered. "He says that Leopold's connections to England, loose though they are, could one day be to his disadvantage politically."

"Oh," said Anaïs. "Well, that is all too complicated for me to grasp. I just think he is handsome. And his wife—someone said she suffers from consumption. I wonder if it is true?"

Charlotte seemed to stiffen slightly. "The Queen is very ill," she answered. "I think she hasn't long to live."

Anaïs leaned very near. "And I have heard the King's mistress is with child," she whispered, dropping one of DuPont's juicier tidbits. "Or may already have given birth."

At that, Charlotte looked suddenly stricken. "But . . . But that is tragic!" she said, one hand going to her breast. "It's said his wife adores him——even if their marriage was politically arranged."

Anaïs shrugged. "Little good that does Leopold now that his father-in-law has been booted from the throne of France," she remarked. "No wonder he is worried about making new French alliances. As to poor Queen Louise, one wonders if love is worth the pain. I am glad, I think, to have married for practicality this time."

Charlotte dropped her gaze to her tea again. "Well, *I* shan't do it!" she said, her voice low and fervent. "I do not disparage your choice, Anaïs. Truly, I do not. But I should rather feel the ache of loss, however acute it might be, than to marry where I do not love."

Anaïs set her teacup down with an awkward clatter. "Poor Charlotte, you are thinking of your husband, are you not?" she murmured, feeling rather like a cur. "I collect you have not been long widowed?"

Charlotte's face softened with a mix of grief and what was obviously affection. "Pierre died last year," she said softly, "but it seems like only yesterday. Some days—*most* days—I wake up, and for a moment, I expect him to be lying there beside me. Then the grief strikes me anew when he is not."

Anaïs reached out and touched her hand. "How inconsiderate I am," she murmured. "Charlotte, I am so sorry. But you do not need to marry again. You have your uncle. He has not suggested you should leave him, has he?"

But Charlotte did not look up. "I have thought of you,

Anaïs, so much since that day we first met," she said out of nowhere. "I have thought about how much we have in common. We both married for love, and against our family's wishes, to men who were not wealthy—and we have neither of us regretted it. Have we?"

Anaïs felt a shaft of remorse pierce her heart, but she shook her head. "No, never."

"And we both have dear daughters," Charlotte continued. "We are young widows of similar background in a foreign land where we cannot always speak the language."

Yes, thought Anaïs guiltily, *or so you believe*.

"But you have remarried," Charlotte added. "Happily, it is to be hoped?"

"I think so," said Anaïs tentatively, searching her mind for yet another lie, and hating herself for it. "But Charlotte, my father is elderly, and wanted me to marry so that I would have someone to care for Jane and me when he is gone. You have your uncle. He obviously adores little Giselle."

"Oh, yes," she said almost wistfully. "Not dotingly, no. But he frets constantly about her welfare—and wants her treated as if she is made of spun glass."

"And I sense that all this has you worried," Anaïs went on.

"Yes, I think that is not too strong a word, my dear. I do hate to see you distraught, however well you hide it. Do you want to tell me what is wrong?"

"It is just that sometimes . . . sometimes I am *so confused*, Anaïs." Her words fell to a whisper. "So confused, and I have no one here to talk to."

Which was exactly as Lezennes had planned it.

They were all of them, it seemed, using Charlotte.

Anaïs was beginning to feel filthy. Again she was tempted to confess all. But she had to remember the child, and Charlotte, she feared, was not strong enough to hear the truth. The expiation of Anaïs's sins would have to wait.

"But you do have someone to talk to, Charlotte," she replied. "You have me. Now I am not, perhaps, the most intelligent creature on earth, but I am your friend and you can confide in me. And even a goose could see, frankly, that there is something about Lezennes that troubles you."

Charlotte swallowed hard, the muscles of her pale throat constricting until Anaïs wondered if she mightn't choke on her words. "Well," she finally whispered, "it is just that he is *not* my uncle."

"But he is your husband's uncle, my dear," said Anaïs soothingly, "and that is the very same thing according to canon law."

Charlotte's gaze had turned faintly inward. "Well, I always *believed* him to be my husband's uncle, though they were never close," she said. "But the truth is, Pierre's mother was just a servant on their family's estate. Pierre's parents were never married."

"Oh," said Anaïs softly. "Well. But it still doesn't matter. Lezennes is taking care of you on behalf of the family."

"It doesn't matter?" Charlotte looked at her a little sharply. "I told myself that at first, too."

"What do you mean, at first?" Anaïs looked at her quizzically.

"I thought Lezennes was Pierre's uncle, but now he says—" She bit off her words, cast her gaze into the depths of the room, and shook her head. "Oh, God, why am I even speaking of this?"

"Because it is troubling you." Anaïs reached out to lightly touch her. "Charlotte, my dear, nothing grows lighter than a burden shared. What does he say now?"

Charlotte gave a shuddering sigh, as if pushing away tears. "Lezennes says that his brother always denied being Pierre's father," she whispered. "That his true father was probably one of the many guests who frequented their estate. Or one of the other servants."

"How odd," said Anaïs. "What did your husband believe?"

She lifted her shoulders weakly. "Pierre just said that he was the old vicomte's illegitimate grandson, and so the family had educated him and found him a place at court—a minor position as a clerk. But Pierre's father died when he was three, so I suppose it is possible he was confused."

Anaïs very much doubted that. "And what does Lezennes say now?"

"That Pierre's mother *claimed* Lezennes' brother was the father of her child, and so the family did the right thing," Charlotte answered, still sounding mystified. "But Lezennes has gently suggested that no one ever really believed it. Indeed, he claims his elder brother was . . ." Her words halted, her face flaming.

"Was what?" Anaïs prodded.

"That he was *unnatural!*" Charlotte whispered, eyes widening. "Lezennes says his brother was never interested in women at all. That the old vicomte simply seized upon the bastard child as proof that his son was . . . was not what everyone whispered he was. And that the family thought it a kindness to let the rumor lie."

"Oh, dear. How very odd that sounds." Anaïs furrowed her brow. "And Lezennes is still caring for you and Giselle, even though he does not believe he is . . . Oh, Charlotte! Are you afraid he will turn you out?"

Charlotte shook her head vehemently. "No, no, he won't," she said, staring at her hands. "He seems most protective toward Giselle. He says nothing need change unless . . ."

"Unless what?"

Charlotte lifted her gaze, and Anaïs saw the unshed tears that shimmered there. "Unless I wish to marry him," she whispered. "He says it is the best way—the only way—to protect Giselle. No written record exists of who Pierre's father was. He says there is absolutely no impediment within the Church to our marrying."

"Oh, my."

Anaïs fell silent for a long moment. It was just as DuPont had feared from the first. Lezennes had tried to have it both ways—and in the end, he had twisted matters around until poor Charlotte was in a devil's dilemma. Charlotte was religious; she could never have violated the Church's edict by marrying her husband's uncle. But now her morality was being tested in another way altogether.

Anaïs wondered if Lezennes had counted on *that.*

"So the way things stand now," she finally said, "you are making a home with a man who mightn't be any relation at all?"

"Yes!" Charlotte squeaked. "Oh, Anaïs, what am I to do? I cannot live with a man who is not my family! It seems morally reprehensible, even for a widow. As if I am living a lie. But I cannot—*will not*—marry a man whom I do not love as much as I loved Pierre."

"And have you told Lezennes this? That you do not love him?"

"Yes, yes, of course I have! I cannot lie to him, either." Words were spilling from Charlotte now. "Not when he has taken us in and given us a home. But he was so . . . vexed. Oh, Anaïs, I think he was almost angry with me. He turned red and sputtered, then stalked from the room."

The perfidy of it made Anaïs tremble with rage. Lezennes knew that marriage would make Charlotte his under the law. He would have the ultimate power—the power to control all that was hers, including Giselle. The power to beat her, most likely. Even the power to lock her away in an asylum if he wished.

"The vicomte has no right, Charlotte, to be angry with you," said Anaïs, her voice quiet but firm. "You must not believe he does."

"But he has asked nothing else of me," she cried. "And I owe him so much. We had no one to turn to when Pierre died. Nothing of value to sell save a little jewelry, which is long gone. It was like a godsend when Lezennes showed up on my doorstep to offer us a home."

"And what did he say when he had regained his composure?"

"That I should not choose hastily," said Charlotte. "That he did not wish to replace Pierre, and that we simply needed more time alone, the three of us. A holiday, perhaps, he said. It does sound lovely—Giselle might like the seashore, perhaps—but I don't know how to tell him . . ."

"That you don't think you will ever come to love him?" Anaïs supplied, lifted one eyebrow.

"But I shan't, Anaïs!" she cried. "I know it. He is so . . . strict sometimes with Giselle. He is so suspicious of everyone we meet. Sometimes I feel as if he watches my every move, and on the next breath I realize I am imagining it! How can I be angry with him when he has done nothing unkind? What an ungrateful wretch I am!"

"No, Charlotte. You are not ungrateful in the least."

Anaïs reached out and took one of Charlotte's hands in her own. But inwardly, she was a little shaken.

One had to wonder if Lezennes' frustration was not rising to the boiling point. Likely he had imagined Charlotte would be so glad for a roof over her head, she would set her moral quandaries aside. Certainly it is what Lezennes would have done.

For a moment, Anaïs was tempted to reach inside her pocket and show Charlotte the letter from Sutherland. But that's all it was—just a letter from Sutherland, not Charlotte's parents. And there would be a great many difficult explanations that would have to be given along with that letter.

Charlotte would distrust her instantly. Indeed, the whole operation could collapse, for who was to say Anaïs was any less evil than Lezennes? Nonetheless, she was increasingly certain that Charlotte was headed for disaster. If Charlotte tried to take Giselle and leave Lezennes, what might the man do to stop her?

They must tread very carefully indeed.

Anaïs forced herself to relax, then patted Charlotte's hand. "My dear, perhaps you *will* come to love him," she murmured. "Stranger things have happened. Do not fret so. And do not, I beg you, rush into anything. Give yourself time, and perhaps . . . well, perhaps you will begin to feel an affection for him."

"But how long? And how could I ever, Anaïs, when all I feel now is a—a near revulsion?" Charlotte stopped, all color draining as she slapped a tremulous hand over her mouth. "Oh, God! I should not have said such a thing. That was vile. I truly am ungrateful."

Anaïs carefully considered her next words. "You are neither vile nor ungrateful," she answered. "You are a mother—which means you must tread carefully, Charlotte. You must always trust your instincts. You must. They will keep your child safe."

"*Safe—?*" she said sharply.

Anaïs flashed a wan smile, and snatched Charlotte's hand again. "I speak too strongly," she said at once. "We have become histrionic, the both of us. We are imagining things that will not happen. Look, I know what we need. We need a glass of sherry instead of this tea."

"Oh, I would be so grateful!" Charlotte's color began to return. "And you are right. I am imagining things, am I not?"

"Yes, so what is called for here is a diversion." Anaïs

forced a wide smile, and leapt up to ring the bell. "And I have just the thing. I have cards."

"Cards?" Charlotte looked at her curiously. "Shall we play piquet, then?"

"No," said Anaïs. "Wait here—ah, Petit! There you are. Be so good as to clear the tea things away, and bring us some of Bernard's strong sherry, please."

The footman bowed. "Certainly, *madame*."

"I shall be but a moment," said Anaïs before dashing from the room and up the stairs.

In her bedchamber she plucked Nonna Sofia's ebony wood box from her night table and went back down the stairs to find Petit already pouring two glasses of wine. The tea tray having been cleared away, Anaïs set the box on the edge of the table and opened it. The cards had not recently been purified, she remembered a little guiltily. But in this case, did it really matter? She was not really going to read.

No, she was going to tell another vile pack of lies. She was going to spin a mound of silly froth laced with just enough truth to keep Charlotte on her guard. It was beginning to feel as though kidnapping both Giselle and Charlotte would be easier than this—one lie spackled upon another like so much lime and horsehair plaster stuffed into a crack.

"Oh, my!" Charlotte was leaning over the box. "What are you up to, Anaïs?"

Anaïs forced a light laugh, and got on with it. "I am going to set your heart at ease, Charlotte," she said. "I am going to tell you what the future holds. How do you like that?"

Charlotte drew back, her eyes large. "Is that a tarot?" she asked. "Can you really use it?"

"A *tarocchi*, yes," said Anaïs, dumping the box into her hand. "That is what my great-grandmother called it."

"Heavens, I have heard of such things, but never seen one," said Charlotte. "Those look almost ancient."

"Indeed, they are," said Anaïs truthfully, setting the pack down. "And frightfully delicate. We never let light get to the cards unless we are reading. They have been kept in that ebony casket for two centuries, at least."

The pack had slid a little to one side, fanning across the table. Tentatively Charlotte touched the top card with the tip of one finger. "This one—*le Re di Dischi*—he looks more faded than the others," she said. "Where ever did you get such a thing, anyway?"

Anaïs looked directly into her eyes. "The Gift of *i tarocchi* runs in the blood of my family," she said honestly. "But it usually skips a generation or two. My nonna was the last, and then the Gift—the skill and the cards, I mean—they passed to me."

At the word *gift*, Charlotte's breath caught, but she quickly recovered. "Could your nonna really tell the future?"

"She lived to be ninety-two, and I never knew her to be wrong," said Anaïs, her heart sinking a little as she said it. There were, regrettably, one or two things she wished Nonna Sofia could have been wrong about.

"But . . . but you cannot be serious." Charlotte pressed one hand flat to her chest. "Can you?"

"Watch, and you will see," said Anaïs, delicately shuffling the pack. "Then you may decide the truth of *i tarocchi* for yourself."

She set it down in the middle of the table. "Now, take the cards up and hold them," Anaïs instructed. "Let the cards feel your energy, Charlotte. Your emotions. Shuffle them if you wish. Then, when you feel ready, set the pack down, and cut them into three stacks with your left hand, dividing it any way you choose, but moving only to the left with each stack."

Charlotte cast her a chary glance. "Very well."

Anaïs watched as Charlotte did as she was bid, eventually dividing the pack into fairly even thirds across the table. "Excellent. Now restack them, in any way you choose."

When this was done, Anaïs laid the cards out, using her nonna's favorite pattern, the crossed circle.

"Now the tarot is truthful, Charlotte, but often capricious," Anaïs murmured, snapping down the last card. "We cannot command it. But tell me if there anything you should particularly like to know, and I shall do my best to elicit an answer."

"N-no," said Charlotte. "Just . . . my future, I suppose." Then she gave a little laugh.

Anaïs wished she were so lighthearted about it all. But suddenly it seemed less like a lark, and more like a burden. Rarely had she attempted to use the cards, even in jest, for it was something she instinctively resisted. Anaïs had seen enough strange things at her great-grandmother's knee to respect the power of *i tarocchi*, if not her own abilities.

Closing her eyes, Anaïs skimmed her hand palm-down around the circle, not quite touching them. It was a tradition—a way of asking for God's guidance in interpreting the cards—but this time the pack seemed to radiate a shocking warmth.

Lifting her lashes in alarm, she looked at the circle. It appeared perfectly ordinary. No supernatural force had set it afire, or piled hot bricks beneath the tea table. These past few days had left her nerves unaccountably jangled, that was all.

Still, it was with a measure of unexpected reluctance that Anaïs turned the first card. It was the three of Swords—a trio of swords driven deep into a bleeding heart—a most significant card, and one that she'd never seen turned at the opening.

Charlotte had recoiled. "How frightful," she said, her voice thready. "Please tell me that card has nothing to do with me."

Anaïs's faint sense of dread was growing. "It is rare that any one picture or number predicts anything," she said. "The interpretation of each card changes based on its position in the circle, the cards it lies in proximity to, and many other variables."

"So you will turn more cards?"

Anaïs nodded and turned three more. "Ah," she said.

Charlotte gave a nervous laugh. "What do you see? Something that does not involve swords or blood, I pray."

"Nothing definitive, no," Anaïs murmured.

She continued her way around the circle, feeling remarkably ill at ease, as if her clothes were too tight or the room too hot. The palm of her right hand felt almost sunburned, and Anaïs's skin seemed to be prickling with an unpleasant sort of awareness—just her own needling guilt, no doubt.

Still, she wished very strongly that she had not gone upstairs for the cards. They felt strange to her today. It was just her fear over Lezennes, she told herself.

With the circle turned, Anaïs sat back in her chair, and rolled her shoulders back to loosen them. Charlotte touched the card nearest her. "This card is pretty," she said. "What can you tell so far?"

"Little yet that we do not already know," said Anaïs, sweeping her hand around the left side of the circle. "Here we see you have come on a long journey—the order represents your travel from England, I think, not your journey to Brussels. You have had a happy life, for the most part."

"Oh, yes," said Charlotte wistfully. "I was blessed."

Anaïs turned the next card, and felt a sudden jolt, like a little discharge of static into her hand. For a moment, she hesitated. It was not too late to laugh, and sweep the cards from the table.

"Anaïs?" Charlotte's voice came from far away.

"I am sorry," said Anaïs, wiping the back of her hand across her temple to brush back a curl that had sprung loose. "I lost my train of thought."

Charlotte touched the card lightly with her finger. "He looks sad."

"He is sad," Anaïs replied, a little quaver in her voice. "This card—the warrior Carbone—he represents the one who has left you. Do you see the way he faces away from us? And the waning moon?"

"Yes," said Charlotte, drawing out the word uncertainly. "Who is he? A real person?"

Anaïs knew without a doubt. "This mighty warrior is your husband," she answered. "He is God's messenger who has passed from this world to the next."

"Oh!" said Charlotte. She jerked upright in her chair. "Anaïs! Surely you are making this up?"

Anaïs shook her head, but could scarcely pull her gaze from the spread of cards. "No, this is very clear," she murmured, her hand trembling a little. "This is a man who was your strength and your light. The waning moon near this card, the four of Chalices, tells us this. But the light is fading. He has passed happily, Charlotte. He is at peace, and waits for you beyond the veil."

"Does he?" she whispered.

"I am certain of it," she said honestly—for honesty did indeed seem the best policy now. She turned the card beside it. "Now this card—the six of Swords—this person carries a mighty burden," said Anaïs. "Do you see the heavy bag he carries? A bag full of weapons. This represents your more recent past. You have been fighting a long and wearying battle, Charlotte, and you have much responsibility left to you here on earth."

"Oh!" said Charlotte sharply.

"This duty, like the bag of swords, weighs heavily upon your shoulders. But this previous card—the warrior Carbone—he sits above you, metaphorically and celestially. He watches over you. He trusts you to carry out your duties well, and act with utmost care. He is confident you will choose rightly."

Charlotte's face twisted as if with grief. "I wish *I* had such faith in myself!"

"But here"—Anaïs turned the next card and lightly tapped it—"here we see a threat to your peace. This card—ah, yes, it represents a grave concern. Something that has followed you for a while now, I believe."

"Yes?" said Charlotte a little anxiously.

Anaïs turned the card below. "*Le Fante di Dischi*," she murmured. "And this, I believe, is . . . yes, this is Giselle."

Charlotte gasped. "Giselle! But . . . that is a young man. Isn't it?"

"Yes, but it is the symbolism one must understand," Anaïs answered. "There is something about Giselle which troubles you, is there not? Something your husband understood. And now you feel lost. In over your head."

The card depicted an androgynous young warrior holding a falcon in one hand. He wore but one boot, and had laid his shield aside. The meaning could not have been clearer. A little weakly, Anaïs turned the next several cards, resisting the impulse to cast them from the table with one swipe of her arm.

"Charlotte," she said quietly, "do you understand the term *augury*? The original meaning of the word?"

"I . . . yes. Why?"

Anaïs drew her fingertip along the card's worn edge. "*Le Fante di Dischi* represents a young person who holds a secret," she began. "The bird is the symbol of things unseen. Of knowledge to be unleashed. Of augury, quite literally. But this is a power the young warrior cannot yet control, and is loath to use. She has her shield—for battle, you see?—but she has not yet taken it up. She is not ready. Instead she looks to her right—to the warrior Carbone—her gaze questioning."

"Yes?" Charlotte rasped. "Go on."

"This young warrior, she seeks guidance," said Anaïs simply. Lightly, she touched the first warrior card again. "But Carbone is walking away into the waning moon. New guidance—a new mentor—is sorely needed."

"But . . . but what does it all mean?" Charlotte's voice was thready.

"That Giselle's burden is heavy, Charlotte, and you cannot keep carrying it. You need help."

Anaïs looked up to see that Charlotte had begun to cry, the tears trailing silently down her cheeks, as if she dared not dab at them and make them real. Anaïs felt sick inside—as if she watched some gruesome accident, yet dared not look away. She had not wanted this. Ought never have started it.

"*The power of* i tarocchi *is strong, bella,*" she heard her great-grandmother saying. "*Take it up as one might a serpent, holding it tight behind the head.*"

"Do you wish me to stop?" asked Anaïs, almost praying the answer would be yes. "Say the word, Charlotte, and I will wipe these cards from the table."

Charlotte gave a shuddering sigh. "No. Go on."

"Then we have seen the past and, I think, the present," said Anaïs pensively. "Let us look to the future." She turned all but the last two cards. "When did you first leave home, Charlotte? Leave England, I mean?"

"Over ten years ago." Charlotte's voice was unsteady. "I left to attend school in Paris."

Anaïs flicked an assessing glance up at her. "And you have no family, you said," she murmured.

"N-no."

"No." Anaïs lifted one eyebrow. "And yet . . . ?"

Charlotte was dashing away her tears with the back of her hand. "And yet what?"

"This card, the eight of Pentacles—a basket full of staves—it means your world was full," said Anaïs. "Your harvest was bountiful, Charlotte. There was richness and love in abundance. A simple world, but filled with . . . yes, many people, I think. But all this you left behind?"

"I . . . did not wish to," said Charlotte weakly. "I went away to school. I always meant to go back. But then I met Pierre, and everything changed."

Anaïs turned the next to the last card. "And this man, *il Cavaliere di Spade*—the Knight of Swords—he is a warrior who grieves for you," she said, wishing to God the dreadful reading was over. "You have left him behind. He is ready to fight for you, Charlotte, but his heart is heavy and his sword—you see here—he has let it fall."

On a little cry, Charlotte touched her fingertips to her mouth. "Is it . . . my father?"

"Well, it is not a man who is dead," said Anaïs warningly. "That much is certain. But I cannot think who else it might be."

"Oh!" said Charlotte again, her color rising. "Oh, I so *very* much wish I could go home!"

"Is that what you want, Charlotte?" she asked sharply. "To go back home?"

"I . . . I cannot."

Her gaze had turned deeply inward, and Anaïs wisely let it go. Instead she reached out, her hand visibly trembling now, and turned the last card, which felt as if it might burst into flames at any moment.

"Good God," she muttered, staring down at it. "So many swords."

"The two this time," whispered Charlotte. "Anaïs, what does it mean?"

"The young warrior, and the old warrior," murmured Anaïs, studying the two figures. "Giselle is looking up to him for guidance. See these little arrows? The evils of the tangible world fly at them but they have their weapons at the ready. They are fully prepared for the battle to come."

"Why are there two?" asked Charlotte.

"Because the young warrior has found her new mentor," said Anaïs. "See, she touches her knee to the ground in deference to his power. He looks down, and offers her his arm. His strength."

"But it is not . . . Lezennes, is it?"

Slowly Anaïs shook her head. "Assuredly not," she said. "This man is one of her own kind. He can be no other."

"Her own kind?"

Anaïs lifted her gaze to Charlotte's, and planted her fingertip firmly on the card. "He is not Lezennes," she said again. "He is her Guardian."

Charlotte sucked in her breath. "Her . . . *guardian*?" In her eyes Anaïs could see recognition.

"Yes," said Anaïs sadly. "He is the man you are seeking, Charlotte. Lezennes cannot help you."

"But who is he? His name, I mean? And where shall I find him?"

"I do not know," Anaïs answered truthfully. "But he waits for her. *Il Cavaliere di Spade*—the grieving man—he will be the means by which all this will happen. You can tell this by his position in the center of the circle."

"Oh." Charlotte reached out and set her palm in the center of the cards. "And all this . . . this is what is going to happen to Giselle?"

"It is what *should* happen to Giselle," Anaïs answered, tracing her finger back around the circle of cards. "But you see here? And here? These cards represent the many hard choices which must be made in the interim. Many bridges which must be crossed."

"What must I do?" Charlotte whispered. "How must I begin? Oh, Anaïs, I cannot make a misstep. This is my *child* we are speaking of."

At last Anaïs swept up the cards. "You begin with utmost care," she answered. "You do nothing—*say* nothing—until matters come clear to you."

"And they will?" Charlotte looked at her a little pleadingly. "Come clear, I mean?"

Far more shaken than she appeared, Anaïs returned the cards to the wooden casket. "They will," she said quietly. "When, precisely, and in what way, I do not know. Just do nothing foolish. Watch, and wait."

"Watch and wait." Charlotte's echo was a little hollow. She had crushed her handkerchief in her hand, and fallen back into her chair, looking almost beaten. It had been too much. It had been a near cruelty. But none of it, alas, had been untrue.

Anaïs's plan to use the cards as a diversion had failed utterly. Indeed, she would be lucky if, in the end, she had not made matters worse. Lucky if her spackled mess of lime and horsehair did not crack and come crashing down upon their heads.

A few minutes later, Anaïs was escorting her guest to the front door. Charlotte still looked a little dazed.

"Charlotte," she said, returning to her earlier, happier persona, "I really do not understand any of this. I just read the cards. Perhaps all that I said meant something to you, but it means nothing to me. Do you understand?"

Charlotte nodded, and turned to go.

"Still," said Anaïs after her, "I think it might be wise if you told no one of what just happened, don't you?"

Charlotte's head swiveled slowly around. "How could I begin to describe it?" she replied. "I do not even *understand* what just happened."

On a sudden impulse, Anaïs reached out and gave Charlotte a swift hug. "Perhaps it will make sense to me later," she suggested. "But Geoff says I'm a bit of a ninnyhammer."

"I don't believe that," said Charlotte, who clearly didn't know what to believe. "But you will tell me, Anaïs, if anything comes clear to you?"

"You may count on that, too." Anaïs seized both her hands, and gave them a reassuring squeeze. "Now go, Charlotte, and be at peace if you can. I shall see you tomorrow night. And in the meantime, I shall think on what I might do to divert Lezennes' interest—at least temporarily."

Anaïs watched her go down the steps and dash between two passing carriages. Hands fisting at her sides, she shut the door and fell back against it, resisting the urge to pummel it.

Good God, what an idiot she was! What had begun as a lark had turned into a potential nightmare. Anaïs drew her hands down her skirts as if she might wipe away the filth of what she had just done. But she could not. She had been a fool to disrespect *i tarocchi*. To treat it as a joke. No, worse—to treat it as a means to manipulate an innocent person.

The whole afternoon left her feeling defiled. Used. And by her own hand, at that. She had done nothing save frighten the wits out of Charlotte.

Cursing beneath her breath, Anaïs came away from the door like an overtight spring, and bolted up the stairs.

CHAPTER 12

*He who knows when he can fight,
and when he cannot, will be victorious.*
Sun Tzu, *The Art of War*

*G*eoff returned home from an afternoon of haunting the art galleries and coffeehouses of Brussels, a venture that had included a deceptively casual meeting with one of DuPont's contacts, a man who was keeping Lezennes under surveillance.

It was a difficult exercise at best, the contact had explained, for much of the vicomte's so-called diplomatic work was conducted within the walls of Brussels's palaces. The contact had witnessed, however, a passing exchange at La Monnaie, the royal opera house, the previous evening with a man believed almost certainly to be a minion of the *Ancien Régime*.

It was looking more and more as if Lezennes had Legitimist leanings—not that Geoff gave a damn about France's politics. He cared only about Giselle Moreau. When she was old enough, and emotionally strong enough, she could fall on her sword for the old Bourbon kings if she wished. Until then, however, the Guardians of the *Fraternitas* had to protect her.

Geoff just didn't yet know how he was to accomplish it. So it was with a measure of weariness that he let himself into the house in the Rue de l'Escalier and tossed his hat onto the hall table. He went at once into the parlor and poured himself three fingers of whisky, tossing it down in two swallows before going up to change for dinner.

Upstairs, however, he could hear faint thuds, as if someone was bouncing a ball in one of the upper floors. He shrugged it off and, after tossing his coats across a chair, rang the bell to order hot water for the tub. He was already yanking off his boots when his valet came in to see what was wanted.

The rhythmic thudding upstairs had become more intense.

"What the devil is that racket, Mertens?" he asked, stripping off his waistcoat.

"I believe it is Madame MacLachlan," said the valet, picking up his coat and shaking the wrinkles from it. "She seemed in a bit of a mood, sir, if you'll pardon my saying. She went up into the attic an hour ago."

"Into the attic?" he echoed, throwing off his shoes. "To do what? The Ghillie Callum?"

This, apparently, did not translate well from the Gaelic to Mertens's Flemish ear, for the valet just looked at him blankly.

"Never mind." After a glance at the clock, Geoff sighed and began hitching the fall of his trousers back up.

Something had gone awry with Charlotte Moreau's tea, he was willing to bet. Perhaps the lady had not turned up again. Or perhaps she had . . .

Slipping the last button into place, he started toward the door. "Tell Mrs. Janssen not to trouble with dinner," he said. "We'll have something cold brought up later. I'm going upstairs to discover the source of Mrs. MacLachlan's *mood*."

After bounding up the two flights of stairs in stocking feet, Geoff pushed open the door to Monsieur Michel's gentlemen's playground and looked round the corner. To his shock, Anaïs stood in the vast, sunlit space that surrounded the boxing bag, a long, wicked rapier glinting in her hand.

Her left arm lifted elegantly behind, Anaïs stood *en garde* before the bag, which was swinging slightly on its rope. She wore nothing but a pair of snug nankeen trousers and a loose white shirt, her hair caught back in a braid tied with a white ribbon. As if she moved to a music she alone could hear, Anaïs dropped her point and lunged, driving her blade through the heart of the bag.

Indeed, it was obviously not the first time she had done so. The bag was spilling its guts through various slits and punctures, bleeding wads of cotton wool and sawdust onto the floor. Yanking out her blade, Anaïs performed a flawless double retreat, then danced back and forth across the floor, engaging with her unseen enemy, executing her steps with a deftness of footwork Geoff had rarely observed.

For some moments, he lingered there, one shoulder set to the door frame in such a way as she was not apt to see him. He wondered if she might not sense his presence, but for once the sole object of her focus was the leather bag, and she had clearly been at it for some time. She was breathing audibly yet not quite panting, the wild curls round her forehead damp with perspiration.

He knew, of course, that it was a trifle impolite to observe someone unannounced. And yet he was enjoying it too much to bring himself to step into the full light of the attic.

Back and forth she went, her slender spine in perfect alignment, attacking the bag as if bent on an elegant, methodical destruction. The rapier was a long weapon requiring patience and methodical timing. Despite her obvious temper, Anaïs appeared to possess both in abundance. He sensed an undeniable poetry in her motion, a fluidity and grace that defied the very violence of her actions.

Beneath the shirt, her round breasts swayed and shifted, clearly as unbound as her temper. The nankeen trousers molded to her hips in a way that was at once decidedly athletic and deliciously feminine.

It was also deeply, carnally erotic.

And on her next thrust, he realized something. Something even more troubling than Anaïs's barely suppressed ferocity.

He wanted her.

And he was getting tired of it.

He wanted Anaïs in his arms. Beneath him. Arching to meet him, gasping for breath.

Oh, the desire itself was nothing new; he had wanted her at first sight. But the wanting had not waned. No, quite the opposite. Living in close quarters with her these last few days had become sheer hell. Looking at her across the dinner table each evening, an exercise in physical restraint. And knowing she lay alone in bed each night just a few feet away had been torture of the worst sort.

And now this.

Why deny himself? he thought, watching her drive her sword deep into her target again. His old logic was beginning to fray. He was an honorable man for the most part, but he was not yet promised to anyone. And she—well, she was still mourning her lost lover and waiting for her prince to come, that much was plain. And whomever she turned to next—well, it wouldn't be Geoff, and that was for the best.

But she did desire him, and had invited him to her bed. She had no expectations, and was not without some experience. But even had he been unaware of that fact, the pure physicality of her movements would have told him that she was a woman in complete control of her body. And Geoff had enough confidence in his skill to know that when at last Anaïs cried out beneath him, she would have long forgotten her Tuscan Romeo—at least for a little while.

Against his thigh, he felt his cock twitch insistently. Shifting his posture, Geoff kept his eyes upon her slender form as she moved back and forth across the wood floor. Eyes flashing, her jaw set tight, at one point Anaïs bounced off the edge of the billiard table, spun about, then landed, drawing her blade mid-center across the bag in a perfectly even slash. There was an unaccountable anger in her motions, but it was a carefully contained sort of rage, for Giovanni Vittorio had taught her well.

In her next retreat, she danced backward into the edge of the billiard table, slamming hard against it as if driven back by a relentless enemy. Then she stunned him by springing up and somersaulting backward, literally rolling across the baize tabletop, rapier still in hand, and landing on her feet on the other side.

She came up panting, but perfectly steady.

He stepped from the shadow of the door, slowly clapping. "*Bravissima!*"

Her chin jerked up, her dark, expressive eyes even larger than usual. "Geoff?"

He walked slowly toward her. "Did Vittorio teach you all that?"

"Some of it." Her gaze wary, Anaïs watched him approach. "How long have you been standing there?"

"Long enough."

As he closed the distance between them, she jerked her head toward the wall. "I'm not done," she said. "Find yourself a blade."

He cocked one hip on the edge of the billiard table. "My, but you are in a mood," he murmured, his gaze running over her. "Still, I do have a soft spot for a woman with a lethal weapon."

Anaïs must have heard something in his tone. She dropped

her point, and sashayed nearer. "You do fence, do you not?" she demanded, looking him up and down.

"What do you think?"

She lifted her chin. "Any good?"

He gave a half smile and lifted one shoulder. "I rather doubt I could tumble backward and come up with my blade still in hand," he said. "But aye, I think I can give satisfaction."

She shrugged. "I think you know that move was pure showmanship. In a real fight, it would likely get your throat slit." Again, she tilted her head in the direction of the wooden rack. "So go on. Let's see what we can do."

"Haven't had enough, eh?"

"Not quite, no."

He came away from the table and strolled to the rack, snatching the first foil that caught his eye. She followed him, trading her blade for one that was blunted.

"Gracious of you, my dear," he said, nodding toward it. "A wiser man might just sit you down and make you tell him what has you in such a lather."

"Another time, perhaps." Drawing back her left arm for balance, Anaïs jerked up her chin and her blade at once. "*En garde!*"

"I think we've had this conversation before," Geoff murmured. But he brought up his point all the same.

They went at it like furies for some twenty minutes, Geoff giving her no quarter. He knew better. Anaïs was good enough she would know if he failed to fully press his advantage.

But his only advantage, really, was his height, his reach, and the fact that she was tiring while he was not. Her aggression, however, did not pale. Several times she lunged, and each time he deflected and beat her back. He feinted a flank cut, then went for her throat. She parried beautifully, then came at him with a swift riposte, catching his sleeve. On and on it went, Anaïs often on the defensive but giving up nothing.

And as they danced each other back and forth across the polished oak floor, feet scuffing and thumping, their blades clashing, Geoff realized the truth of one thing Rance had asserted. In this respect, at the very least, Anaïs was as qualified as any to be a Guardian. Not one man in a hundred would have survived her onslaught.

But he was that one in a hundred—or should have been.

For an instant, he dropped his guard and she came at him low, thrusting in the direction of his femoral artery. *"Fa' attenzione!"* she barked.

But their blades caught and clashed before the words were out of her mouth.

"Oh, I am," he replied, circling her blade then pressing her backward. "Do you realize you're speaking Italian again?"

"I beg your pardon." She smiled a little viciously and parried again. "But you understand, I see."

"Sì, signorina," he said.

Blades striking furiously, the clatter near deafening, he drove her back slowly, his moves heavy and workmanlike, but in the face of her growing fatigue, very effective. She feinted, then went for his cheek, but her timing was just less than perfect. He caught her blade and threw it off, driving her back again.

And it was in that next instant Anaïs made her mistake. She made a swift double retreat, but it carried her too near the thick boxing mat. Her heel caught on the canvas. She tumbled backward, her blade skittering and clanking across the floor. She landed on her arse, sword arm extended, hand empty.

Breathing hard, Geoff came down onto his knee between hers, his blade set across the top of her shoulder.

"*Touché*," she said between gasps.

"*Non*," he replied, tossing the rapier aside. "*Pas de touché*."

"Oh, no." Her black eyes flashed up at him with warning. "Don't you dare."

"What?"

"Don't cede me an inch," she ordered, rolling up onto her elbows. "Damn it, not one, Geoff, do you hear?"

"Oh, for Christ's sake!" Geoff fell onto his hip and elbow alongside her and dragged an arm across the sweat beading on his forehead. "I didn't *give* you anything, Anaïs. Sane and rested, you'd likely match me blow for blow."

She turned her head away from him, her breath calming as she stared into the depths of the room. "Let me catch my wind then," she finally said. "We'll start again."

He slid one hand around her opposite cheek and turned her face back into his. She had lost her hair ribbon, he realized, and her hair was spilling across the leather mat. "Anaïs, what's wrong?"

Her eyes flashed with warning. "I just feel . . . shut up in this house," she complained. "Thwarted. I need to do something physical."

It was his opening, perhaps, to make her an offer he hoped she wouldn't refuse.

He let it go, choosing instead to gaze into her eyes. The air between them crackled with sensual awareness, and yet he sensed a pain beneath it all that troubled him. He meant to seduce her, yes. But not like this. Not yet.

"Anaïs," he said again, "what happened?"

"Why must something have happened?"

She jerked as if she might rise, but he held her still, throwing one leg across hers. "My dear, we've been living cheek by jowl for days on end," he murmured, his hand still cradling her opposite cheek. "I think I know what your unleashed fury looks like."

"Oh, is that your Gift?" she muttered, her gaze dropping to his mouth. "The ability to poke that perfect, Anglo-Saxon nose of yours in someone else's business and leap to a conclusion?"

"Until this mission is finished, my dear, it's *our* business," he said, lowering his head to hers. He brushed his mouth over the little swell beneath her eye.

In response, she pushed him away. "Leave me alone."

But Geoff was not in a cooperative mood. He was frustrated—in more ways than one. "Oh, I think we're done with that strategy," he murmured.

And he was. If she wouldn't talk, then he'd tame her, this wild, fierce thing. He yearned to hold the flame to his breast, even to be burned by it. And suddenly, Anaïs's best interests, Lady Anisha's breathtaking beauty, even Lord de Vendenheim's wrath—none of it seemed to matter.

Rolling the weight of his body over her, he slid his fingers into the hair at her temple and opened his mouth over hers. This time he did not hesitate, kissing her instead in the most carnal of ways, sliding deep on his first thrust, then setting a slow, steady rhythm that made plain what he wanted of her.

As if to protest, Anaïs raised her right knee and shoved at his shoulders with the heels of her hands. Undeterred, Geoff caught her hands in his, then urged them above her head, holding them palm to palm as he continued to thrust and taste.

Trembling beneath him, she was like fire and quicksilver all at once, hot and vibrant and hard to hold. He wanted to lose himself inside her. To make her bend to him, in the way a woman gave to a man. Already his head was beginning to swim with her scent, his ballocks tightening dangerously.

Beneath him, Anaïs squirmed and made a little sound of indignation, rubbing his swollen cock through the fabric of his trousers as she thrashed again, leaving him hard enough to hammer nails.

He slanted his mouth over hers one last time, then reluctantly lifted his head. "Is that *stop*, love?" he murmured. "Seriously?"

Her eyes flashed, but already they were dark with desire. "Would you?"

"Not willingly," he managed. "But aye, if the lady wishes it."

He rose up to see that Anaïs lay beneath him like some wanton earth goddess, the throat of her shirt pulled open to the breastbone, her inky curls fired with a thousand tiny diamonds in the sinking afternoon sun. He looked at her and his heart ached with a longing he did not understand, and it brought home to him the powerful certainty that—at least in that moment—he might well do anything she asked.

She did not speak again. His heart sinking a little, Geoff shifted his weight, but the glint of satisfaction in her eye stopped him.

He cursed beneath his breath, then set his forehead to hers, his breathing still rough. "You said you wanted Mr. Right-for-Now, love," he rasped. "And that's what I'm offering. Do you want me to beg?"

"No," she whispered, her voice dark and suggestive. "I want you to ask—no pretty words, mind. Just say what you want. And then I want *you* to make *me* beg."

She was going to drive him mad.

He was sure of it. He clasped her hands tighter, and pushed them higher over her head, holding her captive beneath the weight of his body. "Anaïs, I want to fuck you," he said. "There. Plain and simple enough? I want you so badly I can't breathe. And yes, I can make you beg. I'll make your eyes roll back in your head."

"*Hmm*," she said. "Now that *is* plain. Keep talking."

His eyes searched her face—her beautiful, remarkable

face. "Sometimes I can't sleep for knowing you're in the next room," he whispered. "If I do sleep, I feel the heat of your body in my dreams. I feel the press of your breasts against my chest, and I feel your hair tangled in my—"

She cut him off with her mouth, lifting her head to kiss him as her eyes closed, feathering impossibly black lashes over her cheeks. He released her hands and took his weight onto his elbows, cradling her face between his palms as he tasted her.

"Anaïs," he murmured, skimming his lips up her cheek. "You are so beautiful."

"Don't say that," she replied, her hands sliding down his shoulders to settle at the small of his back. "Geoff, you don't have to say that."

"Aye, then, I'll show you," he rasped, just before kissed her again. And he did show her, with his tongue, and his hands, plumbing her mouth slowly and sweetly as he weighed one lush, perfect breast in his palm, stroking her nipple with the ball of his thumb.

She sighed with pleasure and he rose up, astraddle her now, and stripped off his shirt. "I'd best lock the door," he whispered.

"Yes," she said, her eyes trailing down his chest. "But Geoff, I—"

She stopped, and swallowed hard. He bent to kiss her again, threading his fingers through her glorious mane of hair. "What is it, Anaïs?"

She winced a little. "It's been a long time for me," she said. "And I'm just not that . . . skilled. Not like the women you're used to."

"Anaïs, love, a woman like you doesn't need skill." He brushed his lips over her forehead. "It's been a while for me as well. But I think I can remember how it's done."

"How long?" Anaïs looked at him earnestly.

He thought about it, and could barely recall. It was as if she had already displaced all others from his mind. "A few months, I suppose," he said. "I've never been the sort of man, Anaïs, to keep a string of mistresses."

"There is no one else, then?" she said with a muted smile.

He shook his head. "No," he murmured. "And when I look at you, Anaïs, I wonder if there ever was."

"Liar," she said. But she smiled all the same; a low, sensuous smile that suggested the possibility of a long night to come. Then she held up her arms. "Undress me, you beautiful liar."

He bent his head, and did as she asked, drawing off her clothing slowly and purposefully, kissing away her faint blushes as he did so. In gradual increments her perfect, pearlescent skin, was laid bare, Geoff pausing to touch and stroke at will. Her breasts were more beautiful than he remembered, not that he'd ever seen them quite this exposed. Her legs, not surprisingly, were long, and more muscular than thin, which oddly pleased him.

Her hair had fallen completely free from its braid. It ran like silk through his hands, and made him think of the night he'd held her on the *Jolie Marie*—of all he had burned for. Of all he had feared. That this woman was different.

That this one might cost him dear.

The sun was fading now, and Geoff realized dimly he had lost track of time. He shucked off his own drawers last, and watched in male satisfaction as her eyes widened with disconcertion, then warmed again.

He turned and came down on top of her.

Anaïs drew up her knees, cradling him intimately as she tilted back her head. "I want you," she whispered. "Geoff. I ache for you inside."

The simplicity of it touched him to the heart. He kissed her on the mouth again—he thought he could die a happy man from just kissing her—then slowly trailed his lips down the long, supple column of her throat. He kissed her along her collarbone, then set his mouth to her nipple, suckling gently.

Anaïs felt Geoff's mouth close around her breast, and cried out at the intimacy. Spearing her fingers into his hair, she tilted her head back and gasped at the sensation. She could feel that exquisite longing go twisting through her, pulling and aching, all the way to her womb.

Lightly circling with his tongue, he stroked and teased her nipple to a perfect, hard peak, then turned his attention to the other breast.

"*Geoff.*" She tilted her pelvis invitingly. "Geoff, please."

"I'm supposed to make you beg, love, remember?" he whispered, spreading a row of little kisses down her belly.

"That . . ." She paused to gasp. "That wasn't begging?"

"Not even close." He stroked the tip of his tongue round her belly button, then trailed lower.

"Geoff?" she whispered uncertainly.

He set his lips to her inner thigh. "Shall I?" he murmured.

Dimly, she understood what he asked. She was not naïve—not entirely. She set her hands flat against the canvas mat and clung to it.

"I don't know," she finally whispered.

He kissed the other thigh. "Ah," he said. "Then we must find out."

As gently as one might a flower, he opened her with his thumb and forefinger, then let his tongue slide into her warmth, drowning her in desire. The ache that had curled inside her began to well up at once. He touched her lightly, delicately, teasing her in a way so intimate she would have died of embarrassment if it hadn't felt so exquisitely wonderful.

Instead it felt as though she was more apt to die of pleasure.

"Anaïs, so lovely," he murmured, his lips soft against her most intimate place. "Let me show you."

This time he stroked his tongue deep, causing her to shudder. She made a sound of sorts, a soft moan deep in her throat, and any hope she might have had of resisting his charms melted away. Anaïs wanted to lose herself to this thing—this magical, aching touch that seemed designed to break her entirely to his will.

Over and over he stroked, teasing with his tongue until she shook, and sliding first one finger, and then another, into her warmth. She was wet and aching; her womanly passage pulling almost traitorously on his fingers, begging him for more.

And then something impossible edged near.

Something new, and unexpected.

Her breath came fast and short, her hands dug into the canvas as she writhed. It was as if she lost consciousness; as if her mind became one with her body, or went to another place altogether. The *little death*, the French called it—and Anaïs was beginning to fear she knew why.

When the pleasure struck full force, it came at her like a warm ocean, rippling through her body and drowning her in bliss. Anaïs gave in to it; lost herself in it, allowing herself to be carried far, far away on a swell of exquisite, erotic delight.

In gradual increments, she returned to the living, becoming slowly aware of the world around her. She could feel Geoff's head lying comfortably on the swell of her belly, and the faint rasp of his beard on her skin. Could hear the last of the day's birdsong beyond the windows. She lifted her head to see that the sky was now striped with purple and azure, the last burst of life in a dying day.

And in that glorious afternoon light, Anaïs could not miss the unmistakable mark inked into Geoff's flesh, blue-black against the creamy swell of his left buttock. The mark of the golden cross—the *Fraternitas Aureae Crucis*—overlaid upon a thistle to indicate his descent from the order's most powerful line. The Scottish line.

It surprised her, and brought home to her once again precisely who he was. Why they were there. And how very short-lived this pleasure would be.

On a groan, she let her head fall back onto the mat. "All right," she said, setting the back of her hand to her brow. "I haven't the strength even to beg now. Do with me as you will."

He chuckled without lifting his head, a low rumble in his chest that vibrated through her as if they were one.

As if they were one.

Oh, she could see how it began, the losing of one's self. She was reminded again how the hunger might sweep you away from your better, more sensible nature. And she didn't care. For once she didn't want to think about anyone but herself; about the pleasure this beautiful man could give her. She caught his hand and drew him up, widening her legs to take him.

Closing his eyes, he knelt there, one hand easing down his erection, which was thick, heavily veined, and a little disconcerting in its length.

Yes, he was exquisitely, magnificently made, this man she did not deserve yet longed for. Geoff's chest was wide and smooth, his muscles hard and finely delineated, as if carved from creamy marble. She set her hands to his chest and felt him shiver, felt the life and warmth that burned there.

His mouth turning up into a soft smile, Geoff leaned over her, his curtain of shimmering bronze hair falling forward, shadowing the hard turn of his cheekbones as he moved, and began to push himself inside her.

He made a sound, a little grunt of exertion—or more likely restraint. In answer, Anaïs set her hands at the turn of his waist and pulled him deeper, drawing up her knees as she did so. Bracing his hands on the mat above her shoulders, Geoff brought his weight forward, pushing and filling her so deeply she began to fear they mightn't fit at all.

They fit.

Oh, they fit. Perfectly.

Eagerly she tipped her hips to allow him to deepen the intimacy. He groaned again, the tendons of his neck cording like ropes drawn taut. He drew out, and pushed again, deeper still, pulling at her flesh and making that deep, sweet trembling start all over again.

"Ohh," she whispered. "That is . . . *delicious.*"

And it was. If his mouth had been exquisitely sinful, this was beyond it. Beyond it, and yet entirely natural—like breathing. Like something meant to be. Something perfect.

Thrusting again, Geoff stiffened his arms, which were layered with muscle and roped with tendons. "Anaïs," he whispered. "This is *us*, love. We are perfect together."

But what they were together, it soon seemed, was more like kerosene on a banked fire.

He set a rhythm, thrusting deeply and slowly, pushing into her with relentless precision. Anaïs rose to him instinctively, felt her body come to his in a symphony of pleasure, as if they had done this a thousand times. And yet it was wholly new. She began to fear it always would feel this way; forever old, forever new, and that a part of her might feel stripped away when he stopped.

But that was a fear for another moment. Not this one, not this timeless stretch of perfect joy. Anaïs stroked her hands down his back, taking in the pleasure of the hard, curving breadth of his shoulders, then down the sculpted muscles of his back, all the way down to the round swells of his backside that tightened and shivered as he thrust.

His very essence surrounded her in a sensual cloud; male musk, a hint of tobacco, and the rich, warm scent of his cologne. Anaïs tipped back her head and breathed him deep. Drew him deep. Curled one leg around his waist and pulled herself to him, as if they might melt into each other.

He looked at her with an age-old knowing, his face shadowed with afternoon beard. Stroking one long-fingered hand down her calf, he shocked her by lifting her legs in turn, hooking them over his shoulders, and pulling her hips hard against his pelvis, opening her fully to his thrusts.

At once something changed and shifted. Geoff groaned deep and choked out her name. His ice-blue eyes were melting now. Anaïs felt herself quicken and rise to him. She matched his pace, taking him deeper and deeper, right inside to the very heart of her, his gaze never leaving hers as he pushed inside her, spiraling them higher and higher.

Those eyes. Those amazing, ageless eyes; so hot and so cold. She was going to drown in them this time. The warm blue of his ocean was drawing her relentlessly back into the waves like a riptide. Anaïs felt herself torn from whatever earthly mooring had held her fast. After that there was nothing but the brilliant light, a perfect crest, and the whisper of her name on his lips.

They came together as one, and it was as if her soul flew to his. The rich, churning depths washed over her, and Anaïs knew that this time she was lost.

CHAPTER 13

Strategy without tactics is the slowest route to victory.
Tactics without strategy is the noise before defeat.
Sun Tzu, *The Art of War*

*A*fterward, they lay together in the dying light curled round each other like cats. Geoff had settled behind her, her hips pulled to his pelvis, his left arm banded tight about her waist, spooning her body to his. He bent his head to the turn of her neck and set his lips to her pulse point, lingering so long she began to wonder if he'd fallen asleep.

"Geoff?" she muttered drowsily.

He stirred and nibbled lightly at her earlobe. "*Umm*," he said, the sound vibrating against her skin. Then he tucked his head against hers and fell silent again. For an instant, she felt herself slip from sensually sated into something perilously like a deep sleep, then jerked herself awake.

"Time for dinner?" she managed, stretching one arm.

His kissed a trail down her throat. "I canceled it," he said, "before I came up."

"Oh?" she said, crooking her head to look back at him. "That sure of yourself, were you?"

"Lord, no." She felt him lift one of her curls and begin to twine it round his finger. "No, Anaïs, I'm never sure of anything with you, a circumstance which I find—and I oughtn't admit this—utterly refreshing. And a little maddening."

"Maddening?" Her curiosity piqued, she squirmed around in his arms, vaguely embarrassed by her naked state.

As if he instinctively understood, he reached behind him, snagged his shirt, and threw it over her. "Here," he said. "*This* was the greatest madness, I daresay. We have two perfectly good beds downstairs, and I'm apt to have given you a chill."

But she was still mulling over his previous words. "Geoff," she murmured, her gaze searching his face, "can you not . . . see us? Could you not have predicted this, I mean, if you wished?"

He crooked his head to look down at her. "I told you, it's not like that for me."

"What do you mean?"

He pulled her closer, and tucked his chin atop her head. "A Vates can't see his own future," he said quietly, "and rarely that of another of his kind. I often feel things when I'm near other people—emotions, especially strong ones—if I open myself to it. Things like fear or malice or just plain dishonesty."

"Yes," she murmured, "I've noticed that about you."

"But I don't just *see* things involuntarily," he went on. "Not unless I'm ill, perhaps, or in some sort of weakened state. When I was a child, yes, odd visions often went skittering through my head. A touch or even strong eye contact could set me off. I was like Ruthveyn in that way."

"Until you learned to keep your curtain drawn," she murmured.

"Yes, and now it's the other way round," he said. "Almost always now, I have to *try* to see—which I rarely choose to do."

"And intimacy does not . . . open any sort of connection?" she asked.

For a moment, he considered it. "It could, perhaps, but never has," he replied. "And it depends on what one means by intimacy, I daresay. I've bedded my share of women, aye, but I can't say as I was ever intimate with any."

"So something like this . . . is just sex for you," she remarked, cutting her glance away.

"No." He seized her chin almost roughly, and turned her face back to his. "*No.* I'm speaking of other people, Anaïs. Besides, it could never be like that for you and me."

"How do you know?"

"I *know*," he said again. "Besides, you are of the Vateis, Anaïs. Like Giovanni Vittorio, you are descended from the great Celtic prophets, or perhaps even the people from whom *they* descended. And the Vateis cannot read one another. Not deeply. Not like you mean. That's just how it always is—one of God's small mercies, Ruthveyn says."

Anaïs just shook her head. "But how could Celts even get to Tuscany?"

Geoff shrugged one shoulder. "Have you read much Tacitus?"

She cast him a withering look. "Vittorio made me," she said. "I did my best."

He smiled and stroked his hand down her hair. "I'm sure he taught you, too, that there was a strong Celtic influence in the provinces north of Rome," he said. "Some believe Tacitus himself to have been a Celt."

"Yes, I remember."

"But more importantly, his writings suggest that Celtic priests—all of them, especially the Vateis and the Druids—fascinated the Romans. They were sometimes captured and taken to Rome, and eventually Romans even intermarried with the Celtic tribes."

She shook her head, her hair scrubbing on the mat. "I daresay all that's true, Geoff, but I am not like you," she said quietly. "I am not like Ruthveyn."

"Almost no one is," he replied. "And thank God for it. But the Gift is an amorphous thing, Anaïs. Surely you know that. Some people dream of what is to come. Some have only keen intuition. Some divine from tea leaves in the bottom of a cup—and yes, almost all of those are charlatans. But a few—a very unlucky few like Ruthveyn—can hold your hand, look into your eyes, and tell you the means of your death."

In his arms, Anaïs shivered. "I don't fall into any of those categories."

"No, you have something a little more subtle," he said. "Vittorio saw it, and honed it, because he knew how."

She dropped her chin, and did not answer.

"You have a sixth sense, Anaïs," he said, brushing his lips over her hair. "Like Maria Vittorio said, you're like a cat in the dark. And perhaps you could not stab someone through the heart blindfolded, like Vittorio, but you can feel the human psyche, I think—unless, of course, you're completed absorbed by something. Fencing, for example. Or lovemaking." He paused to cup his hand round her face. "And then there's the tarot."

She jerked her chin up. "What about it?"

He brushed his lips across her cheek. "Your great-grandmother was a practitioner, was she not?" he murmured a little too casually. "And honestly, I saw a tarot card propped against the lamp on your night table the other day, so I just assumed . . . well, I assumed that's what you kept in that old black box you cart around."

Anaïs didn't respond. She had no wish to think about her nonna's old predictions; one of them in particular. Not just now, when she was aglow from Geoff's lovemaking. Instead she wiggled firmly onto her side, and buried her face against his chest. He smelled of sweat and man and something that felt—at least for now—like comfort.

For a long moment, she simply lay there, covered by his shirt, secure in his arms, and thought about the one thing—well, the second thing—she tried never to think about.

Always, always Anaïs had been willing to do what was asked of her. She was willing to work hard to be a Guardian if that was what her great-grandmother wished. She was a dutiful daughter to her parents—well, most of the time—and a loyal sister to Nate and Armand and the children. She had been a good cousin, too, sitting by Giovanni's bed spooning him broth and clinging to his hand until the cancer inside him had stripped the soul from his body and set it free.

She had even been a good girl—at least in the end—when Giovanni and Maria had sat her down and explained to her, through their tears and hers, that she had to let her dreams of Raphaele go. That he had a wife and a child, and that while he might be an egregious liar and a scoundrel, he had a family who depended upon him for their living.

So yes, she had been a good girl. She had set away her silly dreams.

But what she did not want to be—what she could not *bear* to be—was a damned fortune-teller.

And she was mightily sick and tired of being a good girl, too, now that she thought on it. She would far rather be a bad girl—far rather let the wicked Lord Bessett strip her naked and do the wickedest of his wicked things to her. For after one hour in his arms, being a good girl had truly lost its allure.

But some things, she knew, would never change. Some things, Nonna Sofia always said, were fated. Raphaele had not been her *Re di Dischi*. Certainly Geoff, the elegant and quintessential Englishman, was not. But her Tuscan prince was coming, sooner or later. And Anaïs was destined to be—well, if not forever a good girl, then at least forever honest.

She sighed, and shuddered a little in Geoff's arms, feeling oddly as if she might cry.

"I read for her today," she whispered into the soft hair that dusted his chest.

She felt rather than saw him look down at her. "Who?" he murmured. "Charlotte?"

"Yes."

Geoff sounded fully awake now. "So you can read?"

She shrugged both shoulders. "Anyone can, can't they?" she said. "It does not require the Gift."

He gave a bark of laughter. "I don't believe that for a minute."

Anaïs sighed. "You're likely right," she muttered. "Indeed, I did not mean to do it today. It was a lark. A *stupid* lark. I meant simply to tell her what I wished her to hear. But the cards, Geoff, they—"

She stopped, and shook her head.

"What?" he gently pressed.

She lifted her head from his chest and looked up at him, feeling more than a little lost. "The cards—they fell true from my hand. And I knew it. They took on a life of their own, Geoff. Yes, I read them. I had no choice."

"You mean you read from *here*—" he murmured, settling a hand over her heart.

She slowly nodded. "And I knew what they meant—not just from years of watching Nonna, but . . . in some other way, I knew. So I told her. And I . . . I frightened her. Good God, I frightened myself."

"Anaïs," he murmured, pressing his lips to her head. "Poor girl."

"Poor Charlotte!" Anaïs corrected. "At first I merely felt dirty—as if I were using her. Lying to her. But afterward, I was furious. With myself, I mean. The tarot is dangerous, not something to be trifled with. I knew that."

"The tarot is dangerous for someone who has the Gift of reading it," said Geoff softly. "For one who does not, love, it's just a pack of cards."

Anaïs set her cheek to his chest. "I suppose, Geoff, I have been simply deluding myself," she muttered. "But I don't want the Gift of *anything*."

"I know that," he whispered. "Oh, trust me, Anaïs, I know too well."

But before she could speak, Geoff gave her a swift, hard hug, then urged her away. Rolling onto his back, he lifted Anaïs over him until she was balanced on top of him, her knees set to either side of his ribs. Until they looked at each other face to face.

Gently, he picked up his shirt and tucked her into it, then lifted his hand to push a stray curl behind her ear. "So that's what all this was about," he murmured, his gaze drifting over her face. "This fury. This hell you unleashed on Monsieur Michel's poor boxing bag."

She rolled her shoulders uncomfortably. "Geoff, I just want this to be over," she whispered. "I don't want to go on lying to Charlotte about who and what I am. And I don't want to have to think about what I am."

"I want it to be over, too," said Geoff calmly. "But I daresay you probably told Charlotte more truth today than she has heard from anyone since her husband died. None of this is your fault."

Anaïs cast her eyes up at the skylight, the scant clouds above now lit with violet. "I saw it, Geoff," she whispered. "The evil you spoke of. The blackness. Charlotte is in trouble—more trouble than Giselle, perhaps."

"What sort of trouble, do you reckon?"

She bit her lip, and shook her head. "I wish I knew," she

said. "But there was something there, just beyond my grasp. Something the cards wanted to show me. I have the most awful sense we are missing a part of the puzzle here. I do know we cannot leave her here. We must get the both of them away, and soon."

Geoff's hands still sat at her waist, his gaze intent as he looked up at her. "All right," he said calmly. "We need to end this. But first we need as much information as we can get, as fast as we can get it."

"Of what sort? And how?"

Geoff's brow furrowed. "Tomorrow night we'll dine with them," he said. "Lezennes will keep the child away from us, I am sure. One of us must distract him. I need an object—something belonging to Giselle, perhaps, that her mother has given her. Something that might be imprinted with *both* their emotions. That, and Charlotte's handkerchief together—yes, perhaps that will help us time our approach."

"Or our escape," Anaïs grimly added. "And I'll find you something that belongs to Giselle, trust me. By the way, Lezennes has already proposed marriage to Charlotte, and he's pressing her hard. Perhaps I can give her a little breathing room."

"And how would you do that?"

Anaïs let her gaze drift over his beautiful face. "I shall bat my eyes outrageously at Lezennes," she said. "Perhaps he will think to use me to make Charlotte jealous."

"Too dangerous," he said. "Don't even think of it."

"But you will be with me," she said. "And—"

There was a sharp sound somewhere within the house, like the *clack!* of a broom handle striking a wall. Geoff's eyes widened. "Good Lord," he said. "The real world returns. And I forgot to lock the door."

Anaïs smiled. "I shall take that as a compliment," she murmured.

"Aye, you should," he said, his gaze heating as it drifted over her. His warm, long-fingered hands slid up her ribs to cup her breasts. "Ah, Anaïs, is there anything about you that is not utter perfection?"

"Oh, I think you know the answer to that," she said, hitching one leg over him to sit down on the mat at his side.

He shot her a chiding glance, then rolled gracefully to his feet like a great cat bestirred, and strode across the room to lock the door. "We had better get dressed," he said. "I'll have something cold sent up for dinner."

Anaïs did not answer, but watched him as he strolled to the high, dormered window, then leaned on his elbows as if watching the street below. Ever the gentleman, he was giving her a moment of privacy in which to dress, she realized.

After sparing his naked glory one ⸺st glance, Anaïs dressed in haste, shinnying out of his shirt and into her own, then hitching up the buttons on her trousers. Not once, oddly, had he commented on her mark. Perhaps he had not seen it. She picked up his shirt, carried it across the room, and held it out for him.

Geoff turned from the window and flashed one of his quizzical, sideways smiles. "Where did you get those trousers, anyway?" he said, thrusting his arms into the shirt-sleeves, then shrugging it on.

Anaïs glanced down a little sheepishly. "They used to be Armand's," she said. "I brought them along, just in case I needed some hing to climb in."

Or s mething to seduce you with, she thought.

But Geoff had crossed to the mat, his long, muscled legs bare beneath his shirttail. And she wanted, suddenly, to follow him. To lift the fine can bric of his shirt and set her lips to that mark high on his hip; the mark that had propelled him toward his destiny, perhaps in part trapped him into a life he wanted no more than she.

Good God. Was that how she felt?

Geoff obviously would have surrendered his Gift in a heartbeat, were he to be given the chance. But perhaps it went deeper than that for both of them. Did she resent having lost her chance at a so-called normal life, and having to set forth on this strange path? Did she resent what Nonna had called her destiny? Or had she simply grown tired of waiting for her prince to come?

Surely, at her age, she did not long to become ordinary? To become just another of society's butterflies, flitting from garden party to tea to soiree, all in the search for a husband? But if not, why this heavy feeling in her heart? This sense of having lost . . . *something*.

Anaïs did not know. And there was really no point in thinking about it. Life was what it was, hope and heartache included.

Geoff dressed in silence, and together they strolled back downstairs.

Inside the privacy of her bedroom, he drew her into his arms. "I don't know how much longer we'll have together, Anaïs," he said, gazing into her eyes. "Not long, I think. And I will miss you."

"And I you," she whispered.

But it was not so simple as that. Not anymore.

He slipped a finger under her chin, and lifted her gaze back to his. "We'll be back in London soon, God willing," he said. "Back in the real world, with all its expectations."

"Yes," she said simply.

Some nameless emotion sketched over his face; then, as if to obscure it, he bent his head and kissed her again, slowly and sensually, plumbing the depths of her mouth with his tongue. They came apart a little breathlessly.

"Am I still Mr. Right-for-Now, Anaïs?" he asked, his

voice warm and raspy against her ear. "And if I am, will you spend this one night in my bed?"

"Yes," she said.

Yes, she thought, *and the next and the next and the one after that, too, if you would just invite me . . .*

But that was a foolish notion.

He had a life in London to return to.

And fate had other plans for her.

CHAPTER 14

The quality of decision is like the well-timed swoop of a falcon which enables it to strike and destroy its victim.
Sun Tzu, *The Art of War*

$\mathcal{A}$naïs woke the next morning snuggled in Geoff's embrace. The sun was already limning the draperies with a warm, golden glow. After easing herself gingerly from beneath his arm, she rose and went through to the bathroom. Bracing her hands wide on the washing table, she stared at herself in the mirror.

Her plain, rather long face stared back at her beneath a tumbled mess of unruly hair.

But I'm not precisely ordinary, Anaïs consoled herself.

No, she was plain in an extraordinary way—or, as her mother had always diplomatically put it, she was *handsome*. Sometimes, in the right gown and the right light, even *striking*.

Then she let her hands fall, and sighed. The hours spent in Geoff's embrace had made her feel beautiful—sensual and deeply desirable—and that would have to be enough. She was not the sort of woman who ordinarily gave her looks a second thought, and it was time she readopted that fine attitude.

After washing her face and hands in cold water from the tap, Anaïs went through to her room and flung open the doors to her wardrobe. Absent Geoff's sheltering arms, she was cold. Lifting the robe from its peg on the door, she noticed the dress she'd worn the previous day. The dress she'd stripped off in a temper, and flung across the bed for poor Claire to deal with.

And dealt with it she had, even going so far as to press it, and stitch up the little bit of lace Anaïs had ripped from the cuff in her furor.

Suddenly, Anaïs recalled Sutherland's letter she'd shoved deep into her pocket. Mildly alarmed, she rummaged through the folds until she found the pocket slit.

It was still there, precisely where she'd left it.

She breathed a sigh of relief.

Still, it had been careless of her. Of course, she trusted the servants, and Sutherland had worded his letter carefully; initials rather than names, and otherwise vague references. Nonetheless, a dress pocket was hardly the place for such a thing.

Strolling slowly back to Geoff's room, she let her eyes run over the Preost's words again, taking comfort in his assurances. If they could get Charlotte and her child safely to England, all would be well.

On the threshold, she looked up to see that Geoff still slept as she'd left him; turned almost flat on his belly, one big arm still outstretched over the hollow she'd left in his mattress, his wide shoulders rounded with muscle and glowing warmly in the early sun.

A shock of his gold-bronze hair hung over one eye and his face was heavily shadowed with black bristle, offsetting the aristocratic perfection of that harsh, aquiline nose, and lending him an almost piratical air. The bed linen had been shoved away, only to catch on the swell of one perfect, well-muscled buttock, drawing the eye to his black tattoo just above.

At the sight, something in her chest gave a traitorous little flip-flop—her heart, she feared—and she started toward the bed, intent on rousing him. Then she recalled the letter in her hand.

Geoff's traveling desk, where he kept all their pertinent papers, sat open on a little table by the window. Hastily crossing the room, she tucked the Preost's missive under a stack of what looked like ordinary personal letters, wedging it inside the fat fold that she recognized as Monsieur DuPont's dossiers.

As she turned, however, a stack of books on the other side of the table caught her eye. After cutting a surreptitious look at bed, she shuffled through them. Geoff, it seemed, was a bit of a Renaissance man. His reading included poetry by Coleridge and Burns, a well-worn copy of Scott's *Castle Dangerous*, an engineering manual—something to do with valves and steam—and below that a book of Grecian architectural drawings.

But it was the topmost book which most interested her— *L'Art de la Guerre* by the famous general and philosopher Sun Tzu. Translated into French by a Jesuit priest, the ancient manual of military strategy—the art of war—had been a favorite of Giovanni's, and it had come to be a favorite as hers as well.

Anaïs smiled a little at the memory and moved as if to leave. Then, as a woman in love will often do—in the vain hope that a personal possession will reveal some hidden, intimate insight—she took a second, more curious, look at the traveling desk.

It was a big, old-fashioned box made of mahogany bound in brass with one of the inkwells empty, the other filled to the brim. The leather writing surface was folded shut, and in the main compartment, Charlotte's handkerchief lay neatly on the right of his correspondence, beneath Giselle's yellow hair ribbon.

Carefully, Anaïs tilted the lid to see the brass plate on the top bore Geoff's monogram, and beneath it the full mark of the *Fraternitas*. There was no coat of arms, no heraldry whatever. Obviously, this was something he had owned a long while; since before coming into his title, almost certainly.

She tilted the lid back again, and this time her eye caught on the top letter, which was penned in a tidy—and obviously feminine—script. Tilting her head, Anaïs saw that it was from his mother.

Lady Madeleine MacLachlan was a renowned beauty who had surprised society by giving up the title Countess of Bessett upon her remarriage to a commoner, though by custom if not law, some widows did not, preferring instead to cling to their dead husband's higher rank. Anaïs thought rather more of the lady for it, and wondered if mother and son were much alike.

Unable to contain her curiosity, Anaïs glanced more closely at the lady's letter.

As with eavesdropping, reading another's mail usually comes to no good. The first paragraph, however, was innocuous enough; warmest wishes for Geoffrey's good health, and an inquiry about the weather. The second paragraph, however, was not so benign:

> *As you asked, I had Lady A. to tea again. Oh, Geoff, the more I see of her, the more I am persuaded you have set your sights wisely. I only hope you have chosen for love, and not just duty, as you are wont to do . . .*

Anaïs dropped the letter as if it had burst into flames. For an instant, she could not get her breath; it was as if all the sweetness of the previous moment was sucked from the room, taking the air with it.

She turned to look at Geoff, still sleeping. Then somehow she commanded her shaking legs to move, and pushed blindly through to the bathroom. Locking the door behind, Anaïs sat down on the lip of the tub and clapped a hand over her mouth, the horror of it roiling up inside her.

I only hope you have chosen for love.

The words taunted her. She ran through them all again, struggling to ascribe to them something save the most obvious meaning.

There was none.

There was none, because it was happening again.

No. No, it was not.

This was not the same thing. He was not married. He had simply *chosen wisely.*

But what did it matter? She had already fallen in love with him, however much she might try to deny it. And the result was going to be the same. A broken heart. A life tinged with disappointment, if not full-blown shame. And she had brought it on herself, too—and this time, she could not even console herself that she had been naïve, that she had been seduced by someone experienced and cynical.

No, she had sauntered right up and asked for it.

Anaïs wasn't sure precisely how long she sat there, one hand over her mouth, the other trembling in time with her knocking knees. But eventually, the numbness receded and full awareness flooded back, painful as the warmth of a raging fire after a long chill. It brought with it a heavy, swamping grief that filled her chest and weighed down her extremities.

If what she'd done to Charlotte had left her hands dirty, this left her tainted from the inside out. It was almost— *almost*—the unspeakable all over again.

Hands shaking, she got up, corked the tub, and turned on the tap. It sputtered and spewed, then began sluggishly to run as Anaïs stripped off her thin nightclothes and stepped in. Ice-cold water washed round her toes, and only then did she remember there was no boiler, no way to draw hot water.

Dear Lord, she could not even run a bath properly.

It felt like the last straw. Plopping down in the cold water, Anaïs pulled her legs tight to her chest and let her forehead fall to her knees on a stifled sob.

Just then she became aware of the presence beyond the door. Forcing herself to attend, she picked up her head and turned her ear but heard nothing for a long moment. She knew, though, that he was there.

"Anaïs?" Finally Geoff's voice came, barely audible over the loudly tinkling water.

She turned off the tap—a frightful, wrenching sound that had likely awakened him—and willed her voice not to shake. "Yes?"

"What are you doing?"

It seemed an oddly personal question. "Taking a bath." The words echoed hollow as her heart in the cold, tiled room.

He paused for a long moment. "And you know there's no hot water on tap, right?"

Anaïs closed her eyes, and let her head fall forward again. "Yes, thanks," she said, staring down at the shimmering water. "I'm fine."

Another few heartbeats passed, then, "All right, then," he said softly. "I miss you."

She listened as his footsteps trod away from the door; could even envision him in all his naked, long-legged glory as he moved toward the bed. He sat down on the edge of the mattress, legs spread wide, elbows propping on his knees as he let his head hang.

She knew that was precisely what he was doing; she could feel it. She could feel *him*, though not as clearly as she felt some people. It was like that for her sometimes, and she didn't know why, but she could all but see Geoff's long hair falling forward as he bent. See his fingers laced pensively together.

So if he was betrothed—or all but betrothed—to another woman, why the hell couldn't she sense *that*?

Perhaps because he was a Vates? Or perhaps because he wasn't betrothed?

Perhaps he had not even lied to her. Not with words, at any rate.

Yes, he had said. *I mean to do my duty to the title.*

He had as good as said he meant to marry. And she had not been surprised. Noblemen were expected to provide an heir. All that they stood for—indeed, much of what England stood for—was predicated upon that assumption.

He had said, too, that he was not the one for her.

And she knew that. She knew it, for her great-grandmother's *tarocchi* had told her long ago, and never had it been wrong—vague and mystical, perhaps, but always unerring. But that thought merely compelled her to choke back another sob. All of this—her belief in the tarot, her infatuation with Geoff, the nagging loneliness that had begun to plague her these last few years—all of it welled up and left her wretched.

And it was only then that Anaïs realized she had allowed herself to hope. Oh, only a little, for she had learned the necessity of restraint in a hard school. The importance of holding back a little of one's self. The imperative of never quite trusting.

But had Geoff lied to her?

I am persuaded you have set your sights wisely.

So he had set his sights. He had set his sights, and shared those hopes with his mother. Anaïs needed to get over it.

Despite the nausea swirling in her gut, and the fact that she was still shaking inside, she told herself Geoff was not so much a liar as an opportunist.

And why not? What had she offered him? *Said* to him?

That she was waiting for someone. That she was only looking for something temporary.

She drew a deep breath, stabbed her fingers into her hair, and tried to think rationally. Was that so very different from what he had said?

Well, yes. But only if he was betrothed—not that she'd troubled herself to ask that question before throwing herself at him in her bedchamber that afternoon.

So she had fallen in love again, this time far worse than the last. This time everything had gone against her instincts—Geoff was not right for her, he was too implacable and autocratic, too English, too overtly *male*—he was not, in short, The One.

And she had fallen in love with him anyway. Given herself to him anyway.

Given herself to a man intended, at least eventually, for another woman.

And he had given her just what she'd asked for, and not one thing more. There was no point in being angry with Geoff.

With a barely suppressed violence, Anaïs turned the tap back on, seized the sponge, and began to scrub. She scrubbed as if she might never be clean again; anything—anything—to remove the muck of stupidity that clung to her.

And when she was done—when she'd rubbed herself red and nearly raw—she hurled the sponge across the bathroom. She glared at it, wishing it and wishing herself straight to the devil, then she set her head to her knees again. And this time she sobbed in earnest.

She sobbed for that piece of her heart forever lost to Geoff, and because she was twenty-two years old and the loneliness was harder to endure with each passing year. Because her prince had not come, and the prince she had found had already set his sights wisely. She sobbed for all these things, large and small, but oh, so very silently, for Anaïs had long been the master of muted tears.

Geoff returned to his bed and sat for a while, elbows on his knees as he awaited Anaïs's return. He could sense a strong emotion around him now, something very different from desire. He hoped it was not regret. Even loathing, in his opinion, was better than that.

Perhaps he was mistaken altogether. He was not especially capable where Anaïs's emotions were concerned. Closing his eyes, he drew in what remained of their commingled scents, remembering the night. The whispered sighs. The laughter. The exquisite intimacy. He let his mind run over every moment until at last he heard her bathwater chasing down the drain.

But still she did not return. And when the faint *snick* of the unfastened lock sounded, and the door did not swing open, he knew that she did not mean to.

Something in his chest twisted.

He had assumed . . .

Ah, but that was unwise, wasn't it? He drew a hand down his face, pensively scrubbing his hand round a day's worth of beard, then fell back into the softness of the bed. Now that he thought on it in the clear light of day—now that his body was sated and his mind more rational—Geoff had to admit that nothing had really changed between them. But he had pleased her; on that score, he was well satisfied.

Three times they had made love; the first a little awkward and tentative as they learned each other's most intimate desires, the second slow and exquisite. He had planted his hands above her shoulders, thrusting and teasing and wooing her with pleasure, then tumbled her atop him to draw her down and down; all the way down into his heart, he feared.

He had watched in exultation as Anaïs had thrown back her head and impaled herself on his shaft with a sigh, her long hair tickling his thighs, her presence filling the shadows of a room that had seemed, mere hours earlier, entirely soulless.

But the third time, in the wee hours of the morning when he had turned her on her back and wordlessly mounted her, Anaïs had risen to him like the moon and the stars rising into the night sky. Exquisitely. Unfailingly. As if it were the most natural thing in the universe. As if they knew each other now in the most intimate and perfect and permanent of ways.

But few things were perfect, and fewer still permanent.

Turning his face into the disheveled bedcovers, Geoff stretched his arm across her pillow and let himself imagine for a moment that she still lay beside him; that her long legs were still entwined with his, her wild black tresses still spread across the linen like so much spun silk. He let himself breathe her in. Anaïs always smelled of something sharp and sweet—like some odd combination of rosewater and anise. Like her very nature.

But in this moment, all that was just a memory. And not likely to become anything more, if her disappearance into the bathroom was any sign. Last night, he had been what she called her right-for-now lover, a phrase he was quickly coming to hate. Nonetheless, those memories of her warmth and her laugh and her scent might have to sustain him for a while.

He shut away the sudden, faintly irrational swell of frustration. There was the day to be got on with, and important work to be done. Whatever was to be settled between Anaïs and him—and it *would* be settled—had to wait. But the lady, he feared, might have to give up her dream lover and settle for something different.

No, he was not at all sure he was going to allow her to walk away from him as blithely as she might hope.

Fate might not permit it, either.

There could always be grave and unforeseen conse- quences of a long, passionate night of lovemaking. *That* was one thing they had not discussed amidst all their breathless sighs and laughter, despite his reputation for being unerr- ingly cautious. It was an oversight Geoff was loath to exam- ine too closely just now.

No, for now, he had pressing business to attend, all of it centered on the dark events unfolding across the street. But before he could turn his attention to Lezennes, there were a couple of urgent letters that wanted writing, the first of which would be to his mother, for in Geoff's experience, the sooner hard things were said—or *un*said—the sooner they were halfway behind a man.

In one motion, Geoff sat upright, and came off the bed. He went at once to the bellpull, and rang for hot water. Anaïs might steel herself to a cold bath, but he had a day's worth of bristle to scrape off. And just now it felt as if the chill settling over his heart would be enough to do him for a long time to come.

Anaïs dawdled as long as she dared before going down to breakfast. Upon her arrival in the sunlit dining room, all was civility and silence, save for the rhythmic *tick-tock* of the ormolu mantel clock, which seemed unusually loud today.

As she'd expected, Geoff was there before her, looking resplendently severe in his charcoal morning coat and an impossibly high, white collar. His face freshly shaven, his expression inscrutable, he was reading a letter and sipping at a cup of the thick, black coffee he favored.

For an instant, she hesitated on the threshold. It appeared he had already dined, for his plate had been swept away.

"Good morning, Geoffrey," she murmured as Petit drew out her chair.

His pale, wolflike eyes darkening, he flicked a cool glance up at her, then laid aside his letter and rose, his faint bow supremely formal. "Good morning, my dear," he said. "I trust you slept well?"

"Thank you, yes." She nodded to Petit to pour her coffee. "Have you had a letter already this morning?"

"Aye, from van de Velde's contact here in Brussels," Geoff said. "It looks as though I'm to be away for much of the day."

Anaïs felt a flood of relief wash through her. "Oh," she murmured. "Has something happened?"

Frustration sketched across his face. "There is a retired government official he wishes me to meet," he said. "A fellow in Mechelen who may—or may not—have observed Lezennes paying bribery to some of the fellow's coworkers, and who may—or may not—know why he was paying it."

"My," she said. "There were awful lot of *may* and *may-nots* in that sentence."

"Aye, so it's probably a long drive for nothing," he replied. "And even if I learned something, I'm not sure it would improve our situation since I'm not especially concerned about the welfare of the French government—or the Belgians, come to that. I'm just here for the child."

"Still, one never knows in what way it might help us," said Anaïs pensively. "If some sort of proof of Lezennes' character were to come of it—something we could show Charlotte?"

"Precisely," said Geoff. "So I'll go. There's nothing else to be done at the moment anyway."

Just then the butler passed by the dining room doorway. "Your carriage has come round, sir."

"Thank you, Bernard." Geoff laid his letter face down upon the tablecloth, and pushed back his chair. "Petit, how is your Flemish? Can you read it?"

The footman snapped to attention. "Oh, yes, sir. It's much the same as Dutch."

"Kindly come with me today," Geoff ordered. "And excuse us for a moment, will you?"

Anaïs's stomach sank as the footman left, pulling the door closed.

But Geoff did not rise. Instead, he toyed almost absently with his coffee cup, then dragged a hand through his shock of dark hair. "There's something I need to say to you, Anaïs," he finally said. "About last night."

"Yes." Anaïs cleared her throat. "And I to you, Geoff. Last night was . . . magical."

He flicked a sad, almost cynical look up at her. "Yes, it was," he agreed. "And frankly, it did not have to end so soon."

"But it did, Geoff," she interjected, rising from her chair. "It did have to. All good things must come to an end. And I've been thinking about last night. About how it felt."

"So have I," he cut in, his voice a little raspy. "And this warrants a longer conversation at a better time, but—"

"Now," she said abruptly. "Now is fine, Geoff." She had begun to roam restlessly about the dining room, passing by the sideboard laden with food that didn't tempt her appetite. "Last night was not precisely a mistake—"

"I'm glad to hear you think so," he said.

"But it was probably unwise." Pausing before the hearth, she turned to face him, hands clasped before her. "Oh, Geoff, you are . . . you are wonderful, though even that word does not do you justice. You left me breathless."

"But—?" His expression had darkened.

"But that should probably be the end of it," she said, forcing herself onward. "I can see myself, Geoff, so easily growing overfond of you, and complicating our both lives. You are so handsome. So very dashing. And so very—well, let us call it *gifted*—and I don't mean metaphysically."

"Thank you," he said stiffly. "But forgive me if I fail to see the problem in that."

"It's me, Geoff," she whispered. "The problem is me. I thought I could do this lightly, but—"

"Lightly?" he uttered.

"Yes, but you—" Here she paused to smile wistfully. "Oh, you are not the sort of man a woman takes lightly. I'm just playing with fire. And I'm wise enough to have figured out I'd better quit whilst I'm ahead. We have obligations at home, you and I."

A bitter smile curved his fine, full mouth. "So I am to be a victim of my success? Is that it?"

Anaïs forced a brighter expression. "If one is to be a victim of something," she replied, "I daresay that is as good as it gets."

"Balderdash, Anaïs," he fired back. "That's utter balderdash and you know it. Besides, it might not matter what either of us thinks or wants."

She faltered, and felt the chimneypiece at her back. "I beg your pardon?"

His gaze fell to the slight swell of her belly. "Sometimes fate takes over when two people behave rashly—and we behaved rashly *several* times."

"Oh." Instinctively, Anaïs set a hand on her abdomen. "Oh, no, it should be fine, Geoff. Truly. Do not worry yourself. The timing of things . . . well, it should be fine."

"Should be," he gritted. "But mightn't be. You cannot know, Anaïs, can you?"

She nodded, unable to tear her eyes from his. "It will be," she answered. "It will have to be."

He cut his gaze away at last, his hand going to the coffee cup again; covering it, actually, as if by doing so he might hold his own emotions in. "It's not so simple as wishing it so," he said quietly. "But I should have been more careful. Forgive me."

Somehow she dredged up the courage to go to him, and set her hand on his shoulder. "I should ask you to forgive me," she whispered. "I threw myself at you. But I . . . I'm taking myself back now, Geoff. We'll be in England again soon. Back to our old lives, and the hopes and dreams we left there. We must be free to pursue them willingly, without any lingering guilt."

For a long moment he said nothing, as if he were turning something over in his mind. "So tell me, Anaïs," he finally said, still toying with his cup, still refusing to look at her, "is this about your Mr. Right? And why do I begin to suspect this chap has a name?"

Anaïs closed her eyes. "Doesn't everyone?" she said quietly. "And as to expectations, I daresay your family has a few, too."

"So this is about what your family expects?" His voice was cold. "This match is something they have arranged?"

"In a way, yes," Anaïs whispered. "When I was young, Nonna Sofia said—"

His explosion cut her off. "Oh, God spare me Sofia Castelli again!" he said, shoving back his chair and jerking to his feet. "Tell me, Anaïs, does that woman pull your family's strings from the damned grave?"

"I beg your pardon?" she whispered, setting a hand to her breastbone.

"Well, does she?" He towered over her now, one fist striking the table so hard the silver jumped. "She has you trained up as if for a suicide mission—as if you were a *man*—which you are not. And from the grave she still dictates who you'll marry? Must everyone jump to that meddling old woman's tune? Well, by God, I won't."

Anaïs felt her temper spike. "I fear that overweening pride of yours has overcome good sense, Geoff," she said, her voice tremulous. "You cannot simply bed me, then expect to own me. You don't even want to."

"No, I don't," he snapped, "for you've a damned shrewish tongue. But if the worst should happen—"

"Oh, back to that, are we?" Throwing up her hands, Anaïs cut him off by turning and heading straight for the door.

"Anaïs, do not walk away when I am speaking to you."

"We are done speaking," she said, jerking open the door. "And yes, Geoff, if *the worst* should happen, you'll certainly be the first to know—and then may God help me."

She slammed the door hard behind her, listening in satisfaction as one of the landscapes thumped against the wall.

"Anaïs!" he bellowed. "Damn it, get back in here!"

But Anaïs just kept walking—right past poor Petit, who stood straight-faced in the passageway pretending he hadn't heard the slams and shouts, and past Bernard, who stood sentry by the front door—then straight up the staircase to her room. And once there, she pitched herself onto the bed again, willing herself not to cry.

She would not cry, damn him.

She *would not.*

Half an hour later, Geoff watched as the outskirts of Brussels went flying past his carriage window and the flat, lovely landscape of rural Flanders began to unfurl. Green fields, water glistening with the reflection of clouds and sky, even the occasional windmill wheeling in the sun; all of it was stunning. But even the perfection that was Flanders could not distract him this morning.

He fisted his hand, lifted it, then resisted the urge to pound it on something and let it bounce back onto his thigh.

On the banquette opposite, Petit lifted his gaze from the translated notes he was reviewing. "Sir?"

Geoff turned his face back to the window. "Nothing, Petit. Thank you."

He watched the landscape skimming past until at last the sun struck the window at an angle, throwing his own glowering expression back at him. Almost dispassionately, he let his gaze drift over his face.

He was a handsome man, he supposed. Women always told him so, at any rate. Save for his hair, he looked very like his mother, thank heaven. If he had looked like his father—well, God help them all.

But he did not; he was an Archard through and through, for his mother had been Lord Bessett's cousin. Their May-December marriage, if one could call it that, had been arranged by his grandfather for the purposes of political expediency. The Earl of Jessup had wished to be rid of his only daughter—and his future grandson—as quickly as possible. So he had dumped them upon his late wife's family and pressed on with his ambitions.

But Geoff's Archard blood had held true, at least outwardly. He was tall and lean, and possessed the traditional Archard eyes, though his were cold while his mother's were anything but.

Perhaps that burning blue warmth came from within a person? For as often as Geoff's lovers had whispered to him of his handsomeness, to a one they had told him—in the end, and not in a whisper—that he was cold. Eyes like winter's ice on a February day, his last had said.

He looked at himself again, his image like water in the wavy glass. Did Anaïs think him handsome? She had said so, yes, but she'd not seemed overly impressed by it. Perhaps a woman such as she did not value outward appearance so very much. Not that she wasn't beautiful; she was. Dramatically so. Not in the way of a pretty flower or a sunlit garden, though.

No, Anaïs possessed the beauty of a cool, dark forest.

And the tongue of a shrew. He had not lied about that.

Again, he fisted his hand. An awful longing rushed over him; an emotion such as he had never expected to feel, and still did not quite understand. Was it love? Would it fade? He feared the answers were yes, and no, in that order.

He wished he could speak to his father just now. He would ask him what it was like to suffer unrequited love for years on end. Would it eat the heart out of a man? Was *that* where he was headed? And was there nothing to be done but suffer it?

Or could a woman be bent to one's will?

Oh, knew the answer to that one.

Anaïs de Rohan would be bent to no man's will. And he would not want her if she could be.

CHAPTER 15

Of all those in the army close to the commander,
none is more intimate than the secret agent.
Sun Tzu, *The Art of War*

For Anaïs, the evening at the Vicomte de Lezennes' began as a strained affair, and did not much improve.

Geoff arrived home just in time to dress and go across the street after a fruitless trip to Mechelen to find a man who apparently did not wish to be found. Based on what little she could learn amidst his scowls and grumbling, Anaïs concluded he and Petit had been taken on a merry chase, in the end learning little save for the whereabouts of all the back lanes between Brussels and Mechelen.

At Lezennes' they were received warmly by Charlotte and with overpolished charm by the vicomte. Throughout the first half of dinner neither gentleman said a great deal, leaving Anaïs to lead the conversation. Lezennes did not seem to mind, choosing instead to lavish an almost cold, relentless attention on Charlotte.

Anaïs did her best to be witty and flirtatious, albeit in a lighthearted, almost silly way. It seemed to smooth the evening, by the time the last course was removed, she had succeeded in deflecting some of the attention from Charlotte, thereby allowing their hostess to relax and make light conversation with Geoff.

Afterward, Lezennes declined the bottle of whisky Geoff had brought, suggesting that perhaps they should accompany the ladies into the salon for cards.

Geoff was happy to oblige him.

"Shall we play bouillotte?" Charlotte proposed, taking out the deck.

"Oh, I'm afraid I do not know that game," Anaïs lied.

"Just a rubber of whist will do," said the vicomte in a blasé voice. "That is what the English prefer, *n'est-ce pas*?"

Anaïs caught Lezennes' arm, and insisted they partner—which they would likely have done in any case. But the move coaxed a doting smile from the vicomte, and she proceeded to play like a featherbrain amidst a vast deal of giggling—and a little more flirting. Geoff, however, merely got quieter, his eyes colder.

They were ten tricks into the last hand when Charlotte raised the topic of their holiday. "And you will never guess, Anaïs, what Lezennes has planned for Giselle!"

Seated at the card table, Anaïs tossed down a deuce by way of a sacrifice.

"No, no, Charlotte, I am sure I cannot," she replied, cutting a deliberately warm glance at Lezennes. "Something splendid, I am sure, given the gentleman's exquisite taste."

"Splendid, indeed," said Charlotte as Lezennes trumped the hand, snapping down his card victoriously. "He has taken a beautiful cottage by the sea for a whole fortnight—just for the three of us."

Anaïs tried to hide her alarm. "How lovely," she said, turning to Geoff, who sat at her elbow. "Perhaps we should do that, my dear, if Brussels becomes a little dull?"

"Why should Brussels be dull?" Geoff's tone was cold,

his attitude at breakfast having followed him across the street for dinner. "Brussels suits my purpose admirably. Besides, a cottage by the sea would come too dear, I am sure."

Anaïs feigned a little pout. "Tell us, Lezennes, all about this cottage," she said wheedlingly. "Is it quaint and charming? Shall you have sand and sea at your doorstep?"

"Yes to all those things," said the vicomte in obvious self-satisfaction, "or so I am told. And it is a little more, Charlotte, than just a cottage. We've been given the loan of it by the French ambassador himself."

"See, my dear?" Geoff interjected. "Lezennes is well-placed in the government. We may not look so high, I fear, in our amusements. You'll have to content yourself with an afternoon stroll along the Senne."

Lezennes laughed. Anaïs wrinkled her nose. "Charlotte, when do you go?" she asked. "I shall miss you both, for the two of you are my only friends here in Brussels."

"The day after tomorrow." Charlotte turned an almost brittle smile upon her benefactor. "I am so happy for Giselle. She has never really been to the seashore."

The play was finished with Geoff taking the remaining tricks. He and Charlotte had beaten them soundly, but at Anaïs's dithering apology, Lezennes tossed his elegant hand and said, "Oh, it scarcely matters."

Nonetheless, the vicomte kept one eye upon Charlotte at all times, and once the cards had been put away, he suggested she might go to the pianoforte and play for them. She agreed a little shyly, and went to choose her music.

It was time, Anaïs realized. She mightn't get another chance.

Her hand shaking a little, she reached up and removed a strategically placed pin from her hair, then edged up alongside her hostess.

"Oh, drat!" she said. "Might I trouble you, Charlotte, for

a place to repin my hair? Really, I must have the silliest maid in all Christendom, for she cannot keep a curl of it in place."

As if it were second nature, Charlotte flicked an uneasy glance at Lezennes. "Why, I daresay you might use my room," she finally said. "It is on the next floor, the last door on your right."

"Oh, thank you," said Anaïs.

After exchanging a quick, knowing glance with Geoff, she started up the steps just as the opening notes of a Chopin waltz rang out.

Upstairs she went straight to Charlotte's room, a small but comfortably fitted chamber at the back of the house. At the foot of the bed a small traveling trunk sat open, soon to be heaped with clothing, no doubt.

Moving swiftly, Anaïs shut the door, unlocked both windows—just in case—then went to the mirror to twist up her hair. In less than two minutes, she started back out into the corridor, glancing surreptitiously in both directions.

Just as she moved to pull the door behind, however, she felt a presence stirring. Someone very near. *Not Lezennes*, said her instincts. She breathed a sigh of relief. Just then the door across the passageway swept open to reveal a large, far more lavishly furnished chamber. A slight, well-dressed man came out.

Upon seeing her, his gait hitched, then he gave a small bow. "*Bonsoir, madame*," he said before moving swiftly past her and up the next flight of stairs.

Lezennes' valet. It had to be. He had the downcast gaze and quick step of a much-harried servant. Still, his eyes had been furtive, and Anaïs trusted no one.

When his steps had faded, she drew a deep breath, willing her nerves to settle, then hurried about her business.

The first door she opened was a sort of maid's pantry filled with linen and housekeeping supplies. The next was a small, obviously unoccupied bedchamber. Thwarted, Anaïs looked up and down the passageway, trying to figure where she'd gone wrong. Petit had been sure Giselle's room fronted the house.

Beyond the staircase the corridor made a sharp turn. There had to be another room, but the corner would make it far harder to hear anyone's approach.

Downstairs, Chopin still tinkled from Lezennes' piano keys. Surely no more than three minutes had passed. With a quick glance at the stairs, Anaïs passed them by and turned the corner. There was but one door beyond. Swiftly she opened it.

It was a small, narrow room. Giselle lay curled in a tiny wrought-iron bed to the left of the single window. A lamp burned low near the sill, and on the opposite side an uphol- stered chair held a basket of darning. One sock lay across the arm, as if someone had just walked away for a moment.

It would be just like Lezennes to never leave the child alone, Anaïs realized.

Peeking behind the door, she indeed saw another bed, this one not much larger than the child's. She shut the door, drew aside the drapery to unfasten the window lock, then looked hurriedly around the room. A basket of toys sat near the hearth. Anaïs hastened toward it, rifling through in search of something small, soft, and well-worn.

A stuffed dog with a tattered ear and one missing eye looked promising, but it was a trifle too large for her pocket. It was just the thing, though, that a doting mother would have given her child.

Thinking quickly, Anaïs snatched it, hitched up her skirt, and stuffed it down her drawer leg such that it hung just behind the crook of her knee. Then, gingerly readjusting her garter, she secured both stocking and drawer leg as one.

But when she straightened, every hair on the back of her neck prickled.

Anaïs went perfectly still inside. Closing her eyes, she opened herself to the space around her. There was a presence. Something moving through the house. Very near. It felt . . . *malevolent*. And this time it was not Lezennes' valet.

There was no point in hiding. The vicomte had seen her go up the stairs. He would search until he found her. And situated around the blind corner as she was, with only the one door . . .

Hastily she jerked a handkerchief from her pocket, and thought of the most painful thing she could bring to mind. She thought of Giovanni lying cold in his coffin in the Grand Salon at San Gimignano. Of Raphaele standing in the doorway, his hat in his hand, his brown eyes pleading.

She yanked open the door, and slumped against it. She had no more drawn breath when she was seized with a violence, and hauled into the passageway.

"*Madame*, how dare—"

Anaïs cut him off with a hideous, sniveling sob.

Lezennes' words broke away, but his grip did not relent. "*Nom de Dieu!*" he uttered. "What are you about here?"

"Oh, my lord, do forgive me!" she whimpered into her handkerchief. "But I just slipped round for one quick peek!"

His hand fell away, but Lezennes stood so near Anaïs could feel the heat and the anger that emanated from him. "You have no business here!" he hissed. "Where is the girl?"

Anaïs widened her eyes and felt a tear leak out. "Why, she is right there, my lord!" she whimpered. "Asleep in her own dear little bed! And I did not wake her. Indeed, pull the door shut, pray, before we do so! Children must have their rest."

A shade of red passed over Lezennes face as he reached past her. "I meant the servant girl," he gritted, closing it.

"Why, I'm sure I do not know, sir," Anaïs whispered. "I peeked in just this instant to have a look at the poor, wee thing, and she was quite alone."

"And why would you do such a thing?" he demanded, his eyes narrow slits in the gloom.

Anaïs let her face go slack. "Why, as I said, I j-just wanted to see her," she whimpered, "for the little mite does put me so in mind of my own dear Jane, and I am s-s-so afraid . . . Oh, bless me, sir! I'm so afraid I shall never have her *with m-me again—!*" This last was said on a sob as Anaïs clasped the handkerchief to her face again.

"Mon Dieu, madame, what can you be talking about?"

But Anaïs was trembling now. "Oh, my lord!" she whispered. "Pray do not tell my husband!"

"Your husband?" At last Lezennes was looking more irritated than angry. "What can your husband have to do with any of this?"

"Oh, it really is too terrible!" Anaïs said it witheringly, dabbing at her eyes. "He does not love her. Indeed, I really don't think he wants her at all!"

"Who?" he demanded. "What are you babbling about?"

"I'm n-n-not babbling," Anaïs wailed softly. "I'm talking about Jane, my lord! Did Charlotte not explain? My father arranged my marriage without telling him *about Jane.* And I ask you—how can I be blamed for it? How can little Jane be blamed for it? But you—oh, *you* have taken little Gisette in, and loved her like your own!"

"Giselle," said Lezennes, an edge of suspicion still in his voice. "And a child, you say? How old is this child, Madame MacLachlan? Surely not so old as Giselle?"

Anaïs felt his gaze drifting over her, assessing her age.

"No, Jane is just four, my lord, but her coloring—well, 'tis so very like Giselle's." Here, she paused to dab at her eyes. "Or perhaps my grief has made me fanciful. But Geoffrey does not miss her at all, I vow."

She sensed Lezennes begin to relent. "Perhaps in time he will grow fond of the child."

"Perhaps, but why can he not be more like you?" asked Anaïs. "Here you are, so very good! So kind to dear Charlotte and her little angel. Indeed, you are quite put out with me just now, but how could I be angry about that? *You* love Giselle. You have her best interests at heart."

The last of the anger had fallen from his face.

Perfect timing.

Anaïs launched herself at him, and fell into his arms. "Oh, how can she be so fortunate as to have you, sir!" she whispered, throwing an arm around his neck. "What poor widow would not account herself lucky indeed to have your broad, good shoulder to lean upon?"

Lezennes let his hand snake up her spine, then gave her a perfunctory pat between the shoulder blades. "You are too kind, *madame*, I am sure," he said.

Anaïs released him, giving him a generous view of décolletage as she did so. "Oh, no. I speak with a mother's heart."

An awkward silence settled over them. The vicomte opened his mouth as if to say something, then apparently thought better of it.

Anaïs dabbed away the last of her crocodile tears. "There, I believe I am presentable." She managed a watery smile. "Will you show me back down, my lord?"

Lezennes offered his arm, and they fell into step with one another. "Perhaps you might explain to Charlotte how fortunate she is, Madame MacLachlan?" he suggested as they neared the bottom of the stairs. "I sometimes fear for her welfare. I am not entirely certain she understands how very hard life can be for a widow alone."

"I shall tell her, of course, and most strongly, too." Then Anaïs feigned a look of chagrin. "Oh, what a watering pot I am!" she whispered just beyond the drawing room doors. "I will make you think very ill of my husband, I fear. I daresay he is a very good man."

"You *daresay*?" The vicomte crooked one brow as they went in, still arm in arm.

The piano music was mounting toward a crescendo now. Geoff, who was turning pages for Charlotte, glowered at her. She shot him a quick nod to let him know her mission had been accomplished, then turned back to Lezennes.

"The truth is, I hardly know him," Anaïs quietly confessed, edging nearer so as to afford him a better peek down her bodice. "It was arranged—though once I introduced him to Jane, he turned three shades of red and I thought, truly, that he meant to call it off! What can Papa have been thinking?"

"I'm sure I do not know," said the vicomte, his gaze warming. "Children are a blessing."

"Just as I always say, sir!" Anaïs softly exclaimed. "Well, there's nothing to be done about it just now. I promise never to peek at Gisette—*Giselle*—again if you really wish it."

"She is delicate." But the vicomte's attention, Anaïs noted, was not on her face. "Giselle has a—a nervous condition. I fear I must . . ."

"Yes—?" Anaïs prompted him.

The vicomte lifted his gaze back up. "Er, insist," he finished. "I am afraid I must insist."

"Very well, then." Anaïs cut him a slightly suggestive smile. "But you must promise to tempt me with some other sort of entertainment instead. Something which might distract me from my lonely plight."

"Indeed, *madame*?" Speculation kindled in Lezennes' eyes. "What did you have in mind?"

"Oh, la, sir!" she said breathlessly. "I really could not say. Perhaps you might tell me of something exciting—your life in Paris? Or some of your adventures?"

"Adventures?" he murmured.

Anaïs leaned into him. "Surely, my lord, a sophisticated gentleman such as yourself has had many adventures?"

"*Bien sûr, madame.*" A smile twitched at his mouth. "One or two."

She laughed a little too loudly and again Geoff shot her a dark look. Anaïs ignored him, and reminded herself of her goals. To delay Lezennes from forcing his proposal on poor Charlotte. To convince him she was as empty-headed and harmless as possible. Perhaps if he came to trust her, she might even kindle a relationship with little Giselle, though that still seemed unlikely.

And perhaps—just perhaps—she was enjoying Geoff's fury just a tad too much.

Anaïs did not wish to think too hard about that.

Instead, she nodded in the direction of the piano. "Well, they seem happily occupied with one another," she said with a teasing smile. "Might we have a little stroll in your garden? I find the darkness so very . . . refreshing. You do have some smallish sort of garden, I daresay?" She knew from Petit's reconnoitering that they did not.

Lezennes was beginning to look at her as if she were a tasty morsel. "I fear, *madame*, that we have none," he murmured, pointing at a very small, plumply upholstered settee. "But why do we not sit just there, and I will tell you stories of my time in the French army?"

Anaïs widened her eyes. "The *French* army?" she said, drawing him toward the seat he had indicated. "Which regiment, sir? Oh, do say it was a cavalry regiment! I always say there is nothing so enjoyable for a woman as to look up and see a handsome man mounted atop . . . well, almost *anything*, really."

For an instant Anaïs feared she'd played her cards too boldly. But once the shock had faded from Lezennes' eyes, the heat returned threefold. He urged her into a chair and regaled her for a time with his war stories—a process that involved very little war and a vast deal of pomposity.

It also involved a great deal of laughter, and increasingly intimate glances.

From time to time, however, the vicomte glanced at Charlotte, too, as if measuring her reaction to his having turned his oily charm elsewhere.

But Charlotte was not looking, and by the time her long piece had ended and Geoff could excuse himself from the pianoforte, Lezennes had hold of Anaïs's hand, and was proposing they might ride out together the following day to the village of Waterloo, near the *Grand Armée*'s last stand.

Anaïs was willing to bet he meant to make it no farther than an inn on the outskirts of Brussels.

Geoff, however, was willing to bet they would not go at all.

"I'm afraid it is out of the question," he said. "I mean to go sketch the interiors of the Kapellekerk tomorrow. Perhaps we might all go together at another time."

Anaïs shot an exasperated look at him. "But you do not need me for sketching," she said. "And Charlotte is not interested in military things, are you, Charlotte?"

Charlotte agreed that she was not.

"But I wish you to accompany me," said Geoff coldly. "I'm afraid I must insist."

Anaïs managed to thrust out her bottom lip a tiny fraction, then bite it ever so slightly as she swept her lashes downward.

Lezennes reacted, his eyes warming again. But all the

while, he also watched Charlotte from the corner of his eye. He was taking a malicious enjoyment in this, Anaïs realized. And if he could not make Charlotte jealous, then he expected to get—at the very least—a good tumble out of the bargain, and at little inconvenience to himself.

Anaïs was willing to offer him that—or rather, to seem as if she might.

"The hour grows late," said Geoff, still standing. "Anaïs, get your shawl. We have kept our hosts dancing attendance on us far too long."

After a flurry of shawls and kissed cheeks, followed by good-byes said at the front door, Anaïs and Geoff crossed the Rue de l'Escalier to their house. She could feel Geoff radiating almost unbridled anger.

Well, let him stew in it, Anaïs decided. She went up the steps, rummaging for the key in her reticule. In response, Geoff extracted his own, and shoved it roughly into the lock. "Don't you *ever* pull a trick like that again," he said, his voice cold as the grave.

"We had work to do." She pushed past him when he opened the door. "I was getting it done."

Anaïs went inside, and tossed her shawl onto the foyer table. Behind her, the bolt clicked shut. After that, everything was a blur. Geoff caught her shoulder, forcing her around. In a trice Anaïs found herself imprisoned against the door.

His handsome face twisted. "Damn it to hell, Anaïs," he rasped. "Do you mean to drive me mad?"

She felt her eyes flash. "Is that even possible? I thought you were so—"

"I'll tell you what I am," he cut in, giving her a little shake. "I'm tired of watching you throw yourself at Lezennes. I told you not to do it. And to go off with him in a carriage—?"

"Geoff, he caught me in Giselle's room," she whispered. "I had to do something. Besides, I knew you would never agree to that drive, nor am I stupid enough to go. Now kindly take your hands off my arms."

But he had no intention of that. By the faint light of the hall lamp, she could see his eyes, colder and more implacable than ever before. The weight and the width of him pressed her back against the solid slab of oak. She could smell the mix of irritation and lust rising from his skin; the scent of citrus and warm tobacco mingled with sweat, teasing at her nostrils.

She looked up, far up, and knew he was about to kiss her. And—shame of all shames—that she was not going to fight it. Not really. Not in the end.

Perhaps not even in the beginning . . .

Slanting her head ever so slightly, she let her lashes drop half shut, and heard him curse softly beneath his breath.

Geoff watched Anaïs's long black lashes fan across her cheeks and felt himself fall a little deeper. Fear and frustration and desire run rampant still warred inside him. Shoving his fingers into the soft hair at her nape, he stilled her to his kiss, his tongue sliding deep, invading her.

Anaïs opened to him, and made a low, soft sound in the back of her throat. Dimly, he heard a hairpin strike the floor. Geoff eased his hand beneath her hip and did not hold back. He felt incapable of it. He needed her to understand that *she was his*.

They parried kisses as they had parried blades, taunting and a little dangerous. Tongues slid like warm silk round one other. And when it seemed as if the swell of passion might drown him, Geoff lifted his mouth to slide his lips down her throat. Whispering her name, he nipped and tasted, then trailed his tongue across the sweet throb of her pulse point.

"Anaïs," he murmured against her skin. "Oh, love, 'tis too late."

"Too . . . late?"

"We can't escape it, this thing between us."

His cock was pressed into the softness of her belly, hard and insistent. It was as if he were someone hot and crazed, not cool and dispassionate. He burned for this woman; wanted her as he had wanted nothing in his life. Watching her tonight—watching Lezennes ogle her—it had maddened him. For surely a man was mad to do this.

Nuzzling his face into the turn of her neck, he skated his hand upward to weigh the soft orb of her breast. Anaïs gasped. Geoff caught the ruched edge of her décolletage with his thumb. He dragged it down until the lush mound was free to be tasted.

After that, everything happened in a lust-fueled rush.

Still holding her prisoner with his body, he took her nipple into his mouth. He suckled deeply, then slid the tip of his tongue back and forth over the resultant peak. On a soft cry, her head fell back against the door.

Madness, yes. Roughly he fisted up her skirts. Now. It had to be now.

Later he was unable to recall that moment when he had released himself. He knew only one need; the need to be inside her. The fact that a bed was little more than a staircase away—that a servant might come upon them at any moment—none of this came to mind. He knew only the fierce, dark desire to thrust. To lay claim to her. To spill himself deep inside.

He didn't ask permission. He found the slit in her drawers. Pressing his fingers into her wetness, he felt his entire body tremble. "*Leg—*" he rasped. "Put it—*ah—*"

And then he was pushing himself deep inside her, scarcely realizing how it had come to be.

Oh, he had done this before—a quick, furtive coupling

stolen at some opportune moment, with a woman who knew what she was doing. But burning in the back of his consciousness was the fact that this was Anaïs.

Anaïs, who deserved better. The woman he was falling heart over head in love with.

And still he could not stop.

He was not sure Anaïs wanted him to.

"*Aah*," she sighed. "Yes . . ."

He held her perfectly balanced, his hand cupped beneath the swell of her bottom, her spine set to the door. Anaïs had curled one leg about him, lifting herself eagerly. In his arms she felt no more than a feather, as if she were a part of him. As if this was something perfect, instead of something tawdry.

He lifted her another increment and shoved his entire length into her warmth. She was slick with need, her passage tightening against the invasion, and he thought at that moment he might explode. He thrust and thrust again, impaling her against the door, Anaïs's breath ratcheting up with his every stroke.

Her lashes were nearly closed, her mouth slightly parted. "*Yes*," she whispered. "Like that—Geoff, *oh*—don't stop . . ."

Her climax came swiftly, in the heat and rush of the moment. Geoff felt the release shudder through her, watched in delight as her head fell back against the door, and her lovely throat worked up and down. Around his cock, she pulsed and tightened, her leg curling hard about his hips as she urged herself against him.

He felt his release surge forth, pumping into her stroke after stroke, the pleasure like the parting of the heavens. As if he were being drawn body and soul into that glorious white light.

Long moments later he became dimly aware of a sound. The doleful *tock-tock-tock* of the longcase clock at the turn of the stairs. He still held Anaïs to him, bound chest to chest in his arms, their foreheads damp and lightly touching.

"Geoff?" She fell back against the door, gasping for breath. "Are you . . . finished?"

"Hell, no," he growled. "Not by a long shot."

CHAPTER 16

Victorious warriors win first then go to war,
while defeated warriors go to war first then seek to win.
Sun Tzu, *The Art of War*

But the reality of what he'd just done was sinking in on Geoff. Good God, he'd taken her against a doorway as if she were a two-penny whore. And in their own front hall, where a servant could have come upon them at any time.

But all around them the house still lay in silence. The servants had gone to bed just as he'd told them to do. The clock was ticking away as it always did. Farther down the street, he could hear the rumble of a late-night carriage crossing over the Rue de l'Escalier.

Then all fell quiet again. No one had been disturbed.

Gently, he lowered Anaïs, and felt her leg slip over his hip, then lightly touch the floor. "Oh," she said again.

Kissing her softly one last time, he tugged up the sea-green silk of her dress, then caught her up gently in his arms. Only then did he notice the soft wad of fabric at her knee.

"A stuffed dog," she whispered. "Don't drop it and trip."

The day wanted only that—the two of them rolling back

down the stairs in a state of dishabille with servants hastening upstairs to see what the commotion was about.

He carried her carefully up to her bedchamber. Elbowing his way through the door, he set her down at the edge of the mattress, where the lamp burned low on the bed table. The soft light flickered, casting half her lovely face in shadow.

"I am going to undress you, Anaïs," he whispered, "one lovely inch at a time, then lay you down in that bed and make love to you properly."

"Ah." She looked at him through eyes still sated, a quizzical smile toying at her lips. "And am I to have any say in this business?"

"Dashed little," he replied, reaching around to unfasten the buttons of her green gown. "You could say no, I suppose."

"And you would . . . ?"

He trailed one finger along the edge of her bodice, watching her nipples harden. "Convince you otherwise," he rasped, tugging the bodice down just far enough to expose the tips of her lovely breasts. "Shall I start?"

She reached up, and set her hand to his cheek. "Geoff, I—"

"Don't," he said, kissing the word from her lips. "Don't waste what little time we have together, love. It's fate, and we'll madden ourselves fighting it."

Her lashes swept down almost shyly, and he felt her tremble inside.

He meant for her to do a great more than tremble before the night was out.

He dipped his head and stroked the tip of his tongue round her sweet, rosy peak, and watched in satisfaction as it hardened. He laved it slowly, with tiny flicks followed by a long, slow circle, and when she gave a breathy sigh, he turned his attention to the other.

"You are relentless," she whispered, her voice so soft he scarcely heard it.

He kissed his way up her breastbone, then finished slipping free her buttons. Anaïs's gown was exquisite—a shade of shimmering green like the Adriatic's shallows at sunset—and when it slithered down and took her shift with it, he saw her garters were made of the same color silk, and trimmed with dainty white lace.

On a sound of appreciation, he knelt and began to roll them down, taking her silk stockings along with them. The stuffed toy dropped down her drawer leg and rolled under the bed.

She lifted her lashes and looked down at him shyly. "No one ever undressed me like this," she whispered.

"I would undress you like this every night of the week," he answered, skimming his hand down the back of her calf.

But he could not. Not for long. She was not his, and likely never would be.

The realization drove him, riled him as nothing ever had. It was as if, before Anaïs, his life had held nothing but pale imitations of passion. Vague sentiments masquerading as love and lust and yearning.

Her stockings and garters down, he remained on his knees, untying the ribbon of her drawers. They slithered down her thighs at once, settling in a heap at her ankles. Geoff kissed her thigh, then kissed higher still, delving into her curls with one finger.

"Oh!" she cried, her voice thready.

"Open a little for me," he growled. Anaïs seized the bedpost as if for strength. He touched her intimately with his fingers, sliding through the warmth. She closed her eyes tight and began to make a soft sound in her throat.

He spread a row of kisses across the swell of her belly and thought again of the darkness and the mystery of the forest;

of Anaïs's shadowy depths as yet unexplored. She was so sensual, this dark, fey creature. So naturally erotic, in ways he was sure even she did not comprehend.

He wanted very much to tutor her, to watch Anaïs become the beautiful, voluptuous woman she was meant to be. To entice her feminine nature to unfurl like a flower to his touch.

Suddenly impatient, he rose, and began to strip off his cravat a little roughly.

She opened her eyes and let go of the bedpost. Her fingers went at once to his throat. "Stop," she chided, "and lift your chin."

With a slight smile, he did as he was told.

"You have an arrogant jaw," she said, stripping loose the knot. "Did you know that?"

He said nothing as she drew the neck cloth free from his collar. She let it drop to the floor, then pushed his coat from his shoulders. Her clever, slender fingers made short work of his waistcoat buttons, and that, too, landed on the floor with a soft *whuff!*

He could not take his eyes from hers now. She wanted him still—wanted him too much to refuse him, thank God—but she was none too happy about it.

He vowed to make her happy.

He vowed that by sunrise there would be no turning back for either of them.

With one hand, he swiftly dragged his shirt off over his head, and flung it aside. His gaze fixed to hers, he toed off his shoes and unfastened the only trouser button still hanging.

Her warm hands settled at his hip bones, and pushed the wool and linen down as one. His manhood sprang free from the tangle of clothing, already hardening. Anaïs took the weight of him into her hand and stroked. Breath and belly seizing at once, Geoff closed his eyes and wondered if it was possible to come from the mere brush of a woman's fingers.

Perhaps. If it was the right woman.

He could not wait. He took her into his arms and kissed her deep, then tumbled with her onto the bed. She opened her legs to take him. "Come inside me, Geoff," she whispered.

Geoff obliged her, but this time he slid into her slowly. Still, she was tight. He closed his eyes, felt his arms shudder, and willed himself to hold back. This time he wanted to love her for a long time; love her until her breath became soft, sweet gasps in the night.

In response, Anaïs whispered his name again, curled one leg around his, and drew him down, enveloping him with her warm, slick passage. He sank into her womanly flesh like a man embracing his fate. He closed his eyes, and felt as if he was precisely—and finally—where he belonged.

How many times had he made love to a woman, only to leave her bed a little more lost and a good deal emptier? Not this time. Not with this woman. There was only the yearning, stronger and more heart wrenching. Geoff closed his eyes and eased himself back and forth inside her. Anaïs cupped her hands round his face, kissed him long and hard, rising to meet his every stroke.

She was his.

And he was hers.

The sooner they gave in to that truth, the better it would be.

She was so lovely, his forest nymph. In the cool stillness of the room, he drove himself inside her, reveling in the effort of it. He thrust and thrust, matching her pace and her sighs until sweat slicked his body. And still it was not enough.

It would never be enough. Oh, he would slide deep into Anaïs that one last perfect time and, yes, spill himself in relentless thrusts against her womb. But he was fast coming to need so much more than just release.

Just then, Anaïs hitched her leg higher around his waist, and swallowed hard. Much of her hair had tumbled down now and was spread across the counterpane in a beautiful silken swath. Lamplight shifted and danced over her nakedness, warming her skin. On a breathless sigh, she pressed her head back into the softness of the pillow, her face strained with that exquisite search for pleasure.

Cupping his hand beneath the lush swell of her buttock, Geoff lifted her ever so slightly, then stroked another fraction higher in search of that sweet, aching spot.

He found it. He found her, and bound himself to her, heart and soul. She arched to him, her body stiffening like a cord drawn taut, her eyes flying wide as her nails raked down his back. And then she shuddered and convulsed beneath him, crying out his name.

She was his. And he was hers.

And so he claimed her. Claimed her in the most carnal and wild of ways as her womanly flesh pulsed around his. A triumphant sound coiled up in the back of his throat, something almost savage, as if it had been dragged up from deep in his chest.

Stabbing his fingers into her hair, Geoff held Anaïs still to his thrusts and sank his teeth into the soft flesh of her throat, still pumping furiously inside her. When he came, it was in a bone-shuddering jolt of white-hot pleasure. His ballocks convulsed and his arms trembled. And then he threw back his head on a deep groan, and thrust home one last time.

He fell across Anaïs, and lost himself in the scent of sex and rosewater and sweat. Then he set his lips to her throat more gently, whispered her name as her arms came round him, and knew that he was lost in her forever.

* * *

Geoff stirred to awareness to hear the clock in the stairwell striking two. He could feel Anaïs's head, still cradled against his shoulder as it had been when he'd drifted off in that sweet, boneless lethargy that inevitably follows sensual bliss.

Crooking his head on her pillow, he looked down to see Anaïs staring up at him, eyes wide, honest, and unblinking.

He kissed the tip of her nose. "We forgot to put out the lamp," he murmured.

"Oh, we forgot a lot of things." Anaïs's smile was a little wry. "But I like the light. I like to look at you."

It was his turn to smile. "Do you?"

Her lashes dropping shut, she rolled into him, and trailed the tip of her tongue round his nipple, causing his breath to catch. "Oh, yes," she whispered. "Your face is beautiful, of course, but this chest—ah, it is magnificent. As I'm sure you are aware."

He chuckled. "You keep saying things like that," he answered. "As if you truly expect the worst of me. Have you had a great deal of experience with handsome, arrogant men?"

She flopped back against his arm, flat on the bed, her breasts like ripe, round peaches in the lamplight. "Oh, enough," she said. "But you're right. That was a precipitate choice of words."

At that, he threw back his head and laughed richly. "Oh, damn me with faint praise, Anaïs," he said. "You expect the worst of me—*eventually*. Is that it?"

"Oh, Geoff, don't let's argue," she said, rolling toward him again, and setting her forehead against his ribs. "Let's just enjoy this for what it is."

At that, he slipped a finger under her chin, and tipped her face up. "What this is," he said quietly, "is a serious business."

Her eyes widened. "A serious business?" she echoed. "Tell me, Geoff, how serious? My feelings and my plans aside, mind. Because I was given to understand your attentions were fixed elsewhere."

At that, he felt the stirring of irritation. "My attentions are my own to fix as I damned well please," he said. "And if some busybody—say, my old chum Lazonby—has managed to suggest to you otherwise, then I'll deal with him soon enough."

She turned her head away. "You mustn't blame Lazonby."

"Who, then?"

"It does not matter," she murmured. "It was just something you said that day in the bookroom at the St. James Society."

It damned well did matter.

But Geoff held his tongue, and let his mind run over all the things they had discussed that day. He had been uneasy about traveling alone with Anaïs, for even then he'd been dangerously attracted to her. God only knew what he might have said. Something about being ready to do his duty to his title, he thought. For a woman as skittish as Anaïs, perhaps that had been enough.

He had been quiet too long, apparently.

Anaïs looked up at him. "I ask you again, Geoff, *are* your attentions fixed elsewhere?" she asked. "And mind how you answer that, please."

He felt a flood of frustration—and no small amount of chagrin. "They were, yes," he confessed, "but in the vaguest of ways."

"It mightn't feel so vague to the lady in question," she murmured.

At that, Geoff felt his cheeks warm, as if he were some chided schoolboy. "I will make my apologies to the lady as soon as we return to Town," he said. "She will doubtless be relieved."

But Anaïs's eyes were sad. "You cannot know that," she said, tucking her head nearer as she curled her leg over his. "Just let this be our secret, Geoff. I could not bear to have anyone else hurt. And this thing—this heat between us—it will burn out, you know. We are destined to go our separate ways."

He felt a knot deep in his throat. "Could you love another that easily, Anaïs?" he rasped.

"I do not know," she said. "I only know that I promised my . . . my family I'd marry from amongst my great-grandmother's people. And if ever I find the right one, I will."

"And yet you are one-and-twenty years of age, Anaïs," he gently reminded her. "You have spent large portions of your life in Tuscany. And you have not found your dream lover so far."

"Thank you, Geoff, for reminding me how thoroughly on the shelf I am," she said, though there was little bitterness in her voice. "But this isn't about me. You've left an iron in the fire back in London, so have a care no one gets burned— someone who doesn't deserve it—for I've been on both ends of that harsh tool, and let me tell you, it *hurts*."

She was right, he realized. And so he mulled on it, and said nothing. But inwardly he cursed his own impatience that day in the temple. He had been angry with Rance, and he had felt sorry for Lady Anisha. So Geoff had stepped up to the wicket; he. He had done what Rance would not—and now he was the one to regret it.

Anaïs, however, spoke again. "And I am twenty-two now, by the way," she said, her tone almost artificially bright. "My birthday was last week."

"And so was mine," he said quietly. "I daresay they would be near one another, wouldn't they? And you are not on the shelf, love. You are in your prime."

"*Hmph*," said Anaïs.

At that, he paused and stroked a fingertip over her hip; across the finely drawn tattoo that marked her fate as surely as it marked his. "I did not quite believe Lazonby when he said you bore this sign," he murmured. "I cannot imagine a family so marking a woman. But he assured me he had seen it."

"If he assured you of that, then he lied," said Anaïs flatly.

Geoff stared down at her.

"What?" she said incredulously. "Did you think I'd flash my bare arse at Lazonby?"

"Didn't you?"

She relaxed her head onto his chest again, and settled her hand almost protectively over his heart. "Well, I would have done, I suppose, had it come to it," she said musingly. "After all, he has doubtless seen a thousand bare bottoms in his profligate life."

"Oh, doubtless," Geoff sourly agreed.

"And he didn't quite believe I had the mark, either," Anaïs acknowledged. "I suggested he send for one of the servants, if he wished. So he fetched his housekeeper—a great battle-ax of a woman with a brogue so thick you could have driven nails into it—and she had a look. She knew at once what it was."

"Ah." Geoff felt a strange sort of relief at that.

Still, as she had said, she would have shown Lazonby had it been necessary. Anaïs was dutiful, he coming to understand, almost to a fault. It was one of the traits he most respected in her. And it was the very thing that was aggravating the devil out of him just now.

Ah, but a man could not have it both ways, could he? A fickle, fainthearted woman would have been intolerable. And Anaïs would never be either of those things.

But her fidelity had not always been rewarded, he was beginning to think. Someone had put that bitter edge in her voice. Someone had left that hint of world-weary sadness in her melting brown gaze. Geoff's hand fisted in the sheet as if he might throttle the man.

But Anaïs did not need him to fight her battles. She was strong; whoever he was, he had come up against a formidable adversary. He relaxed his hand and pulled her closer.

"Do you want to talk about him, love?" he murmured.

In his embrace, Anaïs fleetingly stiffened. "I thought you could not read me."

"I can't," he said. "I don't need to. I know you like a lover, Anaïs. And I know, too, that you don't deserve disappointment."

That, at least, made her laugh a little. "Oh, Geoff, after what I just experienced, I think the word *disappointment* has vanished from my lexicon. And no, I don't want to talk about him. He is not worth wasting one moment of my short time with you."

There it was again. That phrase he was coming to hate.

Geoff felt his days with Anaïs racing past, and he yearned to reach out, to rein them back as if they were a team of wild horses that might be somehow slowed. But that would leave Charlotte and Giselle at risk. That would compromise the mission.

"Still, you once loved him," he said, more to himself than to her. "He was the man whom you believed was the one. And I . . . well, I find myself unaccountably jealous."

For a long moment, she lay silent in his embrace, and he thought she might refuse to answer. Then finally she sighed. "He was my Florentine fencing master," she said. "The man Vittorio hired to train me."

Geoff felt his heart sink. "Good Lord," he said. "How old were you?"

"Seventeen," she said. "And I was not naïve, Geoff. I should have known better. But what can I say? Raphaele knew how to get his opponent's guard down."

Still, seventeen was very young, or seemed so to him. "And he seduced you?"

"Oh, thoroughly," she said. "After saying how much he loved me. That he could not live without me. That he wanted to marry me. After a few weeks of it, he simply wore me down with his looks and his charm."

"The lying rotter," he gritted under his breath.

Her gaze had turned inward now. "A rotter, yes," she said. "But you know, I don't think he was entirely a liar. I look back on it now that I'm older, and I think . . . I think that in his way, he meant it. That he did love me, insofar as a man like that can love anyone save himself."

"And were you desperately in love with him?"

"Oh, yes," she whispered. "In that dramatic, heartbreaking way a young girl first falls in love. But I think about it now, and I wonder if perhaps I was just in love with the idea of him."

"And would it have been a bad match?" he asked. "Was your family opposed?"

Again, she hesitated. "My family did not know at first," she finally said. "Nor did Vittorio. Raphaele said we should keep it secret until I was a little older. That Vittorio would think ill of him for having come to San Gimignano and seduced me when he was supposed to be tutoring me."

"And you agreed to that?"

She nodded, her hair scrubbing on the pillow. "I was a fool," she said. "I adored him. He was older—all of twenty-four!—and wiser, I believed. And I imagined I was the luckiest woman in the world. That a man so beautiful should wish to marry me . . ."

"Anaïs, hush," he commanded. "He was fortunate to have you—and deserved to lose you, too, I daresay."

Anaïs, however, seemed lost in her memories. "But yes, I thought he was the one. He was so dashing. So witty and charming. And to see him with a blade—!" Here, she made a very Italian gesture, setting her fingers to her lips. "Like poetry, that man. So I let myself love him. But all the while, the dream seemed so tenuous. So fragile. And eventually, I realized why."

Inexplicably, a chill fell over his heart. "Why?"

Anaïs closed her eyes and swallowed hard. "Because he could never have married me. Not then."

"Why?"

Her smile twisted bitterly. "Because he already had a wife," she whispered. "A wife of less than a year. An arranged marriage. Vittorio didn't know, and Raphaele—well, he found it convenient not to mention it."

Geoff's hand fisted again. "That *bastard*."

Anaïs gave another sharp laugh. "That's just what Vittorio called him," she said. "That, and much, much worse. Raphaele was from a family with long connections to the *Fraternitas* in Tuscany. They were people Vittorio trusted with his life—and with me."

"Good God," whispered Geoff. "What did Vittorio do?"

Anaïs looked at him in vague amazement. "What did he do?" she echoed. "He was Tuscan. He was *Vittorio*. He seized his favorite rapier, and carved up Raphaele's face like a turnip."

"Good God," said Geoff again.

"Yes, let's just say that when Raphaele's wife got him back again, he was not quite as beautiful as when he'd left her."

The horror of it sickened Geoff. *A married man.*

And a handsome, relentless lothario secretly committed to another woman . . .

That was part of the horror that sickened Anaïs. Of course it was.

But he was not Raphaele. He was not married, or even betrothed. He had simply asked to pay court to an eligible lady.

Which, in his world, was perilously near to offering a lady marriage.

He was not going to offer marriage to Lady Anisha Stafford. Not now. Not under any circumstance. But she was still a dear friend—and a fine, well-bred lady of exquisite beauty who was received in London society with something less than unbridled enthusiasm. This, merely because her skin was not quite pale enough, her blood not quite English enough. She did not deserve to be hurt by him, too.

Anaïs was right. He had left an iron in the fire. A very hot one.

And it suddenly came clear to Geoff what he was going to have to do, for all their sakes. He was going to have to explain this disaster of his own making to Lady Anisha herself—and not in a letter. Writing to his mother and to her brother was simply not sufficient. And Ruthveyn, who was stuck on a Calcutta-bound East Indiaman right about now, would likely not even receive his letter for some months.

He sighed aloud, and rolled up onto his elbow to better look at her. "I will make this right, Anaïs," he said quietly. "My situation, I mean. The lady is just a friend, and we both wish one another happy. We were neither of us besotted. It would have been—if anything—a marriage of mutual convenience."

Anaïs only shook her head again. "That sounds like something a man would say—and perhaps even believe," she whispered. "Please say no more. I could not bear being the cause of—"

"Hush," he interjected, touching a finger to her mouth. "You've caused nothing."

But she merely thinned her lips, and looked sad.

"Anaïs, love, I am not Raphaele." He reached down and tucked a wayward curl behind her ear. "And Raphaele is gone. He is in your past. Dead and buried, practically."

She gave a sharp laugh. "Oh, hardly that," she said. "No, Raphaele is persistent, I'll give him that. It wanted only Vittorio's death, and I suppose he thought himself safe."

Something jolted in Geoff's brain. "Aye, you saw him at the funeral Mass, you said."

"Not just then." Her gaze was fixed somewhere in the depths of the room. "He came to Vittorio's villa. Just beforehand."

"Pretty bold of the bastard," Geoff gritted. "What did he want?"

"His way," said Anaïs bitterly. "He wanted his way, that is all. But he didn't get it. Raphaele is not the sort of man who graciously accepts what he cannot change—and he cannot change my mind."

"He thought he would simply pick up where you left off?" asked Geoff, outraged. "He thought you would willingly commit adultery with him?"

She fell silent again, her face an emotionless mask. "She died," Anaïs finally whispered, her voice distant. "Raphaele's wife. She died. In childbirth, just after Vittorio sent him back to Florence with his tail between his legs. And with Vittorio gone, he thought . . ."

Geoff did not know what to say. "Good Lord," he managed.

Anaïs looked up at him with a sort of pleading in her eyes. "That, you see, is how well Raphaele knew me," she whispered. "He assumed . . . well, I don't know *what* he assumed. That I had been heartsick all this time? That I had been waiting in the wings? Well, I should sooner douse him with lamp oil and set him afire. But he did not know that—because in truth, for all his fine talk, the truth is that Raphaele never really knew me at all."

"No," said Geoff firmly. "No, he definitely did not. Or he would have known never, ever to cross you and then come back for more."

Anaïs laughed, a faint, almost withering sound. Then she shocked him by pulling him down and kissing him, her palms cupped round his face.

"*Umm*," he said when they came apart sometime later.

But Anaïs was still holding his face. "Make love to me again," she whispered, her eyes pleading. "I daresay once more won't matter. I don't want to talk of Raphaele, or of the past—or even of the future. Just make love to me once more, and give me something real and something true. Something more I can cherish when this night is done."

And so he did. He made love to her with a sweet, unerring slowness, putting to use his every skill, his every masculine wile; doing, in short, all that he could to ensure that she would come to crave him as he was fast coming to crave her.

And he was. He was coming to need her with an awful ache in his heart and in a bone-deep yearning of his soul, and fast coming to fear that without Anaïs his future was going to roll out before him in endless days of a bland, color-less landscape.

Like something never quite real. Never quite true.

But even as he thrust inside her for those last sweet strokes and felt her rise to him again like the moon and the stars rose to the heavens, Geoff knew Anaïs held back from him a little piece of her heart. And he knew, too, that it would be the last time they made love for a long while to come.

He just hoped it wasn't forever.

He drowsed in her arms for a time, but despite the pleasure and lethargy that had flooded through his limbs, Geoff did not rest. It was time to leave Brussels, he sensed. He yearned to go home; to return to London, set his life aright, and lay siege to Anaïs's heart. To see Charlotte and her daughter safely to England, and placed under the vigilant watch of the Brotherhood.

Tonight at Lezennes', he had felt the evil afoot; felt the

dark emotion surging through the house. Not just Lezennes' trifling pursuit of Anaïs, but something deeper and far more sinister than that.

He tried a second time to fall sleep, curling himself more tightly about Anaïs and drawing in her exotic scent, but to no avail. He bent his head and nuzzled her lightly. She made a soft, happy sound in the back of her throat, and snuggled deeper into the pillow. For a moment, he allowed himself to thread his fingers through the soft, silken hair at her temples, thinking of how he would never tire of such a simple pleasure.

But there was no point, he realized, in tossing and turning here, and continuing to disturb her sleep as well as her life. It was time to set about the practicalities of what had to be done.

Extracting himself ever so gingerly, he rolled away and sat up on the edge of the bed. It took him but an instant to snatch up his clothing, which lay scattered about the room. And as he bent down to grab his trousers, he saw Giselle Moreau's little stuffed dog.

He snatched that, too, and quietly slipped from the room.

CHAPTER 17

Be extremely subtle, even to the point of formlessness.
Be extremely mysterious, even to
the point of soundlessness.
Sun Tzu, *The Art of War*

Anaïs dragged herself up from the black depths of a dream to a shaft of feeble moonlight cutting across her eyes. She lifted her hand to block it out, and realized she was shivering with cold. And there was something . . . something just beyond her conscious mind. A heavy thing, like a sense of impending doom. Or the remains of a nightmare.

Scarcely half awake, she considered turning over to bury her face against Geoff's chest. To draw in his scent and summon back the memory of his hands flowing over her, of his lips tasting and tempting. But even the exquisite memory of what they had shared could not offset the weight of apprehension. And the chill at her back told her he was long gone from her bed.

Levering up onto her elbow, she looked about the room. She lay naked atop the counterpane, and the outer draperies had not been drawn. Her evening gown and underthings still littered the carpet, just puddles of white and aquamarine in the gloom. Geoff's clothing was gone.

Anaïs dragged a hand through her hair and tried to remember what had awakened her.

A sound. There had been a sound.

Rising and jerking on the robe Claire had left across her
chair, Anaïs snatched the blade she kept sheathed beneath
her pillow, then moved soundlessly toward the dressing
room. She was fully awake now, her every sense alert.

There. She heard it again. A subtle, almost mournful
sound. And yet something not quite human, either, like the
flow of an underground river. She went through to Geoff's
room, and entered without knocking.

Sheets pooling about his slender waist, he sat bolt upright,
already half out of bed, the pale moonlight casting him in an
eerie white glow. Despite the chill, both windows were flung
wide. The sound came again, like the sough of the wind, but
her entire focus was upon him.

"Geoff?" Anaïs hastened across the room, dropping the
knife into her pocket.

He thrust out an arm. "Stop!" he rasped.

But she stood at the edge of the mattress now. "What's
wrong?" she whispered.

"It's the water," he murmured, his eyes focused not upon
her, but somewhere in the depths of the room. "The water.
Can't you see it?"

He was dreaming.

She perched on the bed, one leg tucked beneath. "Geoff,
wake up," she said, reaching out for him. "There's no water.
It's just a nightmare."

"Hush," he whispered, his palm still held outward. "That's
it. Do you see? The water?"

A faint breeze seemed to stir through the room, rippling
the curtains. She set a hand to his cheek, wondering if she
should wake him. "Geoff, there's no water."

"*The darkness*," he rasped. "The sand. It's in her shoes. She feels it." This time he seized Anaïs by her upper arms, dragging her to him as if she were weightless. "Good God, why doesn't she see?"

She landed awkwardly across his lap. "See *what*?"

"The moon is bright," he said, wrenching her arms hard enough to bruise. "The waves are calm. She can't—she can't . . ."

Anaïs set a hand to his cheek. He was shuddering as if with cold, but his skin was feverish. "Geoff, *who*?"

"It's too late." The choked out the words. "It's too dark. *Tell him* it is too dark."

Vaguely frightened now, Anaïs forced Geoff's face around and into the white moonlight.

Later she could not have said the moment at which she grasped the fact that the chill in the room was not just a chill. That Geoff was not asleep, that he was not even present. Or at least, a part of him was not. His lupine eyes burned down into her, wild like nothing she'd ever seen or could even have imagined. And despite the gloom, his pupils were like tiny shards of onyx, glittering and multifaceted.

As if he saw through the eyes of another.

And he did, she realized. Dear God, he did.

"Geoff?" Her voice was thready. "Come back. *Please*."

Suddenly, the air surged about them in surreal, unpredictable currents. The sheer draperies, already tossed by the breeze, began to float. There was a low sound, like wind roaring in a distant tunnel followed by a loud *thwap!* Anaïs looked around to see that *L'Art de la Guerre* had blown from the desk. It lay upon the floor, its pages ruffling back and forth like a wheat field in the wind. Then the papers in his traveling desk lifted and began to spin about the room in a cyclone of foolscap.

Anaïs cast her eyes about the room as a lock of her hair whipped across her face. "Geoff, what's happening?" she cried, clinging to him now.

His grip on her arms tightened, if such a thing were possible. "She is going to die," he whispered. "She is going to die. He is pushing her under. Holding her. *Killing her.*"

"Who?" she cried. "*Charlotte?* For God's sake, *who?*"

"Charlotte," he murmured. "Poor Charlotte. She did not see . . ."

Then Anaïs felt his grasp go slack. Geoff fell back against the headboard, his chest heaving like bellows, Anaïs tumbling over with him.

For a moment it was as if time held suspended. As if no one breathed. Then the roar receded like a vanishing train. A deathly stillness settled over the room. The draperies fell limp against the sills. The cyclone of white flew apart, the scattered papers hitching up against furniture legs and wainscoting like so many dead leaves.

"*Grazie a Dio!*" she whispered, setting her forehead to his shoulder.

"Anaïs?" The word was all but silent.

"Geoff?" she managed. "Are you . . . here?"

For what seemed an eternity, he said nothing. But she could feel him slowly returning to himself. Then, his breathing rough, Geoff's arms came around her, wide and strong, and she knew that he had returned to the present.

She clung to him, burying her face against his neck, half afraid and trembling inside.

When he spoke, it was as if the words were dragged from him. "It will be soon, Anaïs," he said, still gasping. "We are out of time."

Anaïs pushed herself up and he let her go. His eyes were his own again, and filled with grief. "Are you all right?" she whispered, searching his face for reassurance.

His breath was steadying. "Aye," he finally said. "Well enough."

A shock of his dark hair had fallen over one eye. Gently, she pushed it back. "What just happened?" she whispered. "Can you tell me? Can you even explain it?"

He shook his head, and set the heels of his hands to his eyes. "Not really." His voice sounded hoarse. "I was just . . . trying to see. I'm sorry. Did I frighten you?"

"Not in the least," Anaïs lied. "And you didn't *try* to see. You did see. Something. The water. The sand. Do you remember?"

He dropped his hands as if resigned. "Oh, aye," he murmured. "I found Giselle's toy. That, and the handkerchief. The letter DuPont brought. I used them."

"To try to open the door." She cast her eyes round the disordered room. "And it looks as though it worked rather well."

He shook his head again. "Not at first," he said quietly. "But you see how it is. It's . . . it's like a sort of madness comes upon me. I hate it. It frightens people."

Anaïs thought it was rather more than that. "It doesn't frighten me," she said again.

He gave a sharp, exasperated laugh. "When I was a lad, I hid it from my mother when the spells came," he said. "She was terrified. The doctors . . . they told her I had a mental disorder. That eventually she would have to put me away."

"Good Lord," said Anaïs. "Surely she did not listen?"

He was quiet for a moment. "No, she took me to someone who was not a doctor," he finally answered. "A . . . a sort of governess who had trained in Vienna, and who worked with children who were thought mentally disturbed. Mad."

She laid a finger to his lips. "Stop using that word."

Geoff watched her for a time, his eyes smooth as blue water now. "Your mother," he said quietly, "she is a sister to the Earl of Treyhern, Sutherland said."

Anaïs dropped her hand. "Yes," she murmured. "Why?"

His gaze fell. "It was his wife," he said. "She was the gov-erness."

"Aunt Helene?" Anaïs was amazed. "But . . . but they have been married ages."

"My mother did not know they had married," he said. "She thought to buy her away from the earl. To offer her more money. Mamma was desperate, you must understand. It was that, she believed, or an asylum."

Anaïs laughed. "I should have loved to have been a fly on the wall for that conversation," she said. "But Helene does have a gift for dealing with children—and uncommon good sense."

"It was the latter which saved me," he said. "She told my mother I was perfectly fine. To let me be, and ignore the doctors."

A memory stirred in the back of Anaïs's mind. "And then you found your mentor," she said. "In Scotland, yes?"

His smile was wistful. "Ah, that is a very long story," he said. "Another tale for another night, perhaps."

But Anaïs was not sure they would have many more nights.

She pushed away the thought. "Well, you have the Gift," she said. "And all that matters is that you've learned to deal with it."

"Aye, until I need it," he said, his expression bleak. "And then it's like calling up the devil. But the devil can't help Charlotte Moreau, can he?"

She threaded a hand through his hair again. "So tell me," she encouraged. "Tell me exactly what happened tonight. You took the dog, and the other things. And then what?"

He lifted his broad, bare shoulders. "Nothing came," he said. "Nothing but that awful darkness. It's haunted me, Anaïs, since we got here. But nothing came so I tried to sleep. It happens that way sometimes, just as the conscious mind begins to slip away . . ."

"And you fell into that odd little crack between sleep and wakefulness, didn't you?" she murmured. "I think everyone feels it to some extent. But for you it is—well, you know what it is. And you are all right now?"

"Yes, but Charlotte is not," he replied, grasping her arms again. "Anaïs, think. When did she say they were going on holiday?"

"The day after tomorrow," said Anaïs swiftly. "Why?"

Geoff closed his eyes. "Lezennes is going to drown her," he whispered. "He means to lure her out—a moonlight walk by the sea—and plead his case one last time."

Anaïs jerked upright. "Oh, Geoff. *No.*"

But his gaze had turned inward. "But she . . . she rejects him," he went on. "He all but knows she will. And he is prepared. That is why he is taking her away. Away from the house and the servants. Her priest. Even you, perhaps."

"My God, it would be so easy!" Anaïs whispered. "In the dark, in her skirts and crinolines—she would not have a chance in the water."

"He will say she tripped," Geoff whispered. "That a wave came out of nowhere. That they were wading and he could not save her."

Anaïs clapped a hand to her mouth to still her gasp.

"A romantic walk, hand in hand." Geoff's eyes were closed now. "He . . . he holds her under. The surf crashes over them. It does not take long. She is so small." He stopped, and swallowed hard. "So small and tired. After all she has been through, she has so little fight left in her."

"But—but that's monstrous!" Anaïs cried. "We must tell—"

Just then, the clock in the stairway struck four, the sound doleful in the gloom.

Anaïs squeezed her eyes shut. "Oh, Geoff!" she whispered. "This is Friday! This is *already* tomorrow!"

"Aye, it is that." He sat up, and set her a little away. "Anaïs, we must make ready to leave. We must take them with us in the night. It's the only way."

"Yes." Anaïs rose and went to the window to stare across the street at Lezennes' house "Yes, it is the only way. But first I must go and warn her."

"Will she believe you?"

Anaïs turned, the hems of her wrapper whipping round her ankles. "I shall do my best," she said determinedly. "I know—I shall ask her to go with me to confession this morning. She won't think it odd. And once we get to St. Nicholas's I'll tell her everything. I can show her my mark if it comes to it."

"Aye, now that she'll recognize," said Geoff, unfolding his long, lean, and very naked body from the bed. "It might do the trick. At the very least, I don't think she'll tell Lezennes what we're up to. But somehow you must convince her that she is safer with us than with him. Still, I cannot like it. I have not gained her trust—and you may not have done, either."

"Then we resort to ladders and laudanum," said Anaïs grimly.

"So you managed to unlock the windows?"

"Yes, all of them."

"Good girl," he said, snatching up his drawers.

"Oh!" she said witheringly. "I do wish—"

He froze, and flicked a glance up at her in the gloom. "What?"

"I do wish you did not have to put those back on," she blurted, then snagged her lip in her teeth. "Ah, but now is not the time, is it?"

And if she were wise, there would never be another time . . .

Was she? Was she going to be wise this time?

His mouth twisted. "Afraid we must press on, love," he said, shoving a leg in. "Wake the house. I want everything packed, loaded, and on the way to Ostend by midmorning. Petit must go along, and tell Captain Thibeaux to make ready. We sail for England tomorrow."

Promptly at half past ten, Anaïs stood on the Vicomte de Lezennes' doorstep in her most demure dress, her prayer book tossed into the market basket swinging from her elbow. To her surprise, one could not actually hear her knees knocking.

The door was opened by a gray-garbed servant whom Anaïs recognized vaguely as one of the downstairs maids. She bobbed a curtsy but did not open the door very wide.

At Anaïs's request, she shook her head.

"*Très* sorry, *madame*," she said in stilted English. "But Madame Moreau is *mal de—de—*"

Fear stirred in Anaïs's chest. "She is ill?"

"*Oui, merci*—ill, and not to receive the callers."

"How very dreadful." Gingerly Anaïs pushed a foot over the threshold. "She seemed quite the thing last night."

The maid bobbed again, and cast her gaze down. "*Désolé, madame*," she said again. "It was—how do you say—*oui*, quick? She will be well soon, it is to be hoped."

She moved as if to close the door, but Anaïs did not extract her foot, and in fact managed to wedge an elbow against the door frame. "Oh, but if I could just see her a moment," she pleaded. "Just long enough to assure myself that it is on no account my fault! Oh, but this is frightful. We kept her up late—playing the pianoforte to entertain us, no less! How thoughtless we were. I feel quite horrible about it now."

"*Non, madame*," said the girl, her voice a little unsteady now. "It is the wish of His Lordship. *Madame* is not for disturbing."

Anaïs put the other foot over the threshold, and wedged her basket in as well. As she'd hoped, the girl finally backed up a pace. "The vicomte, then?" she said, left with no alternative. "Might I speak with him? Just to reassure myself?"

The girl flicked a quick gaze up—almost a warning shot across the bow—then, after a final moment of hesitation, threw the door fully open. "*Bien sûr, madame*," she said. "If you will just take the chair?"

Anaïs sat as instructed, and looked about the entrance hall. A longcase clock by the stairs. An umbrella stand by the door. A very fine rug. All appeared perfectly normal. For a moment, she closed her eyes and tried to move through the house in her mind. This was not the first time she'd done it, either. And she might well have to do it in the dark tonight.

Eyes still closed, she tried to relax. Perhaps something would come to her if she tried to open herself to the void. Some snippet of meaning, or hint of what Lezennes was thinking.

It was no use. Nothing came—not that she had really expected it would.

In short order the girl returned, eyes still downcast, and motioned for Anaïs to follow.

Anaïs rose and trailed after the maid, counting off her steps, mentally noting the distance from hall to stairs. The number of steps. Two paces across the landing. Six more steps.

Lezennes met them at the top of the staircase, and bowed smoothly. He wore an elegantly embroidered banyan over his white shirt, the sleeves folded back to reveal a band of black satin, and had not put on a cravat.

"Madame MacLachlan, you have returned," he murmured, his gaze running almost clinically up her length. Perhaps seen in the light of day—and absent the lubrication of fine wine—Anaïs's actions of the previous evening seemed suspicious to him now.

"Oh, Your Lordship!" she said, setting a plaintive hand on his arm. "Do tell me how poor Charlotte goes on. Do, pray, reassure me. Oh, I am just beside myself at the thought we may have overtaxed her or overset her in some way last night?"

He smiled thinly, and gave one of those airy, elegant waves of his hand. "Not at all," he said. "Do set yourself at ease. It is nothing—a little headache. I merely wished her to rest."

"Well, thank heaven," said Anaïs. "I had hoped she and I might walk to church together this morning."

"I'm afraid that is out of the question," said Lezennes.

Anaïs tried to look wide-eyed and innocent. "Might I go in to see her, then?" she begged. "Just for a moment? Perhaps I might bring her something. A little calf's-foot jelly, perhaps?"

He hesitated, a sort of smirk upon his face, then Lezennes gave a little bow. "You are all kindness, *madame*," he said. "A brief moment will not hurt. But you will see that all is well. Please follow me."

It was on the tip of Anaïs's tongue to tell him she knew quite well where Charlotte's room was, but she suspected at once that the vicomte did not mean to let her from his sight.

She was to be proven right. They strode through the passageway and past Charlotte's room to a door at the very end of the hall. Lezennes opened it to reveal a small, elegantly furnished sitting room with additional doors to either side—a connecting room, she realized, between Lezennes' bedchamber and Charlotte's. The man was utterly without shame.

Charlotte reclined upon a divan by the windows, the door to her bedchamber open. "No, Louisa, the red shoes, please," she said, motioning to someone beyond Anaïs's line of sight.

"Look, *ma petite*, who I have brought you," said Lezennes, striding into the room.

Charlotte's head turned slowly. "Anaïs!" she said, moving as if to rise.

"No, no, you mustn't get up!" said Anaïs. "I know you are unwell, and I can stay but a moment."

A ghost of some inscrutable emotion passed over Charlotte's face. "Lezennes wishes me to rest," she said. "Tomorrow we travel. But how lovely to see you. Do sit down."

"Only for a moment," said Anaïs, glancing up at Lezennes as she sat. "Perhaps the vicomte will join us? We promise not to chatter about bonnets or ribbons, sir, if you will? And then you will see that I mean to keep my promise. I will stay but briefly."

Some of the suspicion seemed to leave his face then, and he took the seat next to her—which he had doubtless meant to do all along.

"Thank you both, by the way, for a lovely evening," Anaïs said, neatening the folds of her skirts. "It was quite the best meal we'd had in an age, my lord. Perhaps, Charlotte, your cook can be persuaded to give her soufflé recipe to Mrs. Janssen?"

"I shall see to it before we leave." But Charlotte was looking wan and uneasy.

It was only then that Anaïs realized a maid stood in the doorway to Charlotte's room, her arms heaped with clothing.

"Yes, all those, Louisa," Charlotte said to her. "Thank you. You are too kind."

"Oh, you are packing!" said Anaïs.

"Yes. Well, Louisa is doing it for me."

Anaïs wagged a finger at her. "Well, if you mean to take the train, Charlotte, do be careful."

"Careful? In what way?"

"Pack all your most important things in one small bag

and keep it to hand," said Anaïs warningly. "Things of sentimental value, especially. I once had my trunks stolen—in Gloucestershire, of all places! I was going to visit my grandmother, and one way or another my trunks were snatched! Can you believe it?"

"But how dreadful!"

"Oh, it was," said Anaïs earnestly. "Luckily, Mamma had the foresight to pack all my keepsakes and a change of clothing in my handbag, or I wouldn't have had so much as a pair of clean drawers when I got to—oh, your pardon, my lord!"

Lezennes lifted one eyebrow. "Not in the least, Madame MacLachlan," he said coolly. "We all wear them, *n'est-ce pas*?"

Anaïs giggled. "To be sure, we do!"

They spoke on for a time about the pleasures of the seashore, and their various childhood memories. Anaïs had none, for her family had been too busy with the farm and their vineyards abroad—and she with her travels to Tuscany.

But she spoke of none of that, maintained her bourgeois façade, and spun instead a hilarious story about how her sister had once fallen headlong off the Cobb at Lyme Regis—and if anyone noticed that the tale was only slightly altered from one Miss Austen had once told in a novel, they were kind enough not to mention it. Anaïs's fictional sister limped away with only her pride and her petticoats wounded, their family holiday intact.

Charlotte then began to speak of her plans to entertain Giselle with sandcastles and seashell hunting during their coming trip to the shore. But as if the topic made him uncomfortable, Lezennes jerked at once to his feet.

"Charlotte, really, you must have your rest if we are to travel tomorrow."

Anaïs knew it was her cue to go.

"His Lordship is quite right, of course," she said, swiftly

rising. "Now, Charlotte, don't get up. I am going to run home and send the kitchen girl back over with a little bowl of my calf's-foot jelly. You must warm it up and spoon it slowly, now—oh, and a book!—I have a book I think you might like."

"One of your unusual novels, *madame*?" enquired the vicomte, with only a faint curling of his nose.

Anaïs managed to blush. "Oh, no, my lord, 'tis just a volume of Mr. Coleridge's poems," she said. "But I thought it might make for easy reading during your travels tomorrow."

"Thank you," said Charlotte swiftly. "I'm sure it would prove diverting."

Anaïs bowed her way from the room, wishing them a marvelous holiday and counting her steps as she went. And all the while she looked about for obstacles that one might most easily trip over in the dark.

Lezennes abandoned her at the top of the stairs after wishing her a good day, then returned to Charlotte's sitting room. Anaïs watched him go, more certain than ever that she was grateful not to have Geoff's gift. Grateful not to know—not to *feel*—the evil that lurked inside such men. For it did not take a gift to see that Lezennes watched Charlotte like a hawk, and meant to keep doing so until she was either betrothed or dead.

Anaïs was determined it would be neither.

Pensive and deeply worried, she went back across the Rue de l'Escalier and let herself in. After setting her basket aside, she trailed through the public rooms of the house. Seeing no one, she peeked through the back window to see a fourgon sitting in the alley at the end of the rear yard. Attired in tall boots and snug breeches, Geoff was on board, helping Petit strap the baggage down.

After permitting herself a few moments to admire the

view, Anaïs let the curtain drop, then went directly upstairs and through her room into Geoff's.

His volume of Coleridge poems still lay amidst the tidy stack of books. After flipping through it to be certain it contained the poem she wished, and that the flyleaf bore no sentimental inscription, Anaïs carried it back through the dressing room.

She tossed it on the bed, opened Nonna Sofia's box, and shuffled through the tarot until she found the card she wanted.

Il Cavaliere di Spade. The Knight of Swords.

For an instant, she closed her eyes and pressed the card to her breast.

It was entirely possible, she knew, that she would not see the card again. After more than two centuries of being handed down from one generation to the next, her family's *tarocchi* would be incomplete—and it would be her doing. The pack would be rendered utterly useless.

The thought left an odd catch in her throat.

At least it was not her card. It was not *le Re di Dischi*.

And yet, strangely, Anaïs no longer wished to take that card from the box, either. Her girlish fantasy—and her nonna's prediction—seemed far, far in the past, and there was a longing inside her now that had nothing to do with a foolish pack of cards.

Anaïs had begun to feel the passage of time most acutely. She was suddenly tired of waiting. Indeed, she felt almost silly for having done so. She wanted a life, a husband and children to love. She no longer cared if her beautiful Tuscan prince never turned up.

In fact, she almost wished he would not. She almost wished . . .

Ah, but that would not do.

Still, while Anaïs had no wish to dishonor Nonna Sofia,

there was no mistaking the fact that something had changed inside her. She was beginning to question the wisdom of waiting for the perfect man. In truth, the whole prediction seemed so harebrained, she wondered she'd ever believed it at all. And save for Maria, no one else knew. The story was too outlandish to bear repeating.

But Nonna Sofia had repeated it—or at least her tarot had. Time and again, the card had turned up for Anaïs. Time and again, the King of Pentacles had been her destiny.

But if she tossed *le Re di Dischi* to the four winds, if she never got *il Cavaliere di Spade* back from Charlotte, did it really matter? She did not want to read *i tarocchi*. She did not mean to consult the cards ever again in any seriousness. The reading she'd given Charlotte still troubled her. She did not want this Gift her blood had cursed her with; no, not even this faint, watered-down version of it.

It made her think again of Geoff; of the young boy he once had been, frightened and floundering in the dark with no one to guide him.

And suddenly the oddest thought struck her.

Why had there been no one?

How could his mother not have known the Gift for what it was? The blood had come either from her or from Lord Bessett. One of them should have recognized the signs, should have known Geoff needed help—and should have found it for him. A Guardian, a Preost to counsel him, a mentor within his circle of blood—*someone*, for God's sake. It was how the Gift had been protected for eons.

Instead, his mother had taken him to doctors. She had feared him mad.

For the first time, Anaïs realized how little sense that made.

Good Lord, no wonder he had felt so deeply for Giselle Moreau—and for Charlotte, too. No wonder he understood so well the fear and uncertainty she suffered as a mother;

why he had been unwilling to hurt her, to take the child away. It was likely what the doctors had tried to do with him.

And Charlotte *knew* her daughter possessed the Gift. How much harder her life would have been had she not known! Anaïs could scarcely fathom the concern that such a strange, fey child would instill in an unsuspecting mother's heart.

But Geoff's background was a mystery that would have to wait—and wait forever, perhaps, for both Geoff's past and his future were swiftly becoming none of her business. For good or ill, her days with him would soon be at an end. And she could not help but wonder—once he had returned to England, the Brotherhood, and his almost-fiancée—if he would not find himself a little relieved to be shut of her.

She had no wish to think about that, and her pathetic sniveling would not help Charlotte. Taking the book and the card, Anaïs bounded off the bed and went to her desk by the door, then yanked open the drawer to snatch a pencil. Turning the card to the light, Anaïs drew a fingertip down the drawing, taking in the knight's bowed head. His drooping sword. The backdrop of a barren, colorless landscape.

An empty life. An abandonment. A swordsman with no enemy to fight.

It was similar, she thought, to the life of a Guardian denied.

Anaïs slammed shut the desk drawer and bent her head to her task. In the thin margin at the bottom of the card she wrote but three words:

Tonight. Be ready.

Laying the pencil aside, she looked at it.

It was vague, but it would have to do. It was almost unnoticeable, too. Indeed, at first glance, it was merely an old card such as anyone might tuck into a book to mark one's place. A worn and slightly unusual one, yes, but most people would not likely give it a second glance.

Charlotte, however, would remember it well. It was the card that had brought tears to her eyes. When she saw it again, she might well study it in great detail, searching for some small sign of her father.

The father who was far, far from dead.

The father who wanted her very much.

Swiftly, Anaïs paged through the book of poetry looking for her favorite poem. It was "Frost at Midnight," Coleridge's ode to the longing he felt for his home, for his birthplace in the English countryside.

She found it, and circled just a few words:

> *Presageful, have I gazed upon the bars,*
> *To watch that fluttering stranger! and as oft*
> *With unclosed lids, already had I dreamt*
> *Of my sweet birthplace . . .*

It was unlikely anyone would look closely at a few circled words. Almost everyone marked passages of poetry, or bits of prose one wished to study or to remember.

It was also unlikely Charlotte would look closely. She probably wouldn't even open the book tonight.

Anaïs cursed aloud, and heartily. No, Charlotte would likely tuck it amongst her things—perhaps into that one piece of hand baggage Anaïs had warned her to prepare.

She heaved a great sigh. *That* likely had not occurred, either.

Indeed, it was rather more likely Charlotte would have tossed the book into the bottom of a traveling trunk, and would scream bloody murder when awakened tonight. And if she did not—if, by some miracle, Anaïs managed to quietly rouse her and plead their case—it was probable Charlotte would wish to dress, to pack a portmanteau, to search

out her favorite hair ribbon or shoes . . . to do all those silly
things women were apt to wish to do when leaving home—
or in this case, leaving everything behind.

And then they would have to get past Lezennes' maid, and
snatch Giselle.

Dear God, this was going to be impossible.

Anaïs felt her shoulders slump. But what choice did they
have? Lezennes clearly did not mean to leave Charlotte's
side, for he had been dressed for the privacy of his home.
He certainly did not mean to permit Anaïs to speak with
her alone.

Just then, there was a knock at the open door and Geoff
strode in, his boot heels heavy on the floor, a riding crop
in hand. Anaïs turned in her chair to look at him. He was
breathtakingly handsome in his snug coat and form-fitting
breeches, his long hair tossed into disarray by the spring
breeze.

His eyes, however, were somber and questioning. "Well?"
he said.

Anaïs shook her head. "He is suspicious," she said. "He
says Charlotte is unwell."

"So you did not see her." His voice was flat with disappointment.

"No, I inveigled my way in, though it took some doing,"
she said.

Geoff sat down on the edge of her bed, looking discon-
certingly as if he belonged there. "That's my girl," he said,
his smile wan. "Ever the devious one."

"But Lezennes would not leave us alone," she went on.
"Not for an instant. But the maid is packing, and they go in
the morning by train."

"At least we know that much." But he was tapping the crop
pensively against his boot top.

Anaïs showed him the book and the card, and explained her plan. "What do you think?" she asked, perching on the bed beside him. "Too risky?"

Geoff cocked one brow, and read over the verse. "Well, the verse proves nothing," he murmured. "I've circled a dozen such passages in the book myself. As to the card, it's old, it's worn, and the words almost blend into the design. One would have to look awfully closely to notice. No, by gad, it could be brilliant."

Anaïs beamed up at him for a moment, then her face fell. "Ah, Geoff, what are the chances?" she asked. "Why would she look at it tonight? What if she really does have a headache? She'll likely just toss it aside."

But Geoff caught her upper arms in his hands. "It is a *good* idea, Anaïs," he said firmly. "Besides, it's all we've got. And if that doesn't work—well, then we pray she doesn't scream the whole house awake, and we try to persuade her to go."

Anaïs held his gaze a little sadly. "Oh, we will persuade her," she murmured. "You should have seen Charlotte today. She looked . . . frightened. I think she knows, Geoff. Is it possible Giselle has—I don't know—*seen* something?"

Geoff had risen, and begun to pace the room. "It's hard to say," he murmured. "Children and their parents generally cannot read one another."

"Nonna Sofia could read my cards," said Anaïs.

Geoff considered it. "But you were the fourth generation down," he said crossing his arms and leaning back against the doorframe. "The blood was thin. Still, who knows? The Gift is strange, especially when it's strong. It is more likely Giselle can read Lezennes, or sense the evil in him. Hell, I can sense that much without laying a hand on the bastard—I beg your pardon. My language suffers from my frustration."

"Lud, never mind that!" Anaïs sighed. "At the very least, I

think Charlotte knows Lezennes means to propose marriage to her one last time. And she knows she means to refuse him."

"Aye, and that alone might be enough to make her run," Geoff muttered, arms still crossed resolutely. "I pray to heaven, Anaïs, that I'm doing the right thing. That Charlotte will be well and that we will get her child safely away. And by God, if I have to stab that bastard Lezennes through the heart to get the job done, then so be it."

And that, Anaïs later realized, was the moment she fell completely, utterly, head-over-heels in love with the formerly cold and aloof Lord Bessett. The moment when the prince of her dreams became not a dark, dashing Tuscan rogue, but a practical and quietly ruthless Englishman with eyes like arctic ice and hair kissed by the sun. The moment when she realized that her great-grandmother's dream was not necessarily her own, and that fortunes, perhaps, could be altered if one truly willed it so.

Of course they could be altered.

Wasn't that precisely what they were doing here? They were saving Charlotte from an awful fate. Snatching Giselle from a man destined to use her ill. None of it was written in stone—and if it was, then why were they any of them there? Of what use was the Gift at all?

The reality—the *possibility*—caught her breath and stole it away with her heart.

Nonna Sofia was gone, and allowing her dream to keep living would not bring her back to Anaïs. It would not make her any less dead—and it need not make her any less important. Nonna Sofia had been right about a great many things—well, everything, really.

Just not this.

On this score, she was wrong—or at the very least, Anaïs prayed she was.

A little unsteadily, she rose from the bed and went to him. Setting a hand to Geoff's cheek, she stood her tiptoes and kissed him lightly. "Has anyone ever told you, Geoffrey Archard, that you are utterly amazing?" she whispered.

His eyes warmed. "Oh, aye?" he answered. "What was that for?"

Anaïs drew away, but did not remove her hand. "I am not perfectly sure," she admitted. "But I'll tell you when I have finished working it out."

At that, he threw back his head and laughed. Anaïs flashed him a wry smile, then went to the bed, and jerked the coverlet off.

His arms fell, his brow furrowing. "What are you doing with that?"

Anaïs draped it over her arm. "I don't think Monsieur Michel will grieve over it when he gets his house back," she said, "any more than he will grieve over those old blades he keeps upstairs."

"His swords?" Geoff's eyes widened. "Rolling them up and taking them along, are we?"

"Just the sharp ones," she said, breezing past and kissing him again. "After all, they do say if you mean to sup with the devil you'd better bring a long spoon."

"Oh, aye, they do say that." He followed her from the room. "And the connection here would be . . . ?"

She turned in the passageway, the coverlet still draped over her arm. "Well, one of us might have to stab Lezennes through the heart," she said breezily, "but I should like us to have a good length of blade when we do it."

CHAPTER 18

Secret operations are essential in war;
upon them the army relies to make its every move.
Sun Tzu, *The Art of War*

*A*s in most large cities, night never really fell over Brussels, and by the time the city's clocks were striking three, traffic in the main thoroughfares had thinned but slightly. Keeping carefully to the shadows, Geoff crouched utterly still against the fence behind the Vicomte de Lezennes' town house, his legs long ago gone numb.

Tonight the moon was peeking from behind gathering clouds, and at times Geoff could barely make out the utilitarian space, which consisted of a privy, a sort of garden bothy at the rear, and a storage shed attached to the house. Far down the alley, the horses were stamping with impatience, their harnesses faintly jingling.

They would not have long to wait, Geoff considered. In a very few minutes, he and Anaïs would have either succeeded, or failed utterly. Silently, he motioned for Anaïs's attention, then tilted his head toward the shed.

Anaïs flashed her fingers. *Eight feet.*

He agreed, and considered their options again. A lifetime ago, it seemed, he had scoffed at her notion of going in a

window. But neither of them had any experience picking
locks, and even had they managed to do it, he had to weigh
the danger of making their way through the house and back
out a ground floor door, as opposed to shinnying in and out
a window. According to Petit, a servant usually slept near
the front hall.

So the window it would be. And much of it would depend
upon Charlotte's bravery. The child—assuming she was
as disciplined as Geoff believed—could be handed down.
Charlotte could not.

Geoff looked again at Anaïs, and marveled at the trans-
formation. Her hair was braided ruthlessly atop her head
such that a hat might cover it in a pinch. She wore, however,
nothing but soft boots, a loose shirt and waistcoat, and her
brother's trousers.

Just an hour earlier, he had watched her prepare much as
he had done; a knife sheathed in a wrist strap, another in her
boot, and a length of rope hitched round her waist. She had
dressed with outward calm, and since leaving the house had
followed his every signal, as if she understood that tonight
they must move and function as one.

Between them, they carried two small pistols, count-
less blades, a vesta box, a candle stub, and a small bottle
of modern ether—one that von Althausen had obtained for
Geoff prior to their departure—and one that he prayed to
God they would not need. He looked at the window again,
and decided.

He set his head very near hers, barely whispering. "Can
you tell if anyone is still awake?"

She caught his gaze, and gave a little jerk of her head.
Slipping from the shrubs, she eased her way up the yard,
moving low and always in the shadows, setting every foot
right. She really was like a cat in the dark.

Geoff followed an arm's length behind. At the back of the house, she stopped and began to move across the length, utterly silent, pausing from one window to the next. When she reached the shed, she knelt and set one hand to stonework.

He leaned nearer.

"Someone is snoring down by the kitchens," she whispered. "Otherwise, no one stirs."

He nodded, rose, and made his way up the side of the shed, setting one boot against a rain barrel, and the other against the door frame, then hefting himself up and over the sloping eave. That done, he reached down and pulled Anaïs up after him. Already balanced atop the barrel, she came up easily and silently.

They had already agreed that Anaïs should go in Charlotte's window first, though he did not like it. But if Charlotte should awaken, she was far more apt to recognize Anaïs's voice. Motioning toward the downspout, she gave it a solid jerk to test its bracketry. It did not budge. Anaïs turned and began to climb, shinnying up like a monkey, using the pipe, the ledges, and even a few chinks in the stonework.

It was perhaps the hardest thing he'd ever done, standing on that shed roof in the shadows of Lezennes' house and watching Anaïs make her way toward possible danger. But she had argued for it, and she had been right. He would follow her up if—and only if—she got the window open.

And that would be the tricky part. It was no easy task to slide up a window from the outside, using only one hand while hanging on to a downspout. But she wedged a palm against the center glazing bar and lifted the lower sash inch by inch, the counterweights rumbling gently in the frame.

He only prayed it would not be enough to awaken Charlotte. He started up after her just as Anaïs braced both hands on the sill and lifted herself through. By the time he stuck his head through the blessedly thin draperies, Anaïs was crouched by a large white object—the bed, he quickly realized as his eyes adjusted.

Anaïs pointed two fingers at her eyes, then stabbed her index left and right. He swiveled his head. A bedside lamp, and a chair on the opposite side of the window. He nodded. Then, maneuvering deftly around them, Geoff slid through and into the room.

Charlotte lay on her side, turned away from them, her body curled round a bolster beneath the covers. Anaïs stood, and set a hand over Charlotte's mouth.

Geoff felt it the instant Charlotte startled awake, fear surging through the room.

"*Shh*, it's Anaïs," she whispered. "Just me. For God's sake, Charlotte, don't make a sound. Nod if you understand."

Geoff heard Charlotte's hair scrub the pillow.

"Thank God," said Anaïs, removing her hand.

Charlotte rolled up onto her elbow. "Anaïs! What on earth?"

"Charlotte, we've no time," Anaïs whispered. "You are in grave danger. I think you know that."

"Y-yes." Her voice tremulous, she dragged herself up in bed.

"Charlotte, we must get Giselle away," Anaïs murmured. "I think you know why. The French Brotherhood of the *Fraternitas Aureae Crucis* has sent us. A man named DuPont. Do you know him?"

Charlotte shook her head, and drew the covers to her chest. "How can I trust you?" she whispered, her voice sharp. "How can I know?"

"I haven't time to tell you everything," Anaïs pressed. "And really, you haven't much choice. But we know about your husband. The French Brotherhood thinks Lezennes killed him."

"Oh, God! I . . . I think so, too." She sounded on the verge of tears.

"Charlotte, now is not the time," said Anaïs sternly. "Now, I am marked—I bear the mark of the Guardian, and so does Geoff."

For the first time, he moved from the shadows. Charlotte gasped.

Anaïs plowed on. "You know what the mark means," she said. "Once we've got some light, I'll show you. You can decide later who you'd sooner trust—me, or Lezennes."

"*You*," said Charlotte tremulously. "Anyone but Lezennes."

"Good, get up and get one bag, Charlotte," Anaïs ordered. "We haven't time to dress."

"I packed it," said Charlotte. "The one bag, as you said. And the card in the book . . . I wondered—"

"Good, now just find it without tripping. We'll get your other things later—if we can."

It was a testament to Charlotte's fear that she did not hesitate. "Just the bag in the chair," she whispered. "It will do."

Geoff felt his way to it, and in a trice had the portmanteau roped and run out the window while Charlotte was up and putting on her shoes. It scraped a little when it hit the shingles of the shed, otherwise all was silent.

It was then that they struck another bit of luck.

"I'm going to get Giselle," said Anaïs. "Is she a sound sleeper?"

"She is here," Charlotte whispered, pointing at the lump, which was not a bolster after all. "She was frightened—has been frightened for days now. Lezennes will not usually let her leave her bed, but tonight he relented."

Her words sent a shiver down Geoff's spine. He knew precisely why the child was frightened, and why Lezennes had relented. The devil believed full well that Giselle would be entirely his in a matter of days—and that Charlotte would be dead.

"Wake her," Anaïs ordered. "We are going to lower her out the window first."

"Out the window?" Charlotte clapped a hand over her mouth.

"We cannot risk waking the footman downstairs," Anaïs pressed. "She will be fine. We do this all the time."

"You *do*?"

"All the time," Anaïs repeated.

Then, in a few short words, she laid out the plan. Charlotte's voice began to shake to the point that Geoff could feel her raw fear. It was best to keep them moving, to press on.

Anaïs understood. "Wake her, Charlotte," she ordered. "Be utterly calm and clear in your directions."

Charlotte nodded, shaking the child awake and speaking to her in a French so soft and swift Geoff could not follow. But in a matter of moments, the child was up but groggy, and nodding at her mother's instructions. As Geoff had expected, Giselle was fully cooperative though she spoke not a word to anyone. It was almost as if she *knew* why they had come—or perhaps she merely understood the evil forces that threatened her mother.

Whatever it was, Geoff thought, it was a burden no child so young should bear, and his heart wrenched again for Giselle Moreau.

But he hadn't long to think about it. With knots that would have made a sailor proud, Anaïs tied the child at the shoulders and waist. Soon he was going back out the window and down to the roof. As Anaïs lowered her inch by inch, Giselle clung a little to the drainpipe, but otherwise made not a sound. Geoff pulled her into his embrace, and at once the child's arms went round his neck. And still she spoke not a word.

Soon Charlotte was coming backward out the window, a heavy wool cloak thrown over her shoulders, her white nightdress flapping in the growing breeze. Though Anaïs had tied a rope round her chest and hitched it tight beneath her arms, Charlotte managed to more or less climb down on her own, losing her footing but once. She made a little sound, a sort of short, sharp scream, but caught the drain-pipe and clung.

Anaïs dragged back on the rope, and Charlotte stopped swaying. She finished the climb, but her whole body was shaking. They would be bloody lucky, though, Geoff thought, if no one heard.

Moments later, they all stood on solid ground. Geoff had the child hitched onto his hip but her arms were still round his neck, clinging as if for dear life.

"Let's go." Anaïs snatched Charlotte's portmanteau, then froze.

"What?" Geoff mouthed the words.

Anaïs tried to listen. "Someone is awake," she whispered. "Someone inside the house."

Charlotte started to speak, but Anaïs clapped a hand over her mouth.

"Quickly," said Geoff. "Through the alley."

Anaïs moved swiftly, her heart in her throat, and one arm hitched through Charlotte's. Thus far, all had gone according to plan, though how much longer Charlotte's nerves would hold was not at all clear to Anaïs.

Dieric van de Velde's coachman had nerves of steel, Anaïs would give him that. He threw open the door and bustled Charlotte and Giselle inside with utter calm, then leapt up onto the box smoothly, as if he fled in the middle of the night once or twice a week.

Geoff untied his mount from the rear, then pulled Anaïs behind the carriage door to swiftly kiss her. "Well done, love," he said, his voice low. "I just pray I never have to watch you do it again."

Anaïs leaned in to kiss him back, but at once, the hair on the back of her neck prickled. Her heart sinking, she cast a quick glance over her shoulder at the house.

Someone had lit a lamp in Charlotte's room.

Anaïs cursed beneath her breath. "We are found out," she muttered. "Mount up, St. George. Your dragon has awakened."

The coachman set off slowly at first, going as quietly as he could, then picking up speed as the center of Brussels vanished. After drawing the curtains down and lighting the small carriage lamp, Anaïs managed to help Charlotte and Giselle dress. She had taken the precaution of having Mrs. Janssen procure a few extra articles of clothing, but Charlotte had packed well in her small bag.

"You took my advice, I see," she said, smiling into the gloom.

"Yes, and I saw the note on your card," she confessed as she wrapped Giselle's cloak tightly round her. "But it looked so old and so strange. Though I did wonder . . ."

Anaïs watched Charlotte's hands tenderly tucking the wool round the child, and felt a moment of admiration—and a little envy, too. Giselle was a lovely, if shy child, and obviously more normal than the vicomte had let on.

"A penciled message on the card was all I dared," she murmured. "Lezennes had become too suspicious."

"Oh!" Charlotte turned to rummage through her bag. Extracting the book, she took out the card and gave it to Anaïs.

With mixed emotions, Anaïs tucked it inside the coat she now wore over a brocade waistcoat and a hastily tied cravat. The whole of it had once been her brother's, and Anaïs had decided that simply wearing it on to Ostend was the wisest thing.

She was quite certain the first thing Lezennes would do after waking his household and searching every room was to go across the street and demand she and Geoff be rousted from their beds. But he would find nothing save a house shut up, and all the servants gone as quickly as they had come.

Lezennes was no fool, however. He would draw his own conclusions. Should he then manage to guess their route and enquire after them along the way—both of which were likely—he would be looking for two ladies, not a lady and a young man.

But they would likely make better time than Lezennes. The roads were good, their carriage light and well-sprung, and drawn by four good horses. They carried virtually no luggage. Petit had gone ahead to arrange for fresh teams along the route. With some luck they would reach the coast by mid-afternoon.

But Lezennes would be driven by temper. And temper was a factor one should never underestimate. He might forgo the comfort of his carriage or simply send his minions on horseback. Or he might be so sure of their plans he would wait for the trains to run, head straight to Ostend, and arrive there before they could sail. None of it was likely, but any of it was possible—and all of it she and Geoff had planned for and discussed throughout the day and half the night.

She simply had to trust their good judgment. *She had to trust in Geoff.*

Charlotte was staring blindly out the window as the last of Brussels flew by. "Where are we going, Anaïs?" she whispered, her voice edged with fear. "Who will take care of us now? The French? The *Fraternitas*? Who—?"

Anaïs reached out, and gripped Charlotte's arm firmly. "The *Fraternitas*, always," she said. "But this time in England. It is more stable, Charlotte. And a new Guardian can be appointed to Giselle."

Charlotte's head whipped round, eyes wide. "Your husband?"

Anaïs felt her face flush. "No, and Geoff is not my husband," she admitted. "That was just a ruse, Charlotte."

"Not . . . your husband?" Charlotte looked dumbstruck. "Then who?"

"Neither Mr. MacLachlan nor I are married," she answered. "And our names aren't even—well, never mind that."

But Charlotte looked pale as milk in the weak lamplight. "And the cards," she whispered. "Were the cards a lie, too?"

"I almost wish they had been," muttered Anaïs. "But no. They were not. In any case, the Gallic Confederation has asked us to protect Giselle until she reaches majority. The *Fraternitas* has good men in Essex. One of them will likely be assigned."

"In Essex?" Charlotte's eyes widened.

"Yes." Anaïs dug about in her bag for Sutherland's letter. "Our Preost has been in Colchester arranging things with your family," she said, handing it to Charlotte.

Charlotte unfolded the letter and turned it to the lamp. Then the letter began to tremble slightly, and for the first time, it was as if a little color returned to her face. "He means my father," she whispered, eyes darting over it. "My God! *He has spoken to Papa!* Is that what it means? That I really may go home?"

At last, Giselle spoke—just a few words, but excitedly. "*Maman! Nous allons à l'Angleterre!*"

Charlotte hugged her tight. "Yes, *ma petite*," she whispered into the child's hair. "I think we do. I think we are going to England at last."

Anaïs reached across the distance of the coach, and tipped up the child's chin. "But we have far to go to get there,

Giselle," she said lightly. "And you will have a grandpapa to meet. It might be better if you slept now."

Lips pressed into a firm line, Charlotte patted her lap. "Good advice," she said. "Put your head here, and rest."

Giselle did as she was told. Charlotte threaded her hand almost soothingly through the child's hair, but after a time her gaze returned to Anaïs.

"I always knew it, you know," she murmured almost accusingly. "From the moment I met you that day at church. There was something—something in your eyes—it did not match your gay demeanor. And then you read those cards— and I . . . I just knew. For good or ill, something very big was about to happen."

Something big very nearly had happened, thought Anaïs ruefully.

Lezennes had meant to drown her in the sea. Save for Geoff's vision—and his ruthless resolve—Charlotte might well have died before this day was out. But Anaïs could see that Charlotte was again blinking back tears—tears of joy, unless she missed her guess. There was no point in revisiting the horrors she had just escaped.

As if by mutual agreement, they said no more for a time. Giselle drowsed as the Flemish countryside rolled by in the darkness, but deep sleep evaded her until they had turned onto the main road toward Ghent.

Then Charlotte spoke more plainly. "We are going to the coast," she murmured. "To Ostend, yes? And Lezennes will be after us."

"Yes," said Anaïs. "A ship awaits us there. And yes, I am very much afraid that Lezennes will not be far behind us."

Charlotte touched her fingers to her lips.

Swiftly Anaïs told her of what she had seen, and of their decision to go by coach rather than wait for the trains to run, for trains were far too public. She silently prayed it was not a decision they would come to regret.

"And from Ostend?"

"Directly to Harwich," said Anaïs. "Our Preost is still there visiting family. Geoff sent a man ahead on this morning's packet. With a little luck, Charlotte, your family will be waiting at the port."

But Charlotte had dropped her gaze. "It is almost too much to be hoped for," she said quietly.

After so many years, Anaïs could understand her feelings. "Charlotte," she whispered, "what do you know of Lezennes' plans for Giselle?"

Charlotte's eyes filled with pain. "At first I was too stupid to realize he had plans, or that he even understood Giselle's Gift," she confessed. "What kind of mother could be so foolish?"

A desperate one, thought Anaïs. "But he did understand, Charlotte," she said certainly, "and he wanted control of her. Do you know why, specifically?"

"I think he wanted to bring her up as his own," said Charlotte, "to have her completely under his thumb. He wanted to force Giselle to use the Gift to see into the future—so that he might turn it to his advantage, politically and economically—or try to alter it entirely."

"Do you know who Lezennes was working for?"

Charlotte's gaze flicked up, wary and uncertain. "For the French government, I assumed," she said, "but late one night . . ."

"Yes?" Anaïs urged.

Fleetingly, Charlotte covered her mouth with her hand. "A man came to the house," she whispered. "A man I knew from Paris—an agent of the old Bourbons, it was whispered. Anaïs, there are many amongst the French nobility who will never stop trying to return them to the throne. They wish to turn history back sixty years! The old monarchy. The old cruelties. And Lezennes is one of them. I know. I put my ear to the door. I had to know. And it was then that I knew I could never marry him. That we had to flee."

It was just as Geoff had suspected, then. Suddenly, another question occurred to Anaïs. "Charlotte," she asked, "what did the vicomte know of your family? Did he know where you were from?"

"No," she whispered. "And I told him what I told everyone—that I had no family. It seemed easier than the truth. That I had been disowned."

That was a bit of good fortune. Anaïs tried to relax.

It was Geoff's plan to drive straight through, stopping only to change the horses. Once they arrived at the port, he meant to put it about that the *Jolie Marie* was bound for Dover. That would make sense to Lezennes. With any luck, if he dared follow, he would head in the wrong direction from Ostend. Perhaps he would not dare follow at all.

Ah, a faint hope, that.

But nothing could be done about it now. Lezennes was not apt to catch them on the road. Nonetheless, Anaïs could not keep herself from extracting Mr. van de Velde's carriage pistols and checking them for about the fifth time as Charlotte looked on, her eyes wide in the moonlight.

"It will be all right, Charlotte," she said reassuringly. "You'll be home in two or three days."

"C-can you use that?" asked Charlotte.

"If I have to, yes," said Anaïs softly. "But it won't come to it. Now try to get some rest."

Charlotte nodded, set her head against the wall of the carriage, and closed her eyes.

The guns returned to safekeeping, Anaïs settled back

against the banquette. Then she, too, let the carriage lull her into something vaguely like sleep. But her senses would not entirely quiet, and when she dreamt, it was of Geoff. Geoff in a damp, pitch-black alley, his hand boldly snaring her assailant's knife. Caught in that place which was halfway between wakefulness and oblivion, Anaïs gave a soft, inward smile, feeling oddly safe, oddly comforted.

CHAPTER 19

*It is essential to seek out enemy agents
who have come to conduct espionage against you.*
Sun Tzu, *The Art of War*

$\mathscr{G}$eoff pushed his way through the surge of humanity
that surrounded the port of Ostend, Giselle set high
on his hip, her arms still round his neck and her mood
eager, as if she understood what was about to happen. This
morning when he had lifted her down from the carriage
at one of the inns, she had begun to talk to her mother in
whispered French, giving what had sounded to his ear like
assurances.

He prayed the child knew something he did not, for his
every nerve was on edge.

Behind him, Anaïs followed with Charlotte, who today
looked pale and drawn. Anaïs still wore her masculine attire,
her hair covered by a beaver hat. Had anyone looked closely,
however, they would not likely have been long fooled. But
no one bothered; another young family at portside was of
interest to no one.

Up ahead, passengers were swarming around the Dover
ferry. Geoff waded into the morass, carried Giselle to the
ticket window, and in his most booming voice, bought a pas-

sage for four. Then they melted into the crowd again, and passed out the other side.

Under the reign of the new Belgian monarchy, the port was in the process of being modernized and expanded by the widening of channels, a fact that merely added to the press of people. Surrounded by the ceaseless racket of this construction, Captain Thibeaux had been occupying a berth near the commercial basin, and his crew taking their ease. But by the time Geoff stepped on board, all hands were on deck, a faint breeze was coming in off the North Sea, and the gulls were wheeling and crying above.

Despite some ominous clouds gathering to the north, Geoff decided to take it as a good omen.

Thibeaux saw them and hastened forward. *"Bonjour, Bonjour!"* The captain paused just long enough to tweak the little girl's chin as Geoff set her down, then motioned for his cabin boy. "Étienne," he bellowed, *"viens ici!"*

The lad scrambled up from the pile of rope he was working and hastened toward them.

After casting a faintly dubious eye over Anaïs's attire, now badly rumpled from having been slept in, Thibeaux bowed to her and to Charlotte. "My nephew Étienne will take you below to refresh yourselves," he said. "Monsieur MacLachlan, if you will please come with me to inspect the ship?"

Geoff caught Anaïs by the wrist, however, and spun her around. Only then did he realize she had slipped her knife from the sheath up her sleeve, cleverly palming the handle. She, too, was uneasy.

"Keep them below till we're well out at sea," he said, his voice low. "Too many people have seen us board."

Anaïs nodded, her gaze sweeping the wharf again, then she fell into step behind the others. He turned at once to the captain. "Thibeaux, we've no time to spare, I fear," said. "Just get us under way."

The captain nodded. "*Oui*, we have been preparing the sails," he said. "To Harwich, Monsieur Petit says?"

"Aye, and run hard," said Geoff grimly. "I think Lezennes is on our heels."

"Alas, *monsieur*, the wind is not what one might hope for," said Thibeaux a little grimly. "But at the very least, we can get you away from Belgium."

But Geoff could not rest, and paced the clipper's deck as Thibeaux's crew hurried to make ready to sail. The afternoon, however, was well upon them, and up and down the wharves the crowds were growing; the same sorts of crowds one saw along waterfronts all over the Continent. Coopers and longshoremen. Prostitutes and pie men. And the ubiquitous clerks rushing to and fro in their long, dark coats, heads bent to their ledgers.

Geoff's gaze picked carefully through them all, seeing no one he recognized. He turned his gaze to the other ships nearby and saw nothing out of the ordinary save for a sleek, three-masted barque. It was a small vessel built for a lean crew and plenty of speed, but it flew no flag. With the lightest of wind, the barque could have run down any other vessel in port, and if ever the term *motley crew* could have been fairly applied, the handful of men stirring above decks fit the phrase.

Geoff motioned for one of Thibeaux's men. "What do you know of that vessel?" he said with a jerk of his head.

The Frenchman gave a sort of Gallic sneer. "Bah, eet eez just smugglers."

"Smugglers?" said Geoff. "In Ostend?"

The Frenchman tapped the side of his nose. "*J'ai du flair*," he said knowingly. "They have lain here two days, doing nothing but drinking and whoring. Moroccans and Spaniards and a couple of Bretons. They speak to no one. Ask no questions. What else could they be?"

What else indeed.

"What sort of flag do they fly?" asked Geoff as the man walked away.

The Frenchman turned back and grinned up at him. "*Vive le France*," he said, winking. "We are all equal now."

Even then, Geoff knew to heed the sinking feeling in his gut. Or perhaps it was something more than just a feeling. He was not sure. But he went below all the same, knocked on the cabin door, and motioned Anaïs out. Her hair was down now, twisted into a long, thick braid down her back, her coat and wilted cravat cast aside. She carried a steaming mug of something in hand.

"Everything all right?" he asked.

Anaïs smiled, but her eyes looked tired. "Giselle is starting to chatter like a magpie," she said. "And young Étienne has made me a mug of ginger tea and God only knows what else—not opium, he assures me."

Geoff managed to smile back. "Perhaps it will help."

"So he swears." Anaïs did not look hopeful. "How are things on deck?"

He shrugged, and set one shoulder to the door. "There's a French barque berthed near us," he said pensively. "I don't like the look of it."

Her dark eyes widened. "You think it could be Lezennes'?"

Geoff shook his head. "I can't see how," he muttered. "But I have a bad feeling."

"That's nothing to be ignored," said Anaïs. "What can I do?"

Geoff shrugged. "Nothing different," he said. "Thibeaux's second mate says they're just smugglers cooling their heels, and he's likely right."

"Perhaps, but what's more opportunistic than a crew of bored smugglers?" Anaïs pointed out.

Geoff considered it. He was suddenly glad Anaïs was down here, and a little disconcerted by how much he'd come to depend on her. To *trust* her. He was oddly confident he could count on her to keep Charlotte and Giselle safe until they were under way.

He dragged both hands through his hair. "We should have kept van de Velde's carriage pistols," he muttered.

"I've got my pocket pistol," Anaïs assured him. "Just stay above deck, and don't worry about us for now."

Geoff nodded, and came away from the door frame. "All right," he said. "But I'm going to go board that barque. Perhaps . . . perhaps I'll get a feel for something."

He moved as if to go, but her hand caught his arm, her hard gaze softening as it searched his face. "Geoff, I—"

He set his head to one side. "Yes?"

Her eyes fell. "Just be careful," she whispered.

A few moments later Geoff was strolling casually past the French ship's gangplank. He kept going for another fifty yards, then turned around and doubled back. In the fading afternoon light, one could plainly see the ship's name written in gaudy script across the escutcheon.

Le Tigre Doré.

The *Golden Tiger*. A man Geoff took to be the boatswain was cleverly balanced on the port gunwale, feet spread wide, bellowing orders up at a sailor who had climbed into the rigging to hammer at something. On impulse, Geoff bounded up the plank. The half dozen men topside stopped what they were doing and glowered. The boatswain, a hulking chap in a greasy leather jerkin, stepped down and growled something at him in a mix of Dutch and French.

"I'm just looking for Captain Reynard," Geoff answered in badly broken French. "He is an old friend. Is he aboard?"

The boatswain's face further darkened, but he shifted

at once to English. "You are mistaken, *mon ami*," said the man, his lip curling. "You need to go."

Geoff lifted one eyebrow, all the while focusing on the man, on the emotions surging round the deck. Animosity. Suspicion. He was being summed up—and they didn't like what they saw.

Across the deck, a lean, pockmarked chap reached inside his waistcoat as if for a weapon. "Sabot," he called. "*Puis-je t'aider?*"

"*Non*, Navarre," said the boatswain, holding up a hand. "No help is needed. Our friend, he is leaving. *Oui?*"

Navarre stood down, his face dark with disappointment. Geoff forced himself to relax, to look amiable and a little sheepish. "I do beg your pardon, Monsieur Sabot," he murmured. "Is this not Reynard's vessel? The *Silver Tiger?*"

"*Non*," said the boatswain, jerking a thumb aft. "Wrong ship, *mon ami*. And I am the captain here. Now take yourself off."

Geoff backed up a step. "Ah, my apologies, sir. My French . . . it is not so good." He extended a hand, trying to lock eyes with the fellow. Tried to open his mind and focus. "I bid you good day, then."

"*Umph*," said the captain—who scarcely looked the part. But he took the extended hand and gave it a quick, half-hearted shake.

At that instant, something flashed through Geoff's mind in a blaze of color and light. Shards of thought, flickering in his brain like sun dappling through trees. And yet there was nothing he could make out, nothing save that awful sensation in his head, a shaft of something that was not quite pain, but something near it.

"*Merci, monsieur*," he managed.

Then, lifting his other hand as if to block the sun, Geoff

stepped backward onto the gangplank, then turned and strolled—with a nonchalance entirely feigned—in the opposite direction of the *Jolie Marie*.

The journey out to the North Sea was not a swift one, for the channel was choked with traffic and the wind still feeble against the *Jolie Marie*'s sails. As the ship finally entered open water, Thibeaux set a course north-northwest, but a layer of high clouds was fast choking out what little was left of daylight.

Cursing their luck, Anaïs stood on the poop deck, following the line of the horizon with her eyes. Though she had found Belgium beautiful, it felt suddenly as if she could not escape it fast enough. She wished the wind would pick up. At least she was not ill. Not yet.

Or perhaps young Étienne knew what he was doing after all?

Geoff stood below, scanning Ostend's vanishing seafront through Thibeaux's telescope, his bronze hair tossed into disarray by the wind. His worry had deepened, she realized, and not without reason.

Just as the *Jolie Marie* had cast off, a man in a dark frock coat had boarded Geoff's suspicious barque and commenced a heated discussion with the fellow who appeared to be the ship's captain. The two had gone below, according to Geoff, and come back up again ten minutes later shaking hands. In short order, the ship was being made ready to sail.

The crew of *Le Tigre Doré* was certainly headed somewhere. Anaïs had a bad feeling.

Gingerly she leapt down to stand beside Geoff.

He dropped the glass from his eye and set an arm about her waist. "Feeling all right?" he murmured, tilting his head to look at her.

"Well, I'm not seasick yet," she confessed. "But these high clouds and still air make me uneasy. And I'm a little afraid we made a mistake in Ostend."

"Aye?" he said. "How so?"

"Perhaps we should have brought Charlotte up to look at that fellow who boarded the *Golden Tiger*," she finally said. "What if it was one of Lezennes' henchmen?"

Eyes narrowed against the sun's rapidly dropping angle, Geoff shook his head. "Not a risk worth taking," he said calmly. "He might have seen her. Still, if anyone asks around port long enough, they'll figure out which ship we were on. But they will have expended precious time doing it."

"And so we wait," said Anaïs.

"And so we wait," said Geoff. Then, after a quick look around, he brushed his lips across her cheek.

"What are you thinking?" she murmured.

He made a sound, a sort of wry laugh. "That I'm tired of waiting," he said. "Seriously, I'm thinking that half of me wishes you were safe at home in England, whilst the other half is bloody glad you're here."

She crooked her head to look up at him. "And I'm glad you are here," she said. "Very glad."

He flashed her an almost wistful smile, tucked a wayward curl behind her ear, then dropped his arm. Geoff returned to his vigil, pacing along the bulwark, the glass at his eye. Anaïs leapt back up, intent on keeping sight of dry land as long as daylight held.

They did not have long to wait. The sun had no more than dropped below the horizon when Thibeaux's lookout in the crow's nest shouted down. "French vessel to starboard, sir!"

Anaïs heard Geoff curse beneath his breath as he adjusted the telescope.

The lad shinnied down and a few moments later and after conferring, Thibeaux hastened toward them. "It might be the French barque," he said, his voice grave. "It will soon be too dark to tell."

Geoff collapsed the glass and dropped it in his pocket. "Any hope of outrunning them?"

"*Non, monsieur*," said Thibeaux, his voice grave. "The wind is all but gone—which means it will take them some time to catch up with us. What do you think they will do?"

"If they have fallen in with Lezennes, they will try to board us," said Geoff, his voice calm. "They want the child. They will do nothing to put her at risk—nor will we."

"You do not wish the guns loaded?" asked Anaïs, looking up at the two small cannon mounted on the poop deck.

Geoff's mouth thinned. "Too dangerous," he said. "Besides, they are flying the French flag. Thibeaux could pay a great price for it—assuming any of us survived. No, I think it better to bide our time."

"*Monsieur*, they are smugglers," said the captain.

"Aye, so they are greedy and venal," he agreed. "But they just want to snatch the child—and possibly Madame Moreau. We must make it inconvenient for them to do so. And they will realize soon enough that they do not have much of a bone to pick with us."

"Very wise, *monsieur*." Thibeaux sounded relieved.

But Geoff was still staring out to sea, as if working out a strategy in his mind. "What sort of crew will the barque run with?" he asked the captain.

Thibeaux scrubbed a hand round his chin. "Very few, I think," he said pensively. "Twenty at most, and ten can do it. I've not seen above six or eight on deck these last two days."

"And what size is your crew?"

"Fourteen, not counting Étienne," said the captain. "Good hands, all—and happy to fight for the *Fraternitas*."

"Thank you, Thibeaux," said Geoff. "Clouds are gathering to the north. Perhaps the dark will work in our favor?"

"They cannot board what they cannot find," said the captain. "We'll light no lamps on deck tonight."

At last Geoff smiled, though it was tight and a little weary, reminding Anaïs yet again that he had spent half the night and much of the day in the saddle, while she had had the luxury of drowsing, however uncomfortably, in a carriage.

"On the other hand," Thibeaux belatedly added, "if they do find us, they could be upon us before we know it."

Anaïs gave an inward sigh. Thibeaux was right. None of them, it seemed, would sleep this night. It would be far too dangerous. Somehow she tore her gaze from Geoff's face and looked out across the water, but it was already too dark to see much beyond the occasional shimmer of the waves.

"Call all hands, Thibeaux," Geoff ordered. "With swords and sidearms, please. Anaïs will go below and secure the aft cabin."

Not for the first time, Thibeaux cut Anaïs a strange look, as if he did not understand why such duties were being assigned to a woman. She still wore her boots and breeches, a fine stroke of luck. She reached the hatch in a few strides, and more or less leapt down the ladder, something she never could have attempted in skirts.

Inside the cabin, Charlotte and Giselle were sleeping. Étienne was still there, unfolding blankets on the other two berths by the light of a single lantern. Anaïs summed him up; he looked quick and smart, and tall enough, too.

"Étienne, *viens ici*," she whispered.

"*Oui, madame?*" The lad came at once.

Anaïs shifted her trouser leg, and tugged her small pistol from her boot. "Do you know how to use this?"

The lad nodded. Anaïs went over it anyway, showing him step by step. "Yes, *madame*," he said in perfect English. "I can do eet."

His round, solemn face looked up at her steadily, and Anaïs believed him. But they went over it again and again, just the same, until the cabin boy was looking up at her in mild exasperation.

"Excellent," she said. "Now, Étienne, I'm going to go above and guard the aft hatch. A vessel is nearing—the smugglers, perhaps—but they will not cause us too much trouble, I do not think."

The boy smiled bemusedly. "*Non, madame,*" he said. "Uncle has a brave crew. But you—*pardon, madame,* but you are a woman. Do you not wish me to guard the hatch?"

Ah, men were the same the world over, it seemed.

"I think I can manage," she said, seizing one of the small chairs from the table. "Now, once I am gone, take this chair and wedge it tight beneath the doorknob. Do not remove it for anyone. Not unless you recognize the voice—me, Mr. MacLachlan, or one of the crew."

"*Oui, madame.*" He nodded.

She bent, and tucked a finger beneath his chin. "Now, here is the hard part, Étienne," she said. "If anyone tries to force the door, you must—"

"—shoot them," said the boy.

"*Before* they open the door," Anaïs stressed, showing him again the mechanism. "One barrel through the door as a warning shot. The second only if you must. And brace your back against the wall, or the recoil will knock you down and you won't get another shot."

"*Oui, madame,*" he said gravely. "Uncle has taught me. I can do eet."

"I believe you can," said Anaïs, going to their small pile of baggage.

She extracted Monsieur Michel's counterpane, tucked it under one arm, and left, waiting only long enough to hear Étienne wedge the chair as instructed.

"*Alors, madame*," he called through the door. "The water is very calm. Have you the seasickness yet?"

Anaïs froze, set her empty hand to her belly, and smiled. She felt . . . fine. Perfectly normal. And it had little to do with the stillness of the water, not if past experience was any guide. But there was no time to think of it just now.

"No, Étienne," she said quietly. "*Merci*."

CHAPTER 20

The art of war teaches us to rely not on the
likelihood of the enemy's not coming,
but on our own readiness to receive him.
Sun Tzu, *The Art of War*

It had always seemed to Geoff that night fell with surprising swiftness when one was at sea. This one was no different. He watched up and down the deck as Thibeaux's men slowly became one with the gloom, until at last he could make out no one save the fellow on his immediate right. Soon he, too, had vanished, and Geoff was in utter darkness with only the soft *shush-shush* of the sea and the creak of the rigging to bear him company.

He was just beginning to worry about Anaïs again when he felt her warmth at his side. "Here," she said, her voice husky in the dark, "I brought you one of the *épées*."

"Thanks." Gingerly, he found the hilt and took it, then, having no scabbard, drove it into the wood of the deck.

"Good Lord but it's dark," she whispered. "Thank God you're still here."

His fingers were laced through the basket of the *épée*, still warm from her grip. "Aye, still here," he rasped.

Still here—always here—if you will but have me.

But these were mere thoughts, not words to be said aloud, for it was neither the time nor the place.

On the other hand, they lived in an uncertain world. When would his time be? What was his place? In the universe? In her heart? Good God, he was so tired of waiting. And suddenly the doubts and questions rushed in on him. On a sudden, foolish impulse, he drew Anaïs to him and kissed her soundly in the pitch-black night.

She gave a small, breathless gasp, then opened beneath him, taking his kiss and returning it. And for one fleeting instant, all thought of their mission flew from his head, displaced by the desperate need to *know*.

The irony of this was not lost on him—not even as her hands slid over him, warm and caressing, and their tongues twined sinuously together—for in that moment of heated kisses and sudden despair, Geoff would have surrendered everything he owned, everything he was, merely to do what he'd always dreaded—to see into the future—*their* future.

It was Anaïs, however, who broke the kiss, her breath a little shallow as she let her hand skate down his chest, then lower still. "My heavens," she murmured, brushing the ridge in his trousers seductively. "It's true what they say. One never knows what dangerous creatures lurk in the dark."

He jerked her back, lifting her hard against his swelling cock as he skimmed his mouth down her throat. "To hell with the dark," he rasped. "I swear, Anaïs, when we are out of this, I'm going to make love to you in broad daylight—*all* day long—and you are going to let me, do you hear?"

"*Umm*," she said, pushing a little away.

But he refused to let her go. "*Say it*, Anaïs," he ordered. "Say you believe me. Say *yes*."

She gave a faint laugh, dropped her hand, and stepped away. "I fear it will be a long night with a promise like that on my mind," she whispered.

This time, he let her go though he was loath to do it. "Aye," he gritted, "and longer still if Lezennes catches up with us. A case of unslaked lust will be the least of my problems, I daresay."

He heard the soft catch in her throat. Felt her hesitation. "Will he?" she finally asked. "What is your sense?"

He knew what she asked. Knew what he had seen, though it had been just flashes of vision. It had been nothing. Nothing, and everything. The weight of it was still upon him.

"He is coming," said Geoff. "I didn't precisely see it . . . but I know it."

"And it's too dark now to see the hand in front of your face."

"Thibeaux has the ship's lanterns at the ready against the first suspicious bump or scrape," he assured her.

"That should work well," said Anaïs dryly, "since there's nary a breath of wind now to blow them out. What sort of boats did *Le Tigre Doré* carry?"

He thought on it a moment. "Just a little cutter," he said. "About twenty feet."

"Then they'll likely come aside us in that," she said, "coasting in the last bit so we don't hear the oars. By the way, I laid a pair of smallswords and a rapier under a canvas by the aft hatch. A rapier isn't ideal in close quarters, but—"

They both felt it then. The faintest shudder of the ship, as if it had bumped a wharf.

Or another smaller vessel.

Geoff took Anaïs by the shoulders. "Please, Anaïs, go below. Be safe."

She tore away from his side, her footfalls rapid into the gloom. But he knew, even then, that she would not run. That she would stay and fight like a man—better than a man, perhaps.

He felt a second sound, a sort of scrape, and Thibeaux

barked his order. Just as the first lantern sputtered to life, a grappling hook flew across the bulwark, then *thunk! thunk! thunk!* came another three. Everything happened at once then, men hurtling over the rail and onto the deck.

Thibeaux's men were prepared with a volley of pistols. One smuggler screamed and clasped his shoulder, toppling back into the water. Geoff drew a bead on a dark, bearded fellow. He aimed for his leg as he threw it over the rail. The shot missed, but the spray of splintering wood caught the man full in the face. He fell to the deck, clutching his eye.

Men charged one another, boots thundering across the deck, blades slashing and glinting in the lantern light. But Thibeaux's men had the best of it; all around them smugglers were staggering back, caught unawares by the sudden flaring of light.

Pistols were inaccurate and short-lived. Almost at once they were flung aside. Blades came out, metal clashing against metal. Caught in the thick of it, Geoff saw a flash of light. He dodged left just as a cutlass whizzed by his right ear.

"*Alors, mon ami,*" a gruff voice boomed. "We meet again!"

The *Tigre*'s captain. Sabot's beefy, sunburned face grinned in the gloom.

Geoff feinted right then left, warding off his blows with Anaïs's *épée*. "This is not your fight, Sabot," he said, striking back with a flurry. "Go whilst you can."

Sabot's grin deepened. "Ah, but a man's word is his bond." He struck back, again and again, his blows heavy but effective.

Geoff's blade circled Sabot's. "Lezennes' word is as good as a boot full of piss," he said. "Take his money, and forget it."

But Sabot just laughed, his rotten front teeth like black pits in the gloom. For a time, both of them struck and par-

ried, heedless of chaos about them. Geoff tried not to think
of Anaïs; he was of no use to her dead. Instead he drove
Sabot back with a flurry of rapid blows, pushing him almost
to the rail. Sabot began to grunt with his exertions but did
not relent.

All around them, men were fighting. Two gave it up, and
went over the side, but Sabot was undaunted. He laughed
wickedly and swung a wild arc, the cutlass narrowly missing
Geoff's throat. "Ah, *mon ami*," he rasped, "are you ready to
die?"

"Only your men will die," he gritted, driving the captain
back again. "Lezennes lied, Sabot. He's led you into a trap."

Then Geoff saw his opening, and went for Sabot's throat.

At that moment, however, Thibeaux's master rigger drove
one of the smugglers between them. Thrown off balance,
Geoff raked the tip of the *épée* across Sabot's windpipe. He
drew blood, but not much. Sabot's man was reeling, the poor
devil tripping over his captain's foot.

Too late, Sabot jerked back his cutlass, slicing the man
across the shoulder. The sailor fell between them, bleeding.
They eyed each other over the groaning body, both of them
panting now. Then Geoff chose his moment and lunged,
leaping over the wounded man, and driving Sabot back
against the mizzen.

Sabot caught his blade and threw it off. Geoff feinted,
then struck hard, catching the flat of Sabot's blade. The
cutlass flew from his hand, clattering to the deck. Geoff
shoved him against the mast and set the blade to his bleeding throat.

"You have not gained the element of surprise here, Sabot,"
he said, panting. "And you are outnumbered. Your men
know it, even if you do not."

And it was true. Moreover, they had no loyalty to Lezennes; one could see it in their faces, now pale in the

wavering lantern light. Sabot cursed him, but Geoff could sense his uncertainty. He had been told, no doubt, that they could take the ship unawares, and snatch the child before any alarm was raised.

Now, however, there was a skirmish to Geoff's left, just beyond his sight, otherwise the whole of the ship had fallen silent. "Order your men off, Sabot," he said through gritted teeth. "Do it now!"

The captain hesitated but an instant. "*Arrêt!*" he shouted, his voice carrying across the deck. "Stop! We are done here!"

But Geoff did not remove his blade. Already men were vanishing over the side almost as quickly as they had come. "Lezennes is a greater scoundrel than the whole of your crew together," he said. "I want the bastard, Sabot. *Now.*"

Sabot's grin returned, his mouth turning up slowly. "*Et voilà,*" he said, jerking his head in the direction of the hatch. "You may have him, *mon ami*—if there is anything left when the woman is finished."

Only then did Geoff turn to see what the rest of the ship was already watching.

Anaïs had Lezennes backed up nearly to the forecastle, a smallsword in her left hand, her beloved rapier in her right. She met him blow for blow, parrying easily, using the small-sword for nothing save balance. Geoff started toward her, then checked himself, though it was the hardest thing he'd ever done.

But he would do nothing save throw off her balance and sight. And he simply was not needed. Already Lezennes' expression was gritted, like that of a rabid dog; as if he did not believe his own eyes.

Time and again, he came at her madly, clashing his blade against hers. But Anaïs gave him only what distance she wished, retreating elegantly—almost mockingly—then ex-

ecuting a neat thrust to his throat or his flank, but never quite
striking; moving always as it pleased her, playing him as a
cat might a mouse.

"*Stupide pétasse!*" Lezennes cursed, thrusting furiously
but unwisely.

Laughing, Anaïs caught the blow, circled his blade, and
threw him off, very nearly throwing off his balance, too.
The men had backed away. Space was no constraint to her
long blade now. Behind him, Geoff could hear the last of
Sabot's men bumbling their way back down their ropes, retreating while they could.

Lezennes, however, would not be leaving any time soon.
He had doubtless begun this battle of blades with great confidence. But he was going to finish in blood.

No man moved to help Anaïs, nor did Thibeaux order it.
They seemed to know, as Geoff did, it would be wasted.
Again and again, she played the vicomte out, then drove
him back. Again he attacked, driving at her furiously. She
parried and cleverly threw him off. Lezennes swung wild,
catching a run of clew lines with the tip of his blade and
slicing it through. Somewhere above a sail billowed, then
dropped, swinging crookedly down behind him like the curtain in a cheap Punch and Judy show.

In response, Anaïs leaned in, pinking him neatly—and
quite deliberately—in the temple.

Lezennes screamed with rage. His expression was wild
now, blood trickling down his cheek. "You English bitch!"
he bellowed again. "How *dare* you?"

"You're done for, Lezennes," she said calmly, driving him
all the way back this time. "You meant to kill Charlotte—
now I should like to kill *you*."

Lezennes panicked then. He beat at her furiously, to no
avail, retreating inch by inch, until at last he leapt onto a pile
of folded canvas, and hitched up against the gunwale.

It was a fatal error. The wood caught him hard at the back of his legs. Lezennes' arms wheeled, his face a mask of horror. His blade clattered to the deck as he made one last attempt to save himself. Too late. He toppled backward, and over the edge.

A moment of stillness fell across the deck, followed by a loud splash.

Only then did Geoff realize he was almost shaking. Thibeaux's men broke into cheers, one of them turning to shake Anaïs's hand, but they were cut short. A great *ba-boom!* came from below, echoing ominously through the ship, as if something in the hold had exploded.

His heart still in his throat, Geoff leapt for the hatch, catching the lip on his hands, and swinging himself down. He dropped below and bolted toward the aft cabin, Anaïs on his heels.

On the other side of the mizzenmast, he drew up hard. The pockmarked man named Navarre lay spread-eagle in the narrow passage, covered in shards of wood, one leg twisted awkwardly beneath him. The cabin door had a hole the size of a cricket ball blown in it.

Anaïs leapt over the body. "Étienne!" she cried, reaching through the hole and shoving something aside. It hit with a clatter, and she threw open the door. Eyes wide, Étienne Thibeaux still stood with his back to the wall, holding the pistol.

He dropped it at once. "*Bonjour, madame,*" he said. "*C'est fini.*"

Geoff flicked his gaze up from the supine smuggler. Above, on the topmost berth, Charlotte cowered on her knees, Giselle thrust behind her as if to protect the child. She collapsed upon seeing Anaïs, one hand pressed to her heart. "Oh, thank God!" she cried. "Oh, thank God!"

Geoff knelt over the body and pressed two fingers pressed to Navarre's throat. Étienne stepped gingerly over the body, his expression curious.

"Is he dead, *monsieur*?" asked the boy calmly.

"No," said Geoff, feeling for a wound. "No, I think he just struck his head."

"Oh," Étienne's small face fell. "*Tant pis!*"

CHAPTER 21

Bestow rewards not required by law;
impose exceptional governmental orders.
Direct the masses of the Three Armies
as though commanding one man.
Sun Tzu, *The Art of War*

𝒯he Reverend Mr. Sutherland was, above all, a man of faith. A strict traditionalist, he believed that the hand of God could be seen in many things that man was not destined to understand in this lifetime, and Sutherland placed the *Fraternitas* squarely into that category. That said, the good Preost believed strongly in the Brotherhood, and understood that one must occasionally sacrifice for the righteousness of its cause. And on those rare occasions when he found his personal tenets in conflict with his natural inclinations, it troubled him.

It troubled him now as he stood tucked beside one of the brick turrets that flanked Colchester Station, watching the rain hammer down as the last of their baggage was portered from Charlotte Moreau's carriage—or rather, her father's carriage—to the curb. And then the coachman whipped up his horses, and the entourage set off, a cart and a traveling coach rumbling away in the rain.

Charlotte waved good-bye to the three of them until the carriage turned onto the main road. And even then, Sutherland could see Giselle's small, sharp-chinned face at the back glass, watching them as she grew smaller and smaller. Then, at the last moment, she lifted her hand and pressed it to the glass—along with her little nose—and Sutherland could see no more, though whether it was from the rain or the faint mist in his eyes, he could not have said.

On the pavement below, Geoffrey and Miss de Rohan turned, and dashed from the street and under the lee of the station, popping their umbrellas down and giving them a vigorous shake. In their dark, almost formal attire—he in black superfine with blinding white linen, and she in dark aubergine satin—they might have been a wealthy young couple in half mourning.

The earl was still watching the carriage, far in the distance now. "Well," he said, almost to himself, "do you think they will be all right without us?"

Sutherland smiled beatifically. "You are not the only Guardian, my boy, capable of tending to that child—no matter how attached the three of you may have become these past few days."

Geoff laughed.

"Mr. Henfield will do right by the child, Geoffrey." Sutherland set a consoling hand between his friend's shoulder blades. "He is a fine Guardian—and I believe Charlotte likes him very well indeed. You and Miss de Rohan have done the Lord's work here, for He has a purpose for that child, though we cannot yet know what it is."

"She has already predicted the fall of one monarchy," said Geoff a little worriedly. "I shudder to think what she might say next."

"Precisely," murmured the Preost. "And now she will be safe until she learns to understand the Gift. Perhaps she will choose not to use it at all—but at least she will *have* a choice. That is the gift the two of you have given her."

But the rain chose that moment to begin to hammer down again, splattering off the pavement and bouncing up like pebbles. "Come," said Geoff, urging Anaïs toward the door. "Let's go in."

Inside the station, the gentlemen waded into the press of passengers and porters to purchase tickets and direct the luggage. They rejoined Anaïs near the entrance just as a train pulled in, belching and whistling.

"Well," said Sutherland over the racket, "this is where we part company, I suppose. Miss de Rohan, are you quite, quite sure you will not join me? My sister keeps a fine cook, a comfortable house, and she would love to have the company."

For the third time since breakfast, Anaïs shook her head. "You're very kind, sir," she said, "but I find myself a little homesick."

"Then I would be happy to hire you a carriage for your return today," the Preost pressed.

"What is your point, Sutherland?" asked Geoffrey pointedly. "Trains run back and forth to London all day long."

The Preost thinned his lips. "Well, it isn't quite the thing, Geoffrey, even in this modern age," he finally said. "An unwed lady, I mean—on a train, shut up in a first-class compartment? With a gentleman to whom she is not wed?"

At that, Geoff cut Anaïs an odd glance. "Set your mind at ease, sir," he said a little tightly. "I mean to rectify that shortcoming as soon as I can speak to the lady's father."

Both Mr. Sutherland's bushy eyebrows flew aloft. "Do you indeed?"

"Yes, by God, I do. Not that it's anybody's bus—"

"Stop this, the both of you!" Anaïs's expression was dark. "Geoff, that announcement is just a trifle premature, don't you think? Go home and get your iron out of the fire, if you can. As to you, Mr. Sutherland, I have been a great many days in Geoff's company—in the service to the *Fraternitas*, I might add. A trip down to London will scarcely be the worst of it. I think we've left it rather late, this concern for my reputation."

Which was precisely the conflict Sutherland found himself obliged to wrestle. It was all very well to sacrifice in the name of the *Fraternitas* when one was a part of it—and a gentleman, protected from the worst of society's scorn. But it was quite another if one was a lady. A lady who had been denied membership, and yet had gone above and beyond duty's call.

But it was too late to begin struggling with the ethical ambiguity of the thing now. Or the guilt. Still, the latter bit at him like a gnat; unrelentingly, taking one tiny nibble after another of his moral certainty that men were the stronger sex. That women had no place inside the Brotherhood. If even half of what he had heard was true, the young lady had been most remarkably brave.

The train let off another ear-shattering burst, and the swarm of passengers began to surge in the general direction of the doors. Anaïs de Rohan's expression had not lightened.

Suddenly, impulse seized him—or perhaps it was just good judgment. He took off his top hat, and set it on his portmanteau. "My dear," he said, "give me your hand."

Vague surprise sketched over her face, but she did so, placing her long, cool fingers in his.

"Now," he said, "say the words. And quickly, please."

"The words?" Her brow furrowed.

Sutherland waved his empty hand as the train tooted again. "*I humbly ask for admission, et cetera, et cetera,*" said Sutherland.

"For the *Fraternitas*?" She looked at him a little dumbstruck.

"Yes, yes, it's just a formality," said the Preost. "Lazonby already said his part."

Geoff shot him a dark look. "For God's sake, Sutherland," he hissed. "In a *train station*?"

But Miss de Rohan was already speaking, her voice quiet but clear, her Latin precise. "I humbly ask for admission to the Brotherhood," she said, rushing through the words. "I have earned this right with my Devotion, with my Strength, and with my Blood. And on my honor, I pledge that by my Word and by my Sword, I will defend the Gift, my Faith, my Brotherhood, and all its Dependents, until the last breath of life leaves my body."

Sutherland set his opposite hand on her shoulder. "Then may your arm, sister, be as the right hand of God," he said. "And all your days given to the *Fraternitas*, and to His service."

"And so may yours," she answered.

Sutherland dropped both hands and gave a little bow. "There," he said. "'Tis done."

Miss de Rohan still looked a little confused. "And . . . is that it?" she asked. "It's just . . . *done*?"

"Well, we can finish the formal initiation ceremony when we return to London, if you wish it," Sutherland offered.

"Thank you, no," said Anaïs firmly. "I've already thrown my shift away."

"Then yes, actually," said the Preost. "That's it."

"Well, I think there must still be a vote," said Geoff uncertainly. "The St. James Society. The members . . . ?"

She pinned him with her gaze. "And how will you vote?"

His gaze softened. "You know how I will vote," he replied.

"And *I* know how the others will vote," said Sutherland,

snatching up his hat and slapping it back on his head. "Other-wise, they can find themselves a new Preost."

Geoff seized Sutherland's hand and shook it hard. "Then I anticipate a unanimous verdict," he said, turning to Anaïs with a tender smile. "Congratulations, my dear. And much deserved."

"Ah, well." Sutherland cleared his throat sharply. "In any case, I look forward to the resolution of this little mystery of your future together," he said, doffing his hat in Anaïs's direction just as another whistle blew. "And this is my train back to Ipswich, I believe. Let me thank you both again for your exemplary service to the F.A.C."

And with that, he hung his umbrella over one arm, picked up his portmanteau, and strode off toward the platform.

Feeling suddenly awkward, Anaïs watched Sutherland go. Her head seemed to be still spinning from what Sutherland had just done. That, on top of all else, was more than just disorienting. She felt rather as if she'd been shot out of a cannon.

She and Geoff had been nearly three days in Essex, brief-ing Sutherland and Mr. Henfield, reuniting Charlotte with her parents, and settling matters for Giselle. And now the press of the mission was over. The rush of danger was past. It was as if everything had changed between them.

Then Geoff slid his hand around hers, and gave it a firm, sure squeeze, sending everything right side up again. "Come, love," he whispered. "Let's go home."

Up ahead another engine was slowly belching and shud-dering its way into the station. It ground to a halt, and the flurry of activity resumed, this time going in the opposite direction. Anaïs took Geoff's proffered arm, and he snared both their bags in one hand, carrying them as if they were weightless.

It took but a few moments to settle into their carriage and

tuck the hand baggage away. Up and down the platform, doors began thumping shut again. Far ahead, the engine let off two staccato bursts sending Anaïs almost off the seat. She had spent the last five days on edge, and now it felt as if her body was in some state of perpetually heightened awareness.

Geoff reached across the space, and set a hand over hers. "It's like that sometimes," he said quietly, as if he'd read her mind. "Soon we'll be back in London and life will return to normal."

That's just what Anaïs was afraid of, that they would return home as they had left it, wary strangers with lives of their own. She was afraid the days she'd spent with Geoff had been a time out of place, an extraordinary interlude with no bearing on reality—and no place in it, either. That his lust for her was just that, and no more, and that her new-found clarity—about life and love and dreams left to languish—would fade the farther she got from Brussels.

Her doubts were made all the worse by the fact that since fleeing Lezennes' house, she and Geoff had had not a moment alone, save for one heated kiss in the dark aboard the *Jolie Marie*. For days on end, they had lived cheek by jowl together, and learned to trust each other. They had worked, however querulously, toward a common goal. And they had become lovers; lovers with a feverish, extraordinary passion.

And then—as suddenly as it had begun—it was over. The time out of place, the solidarity, it was all ending. And fevers so often burned themselves out, she knew. Yet Anaïs felt an entirely different person. Much of what she'd believed about herself had somehow altered, upending her well-ordered world. And now the thing she'd worked toward for so long—initiation into the F.A.C.—was suddenly hers. So why did she feel just a little apathetic about it?

The train began to shudder and grind, then to move forward. Anaïs watched the empty platform begin to inch away in a hiss of steam and smoke. She turned from the window to see Geoff holding out his hand.

"Come here," he said. And like all his commands, it was gently but firmly made.

Anaïs was in no mood to quarrel. She shifted across and tucked herself onto the seat beside him as the train gained speed and the countryside began to glide past.

Geoff set an arm about her and urged her head onto his shoulder. "Anaïs de Rohan," he said quietly, "I love you."

She must have stiffened in his embrace.

He dipped his head to look at her. "What?" he said. "You didn't expect that to change, did you? You look a little like a prisoner headed to Tyburn."

She looked up at him honestly, unblinkingly. "We've been through some extraordinary days together," she said, "but now we have our old lives to return to."

He said nothing, but merely stared through the window for a time. Then, "I'm not sure I can return to a life without you," he said quietly. "But if you do not feel the same, I'll accept that."

"Will you?" Her heart sank a little.

"Yes," he said, "but only long enough to court you properly. I'm biding my time, Anaïs. I'm going home to do what you have asked of me. And then I mean to try and win you the hard way. By laying siege to your heart. By refusing to take no for an answer."

"Geoff," she said, her throat suddenly too tight. "I haven't said no. Not that kind of no. Just please just try to understand—the sort of guilt I've had to live wi—"

He cut her off, setting a finger to her lips. "Shush, Anaïs," he said. "I *know*. And I mean to run the lady in question to ground the moment I step off this train. I want to explain all this to her myself. It will be done before the sun sets, I do assure you. And she will likely be relieved."

Anaïs did not know what to say. She wanted him, but did she want him at the expense of another?

To her shame, yes. She did. She looked away and swallowed hard. She had to trust that her judgment was good, and that Geoff was right. And that her nonna had been . . . well, *wrong*. But she was sure of her love. Of her choice. And this was her life to live now; her opportunity to seize hard with both hands, for Geoff was a man well worth hanging on to.

They rode on in silence for the longest time, until the next station was reached and the surge of passengers and porters began anew. Geoff crooked his head to look at her from time to time, but saying nothing, merely smiling. Then the doors slammed shut again, one after the other, and the steaming and whistling resumed.

He set his lips to her temple. "I'm afraid it is a long while to the next station," he said.

"Oh," said Anaïs quietly. "That's . . . promising."

"Aye?" He lifted his head, his expression bemused. "Why?"

"Because I have just been wondering," said Anaïs quietly, "what it would be like to make love on a moving train . . ."

That afternoon, the gray clouds over London miraculously cleared to reveal a remarkably azure sky, and a sun so bright the ladies who came out to peruse the shops of St. James were required to pop up their parasols lest their noses freckle.

Rance Welham, Lord Lazonby, was just going down the front steps of the St. James Society—having spared his nose not a thought—when a black phaeton with ruby-red wheels came tooling briskly round the corner into St. James Place, splashed through what was left of the morning's last puddle, then drew up but a few feet away.

The fine-boned, perfectly matched blacks stamped and shook their heads with impatience, but the driver held them easily. "Good afternoon, Rance," Lady Anisha called down. "What a pleasant surprise."

He watched in mild stupefaction as the lady descended, tossing her reins to Belkadi's footman, who had come dashing down the stairs to bow and scrape before her.

"Well, well, Nish!" said Lazonby, leaning on his brass-knobbed stick. "Fending for yourself now, eh?"

"It's a hard life." Lady Anisha smiled, stripping off her driving gloves as she came down the pavement. "Do you like it?"

"It's . . . dashing," said Lazonby, struggling to keep his jaw from hanging. "I'm just not sure it's you."

"Well, perhaps it should be?" the lady murmured cryptically.

Lazonby's critical eye swept over the conveyance, finding much to admire. It was high, but not perilously so. It was perfectly slung, with front wheels reaching to Lady Anisha's shoulder and paint that glistened like onyx set with rubies. It was a carriage no young man of fashion would willingly have given up—and one very few ladies would have driven.

"In any case," Lady Anisha continued, "I'm merely holding on to it, shall we say, for my brother Lucan."

"Ah," said the earl knowingly. "Pup's under the hatches again, eh?"

Lady Anisha's smile tightened. "Quite so," she said. "Baccarat this time. But he's learnt the hard way if he wishes my help, there's a price paid. And this time the price is his phaeton. I confess, I've come to quite like it. I'm not at all sure he'll be getting it back."

Lazonby turned his attention from the phaeton to the beautiful woman. "Have you come to visit Mr. Sutherland again?" he asked, curious. "Because he's still off in the wilds of Essex."

"Well, he could hardly go all the way to Colchester and not visit his sister, could he?" said Anisha. "But I've actually come to fetch Safiyah. I'm going to make her drive in the park with me."

Lazonby drew back a pace. "Well, good luck with that."

"I know." Anisha screwed up her face. "She'll likely refuse. What about you? Dare you trust your life to my hands?"

"I can think of few I would trust so readily," said Lazonby truthfully. "But no, I was just headed across the way to the Quartermaine Club."

"Rance!" she said chidingly. "You are not gaming again."

He grinned down at her. "Not at Ned's, that much is certain," he said. "He won't let anyone from the St. James Society sit at his tables."

"Heavens, I wonder why!" she murmured. "Look, at least ask me up to the bookroom for a moment. I have something I ought to tell you, and I don't want to stand in the street."

With a sudden and grave reluctance, Lazonby inclined his head, and offered his arm.

Two minutes later, they were seated on the long leather sofas in the club's private library, looking at each other a little uncomfortably across the tea table. Lazonby very much hoped Lady Anisha had forgotten the last time she had come upon him in this room.

He had been in a terrible state then, roiling with thwarted rage and something else he would as soon not think about. He had been caught by Nish's brother in what had apparently appeared to be a most compromising position—caught with that little shite Jack Coldwater. Worse, Nish had been with Ruthveyn. He only hoped she had not quite seen . . . well, whatever it was that had been going on.

Her brother most certainly had seen—and had given him a fierce dressing-down for it. Not because Ruthveyn was a judgmental sort of man; he wasn't. No, the scold had been on account of Nish. Nish, who was quite likely the most beautiful woman he'd ever laid eyes on.

He watched her now, her dark eyes flashing, her small, perfect breasts so snugly encased in her black silk carriage dress, her neck long and elegant as a swan's, and he wished a little forlornly that he had not passed her on so swiftly to Bessett.

Not that Nish was anyone's to pass on. She was not. Not any longer. He somehow sensed it most acutely today.

As if to break the awkward moment, Lady Anisha reached up to pull the long pin from her jaunty hat, then set them down beside her. "There," she said on a sigh. "It was poking me. Now, Rance—you were very bad to abandon me in Whitehall the other day. Whatever were you thinking?"

He jerked to his feet. "I did not abandon you," he said testily. "I left you my carriage, my coachman, and my footmen—with instructions to convey you safely back to Upper Grosvenor Street. I thought it best I walk home, for I was in a temper and not fit company for a lady."

"You left me," she said, following him to the window. "Honestly, Rance, I can't think what's got into you these past few months. You are behaving most strangely."

Lazonby stared down at the entrance to the Quartermaine Club, watching as Pinkie Ringgold, one of the club's bully-boys, came out to open the door of a waiting carriage.

He forced himself to turn around and face her. "I'm sorry," he rasped. "What was it, Nish, you wished to say to me?"

She flicked a quick, appraising glance down his length. "Two things," she said. "Firstly, what do you know of Royden Napier's background?"

Lazonby lifted both shoulders. "Not a damned thing, save he's old Hanging Nick Napier's get."

"Lud, Rance, your language!" Anisha rolled her eyes. "In any case, Lady Madeleine told me something interesting over dinner last night."

Lazonby grinned. "Getting awfully cozy with your new mamma-in-law, aren't you?"

Her dark eyes glittered angrily. "Just hush, and listen," she muttered. "A few months ago, when Napier rushed to his uncle's deathbed—"

"Aye, to Birmingham, someone said," Lazonby interjected. "Probably some jack-leg silversmith. What of it?"

"Well, it wasn't Birmingham." Lady Anisha had dropped her voice. "Belkadi misunderstood. It was *Burlingame*—as in Burlingame Court."

For a moment, Lazonby could only stare at her in bewilderment. "To Lord Hepplewood's?"

"Well, Hepplewood is dead, is he not? Or so Lady Madeleine says." Lady Anisha tossed her hand dismissively. "I confess, I know nothing of these people. But I think it odd that Napier is nephew to a peer so well connected."

"Connected, then, on Lady Hepplewood's side," Lazonby murmured.

"Lady Madeleine says not," Lady Anisha countered. "I was wondering if perhaps Napier was illegitimate."

"No, but old Nick might have been." Then Lazonby shrugged again. "But I don't give two shillings for Napier's name. I just want him to get off his arse and do his job."

Lady Anisha looked up at him from beneath two fans of long, inky-black lashes. "Which brings me to my second point," she said, her husky voice suddenly flowing over him.

Lazonby's mouth went just a little dry. "What?"

"I've convinced Royden Napier to let me look at the files in the Peveril case," she said.

"You what?" He looked at her incredulously.

"He's going to let me see the files," she repeated. "I can't take them from his office, of course. But they are a matter of public record—well, sort of—so he's going to let me see them. His father's notes. The witness statements. That sort of thing. So . . . what do you want to know?"

Rance could not take his eyes off her. "I . . . good Lord . . . *everything*," he managed. "Everything you can learn. But how . . . ?"

Nish cut her gaze away. "Vinegar and honey, Rance," she murmured. "You know the old saying. I think you'd best let me deal with Napier from here out—especially since you can't keep a civil tongue in your head."

Lazonby closed his eyes and swallowed hard. "Thank you, Nish," he whispered. "I don't know what you did, but . . . *thank you*."

When he opened his eyes, Lady Anisha was still staring at him, her dark, exquisitely beautiful face a mask of inscrutability, her wide, black-brown eyes deep, unfathomable pools. It was like that sometimes when he looked at her—his breath simply caught. It wasn't love. It wasn't even lust.

"You are welcome," she said quietly.

And somehow—in that one surreal moment by the open window, with carriages rattling past and doves cooing from the eaves above—it seemed the simplest, most natural thing on earth to draw Nish into his arms and kiss her.

She came against him on a breathless gasp, and their lips met. He kissed her gently at first, slanting his mouth over hers as he drew in her scent; a dark, exotic mélange of sandalwood and champaca and the sort of pure, unadulterated femininity that could have stirred a dead man's blood.

Nish kissed him back, rising onto her tiptoes, for her head barely reached his upper chest. He deepened the kiss, sliding his tongue into her mouth, and felt his stomach bottom out and his cock begin to harden. In response, she gave a soft moan that sent a shiver of lust down his spine.

He could want her, he realized.

He could take her to bed this moment and lose himself in her small, sensual body. He could give her extraordinary pleasure, even joy, perhaps. And she could quiet this bone-deep dissatisfaction that seemed forever to churn inside him—at least for a while.

But he could not let himself love her.

He could fuck her. He could use her—oh, splendidly! But she was better than that. Better than he was—by a long, long shot. Lady Anisha Stafford was like a small, exotic jewel—trained by her Rajput womenfolk, if rumor could be believed, in a thousand exquisite ways to please a man—and she deserved someone capable of worshipping that perfection. And that was not he. He'd seen too much. Tasted too much. His palate was deadened with life's excess.

A little ruthlessly, Lazonby tore his mouth from hers and set her away. His breathing was rough, his body ready and begging for her.

"I'm sorry," he rasped, letting his hands fall. "Good Lord, Nish. Forgive me."

She let her gaze drop, and stepped away as if embarrassed. Neither of them saw the shadow that had just passed nearly through the door, and back out again.

Instinctively, he reached out for her. "Wait."

"No," she said, and stepped back another pace. "I'm not waiting. This thing between us . . . it won't ever be, will it, Rance?"

He shook his head. "No," he agreed. "I could make love to you, Nish. I could. I . . . I want to. But Ruthveyn would kill me. And Bessett—*good God*, what am I thinking?"

At last she lifted her eyes to his, her face flaming. "A better question might be what am *I* thinking?"

"You should marry him, Nish," said Lazonby. "He's a good man. He'll give you an old, honorable, untarnished name—something I could never do. And he'll be an extraordinary father to your boys. You should marry him."

Her gaze faltered. "Yes. I should."

"And will you?" he rasped. "Will you do it? I hope you will."

Again, an uncertain flick of her eyes. "Perhaps," she finally said. "If he asks me—and he has not—then yes, for the boys' sake, perhaps I shall."

Lazonby heaved a sigh of relief, and felt his blood flow back where it belonged. "Good," he said quietly. "You will never regret it."

She pinned him with her stare. "And you will never regret it, either," she said, "will you?"

He thinned his lips and looked away. "You do not love me, Nish," he said quietly.

A long, expectant moment hung over them. Then, "No, I do not," she finally said, her voice surprisingly strong. "I occasionally desire you, Rance. You are . . . well, the sort of man who brings out the worst in a woman, I suppose. Or perhaps it's the best. But no, I do not love you."

He looked at her in some surprise, uncertain what to say.

"Is there anything else, then?" she asked evenly. "Before I go back to Whitehall? I don't know how many trips I can make before Napier's patience gives out."

There was something. Something important. Lazonby felt his face flame with heat. It seemed a dashed bad time to ask Nish for a favor. But he'd long been a desperate man.

"Yes," he finally said. "There is one particular thing." He went to the small desk near the door and extracted a piece of the club's stationery. Impatiently, he scratched a name on it, and handed to her.

"John Coldwater," she murmured. Then she flicked an almost irritated glance up at him.

"Or Jack," Lazonby rasped. "Jack Coldwater."

"I know who he is." Her voice was cold.

"Or any name in the file that might be loosely connected to a person named Coldwater."

"And how am I to know that?" she asked a little tartly.

"That's why I was headed over to Ned Quartermaine's," Lazonby replied. "I'm going to hire one of his informant thugs to dig the chap out. Find out where he came from, and who his family is."

"Why?" Lady Anisha's lips thinned with disapproval. "I should have thought you'd learnt your lesson on that score."

Lazonby did not dare ask what she meant by that. "Coldwater is dogging me for a reason, Nish," he answered. "This is more than the *Chronicle* looking for a story, because I'm old news now. No, this is personal."

"*Personal*," Lady Anisha echoed, tucking the piece of paper into her pocket. "I'll tell you what I think, Rance. I think your obsession with Jack Coldwater is *personal*."

"Do you?" he asked a little snidely.

"Yes," she snapped. "And very, very unwise."

For an instant, he hesitated, wondering whether to tell her to go to the devil, or to simply kiss her again to shut her up.

In the end, however, he did neither. He took the coward's way out. "You will pardon me," he said, his voice tight. "I am wanted elsewhere."

Then Lazonby turned on one heel, strode out the door, and turned toward the stairs only to bump squarely into Lord Bessett, who stood just out of earshot, his back set to the passageway wall, his fingers pinching hard at the bridge of his nose.

Lazonby threw up his arms. "Christ Jesus!" he uttered. "Where did you—?"

Too late, he realized Bessett had laid a finger to his lips. "For pity's sake, Rance," he managed, his voice choked with either rage or laughter, "get the hinges on that damned door sanded if you mean to keep kissing people you oughtn't behind it."

"*You!*" said Lazonby again, hands fisting at his sides. "What the hell are you doing here?"

"It appears I might ask you the same thing, old chap," he managed. "But me—well, I've just come by to pull an iron out the fire. Higgenthorpe said I might catch Nish here."

"An *iron* out of the fire?"

"Aye," said Bessett, eyes dancing with mirth, "though frankly, old chap, it looked rather as if you were doing the job for me."

By seven o'clock, Maria Vittorio was drawing the heavy velvet draperies in the withdrawing rooms in Wellclose Square, her heels clicking noisily on the wide, polished floorboards. A carpet was needed, she had often complained, but none had been fitted as yet, for Anaïs had shown little interest in choosing one, preferring to leave the rooms much as they had been in her grandmother's day.

But in her grandmother's day, these rooms had been filled not with upholstered chairs and long, matching sofas, but with massive desks and stacked drawers, and clerks buzzing about like diligent honeybees; Sofia's empire, kept close to hand when she had grown too old to leave the house. The truth was, however, that Castelli & Company had outgrown the space long before the old woman's death. They had simply made do.

And now the rooms were elegant in their near-emptiness; long, massive chambers sparsely furnished and rarely used, for the house was large, and they were but two people. Two people who kept to themselves—who had nothing from which *to* withdraw—for they entertained no one save family.

Now, however, Maria looked about the wide, high-ceilinged rooms, and wondered with a mother's heart if yet another change was coming to these rooms, and to this house. Oh, perhaps she was not, strictly speaking, a mother, for God had not blessed her in such a way. But God had blessed her with Nate and Anaïs and Armand and a whole alphabet of other people who needed her.

She was not sure, however, that Anaïs still did—not in the old way, at least, for Anaïs had come home today amidst another flood of trunks and bandboxes an altered person. Altered in a way Maria knew all too well; with a light in her eyes but a sadness in her heart, yet saying little. And always, always, there was a man at the center of such conflicting emotions and subtle silences.

Maria was just drawing the last of the heavy panels when she heard the front knocker drop. Never above answering her own door, Maria set down her drawing rod and did so, swinging it wide to reveal a very tall, slender gentleman in a midnight-blue frock coat and a tall beaver hat that must have cost, if not a king's ransom, then at least a minor prince's.

She recognized him at once.

And Anaïs had not, apparently, learned her lesson about handsome, dashing men after all.

"*Il bell'uomo,*" she muttered under her breath, not in the least surprised.

"Thank you," said the gentleman, sweeping off his hat. "I'm Geoffrey Archard. Is Miss de Rohan at home?" He presented a thick ivory card, and Maria took it. But the card did not say Geoffrey Archard, she noticed.

"*Sì,*" said Maria, vaguely impressed. "Come in, my lord."

* * *

Anaïs was in the family parlor sorting through the towering heap of mail that had accumulated in her absence when she sensed a presence in the house. A male presence, she thought, but not Nate. Not Armand. She drew a deep breath, willing her nerves to settle.

She had not long to wait until she heard Maria coming up the old oak staircase with another, heavier tread falling softly behind her. Laying aside the butcher's bill, Anaïs pushed back her chair, nervously smoothing her hands down the front of her dark blue dimity gown. It was an old, comfortable dress, and far from her best, leaving Anaïs feeling oddly ill-attired—for she knew, as surely as she knew herself, that it was Geoff.

Oh, she had expected he would come, for he was a man who would always do the right thing. But once he had returned to London and to normalcy, what would he think the right thing was?

Certainly she had not imagined he would come so soon. Not the very same day they had parted company at Bishopsgate Station, going their separate ways in hired hackney cabs, with Anaïs snuffling back tears.

And then he was there, his broad shoulders filling the width of the parlor door, carrying his tall hat in his hands, his hard blue eyes somber.

"You have a caller, *bella*," said Maria, her eyes dark with warning. "I go now—*but not far.*"

Geoff tossed his hat onto a chair, and swept her into his arms, kissing her thoroughly and seizing her breath. "Oh, Anaïs, it has been too long," he murmured, his mouth brushing her ear. "I don't suppose you could do something about that *not far* part?"

Anaïs pushed herself back to study his face, finding nothing but honesty there. And for the first time since leaving

Brussels, she began to feel a sense of certainty. "Why?" she whispered. "Did you miss me?"

He kissed her again, swift and hard. "The longest five hours of my life," he said. "Come, ask me to sit. Pour me a brandy, won't you? It's been one hell of an afternoon."

She motioned toward the sofa by the windows, now darkening, and went to the sideboard. "Where have you been?" she asked, keeping her voice light.

"Where I said I would be," he replied, dragging both hands through his hair. "Doing what I said I would do. It was just . . . strange, that's all."

On second thought, Anaïs poured herself a brandy, too. She was rather afraid she might need it.

She joined him on the sofa, and pressed the glass into his hand. But Geoff merely sipped from it, then set it impatiently away, drawing a deep breath as he did so. "Anaïs," he said, holding his arms wide, "come here."

She did, scooting across the narrow space and burying her face against his shoulder. She drew in his familiar, comforting scent and felt as if, at long last, she had come home.

"Anaïs," he murmured, holding her to him, "I love you desperately. I've come to give you fair warning that I really do mean to lay siege to your heart. I mean to make you forget Raphaele and anyone who ever was, or ever could have been. I've never been unable to do anything I set my mind to—and nothing has ever mattered more than this."

Anaïs lifted her head, and set her lips to his cheek. "You may save yourself the trouble of a siege," she said. "I love you to distraction. And that will never change."

He turned his ice-blue gaze on her then and, tipping her chin up with one finger, kissed her lightly on the lips. "I hope it won't," he said quietly. "You are everything to me, Anaïs. But there is something I need to tell you. Something important."

She felt her breath seize. "About what?" she murmured, her eyes searching his face. "Something to do with the lady you were courting? Oh, Geoff, please don't say she—"

"She is perfectly fine." Then his words hitched for a moment, and he ruefully shook his head. "Oh, she still needs a husband, for her children's sake, I think. But that's a problem I now realize I cannot fix for her, no matter how much I might care. I thought I was willing to try, but I'm not. And she understands. She was actually quite relieved."

Anaïs closed her eyes, sagging inside with relief. "So what did you wish to tell me?" she managed.

"Nothing to do with that," he said, and he sounded as if he meant it. But Geoff's reticence oddly returned, his jaw stiffening almost imperceptibly, and Anaïs was reminded once again of the man she had met with that day in the society's bookroom. He was a pensive, stubborn man, yes—but a good man, too.

And a gentleman to his very marrow.

Whatever it was that troubled him now, it had something to do with that, she sensed. And it had been nagging at him for a while.

He cleared his throat a little sharply. "You came to realize, I think, whilst we were away how deeply concerned I was for Giselle Moreau," he said. "From the very first, her safety—her *future*—was paramount to me."

"You felt a great sympathy for her," Anaïs acknowledged, "and on some deeply personal level I cannot quite fathom. But I cannot know what it is to carry the sort of burden people like you and Giselle carry—and for that, I am truly grateful."

After a moment had passed, he reached out and covered Anaïs's hand with his own, curling his fingers through hers. "My childhood was much like Giselle's," he said. "Or like what hers could have been. Until I was twelve, I had no one to turn to. No one to help me."

"Yes," said Anaïs slowly. "And I have wondered at that, honestly."

His mouth turned up in an almost bitter smile. "My mother blames herself for it," he said. "But it was not her fault. She . . . she was so young; barely seventeen when she conceived me—and she could not have known what to expect."

"That's what I don't understand," Anaïs murmured, dipping her gaze to catch Geoff's. "Wasn't Lord Bessett her cousin? The Gift is carried in the blood. Everyone who has it knows that much."

"My mother was the great-granddaughter of the fourth Earl of Bessett, yes," he said. "However, her marriage to her cousin was but a marriage of convenience—which is to say, it was convenient for everyone save her. And me. And—"

Anaïs looked at him encouragingly. "*And—?*"

Geoff's throat worked up and down for a moment. "For my real father," he finished.

It took a moment for that to sink in. "Ah," she finally said. "I begin to comprehend."

His smile turned from bitter to grim. "I'm sure I need not ask your confidence in this," he said. "The implication is clear."

"Geoff, none of this matters to me," she said swiftly, setting a hand to his face. "I'm sorry for your mother—to have conceived a child so young and out of wedlock must have been an unspeakable horror—but it matters not one whit to me who your father is. You must believe that. You *must*."

He laid his hand over hers where it cupped warmly round his cheek. "I have never doubted it," he said quietly. "You are not the silly sort of woman, Anaïs, to whom such things as blood and propriety matter unreasonably. And I have never been ashamed of who and what I am."

"I would think less of you if you were," she said.

He turned his face into her hand and kissed her palm lingeringly, then laced his fingers through hers and settled their hands in his lap as if to better study them. "I have also never been ashamed of my background," he said quietly. "I was conceived in love by two parents who wanted me very much. I was also conceived in wedlock—or perhaps a day or two before it. And therein lies the complication, you see."

Anaïs felt her eyes widen. "I should say," she murmured. "Do you . . . wish to tell me about it?"

He lifted one shoulder and sighed. "Just a few weeks into her come-out season, my mother eloped with a near-penniless Scot, and married at Gretna Green," he said. "But my maternal grandfather was a cruel man. He managed to catch them soon after, and to convince my mother by means of some forged documents that my father had married her for her money—which was considerable—and that he had paid my father off to annul the marriage. He even showed her the papers."

"Oh!" Anaïs set a hand to her mouth. "But that's monstrous!"

"He was a powerful politician," said Geoff. "He had arranged a political marriage for her, one which served his own thirst for power. He thought he could cover over the elopement and cow her, but he didn't count on me. Now, it is one thing to dupe a young man into taking a wife who is not a virgin, and quite another to foist off a bride who's already with child. Even Lord Jessup—my grandfather—dared not try that. My mother, therefore, became worthless to him."

"But he . . . he would not let her go back to your father?"

Geoff shook his head. "Never," he said. "He was far too vindictive and prideful. Moreover, he'd had my father beaten and left for dead. My mother believed herself abandoned. So Jessup quickly foisted her off on her mother's first cousin— on Alvin's father—for Alvin needed a mother, and Bessett had his nose so deep in his history books he could scarce be bothered to act as a father."

"That sounds selfish."

Geoff hesitated for a moment. "Just self-absorbed, I think," he said pensively. "Bessett was a decent sort, and in his way he cared for Alvin and me—and for my mother, too. He must have done, or he wouldn't have married her knowing she carried me. I console myself with that thought when the night feels long."

Anaïs was turning it over in her mind. The horror of it. The unspeakable sadness of it. "And so you were raised by Bessett as his child though you were only his second cousin," she muttered. "And the Gift . . . your mother knew nothing of it?"

"She knew almost nothing about my father," Geoff replied. "She knew he was a Scot, and possessed of an artistic temperament. She knew she loved him madly. But she'd lived the whole of her life in Yorkshire. She'd been in London scarcely above two months when they eloped. And following her marriage to Bessett—if one can even call it that—they went immediately abroad for several years. Until she took me down to London to find your aunt, she did not even know my father was still there."

"But then she found him?"

Geoff's smile was rueful. "Oh, aye," he said. "She found him—quite by accident. And good Lord, did the sparks fly then. When he realized I was his, hellfire practically spewed out his nose."

"Heavens!" Anaïs widened her eyes. "What did he do?"

"Snatched me up by the scruff like a lost kitten, slung me in his coach, and hauled me off to Scotland before any of us could so much as sneeze," said Geoff. "And I thank God for it. He knew at once, you see, that what Lady Treyhern had said all along was true. That there was nothing mentally wrong with me."

"But this is amazing!" said Anaïs. "Your poor mother. What did she do?"

"She came with us," said Geoff. "Father left her little choice. He still carried their marriage lines in his pocket. And I—well, I spent the next several years with my grandmother, who had close ties to the *Fraternitas* in Scotland. And they were good years, too. They made me what I am. And I know that Charlotte understands, on some level, what Giselle is. But that is not enough, Anaïs. The child needs a true mentor, and in Essex, she will have it."

"And what of your mother?" Anaïs murmured. "Your father? How did they manage?"

"After a time, they quietly married again," he said. "Not that they needed to. It was all for show, Anaïs. All done to preserve the illusion of my parentage, and to keep my mother from being branded a bigamist."

"Oh, Lord," said Anaïs breathlessly. "I never thought of that."

"Well, I have," said Geoff grimly. "And I'll not have it said of her. I'll not make her the subject of gossip. Not for anything."

"So your stepfather isn't a stepfather at all." Suddenly, Anaïs grinned. "Which means that when you signed my drawing in the park, what you signed was your real name?"

"I suppose it was," he said with a faint, inward smile. "And the name I use today—well, that's my real name, too." His face fell a little. "Mother wanted to change it when she remarried, but Father . . . well, he said it didn't matter. That he knew who I was, and I knew who I was, and that the rest of the world could go hang."

"I begin to see where you get your independent streak," said Anaïs. "And you did rightly, I think."

He shrugged. "It was the name Alvin and I shared," he said. "I don't give a damn for the Bessett title, mind—I wish to God I could give it back to him—but I'm stuck with it now."

"But you *are* descended from the Archard line," Anaïs pointed out. "Though the title could never have passed back up and through your mother—or could it?"

He stared pensively into the depths of the room, which were dark with shadows now. "Actually, Mamma says the oldest title and the actual estate would have done," he said. "Something to do with it once being held as an ancient barony by writ. But no, there was no provision for the female line to take the title of earl."

"So . . . have you another cousin somewhere? Someone who . . . who . . ."

"Whom I've cheated out of an earldom?" As he so often did, Geoff lifted a hand and tidied one of her loose curls. "No, Alvin was the last of the lot, both up and down the tree. The earls of Bessett were not prodigious breeders—too busy reading, I collect—so I think my mother might actually might be Baroness Something-or-other now, and I'd be her heir. I don't know, and I don't give a damn. I'll call myself the Earl of Bessett until I die before I'll let my mother suffer an ounce of mortification."

"My heavens, this is confusing," said Anaïs, sagging back against the sofa. "But this—none of it—has any bearing on how I feel for you, Geoff. You did not have to tell me any of it."

"I felt that I did," he said quietly. "But not, perhaps, for the reason you might think."

For about the third time that day, Anaïs felt her heart sink a little. "Then what was your reason?"

He turned sideways on the small sofa—no easy feat given his long legs—and took both her hands in his. "I'm telling you, Anaïs, because I feel that a woman should always go after what she wants," he said. "My mother did not. She was young and timid and beaten down by her father. But worse than all of that, she had no faith in herself. No faith in her ability to have chosen wisely; to know what she wanted and go after it. And we all paid a price for that."

"And how does this affect me?"

"Don't ever be faint of heart, Anaïs," he said. "I think you are probably the last woman on earth anyone needs to say that to, but I have to say it. Go after what you want. I intend for it to be me. But in the end, if it's not—if you think Raphaele or someone like him is really what you need—then throw me aside. But only because *you* want it. Not because your nonna wanted this thing or that thing, or because your family expects something else. Family expectations left my mother longing for an early grave—and had it not been for me, I think she might have found one."

His words were so heartfelt, so humbling, Anaïs dropped her head. "I know what I want, Geoff, and it's not that," she said quietly. "Besides, it was just a silly notion anyway. Something Nonna Sofia took into her head, no doubt, and it played out in the cards because . . . well, because she wanted it to."

"In the cards?" he asked, clearly confused.

Anaïs jerked her chin up, and realized she'd never really told him the whole of it. "Oh, never mind that!" she said on a rush of embarrassment. "None of it matters now, Geoff. I know what I want—at least in part—and it is *you*."

He held her gaze for the longest time, his blue eyes drilling deep, as if he looked straight to the heart of her to make perfectly, perfectly sure. Then he relaxed, released her left hand, and shifted from the sofa and onto her parlor floor, going down on one knee.

"I'm taking you at your word, then," he said in his quiet, calm voice. "Anaïs de Rohan, will you make me the happiest man on earth, and be my wife and countess?"

Anaïs closed her eyes, and tossed at least half of her grandmother's silly dream to the four winds. "*Yes*," she whispered. "Yes, Geoffrey. I love you. And I will marry you, and account myself fortunate indeed."

He kissed her hand and rose. "Thank God that's settled," he said, sitting back down beside her. "I was a little afraid you'd go tearing off to Tuscany to make one last search for Mr. Right."

"I have decided that *you* are my Mr. Right," she said quietly, touching her fingertips to her heart.

"Oh, Anaïs, I have always known that," said Geoff certainly. "I just wasn't sure you did. Now when will your father be back? I must speak to him."

"A few weeks, at most," she managed, her throat constricting. "But he just wants me to be happy, Geoff. He knows nothing of nonna's strange notion. Don't worry."

"How can I not?" His intense hot-and-cold gaze held to her. "You are everything to me now, Anaïs."

She realized she was blinking back tears. "Oh!" she said softly. "Oh, Geoff. I love you so much. And that story—about your mother and father—it's just so tragic. Promise we will never, ever let anything like that happen to us."

"Never. Ever." With each word, he kissed a tear away. "But I have another, better story—one with a far happier ending."

"Oh, good," she said witheringly. "Let's hear it."

"Once upon a time," he whispered, brushing his lips over the shell of her ear, "there was an earl who wasn't really an earl who fell in love with a strange, fey girl with wild black hair and an even stranger name. And they got married, broke the Bessett breeding curse, had a houseful of children, and lived happily ever after. In Yorkshire. Or London, if you like that ending better?"

"I don't care about that last part," she said, settling her head onto his shoulder. "But yes, I like that story much, *much* better."

EPILOGUE

Heaven encompasses yin and yang,
cold and heat, and the constraints of the seasons.
Sun Tzu, *The Art of War*

*A*naïs Sofia Castelli de Rohan was wed on a spring
day in a dashing red and white gown in the gardens
at Wellclose Square beneath a brilliant sun and a swirling
snowstorm of apple blossoms that dappled Geoff's matching
red waistcoat, and caught like fat snowflakes in the brim of
his hat. It was not, perhaps, the most fashionable address
for a London wedding, but having denied Nonna Sofia her
dream, Anaïs decided it was the least she could do to honor
her beloved great-grandmother.

The Reverend Mr. Reid Sutherland officiated—with a bit
of a gleam in his eye—and pronounced them man and wife
amidst a score of their closest kin and half the St. James
Society. Afterward they retired to the massive withdrawing
rooms to mill about on Maria Vittorio's new Oriental carpets while nibbling at tidbits and drinking *Vino Nobile di
Montepulciano*, toasting the happy couple's health, wealth,
and fertility, until Lord Lazonby began to leer a little too
openly at one of the housemaids.

Mr. Sutherland called at once for their carriage—but not
before Lazonby launched into a wild tale about the irony

of having first met the groom in a Moroccan brothel. Lady Madeleine gasped and covered her daughter's ears. The Preost caught Lazonby a little violently by the coat sleeve, and steered him out and down the front steps, lifting his hat in salute as he departed.

From there, the remaining guests began to take their leave in a flurry of shawls and carriages. Including Nate, the earl and his new countess possessed several brothers and sisters, requiring three carriages to haul them back to Westminster. Another ten vehicles carried off the remaining guests as the happy couple kissed cheeks and waved good-bye, until at last no one remained save Geoff's parents.

On the doorstep, Lady Madeleine swept Anaïs into her embrace for about the sixth time in as many hours. "Oh, my dear, dear girl," she said a little tearfully. "It seems that only yesterday I was holding Geoffrey for the first time, frightened out of my wits, and so terrified he would never see this happy day. But now he has, and I am *so glad*, Anaïs. So glad he has found you."

"Oh, Lady Madeleine, how kind you are!" Anaïs drew away, still clutching both her new mother-in-law's hands. "But why were you terrified? Was he frail?"

Lady Madeleine shrugged, and blushed. "Oh, no, but I was so young!" she said. "And I felt so very alone, so unable to grasp what was going on. I passed out from exhaustion, I think, and when I awoke, I just remember the midwives kept whispering, *che carino bambino*—or maybe it was the other way round?—until I began to cry, I was so frightened."

At that, Geoff laughed, and kissed his mother's cheek. "What a goose you are, Mamma! I think they were just complimenting your pretty baby."

She shot him a withering look. "Do not dare laugh at me, young man!" she cried, trembling now. "I was barely conscious and spoke not a word of that language!" Suddenly, she turned to her husband, her eyes welling with tears. "And I somehow took it into my head that *carino* was *carry no.* That they were saying *she carried no baby.* It seems foolish now, but I thought he was gone. That there'd been some terrible mistake. Or I'd imagined it all."

"Oh, Mamma!" said Geoff softly. "You had been under a long, terrible strain."

"Yes, there, there, Maddie," said her husband, opening his arms and folding her to his chest. "You could not have known, my love."

But it was as if the stress of the day had taken its toll on Lady Madeleine. "Oh, Merrick, I thought I'd done something wrong!" she cried, sobbing into his cravat. "By the time they bathed him and gave him to me I was heartsick. I counted his fingers and toes for two days, and dared not go to sleep for fear he might die! And now—just think! He is *married!*"

"He is also thirty years of age," said Mr. MacLachlan, with only a hint of sarcasm. "Your duty is done, my love. And now it is Anaïs's job to keep up with his fingers and toes."

By then, however, no one noticed that all the color had drained from Anaïs's face, for Geoff had gone back into the withdrawing room to pour his mother a tot of brandy. When he returned, Lady Madeleine drank it down a little gratefully, apologized over and over again for her tears, then kissed them both again before taking her leave.

Mr. MacLachlan escorted her down the front steps as if she were a fragile flower, and tucked her carefully into a barouche so elegant half the denizens of the square seemed to be leaning out their windows to gawk at it. Then Mr. MacLachlan waved good-bye, climbed inside, and ordered his coachman to set off.

Anaïs stood on the top step, her hand in Geoff's, as his parents circled the square.

"Geoff," she said quietly, as the barouche disappeared, "where were you born?"

"Rome," he said, following her in and closing the door. "Or near it. A place called Lazio. Do you know it?"

Anaïs stared up at him, her brow furrowed. "Yes, but Lazio is a province, Geoff," she said. "It is quite large."

"And beautiful, I'm told, though I don't remember it," he said, strolling back into the withdrawing room, to the wine they had scarcely had time to drink. "The next year, I believe, we were off to Campania. And from there to Greece. As I said, Bessett was a scholar of ancient civilizations. But when I was born, he was in Lazio digging up ruins near some lake north of Rome. I forget the name."

Anaïs took the glass he pressed into her hand. "*Etruscan* ruins, by any chance?"

He shrugged. "It's quite likely," he answered. "But I never really shared his passion for old civilizations. Bessett was undeniably a brilliant man, but I wasn't surprised, frankly, when I learned he was not my father."

"Geoff," she said excitely, "*which* village?"

He looked up from the glass he was refilling at the sideboard. "Which village what?"

"Which village were you born in?"

He set down the wine bottle with a *thunk!* and furrowed his brow. "Let me think," he muttered. "It had a charming name . . . *Piggly-Wiggly*-something, Mamma called it."

"Pitigliano?" she said breathlessly, sitting down on the sofa.

Clarity dawned over his handsome face. "Yes, that's it." He joined her, settling sideways beside her. "*Pitigliano*. A small place, but some midwives had come from Rome— nuns, I think—to train a couple of local women. It wasn't far from Bessett's lake, Mamma said, so he took a house there for her confinement."

"*Dio mio!*" Anaïs whispered, setting her glass down a little awkwardly on the tea table.

Geoff leaned into her and kissed the tip of her nose. "What? Does it matter? I told you I spent my childhood abroad."

She turned to face him, eyes wide. "But Geoff, this is amazing!"

"Amazing?" He crooked his head to better look at her. "In what way?"

"Well, Lord Bessett might have dug up the whole of Lazio for all I know," she answered. "But I do know this—*Pitigliano is in Tuscany*."

He looked at her curiously. "Are you quite sure?"

"Well . . . yes." Anaïs put one hand over her heart. "It is near the border, but so far as I know, it has always been a part of the Duchy of Tuscany."

"Well, there you go." Geoff flashed his familiar sardonic grin, and raised his glass. "Yet another interesting tidbit about me that even I did not know—albeit a trifle less shocking than my paternity."

But Anaïs had fallen back against the sofa, speechless. Her gaze had fallen to his red waistcoat, where a little white dot of apple blossom still clung tenaciously to the silk.

He set his glass away, and pulled her close against him. "Anaïs, what?"

"*Le Re di Dischi*," she muttered to herself, "in a coat of scarlet. Geoff, you will never, ever believe this . . ."

He slid his warm, long-fingered hand—his beautiful artist's hand—around the turn of her face, heating Anaïs all the way through to the pit of stomach. "No, I won't believe it, my love," he whispered, his gaze fixed to hers, "especially if you don't finish the sentence. Honestly, you've gone a little pale. Have I said something wrong?"

She lifted her gaze from his waistcoat. "No, no, it's just that you are The One," she said. "All along . . . *you* have been The One."

At that, Geoff threw back his head and laughed, his blue eyes alight with merriment. "Oh, Anaïs, I have always known that," he said to her for the second time. "I just wasn't sure you did."

And so she kissed him, her handsome Tuscan prince.

Her handsome, bronze-haired, *blue-eyed* Tuscan prince . . .

Coming Soon

The Bride Wore Pearls

The next book in
Liz Carlyle's fantastic series
Available 2012
From Avon Books

At Avon Books, we know your passion for romance—once you finish one of our novels, you find yourself wanting more.

May we tempt you with . . .

- **Excerpts** from our upcoming releases.

- Entertaining **extras**, including authors' personal photo albums and book lists.

- Behind-the-scenes **scoop** on your favorite characters and series.

- **Sweepstakes** for the chance to win free books, romantic getaways, and other fun prizes.

- Writing **tips** from our authors and editors.

- **Blog** with our authors and find out why they love to write romance.

- **Exclusive content** that's not contained within the pages of our novels.

Join us at
www.avonbooks.com

AVON
An Imprint of HarperCollins*Publishers*
www.avonromance.com